SOLDIER OF ROME:
HEIR TO REBELLION

THE ARTORIAN CHRONICLES THUS FAR

SOLDIER OF ROME: HEIR TO REBELLION

Book Three of The Artorian Chronicles

James Mace

iUniverse, Inc.
New York   Bloomington

Soldier of Rome: Heir to Rebellion
Book Three of The Artorian Chronicles

iUniverse books may be ordered through booksellers or by contacting:

iUniverse
1663 Liberty Drive
Bloomington, IN 47403
www.iuniverse.com
1-800-Authors (1-800-288-4677)

ISBN: 978-1-4401-5715-8 (pbk)
ISBN: 978-1-4401-5716-5 (ebook)

Printed in the United States of America

iUniverse rev. date: 7/15/09

"Nothing except a battle lost can be half as melancholy as a battle won."
— Arthur Wellesley, Duke of Wellington

Acknowledgements

I have to confess that this book has been the most difficult for me to write thus far. In essence it is an interim story, meant to tie two larger parts of the series together. I found it to be much more difficult trying to develop the characters rather than just bouncing from one battle sequence to the next. In the end I am glad to have done this book, as it gives a lot more depth to the characters, as well as the story itself within what I have since dubbed *The Artorian Chronicles*.

I must as always thank God for giving me the strength and fortitude to continue this journey of storytelling, even in the face of many adversities and hard lessons-learned.

To Mum and Dad, I thank you for continuing to support me and for believing in the *Soldier of Rome* story. My sister, Angela, for helping me proof-read and make sense out of what was often times a garbled mess. My 'co-author' Mike Lower, who gives me at least one entertaining line per book, and Don "Praxus" LaMott, without whom this project would never have even gotten off the ground. Thanks as always to Mike Daniels and Rusty Myers of Legio VI, Ferrata; as well as Michael Knowles of the Ermine Street Guard. You are each a credit to Roman historians everywhere; your technical advice, as well as validation from a historical perspective, have been invaluable. Cody Earl for donating your time and photography services.

Special thanks to my other proof-readers: Clint Hanson, Gunnar Klaudt, Jason Gracida (even if all you guys really wanted was to read the story before everyone else!) and to Robbin Christina for continuing to help bring *The Artorian Chronicles* to life.

For some close friends who continue to inspire and motivate me to take this story further: James "Cursor" Philpott, Chris "Camillus" Irizarry, Nic Fischer, Justin "Vitruvius" Cole, David Gehrig, Christopher Harvey, Linda Roehrborn, Ryan "Decimus" Small, Pho "X-Man" Xayamahakham, Martin Shepard, Greg Dolphin, Matt Comiskey, and Lloyd Levin. And of course to my brother "legionaries" in the U.S. Army that have been a privilege to serve with.

Finally, to "Lady Diana," wherever you may be!

Cast of Characters

Soldiers:

Titus Artorius Justus – A Decanus, Sergeant of legionaries
Magnus Flavianus – Artorius' best friend and fellow legionary, he is of Nordic descent
Praxus – A fellow Decanus and friend of Artorius
Statorius – Tesserarius of the Second Century
Camillus – Signifier of the Second Century
Gaius Flaccus – Optio of the Second Century
Platorius Macro – Centurion of the Third Cohort's Second Century
Marcus Vitruvius – Centurion of the Third Cohort's Third Century
Valerius Proculus – Centurion Pilus Prior of the Third Cohort
Calvinus – Centurion Primus Pilus of the Twentieth Legion
Gaius Silius – Senatorial Legate and Commanding General of the Twentieth Legion
Julius Indus – A legendary cavalry commander who distinguished himself during the Sacrovir Revolt
Aulus Nautius Cursor – A Tribune of cavalry serving under the tutelage of Julius Indus
Rodolfo Antonius – A Centurion of Cavalry and Cursor's deputy
Felix, Decimus, Valens, Carbo, Gavius – Legionaries

Noble Romans:

Tiberius Caesar – Emperor of Rome
Livia Augusta – Mother of Tiberius and widow of Emperor Augustus Caesar
Drusus Julius Caesar – Son of Tiberius and his first wife, Vipsania Agrippina
Claudius – Brother of Germanicus / suffers from lameness and speech impediment

Livilla – Sister of Germanicus and Claudius / wife of Drusus

Antonia – Mother of Germanicus, Livilla and Claudius / daughter of Marc Antony and widow of Tiberius' brother Drusus Nero

Agrippina – Widow of Germanicus and half-sister of Vipsania, she mistrusts and despises the Emperor

Lucius Aelius Sejanus – Commanding Prefect of the Praetorian Guard, he is Tiberius' most trusted advisor

Claudia Procula – Betrothed to Pontius Pilate, she is also a distant cousin of Centurion Proculus

Diana Procula – Claudia's older sister and domina of the Proculus family's Gallic estate

Gauls and Rebels

Heracles – Of Greek decent, he was one of Sacrovir's most trusted lieutenants. Opted to go into hiding instead of committing suicide with the rest of the rebel leaders

Radek – A rebel sent to the mines of Mauretania following the Sacrovir Revolt

Broehain – Impoverished Gallic Noble

Kiana – Daughter of a Gallic noble, her lover was slain during the rebellion by Roman soldiers

Tierney – Kiana's older sister, sent by her father to Lugdunum to watch after her

Erin – A slave

Roman Military Ranks

Legionary – Every citizen of the plebian class who enlisted in the legions started off as a legionary. Duration of service during the early empire was twenty years. Barring any promotions that would dictate otherwise, this normally consisted of sixteen years in the ranks, with another four either on lighter duties, or as part of the First Cohort. Legionaries served not only as the heart of the legion's fighting force, they were also used for many building and construction projects.

Decanus – Also referred to interchangeably as a *Sergeant* in the series, Decanus was the first rank of authority that a legionary could be promoted to. Much like a modern-day Sergeant, the Decanus was the first-line leader of legionaries. He supervised training, as well as enforced personal hygiene and maintenance of equipment. On campaign he was in charge of getting the section's tent erected, along with the fortifications of the camp.

Tesserarius – The first of the *Principal* ranks, the Tesserarius primarily oversaw the fatigue and guard duties for the Century. He maintained the duty roster and was also keeper of the watch word. On a normal day he could be found supervising work details or checking on the guard posts.

Signifier – He was the treasurer for the Century and was in charge of all pay issues, so was much-loved on pay days. On campaign he carried the Century's standard (Signum) into battle. This was used not only as a rallying point, but also as a visual means of communication. Traditionally he wore a bear's hide over his helmet, draped around the shoulders of his armor. (A Signifier wearing a wolf skin is a Hollywood invention). Because of his high level of responsibility, the Signifier is third-in-command of the Century.

Optio – The term *Optio* literally means *'chosen one'* for he was personally chosen by the Centurion to serve as his deputy. He would oversee all training within the Century, to include that of new recruits. In battle the Optio would either stand behind the formation, keeping troops on line and in formation, or else he would stand on the extreme left, able to coordinate with adjacent units.

Aquilifer – This man was a senior Signifier bearing the Eagle Standard of a Legion. (*Aquila* means eagle). This standard was the most important possession of the Legion – losing it brought shame and humiliation to the entire Legion. This position carried great honor, though it is debatable whether or not he wore any headdress or animal skin. It is known that he carried a small, circular shield called a *parma* instead of the legionary scutum.

Centurion – In addition to being its commander, the Centurion was known to be the bravest and most tactically sound man within the Century. While a stern disciplinarian, and at times harsh, it is borne of a genuine compassion for his men. The Centurion knew that only through hard discipline and sound training could his men survive in battle. He was always on the extreme right of the front rank in battle; thereby placing himself in the most precarious position on the line. Mortality rates were high amongst Centurions because they would sacrifice their own safety for that of their men.

Centurion Pilus Prior – Commander of a cohort of six centuries, the Centurion Pilus Prior was a man of considerable influence and responsibility. He not only had to be able to command a century on a line of battle, but he had to be able to maneuver his cohort as a single unit. Such men were often given independent commands over small garrisons or on low-level conflicts. A Centurion Pilus Prior could also be tasked with diplomatic duties; such was the respect foreign princes held for them. At this level, a soldier had to focus not just on his abilities as a leader of fighting men, but on his skills at diplomacy and politics.

Centurion Primus Ordo – The elite First Cohort's centuries were commanded by the Centurions Primus Ordo. Though the number of soldiers under their direct command was fewer, these men were senior in rank to the Centurions Pilus Prior. Men were often selected for these positions based on vast experience and for being the best tacticians in the legion. As such part of the duty of a Centurion Primus Ordo was acting as a strategic and tactical advisor to the commanding general. Generals such as Caesar, Marius, Tiberius, and Agrippa were successful in part because they had a strong circle of First Cohort Centurions advising them.

Centurion Primus Pilus – Also referred to as the *Chief* or *Master* Centurion, this is the pinnacle of the career of a Roman soldier. Though socially subordinate to the Tribunes, the Centurion Primus Pilus possessed more power and influence than any, and was in fact third-in-command of the entire legion. He was also the commander of the elite First Cohort in battle. Upon retirement, a Centurion Primus Pilus (and possibly Centurions of lesser ranks as well) was elevated into the Patrician Class of society. He could then stand for public office, and his sons would be eligible for appointments as Tribunes. Even while still serving in the ranks, a Centurion Primus Pilus was allowed to wear the narrow purple stripe of a Patrician on his toga; such was the respect Roman society held for them.

Tribune – Tribunes came from the Patrician class, often serving only six month tours with the legions. Though there were exceptions, many Tribunes stayed on the line only long enough to complete their tour of duty before going on to a better assignment. Primarily serving as staff officers for the commanding Legate, a Tribune would sometimes be given command of auxiliary troops if he proved himself a capable leader. Most were looking for a career in politics, though they knew they had to get as much experience as they could out of their time in the legions. In *Soldier of Rome*, Pontius Pilate is an example of a Tribune who elects to stay with the legions for as long as he is able; preferring the life of a soldier to the soft comforts of a political magistrate.

Laticlavian Tribune – Most commonly referred to as the *Chief* Tribune, he was a young man of the Senatorial class starting off his career. Second-in-command of the legion, his responsibility was incredible, though he was often aided by the Master Centurion, who would act as a mentor. A soldier's performance as Chief Tribune would determine whether or not he would be fit to command a legion of his own someday. Given the importance of military success to the future senator's career, he would no doubt make every effort to prove himself competent and valiant in battle.

Legate – The Legate was a senator who had already spent time in the legions as a Laticlavian Tribune and had proven himself worthy of command. Of all the possible offices that a nobleman could hold, none was dearer to a Roman than command of her armies.

Legion Infantry Strength (estimated)

Legionaries – 3,780

First Cohort Legionaries – 700

Decanii – 610

Tesserarii – 59

Signifiers – 59

Options – 59

Aquilifer - 1

Centurions – 45

Centurions Pilus Prior – 9

Centurions Primus Ordo – 4

Centurion Primus Pilus – 1

Tribunes – 6

Chief Tribune – 1

Legate – 1

The Julio-Claudians

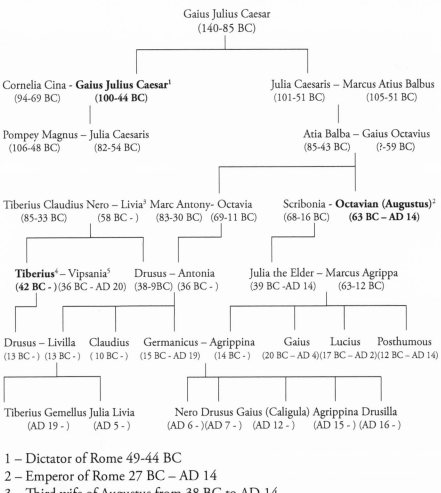

Gaius Julius Caesar
(140-85 BC)

Cornelia Cina - **Gaius Julius Caesar**[1]   Julia Caesaris – Marcus Atius Balbus
(94-69 BC)   **(100-44 BC)**   (101-51 BC)   (105-51 BC)

Pompey Magnus – Julia Caesaris   Atia Balba – Gaius Octavius
(106-48 BC)   (82-54 BC)   (85-43 BC)   (?-59 BC)

Tiberius Claudius Nero – Livia[3] Marc Antony- Octavia   Scribonia - **Octavian (Augustus)**[2]
(85-33 BC)   (58 BC -) (83-30 BC) (69-11 BC)   (68-16 BC)   **(63 BC – AD 14)**

Tiberius[4] – Vipsania[5] Drusus – Antonia   Julia the Elder – Marcus Agrippa
(42 BC -)(36 BC - AD 20) (38-9BC)(36 BC -)   (39 BC -AD 14)   (63-12 BC)

Drusus – Livilla   Claudius   Germanicus – Agrippina   Gaius   Lucius   Posthumous
(13 BC -) (13 BC -) (10 BC -) (15 BC - AD 19) (14 BC -) (20 BC – AD 4)(17 BC – AD 2)(12 BC – AD 14)

Tiberius Gemellus Julia Livia   Nero Drusus Gaius (Caligula) Agrippina Drusilla
(AD 19 -)   (AD 5 -)   (AD 6 -)(AD 7 -)   (AD 12 -)   (AD 15 -) (AD 16 -)

1 – Dictator of Rome 49-44 BC
2 – Emperor of Rome 27 BC – AD 14
3 – Third wife of Augustus from 38 BC to AD 14
4 – Emperor of Rome AD 14 – Present
5 – Daughter of Marcus Agrippa through his marriage to Caecilia Attica

Note: This is not an all-inclusive family tree, but shows the Julio-Claudians that appear or are referenced in The Artorian Chronicles. For example, Germanicus and Agrippina had nine children altogether, three of whom died young. Augustus was also married a total of three times, with Livia being his last wife.

The Families of Artorius and Magnus

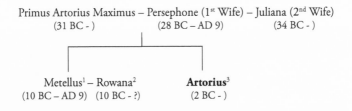

Primus Artorius Maximus – Persephone (1ˢᵗ Wife) – Juliana (2ⁿᵈ Wife)
(31 BC -)   (28 BC – AD 9)   (34 BC -)

Metellus[1] – Rowana[2]   **Artorius**[3]
(10 BC – AD 9) (10 BC - ?)   (2 BC -)

1 – Killed in Action, Teutoburger Wald, Germania
2 – Disappeared soon after the Teutoburger Wald disaster. Current whereabouts are unknown.
3 – Full name: Titus Artorius Justus

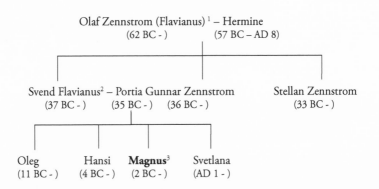

Olaf Zennstrom (Flavianus) [1] – Hermine
(62 BC -)   (57 BC – AD 8)

Svend Flavianus[2] – Portia Gunnar Zennstrom   Stellan Zennstrom
(37 BC -)   (35 BC -)   (36 BC -)   (33 BC -)

Oleg   Hansi   **Magnus**[3]   Svetlana
(11 BC -) (4 BC -) (2 BC -)   (AD 1 -)

1 – A minor overlord in the Nordic realms, he served twenty-five years as a Roman Auxiliary, earning his family Roman Citizenship, before returning to his homeland. Was given the Roman name Flavianus.
2 – The only son of Olaf to remain within the Roman Empire after his father's retirement. Kept the Roman name Flavianus, though as a family tradition he still gives his children Nordic first names.
3 – Full name: Magnus Flavianus

Preface

Gaul, A.D. 21

A year has passed since the end of the Gallic rebellion of Sacrovir and Florus. Retribution has been exacted and the province is at peace once more. And yet there are some who escaped Rome's justice. They are led by a man whose heart burns with hate; an heir to rebellion. Knowing that there can be no victory against the legions; his vengeance can only be wrought through terror and murder. The Gallic city of Lugdunum will be the first to taste his wrath.

The city of Lugdunum flourishes; the Twentieth Legion's Third Cohort having been stationed within the city since the end of the Sacrovir Revolt. For Centurion Proculus and his legionaries their comfortable assignment will soon come unraveled as a series of grisly murders looks to upset the order of the city. Sergeant Artorius inadvertently finds himself at the center of the search to find these mysterious killers before they undermine the city's faith in the protection of the legions; a search that will lead him on a journey into the darkest corners of what lurks in a broken man's wicked soul.

CHAPTER I

▼

REBELLION'S HEIR

Massilia, Gaul
April, A.D. 21

It was a good sword; a bit gaudy for his taste perhaps, but a fine weapon nonetheless. Sacrovir had had an affinity for cavalry weapons, and this spatha had been specially made for him. Well balanced, it rested easily in his hands. Heracles turned it over while running an oiled cloth along the blade. The blade had been honed to a fine edge, working all the nicks and burrs from where the weapon had lain. It had been buried in Sacrovir's heart as his burning estate collapsed over his head. The Romans had made no effort to excavate the ruins, content as they were that the rebel leader was dead.

Romans, Heracles thought to himself as he let out a sigh. *I hate Romans!* Indeed he had plenty of reasons to hate Rome. He had been an impulsive gambler in his past life, much to his wife's chagrin. Things were taken too far when he tried to take on the provisional governor himself.

Heracles had always taken it as a personal umbrage that his native Sparta was little more than a sub province of the Roman Empire. He had sought to humiliate the governor at a gladiatorial spectacle, placing a massive wager that he knew he could not cover. Before the match Heracles was caught trying to bribe one of the combatants into losing. The governor's bodyguards beat him and dragged before the man, in full view of his fellow Spartans. The governor became enraged at how the Greek had tried to humiliate him. He declared that if Heracles was determined to fix gladiatorial fights, he could do so from within the arena. His wife and children were seized and taken away, their property confiscated in retribution to what the governor called "a blasphemous insult against your betters."

Betters, Heracles growled inside. *No Roman is my better!*

Memories enveloped him as he remembered all too well; his wife and children were sold into slavery, while he was beaten once more and left in the hands of the local gladiatorial school where his hatred consumed him. He spent several years in the arena, being cavorted all around the Empire, gradually making his way west. It was not too far from where he was now that he fought his final battle in the arena. His hands trembled at the memory, almost cutting him on the sword's razor sharp blade.

It was during the autumn festival, and the magistrate wanted to celebrate with games and gladiatorial matches. Heracles was amongst the prime attractions. Heracles was not his real name; but rather one given to him for his terrifying feats in the arena. Though only a small percentage of matches ended in death, his high rate of killing made him feared amongst the other gladiators, and loved by the spectators. This time would be no different; he would not be deferring to the crowd as to whether his foe lived or died. Indeed the young whelp that faced him in the sand proved little match for him. He had seen the young man fight before, always with a masked helmet on, and often being overwhelmed by the more experienced fighters. On at least two occasions the crowd signaled that they wanted him slain by his conqueror, only to have the magistrate overturn the crowd and allow the man to live. It baffled Heracles, because the magistrate had had no issue with allowing other gladiators to be executed, even some who had fought far better than this pathetic excuse of a fighter.

He took it as an insult when on the last day of the festival Heracles was slated to fight this man. So tired was he of watching this pathetic gladiator be allowed to live that he stabbed him through the heart with sheer malice as soon as he tripped him to the ground. Then tragedy struck. He roughly ripped the masked helm and gazed on the face of his own son. The lad reached for him piteously as blood streamed out of both corners of his mouth. Heracles' strength left him as he fell to his knees. In an instant he realized the sick and twisted mind of his captors; to have had his own son so close for so long, and yet completely out of reach. Only now did they place father and son in the arena together, knowing that unwittingly Heracles would destroy his own flesh and blood. He sobbed that only a short moment ago he wanted, and looked forward to, killing the young man.

Heracles set the sword down and closed his eyes. He had tried to plunge his blade into his own heart, but was forcibly restrained by guards. He refused to fight thereafter and was cruelly punished by scourging. When the slave master realized there was no fight left in him, he sold Heracles to a noble family. They soon learned that he could read and write and he started his life anew. The family told him news of his wife. She had been sold to a brothel and hanged herself. He would never learn the fate of his daughter.

His new owners treated him kindly enough, but they were still Romans and therefore his enemies. Heracles bore the indignity of teaching their children Greek letters well enough, but he refused to allow any compassion to enter his heart. It was when the father was away that he took the first steps of his revenge on the Roman people. Pity and any sense of remorse had died with his family, making it all too easy to slash the throats of the Roman babes while they slept. The wife took much more doing, for he first had to be rid of her troublesome maidservant. He was pleasantly surprised to learn that if honed sharp enough, a butcher's cleaver could sever a human head from its shoulders. He had at first thought to rape the domina of the house, but so hot was his hatred that his manhood failed him. She had mocked his lack of masculinity as she struggled in his grasp. He then settled for disemboweling her, spilling her entrails with repeated blows of the cleaver. He left her convulsing in agony as death took its time coming for her. With as much coin as he could carry and one of the children's horses he fled. Racing through the night he felt a morbid sense of satisfaction. There was no room in his now blackened heart for anything else. If happiness was gone forever from his life and such feelings were the best he could hope for, then so be it.

It was in the north, outside of Augustodunum, that he met Sacrovir and Florus. The two men were Gallic nobles who sought to plant the seeds of rebellion. Heracles cared little for Gauls, viewing them as unkempt barbarians even after more than seventy years of Roman rule and influence. However, he saw an opportunity to further unleash his revenge. Unfortunately, Sacrovir and Florus were not military men. Florus was the typical pompous noble who only sought rebellion as a means of freeing himself from his debts. Sacrovir, while eager and cunning had made the most of his fortune financing gladiatorial games. He had lost a substantial portion of this when one of his best was killed by a common Roman soldier. Heracles found it ironic that his own gambling lust had long since perished.

Their army that they spent nearly a year raising consisted mostly of thieves, debtors, and former slaves, though Sacrovir had captured the trust of a large contingent of noble youths who also flocked to his banner. Still they proved little match for the legions of Rome. Heracles had taught the rebels how to fight in a phalanx, and yet they broke at first contact with the legions and their auxiliary cavalry. Most fled into the hills, while the noble youths, who served as the vanguard of Sacrovir's force, were either captured or killed. The surviving leaders had fled to Sacrovir's estate, only to be hunted down after a captured rebel betrayed them.

And yet, he could not let it end this way. When Sacrovir and the others fell on their swords while the estate burned over their heads, Heracles slunk away. It was only well after the Romans had left that he returned to find Sacrovir's sword.

The result was a great tragedy for Gaul, for the rebellion of Sacrovir and Florus had seen a generation of their noble youths destroyed; young, impressionable lads who had been brainwashed by Sacrovir's poisoned tongue, only to be utterly savaged by Rome's invincible legions. Those who survived were either ransomed at a heavy toll to their families, or sent to the sulfur mines in Mauretania. Heracles cared little for the Gauls' suffering, and the small numbers of legionaries who died during the campaign did nothing to ease his hatred.

A knock at the door brought him out of his reminiscing. He picked up his sword and stood behind the door.

"Enter!" he beckoned as the door creaked open. A hunched old man entered, bearing a tray of food and a bottle of port.

"Your dinner, sir," he said as he peered into the darkness. The old man gave a jolt as Heracles briskly closed the door behind him.

"Thank you," the Spartan said, his sword hidden behind his back.

"I've got some bread cooking, sir, if you would like some," the innkeeper said nervously. The strange man who occupied this room unnerved him, and under most circumstances he would have cast him out onto the street; however the man appeared to be quite wealthy and had paid him far more than the room was worth. Money could make even the meekest of men brave.

"Yes, that would be fine," Heracles replied, opening the door once again. The old man smiled and shuffled out. Heracles let out a sigh. He was becoming paranoid. He had been in Massila for four months now and his coin had kept the senile innkeeper quiet. The hustle and bustle of the busy port town had lent him an incredible amount of autonomy. No one bothered him here, and no one was looking for him either. For all the Romans knew, every rebel leader had died with Sacrovir.

A year had passed since the disastrous rebellion and it would soon be safe to move about freely again. What he would do then he was not sure. He knew that a province revolution was impossible. If Sacrovir and Florus had failed to gain the support of the masses, he knew he would have no chance. It mattered not; for his quest was one of retribution against Rome, nothing more. His was a personal war against Rome and it was now his life's work. He then decided that he would sow the seeds of discord by annihilating an entire Roman garrison. Surely that would give him some satisfaction; more so than a few dead legionaries amongst the piles of Gallic dead. But where would he strike? Lugdunum was to the north, along the Rhodanus River. It was a large city, and its urban police were reinforced by a cohort of legionaries. These men were from Legio XX, the Valeria Legion; one of the two that had put down the Sacrovir Revolt. The other had been Legio I, Germanica, which shared a fortress on the Rhine with the Twentieth. These men would bear the brunt of Heracles' wrath.

Wiping out this garrison would not come easy; a single legionary cohort was a fearsome enemy consisting of six eighty-man centuries of the fiercest and most disciplined soldiers not seen since the height of Sparta. As much as it wounded his pride, Heracles begrudgingly recognized Rome as superior to Sparta; for Sparta and all of Greece had been defeated by Rome centuries before. Rome had achieved what Xerxes and the entire Persian Empire had failed to do; subjugate Sparta. It had been nearly two hundred years since the combined forces of Macedonia, which now included Sparta, had faced Rome in battle. The Battle of Pydna had been a crushing defeat for King Perseus and was generally accepted as the classic example of how the Greek phalanx had been proven inferior to the Roman legion.

So how did one go about annihilating a cohort of Roman soldiers? Direct assault was impossible; it would take thousands of men and even then victory could not be certain. No, this would require cunning and deceit rather than brute force. Heracles remembered all-too-well what had happened the last time Gauls had tried to overpower Rome. At Augustodunum the army of Sacrovir had the Roman force outnumbered at least three to one, perhaps even more? Heracles had worked diligently to try and teach that rabble of beggars and thieves how to fight in a proper phalanx. Though the phalanx was an inferior formation as opposed to the legion, it was still preferred when one's army was undisciplined amateurs.

Sacrovir had encased his vanguard of noble youths in plate armor, in an attempt to break up the Roman formations. The result was catastrophic. In their ingenuity, the legions had attacked this force with pickaxes, chopping down their foe like small trees. Only the vanguard and Sacrovir's gladiators attempted to withstand the Roman onslaught; the bulk of his army of thieves fled in terror at first contact. A regiment of Roman cavalry, led by a Treveri noble named Julius Indus, had attacked both wings of Sacrovir's force with devastating effect. What spurred Heracles even more was that Indus had at first been one of Sacrovir's confidants, only to betray him and align his regiment with Rome. Indeed, it had been Indus' regiment that along with a single cohort of legionaries had destroyed a far superior force led by Florus; the rebel leader falling on his sword when he saw that all was lost. The Emperor Tiberius had been most generous to Indus, awarding him Rome's highest honor, the Civic Crown. He had also ordered the Treveri regiment to be permanently named *Indus' Horse.*

"Enjoy the spoils of Rome while you can," Heracles said in a low voice. "For the time will come that you will pay for your treachery." A grim smile crossed his face. There was a ship bound for Mauretania leaving in the morning. It was time to visit some old friends.

CHAPTER II

▼

CALM AFTER THE STORM

Vexilation Garrison of Legio XX, Cohort III,
Lugdunum, Gaul

The sun shown over the hills; the city of Lugdunum was slowly waking up to the start of the new day. Artorius stood on the small balcony, stretched his arms overhead and breathed deeply. The cool breeze felt pleasant and invigorating and he enjoyed the view from up there. The glow of the sun as it cast its light on the forum in the distance was a far better sight than the view from his barracks back in Cologne, where all you saw was another barracks block across from you.

The Third Cohort had been garrisoned at Lugdunum ever since the end of the Sacrovir Revolt. Though such postings were not unusual, it was the first for Artorius in his six years with the legions.

Six years, he thought to himself. *Has it really been that long?* Of course six years paled in comparison to the lengths that some of his fellow soldiers had been serving. Master Centurion Calvinus, the Legion's Primus Pilus, had been in the army for twenty-seven years; four years longer than Artorius had been alive. The thought was a little overwhelming, especially with everything that had happened to him thus far in his young career. He was a veteran of many savage battles and brutal campaigns and had been decorated three times for valor or meritorious service. Everyday citizens could never comprehend the magnitude of experience possessed by even the youngest of legionaries. Contrary to popular belief, most Roman men did not join the legions upon reaching the age of maturity. Rome's total combined military force, to include legionaries, auxilia, and urban cohorts, numbered roughly three hundred thousand men under arms. Of these less than half, maybe one hundred and twenty-five thousand, were legionaries; a miniscule percentage of an empire's population that numbered upwards of seventy million souls.

Though he had already seen and done more than most would ever in a dozen lifetimes, his age still reared its head on occasion. Within the Second Century he was the youngest of the Decanii; the Sergeants of legionaries. He was also the youngest chief weapons instructor in the entire Third Cohort. This led to him sometimes being referred to as "the boy Decanus." The fact that he had a young face which required a shave but once a week added to this image. In truth Artorius relished looking so young, for he figured that perhaps when he was forty he would still pass for a man in his late twenties to early thirties.

He was extremely muscular and strong. Though he could not say for certain, but he figured he outweighed even the tallest and best-built men in the Third Cohort; something he took pride in.

Be that as it may, his age had certainly not held him back from becoming Valeria's *Legion Champion*, where his physical power complemented his skill in battle nicely. During the spring before the Sacrovir Revolt, sixty-four of the best close combat fighters in the legion had faced off in a tournament, with Artorius emerging victorious. And he also distinguished himself as a leader of men during the rebellion. During some fierce fighting with a vastly superior enemy force in the mountains outside of Augusta Raurica, he had organized a hasty defense with two other sections that repelled a rebel counterattack.

He let out a sigh. The strain of his position took its toll on him some days, and he was glad for the reprieve that being garrisoned in Lugdunum brought him. He had been so eager for promotion that he took advantage of the opportunity afforded him without thinking through the full consequences brought on by promotion. How the Centurions handled the extreme pressure and responsibility placed on them he had no idea.

"Morning," a voice behind him said through a loud yawn. Artorius turned to see his friend Magnus stretching his arms out to his sides while yawning still. "Aren't you cold?" The Norseman had already donned his tunic, while Artorius was still naked to the waist. Magnus was slightly taller than Artorius and almost as muscular. His skin was much fairer and his head covered with a mop of blonde hair.

"Ah, the cool spring breeze feels good first thing in the morning," the Decanus replied.

"You keep standing out there like that and your nipples are going to get all perky like an aroused whore," Magnus replied. Artorius ignored him.

"You realize that we haven't done a single road march since we've been here?" he asked aloud. Magnus nodded. "Well, we'll just have to fix that. Can't let the boys get all soft on us now."

"Too much wine and prostitutes do you think?" Magnus asked, scratching the back of his head.

"Too much wine perhaps," Artorius consented, "but I wouldn't say too much fornication. Every physician I have ever met says that it is healthy for men to constantly relieve themselves of excess testicular man-load!" His friend laughed out loud at his assessment.

"Yes, and I'm sure they put it as succinctly as you!"

"But of course," Artorius replied with a wink. He then let out a sigh and assessed his physique. "I'll lay off the alcohol but don't think for a second I'm going to stop trying to bury my cock in as many delicate young women as I can!"

"Hmm, well you know it's not just the young ones who have to worry," the Norseman said with a grin. Artorius gave a shrug.

"Well yes, I do in fact like the ones who are a bit older and are more in tune with their bodies. How'd you know?" Magnus gave a shrug of his own and grinned.

"Oh, it's just that some of the lads and I saw a couple of women bearing the *mark of Artorius*." Magnus was referring to his Decanus' tendency to leave visible bite marks on the necks of women he associated with.

"Vitruvius made mention of a Greek gymnasium in the city the other day," Magnus added, changing the subject. Artorius frowned in contemplation.

"That's not one of those places where Greeks get sweaty and naked together is it?" he asked.

"Probably," his friend replied with a laugh. "But hey, if they've got the equipment that will allow us to build enough muscle that we put the statues of the gods to shame, I'm all for it." Artorius grinned. Though he may have been getting a little soft, he still possessed more muscle mass and power than any in the Third Cohort; probably the entire Legion. The thought of tightening up the areas that were growing soft and adding even more muscle to his frame greatly appealed to him.

"Well let's go and find it then, shall we?"

They decided to take a walk through the city first. Lugdunum was a mixture of Gallic, Roman, and Greek architecture; a melting pot of cultures that Artorius found to be both fascinating as well as slightly perverse. He pointed this out to Magnus, who looked at him with a raised eyebrow.

"Artorius, you seem to forget that *I* am a type of cultural melting pot," he said as they walked past an old timber mead hall; a place where Gallic warriors and nobles would come to feast and celebrate martial victories in ages past. "I am a Norseman whose family, outside of my father and brothers, still lives in the Scandinavian regions outside of the Empire. And yet I am also a Roman."

"So how exactly do you go about fitting into both cultures?" Artorius asked. Magnus gave a slight chuckle at that.

"To be honest, it isn't easy some days," he replied. "My grandfather, who won us our citizenship in the first place, still wears his hair in a long ponytail, his great beard braided on both sides of his chin. He laughs and jokes with my father and I about how effeminate we look with our short hair and clean-shaven faces." Artorius started laughing aloud.

"Magnus, you are anything but effeminate!"

"I know that," his friend replied, "and so does my grandfather, even if he did say I looked like the quintessential boy lover! The thing is he spent twenty-five years as an auxiliary to earn Roman citizenship, not for himself, but for his sons. Once his tenure was over he returned home to the old country. His sons at least had the opportunity to put their citizenship to use. Strangely enough, only my father chose to do so … ah, here we are."

They came upon a large marble building, one with massive pillars and stairs leading to the main doors. A large brass plaque was posted on the right-hand side of the doors. It read:

Lugdunum Gymnasium
Only the Strong May Enter

"Think we qualify?" Magnus asked, looking at Artorius inquisitively. Artorius raised and flexed his right bicep. Though softer than was usual for him, the bulging muscles still looked impressive.

"Yeah, I think we'll be alright," he joked as they walked inside. Artorius was in awe as he gazed upon the interior of the gymnasium. Never before had he seen such masculine beauty. There were stones of various sizes, along with bars and other equipment for building strength; ropes hung from the ceiling that men could be seen climbing up and down; a roped off area in a sand pit provided an area for men to box and wrestle; steam poured from the communal sauna; and through the back archway one could see a lengthy pool with men swimming in it.

"About time you two showed up!" a voice yelled at them from over at the strength training floor. They looked over to see Vitruvius, shirtless and covered in sweat. His muscles were pumped up and swollen, ready to burst through the skin.

Artorius grinned broadly and hurried down the steps to join his friend and mentor. "By Apollo, but you two have gone soft!"

"Eh, I was never that hard to begin with," Magnus lied. Artorius raised an eyebrow at the remark.

"Hey, your issues with getting 'hard' are not my concern," Vitruvius replied with an elbow to the ribs. "Well come on, I just got warmed up!"

A passion burned inside each of the men as they sweated their way through exercises meant to add size to their powerful frames. Artorius knew that it had always been there, being that he had built his size and strength in a very crude form of a home-made gym when he was a young lad. Magnus possessed that inborn Scandinavian power and tenacity; his very soul wished for nothing more than to become bigger and stronger. Vitruvius … if ever there was a god incarnate, it was him. Artorius could only match him in size and power because of his extreme work ethics. An unspoken bond was born between the three men; they would meet every day and build their bodies above and beyond what they had ever thought possible. Rank played no role in their relationship of stone and steel. Once they passed through those doors, the only thing that mattered was the formation of brutal strength.

Through each muscle-building exercise they would push each other. Great stones would they press overhead. Each man tried to outdo the others in numbers of repetitions completed. Another stone would he wrap his arms around and squat down until his thighs were parallel with the ground, all the while heeding the shouts of encouragement from his companions as he fought to do one more repetition. A simple bar on a wooden frame they would use for doing pull ups to widen their backs and increase bicep strength.

Several weeks into their routine, Artorius and Magnus were walking back to their billets, Vitruvius having gone ahead by himself. Once they left the gymnasium the boundaries of rank returned and fraternization was avoided. They soon came upon the slave market at Four Corners Road. The stockades reminded Artorius of the ones they had hastily erected following the Battle of Augustodunum to handle the large number of prisoners they had taken. He expressed this to his friend who simply shrugged.

"Slaves are slaves, nothing special," Magnus stated. "To tell the truth, I've always had little use for them."

"Do your people in the high country use slaves much?" Artorius asked as he gazed at the mournful faces that stared from behind the bars while patrons eyed them for possible purchase.

"Of course," Magnus replied, "though not on the scale you see here. Mostly prisoners of conquered tribes are all you see. While my native people don't exactly oppose slavery, they don't market human beings on the scale like you see within the Empire."

They then reminisced about the consequences suffered by the nobles who had been dragged into Sacrovir's rebellion. Thousands of noble youths had been killed in battle; and of those who survived, dozens had been sold into slavery when their fathers refused to pay their ransoms. The ransoms had been severe, and had cost many a noble family their lands and treasure. The lands confiscated had been auctioned off, with many Roman nobles taking advantage of the deals. Centurion Proculus had even taken part, purchasing lands and an estate, which were now under the care of one of his cousins. He had already bought himself a grand villa on Esquiline Hill; however he was quick to jump on the opportunity to buy him and his wife a nice estate in the country. Artorius remembered seeing this cousin once, a rather fetching lady named Diana. He had not had the opportunity to see her up close, as he was on a patrol that morning; though even from a distance he could tell she was absolutely radiant. So enraptured had Artorius been that once off duty he had rushed to the nearest brothel and bought himself the most expensive courtesan he could find, just to get her out of his mind.

"A month's pay blown in one night!" Magnus heckled as they arrived at the Principia.

"Well I didn't require a wank for about a week after that, so I think it was well spent!" Artorius retorted as he went inside for his monthly meeting with the Tesserarius to go over the Century's duty roster for the next month.

✳   ✳   ✳   ✳

Drusus sighed as he walked down the corridor with some reports in hand for his father, the Emperor. He worked to stifle a cough, his health still weakened by a recent illness. It was this very illness that had brought about the death of a man who had in recent years been rewarded by Tiberius for a stirring poetic tribute he had done to the memory of the Emperor's nephew, the late Germanicus Caesar. Drusus coughed once more before knocking on the door to his father's study.

"Enter!" the voice inside boomed. Taking another deep breath, Drusus walked in and saw Tiberius seated at his desk, hands folded in contemplation.

"Message from Lepidus," Drusus said, handing a scroll to the Emperor. Tiberius scowled as he read the message from the senator. He set the scroll on his desk and walked over to the window, his hands clasped behind his back.

"The more the senate tries to please me, the more they earn my displeasure," he said at length. "At least Lepidus had the good sense to try and save us from an unnecessary slaying." The issue at hand was that the man, named Priscus, had written another poem of remembrance as a precaution in case Drusus succumbed to his illness. He had then read said poem in the presence of a number of ladies of rank, who were then frightened into testifying against him when an informant appeared and accused Priscus of seeking the death of the Imperial heir in order to fatten his own purse. The Senate, hastily trying to show its solidarity with the Imperial family, invoked the death penalty on the accused. Haterius Agrippa, the consul-elect, had made the motion for the maximum penalty. Of all the senators present, only Marcus Lepidus showed any common sense and spoke against the sentence with the following speech:

"Senators, if we look to the single fact of the infamous utterance with which Lutorius Priscus has polluted his own mind and the ears of the public, neither dungeon nor halter nor tortures fit for a slave would be punishment enough for him. But though vice and wicked deeds have no limit, penalties and correctives are moderated by the clemency of the sovereign and by the precedents of your ancestors and yourselves.

"Folly differs from wickedness; evil words from evil deeds, and thus there is room for a sentence by which this offence may not go unpunished, while we shall have no cause to regret either leniency or severity. Often have I heard our emperor complain when any one has anticipated his mercy by a self-inflicted death. Lutorius' life is still safe; if spared, he will be no danger to the State; if put to death, he will be no warning to others. His productions are as empty and ephemeral as they are replete with folly. Nothing serious or alarming is to be apprehended from the man who is the betrayer of his own shame and works on the imaginations not of men but of silly women. However, let him leave Rome, lose his property, and be outlawed. That is my proposal, just as though he were convicted under the law of treason."[1] Only a former consul named Rubellius supported Lepidus. The rest voted to have Priscus dragged off to prison and instantly put to death.

"Priscus was a fool," Drusus observed, "but he was a harmless fool. He was a great poet and orator, and it saddens me that he was executed for simply trying to find the words to console his Emperor should the worst have happened to me."

"His conduct was still inexcusable," Tiberius replied, turning to face his son, "though I still concur with Lepidus' assessment. Mere words should not have warranted a death sentence. I will have words with the Senate and see if we can correct this type of rash behavior." There was a pause as Tiberius felt that the issue was done. He raised an eyebrow as Drusus still remained in the room waiting patiently.

"Father, there is another issue I wish to discuss." Drusus dreaded the pending argument he knew he could no longer avoid. He had thought of ways he could bring Tiberius to see reason regarding his Praetorian Prefect without making it seem personal. Unfortunately, Drusus knew he had taken things with Sejanus too far and too publicly. Indeed, he had earned the nickname *Castor*, or "brute" after he physically assaulted Sejanus following a heated argument.

"Well let's hear it," the Emperor replied. Tiberius hoped that whatever it was that troubled his son it had nothing to do with Sejanus. He had recently severely reprimanded both men and made clear to them that he would not have his right and left hands fighting each other.

"It's about the realignment of the Praetorians ..." Drusus started to speak before Tiberius cut him off.

"By the Divine Augustus, why must you question every decision my Prefect makes?" he interrupted, a scowl creasing his hard face.

"Father, please hear me out," Drusus persisted, raising a hand in emphasis. The Emperor made it a point of hearing his son out, no matter what the issue; for whatever lack of communication there may have been between Tiberius and the Senate, he needed to stay close to his son who would become Emperor when he was gone.

"Believe me when I say that my concerns are in no way connected to my personal antipathy towards Sejanus," Drusus continued. "I know he stated to you that by placing the scattered cohorts into one barracks it would strengthen their numbers and resolve; and it would allow them to receive their orders simultaneously. While these points are not without merit, the end result is far different. If you have been out in the city in recent weeks you would know that the populous is terrified of the Praetorians. And did you know he hand-picked the Centurions and Tribunes himself? No other organization within the whole of the Empire, military or otherwise, is so directly controlled by one man."

"I've seen the lists of Centurions and Tribunes of the Praetorians," Tiberius remarked. "They are all good men of status and merit. Indeed his Deputy Prefect, Pontius Pilate, served under your brother, Germanicus, and came to us with the highest recommendations for his valor and conduct."

"I do not deny that Pilate was an honorable soldier," Drusus conceded, though in his mind he believed Pontius Pilate had become little more than a political pawn for Sejanus. "And speaking of Pilate, what is this I hear that he is being sent to the east?"

"I was not aware of this," Tiberius replied, "though if Sejanus thinks it would be useful ..." Drusus threw his hands up in the air in exacerbation before the Emperor could finish.

"Father, when will you open your eyes?" he asked. "Now he seeks to expand his influence to the legions!"

"Enough!" Tiberius barked, slamming his fist onto the table. "I will not have the man who has been my right hand for all these years talked to in such a slanderous tone; not even by my own son!" Drusus nodded quietly and backed out of the room. He knew when he had gone too far with his father; and further discussion on the issue of Sejanus would be counterproductive. He would have to find another way of dealing with the man he was convinced wished to sit where his father sat. His head hurt and he decided to head home. He hoped Livilla would be home; she always had a way of making him feel better after one of his bouts with the Emperor. She never would tell him what it was she put into his drink to make him sleep so well, but he was grateful for it.

*   *   *   *

"Legio XII, Fulminata," Pilate read aloud. He looked up from the scroll bearing his assignment orders and looked at Sejanus, puzzled.

"It's only a temporary assignment," the Praetorian Prefect reassured him. "There have been some issues with the eastern legions, and I need to get a set of reliable eyes on them for a little while. Don't worry, you will still hold the billet of Deputy Praetorian Prefect, and I don't imagine you will be gone for much more than a year or so."

"What do you mean 'need a set of reliable eyes on them?'" Pilate asked, his face betraying his concern.

"Legio VI sent a certain Optio to act as a liaison for the eastern legions," Sejanus answered. Pilate shrugged in reply.

"Yes, Justus Longinus; he's an old friend of mine. What of it?"

Sejanus gave an audible sigh and gave Pilate a pat on the shoulder. "You have much to learn, my friend. Justus was sent to keep an eye on us, well at least *me* at any rate. There have been many grumblings coming from the east ever since the death of Germanicus four years ago."

"Does the Emperor know of this?"

"Of course," Sejanus lied. "Nothing that goes on within the Empire gets past Tiberius; I see to that personally. Right now we need a direct Imperial influence to restore some order to the eastern legions. I could go, but the Legates would see this as a personal affront to their authority. By sending my Deputy they won't feel so threatened. It will show that we are not out to undermine their positions; however, it also lets them know that the Emperor is watching and will not tolerate any lapses in order, discipline, and loyalty." Pilate nodded.

"Whatever I can do to serve the Emperor," he asserted.

"Know that Tiberius will reward those who prove their loyalty," Sejanus emphasized. It was coming together all too easy. Pilate would be his eyes and ears in the east and through him he would extend his reach to the farthest corner of the Empire. All the while Pilate would be under the assumption that he was directly serving the Emperor. Sejanus would reward him, of course; and it would be in such a way that Pilate could continue to do his bidding.

In Sejanus' opinion he needed to keep Pontius Pilate away from Rome as much as possible. Pilate was in the unique position that he had served most of his adult career thus far with the legions, instead of doing the mandatory six months and then moving on to more politically advantageous assignments. The frontier legions had a sense of nobility, almost a naivety about them. The longer Pilate stayed in Rome, the more questions he would ask. During his time in the legions he had developed a strong sense of right and wrong that Sejanus found irritating. Still, he had found a use for Pilate's sense of ethics, as long as he did not keep him around too long. As long as Pontius Pilate felt that he was serving the Emperor, Sejanus could manipulate him into doing just about anything.

CHAPTER III

▼

OUT OF THE SHADOWS

The Mauritanian coast and the city of Caesarea were in sight; however Heracles would wait until dark before disembarking. Like always, no questions were asked. From here it would be but a short journey south to Zucchabar.

The voyage had been disagreeable to Heracles. He hated the sea, though he was choice less when it came to the trip to Mauretania. The seas had been reasonably calm, and Heracles had stayed in the back of the ship, in a small cabin. A few coins to the ship's captain and no questions were asked. Thankfully he had been able to hang his head out the stern window every the swells played havoc on his stomach. He lay down on the hammock strung across the cabin and closed his eyes. He did not recall falling asleep, but yet he was awoken by a quiet knocking at the door.

"The sun has set," a voice said from the other side, "time for you to leave my ship." While the captain liked Heracles' coin, the man made him very nervous and he was glad to be rid of him.

"So it is," Heracles replied. He secured what few belongings he had brought with him; threw the hood of his cloak over his head and quickly walked out the door almost running into the captain. A few deckhands stared in curiosity at this strange man they had brought to the coast of Africa. None could see his face, and in truth they wondered if they wanted to. Rumors had abounded that the man they had given passage to was not a man at all, but a demonic spirit. Heracles had overheard some of the talk and he had smiled inside wickedly at it.

If only they knew, he thought to himself.

Dry land had never felt so good to Heracles though he had to steady himself on against a pillar in order to regain his balance. The docks were fairly quiet, aside from the cargo being offloaded from the ship he had just disembarked. Panic gripped him when he saw a Roman warship a few docks down; dozens of legionaries disembarking. His eyes wide, he grabbed a passerby and pointed towards the Romans.

"Who are they?" he asked. The man shook him off, indignant at being grabbed by a complete stranger.

"*Who are they,* he asks," the man retorted. "That's elements of Legio IX, Hispania; here to help put down the rebellion."

Rebellion? Heracles thought to himself. Of course! He had forgotten that over the last three years numerous Mauritanian and Numidian tribes had become mutinous. Rarely was an empire so large ever fully at peace.

"Seems the Third Legion severely botched things a couple years ago," the man continued. "Cowardice ran rampant and they got punished by decimation for it. Hispania's been sending troops to clean up their mess." With that the man went on his way.

Heracles gave short, mirthless laugh at the mention of decimation. This was the most severe punishment utilized by the Roman army, where one man in ten, regardless of guilt or innocence, was summarily executed. Because of the extreme nature of this punishment, it was almost never used, so the offenses and cowardice committed by Legio III must have been severe indeed!

"If only the legions we faced in Gaul had been so," he said to himself in a low voice.

It was overcast, which was a blessing for Heracles. Spring rains kept the dust down as the cart made its way along the dirt road that led to the sulfur mines. A wheeled cage was towed behind them; his quarry would need to still give the appearance of being slaves once they were bought. The Greek kept his cloak around him tightly, Sacrovir's spatha concealed in its folds. His pouch of gold was heavy, though he knew better than to trust his riches to any man while he travelled. The old man at the tavern had promised to keep his room for him, though Heracles knew it would be picked clean before his return.

"Here we are then," the cart driver said as they gazed upon the depressing sight that was the sulfur mines. There was nothing but barren rock, with few outcroppings of vegetation. Heracles dismounted without a word and walked briskly towards the small group of buildings which housed the slave drivers and the offices of the mine owners. He paid little heed to the row of newly-arrived slaves who were being accounted for by the shift foreman. A pity for them that it was overcast that day; they would not even get a final glimpse of the sun. Heracles found the main office and pushed open the door. A bored clerk was busy writing sales receipts for customers.

"Here to pick up merchandise or dropping off slaves?" he asked without looking up.

"Neither," Heracles replied. "I'm here to purchase a couple slaves." The clerk raised his eyes to assess the Greek and gave a short laugh.

"I'm not sure I understand you," he stated, his eyebrows furrowed. "This is not a place one comes to *buy* slaves. This is where slaves get dumped off because they are of no use to anyone else."

"Yes, well there are a couple in particular that I am interested in," Heracles replied.

"Ah, family members, or lost friends perhaps?"

"You could say that," Heracles answered, his expression never changing. "Mind if I look at your prisoner rolls for those brought in, oh say around September and October of last year?"

"Sure," the clerk replied with a shrug. He pointed his thumb over his shoulder to a shelf lined with scrolls. "Have a look over there, if you wish. Just don't go messing up the order of the books!" Heracles gave a nod and the clerk went back to his work. He grabbed a couple of scrolls and started to read through them. Most of the names were lined through, with the words "deceased" written over them. He gave a mirthless snort at that. Not many survived more than a few months in the hell of those mines. Accidents were common, the sulfur burned the eyes until one went blind, and the very air was a poisonous fume. Indeed even the slave drivers who returned to the surface after their shifts put their lives and their health in great peril by working in such conditions.

Heracles saw one group from the first part of October that gave him pause. There was an asterisk next to many of the names. At the bottom of the page was a note that said " * - *Prisoners of war, do not release under any circumstances!*" Most of these had long since perished as well, though one name stood out. Radek was not a name that Heracles recognized; however he figured the man must have been one of the debtors and thieves that Sacrovir and Florus had taken into their army. Many of the slaves had only one name listed; family names probably unknown to many.

"I want this one," Heracles stated, pointing to Radek's name; the rest of the prisoners of war having perished, quite possibly with some help from their new masters. The clerk laughed and shook his head.

"You can't have that one," he said with finality. "If we released a prisoner of war, the Roman governor would cast us down into those mines!"

"Oh I think I can have this one," Heracles said with an equal air of determination. "Send for the foreman and I will discuss this with him."

"Fair enough," the man replied with a shrug. A few minutes later he returned with a rather burly and hairy man who looked as if he had not bathed in weeks. A short whip hung from his left hand.

"Hey, who in the bloody fuck are you, thinking I'm going to hand over a prisoner of war!" he spat with a vile sneer that exposed his blackened teeth.

"Someone willing to make it worth your while," Heracles replied. He reached into his bag and pulled out a gold piece that he tossed nonchalantly towards the foreman. The coin was worth about seventy-five denarii--a third of a legionary's annual wages--and the grisly man gave a frown of comprehension while he turned it over in his hand.

"Well I'll be buggered," he said. "I wouldn't give a bottle of piss for any one of those scabs, but if he means that much to you ..."

"He means nothing to me," Heracles corrected in his calm but firm voice. "I'll give you three gold pieces for the man; plus one more to each of you for keeping your mouths *shut*. You have never seen me; I have never been here. The prisoner Radek died of a fever on the twenty-second of April. Am I making myself clear?"

"Quite," the foreman replied. Behind him the clerk licked his lips in anticipation.

✱   ✱   ✱   ✱

Radek could not believe his ill fortune to still be alive. The socket where his left eye had once been was a putrid mass, the wounds to his back and leg from a Roman lance in a constant state of infection. He did not understand why he was not allowed to die like all the others who had come to the mines with him. Many had been in finer health than he, having not suffered such grievous wounds as his. These had mostly been young men, boys really, whose fathers had refused to pay their ransoms and had left them to die in the mines. And die they did, for not one of them could have fathomed the sheer torments they would be subjected to. His little plaything had not even lasted a few days. Radek had grabbed the boy so he could have his way with him in the dim cavern where they slept, only to find the boy was dead. Such had ruined his day. It was while he mused on his hard bunk that he saw the torches coming down the passage.

"It can't be time to go back already," one slave whimpered in the dark. Radek rolled onto his side, away from the torchlight. He was beyond exhausted, his persistent cough continuing to grow worse. The butt of a spear jabbed him in the back, where his wounds from the battle at Augustodunum refused to heal.

"You!" the guard bark, "you're coming with us." Radek rolled off the boards and landed roughly on his feet.

"Come to put me out of my misery?" His remark led the guard to rapping him across the face with his spear.

"Move!" As they wandered down the narrow, dark corridor, they came to a place where the passages branched off. Radek instinctively started towards the right-hand passage when the guard jabbed in the back with the spear point.

"Other way," he snapped, which confused the slave. Radek had only been down that passage once, and that was when he was brought to this accursed place. Slowly he made his way up the passage, his bad leg continuously cramping on him. A short flight of stone steps led to a door where a pair of guards stood posted. One forced open the heavy wooden door where Radek was suddenly blinded by the sunlight. He placed his hand over his face protectively. It had been months since he had last seen the sun and the brightness hurt his eye.

"Aren't we a frightful sight," a voice said. Heracles felt nauseated looking at Radek. The man was covered in sulfur burns, his beard and hair matted in knots, puss seeping from his multiple wounds and festering eye socket.

"Who the bloody piss are you?" Radek asked, still trying to shield his eye from the sun. He could not make out Heracles' face, but his voice sounded familiar.

"A friend," the Greek replied. "And now I'm your new master." His face darkened at this last remark. This wretched shell of a man would serve him, even unto death. Radek let out a sigh.

"Well any master is better than the mines," he remarked, his sight slowly returning. He gave an evil grin as he at last recognized Heracles.

"I know you," he said. The Greek nodded.

"That you do. Come, let us leave this place." There were about a dozen other men that had been purchased by Heracles. He had paid less for the rest combined than he had for Radek alone. This was not lost on the clerk as he and the foreman watched the rag-tag contingent walk down the slope towards their waiting wagon.

"What make you of that?" the clerk asked. "This man buys a dozen of our least shoddy slaves for market prices, and yet he pays as much for that one wretched creature as for the rest together." The foreman folded his arms across the chest as a couple of slaves helped Radek into the wagon.

"Our silence has been bought," he replied. "The slave Radek died of his injuries and lies in the burn pit with the rest of the damned."

✳   ✳   ✳   ✳

"How are your men adjusting to their new accommodations?" Tiberius asked. Sejanus walked beside him through the shaded gardens, keeping a respectful half-step behind the Emperor.

"Very well, Caesar," he replied. "Our reaction times to crises have improved ten-fold. Morale is high and the men feel more unified in a sense of common purpose."

"That is good," the Emperor said, feeling reassured. "And what is this I hear about you sending your Deputy to the east?"

"A mere courtesy visit to the eastern legions," Sejanus stated. "There have been some grumblings in the east and I felt a direct representative from us would help to quell any misgivings the eastern legates may have." Tiberius frowned in contemplation.

"I have not heard of any such misgivings," he said after a few moments of thought.

"Forgive me, Caesar; I did not wish to disturb you with what I am certain is a minor matter," Sejanus responded quickly.

"Yes, well I'm certain you'll take care of it," Tiberius replied, waving his hand dismissively. "You have yet to lead me wrong, my friend, and I trust you more than any."

"Surely you don't trust me more than your son," the Prefect said with mock surprise. The Emperor paused for a moment, took a deep breath, and continued his walk.

"Drusus does his best to serve me," he said. "However, his judgment is constantly clouded by emotion, particularly his anger towards you. Did you know he came to me just the other day expressing his concerns about the new Praetorian barracks?"

"But surely Caesar, the reorganization of the Guard has been a resounding success!"

"I know that," Tiberius replied. "Drusus sees it as a means of you consolidating your power and he somehow feels threatened by it."

"I assure you," Sejanus persisted, "that if the time comes while I am still in my post I will serve Drusus just as fervently as I serve you." He was impressed by his own skills of persuasion. Tiberius *believed* him. All the same, Drusus was becoming more than a mere nuisance. Sejanus knew that should anything befall Tiberius, his own life would probably be forfeit; so deep was Drusus' hatred towards him. It was now more than just a mere matter of consolidating his rise in power, his family's very survival would depend upon the removal of Drusus Caesar.

✳　　✳　　✳　　✳

Heracles hated being back at sea once again, though at least now he had some company. He had purchased a handful of other slaves from the mines along with that beast Radek. These particular men had not been prisoners of war; all the same such was their gratitude towards the man who had liberated them that they would follow Heracles into the gates of Hell itself. He contemplated how best they could serve him. Men of such loyalty were not to be expended wastefully; however he knew that his ambitions would involve massive numbers of 'expendable labor' as it were.

Slaves, he thought to himself, *I need large numbers of slaves.* Slave markets were ample in the region so acquisition would be simple enough. It was then that an evil thought struck him; one which would supply him with endless hordes and bring about disruption of the province. Slaves made up a large portion of the population; even the poorest plebeians possessed human property. Most slaves were fairly docile, having been born into their lot in life and they accepted it. Heracles also knew that within the deepest souls of each burned a desire for freedom. He would offer it to them ... at a price of course!

CHAPTER IV

▼

A SAD JOURNEY HOME

As the days and weeks rolled by Artorius found that he was growing beyond what he had ever thought possible. His tunics hardly fit anymore; his strength and stamina, which was already savage, were now that of a warhorse. And yet he found himself mentally more relaxed and focused. The gymnasium provided an outlet for his aggression. In his encounters with women he had become more consciously aware of his brutal strength and veracity, and thereby less inclined to try and break them in half, as had been his habit previously. He still had a tendency to bite, though that was more out of habit than anything. He was pondering such conquests when he strolled into the inn where the Principal officers and Centurions were housed. He was there for his monthly meeting with Statorius, the Century's Tesserarius in charge of the duty rosters and guard details. He was surprised to find Decimus sitting in his chair at the table.

"Decimus, what are you doing here?" he asked, an eyebrow raised.

"I was going to ask you the same question," Optio Flaccus interrupted, walking down the hall with a folded note in his hand which he handed to the Decanus.

"What is this?"

"Proculus put out that we need to start rotating the men through on furlough," Flaccus explained. "And since you and Magnus are both from the Ostia area, you two are going together. There's a river barge leaving at dawn tomorrow; take it to Massila, where you will catch a transport ship heading to Ostia."

"*Home,*" Magnus mused. His pack was laid out on his bed as he stuffed it with everything he wanted to take with him. "How long's it been?"

"Four years next month," Artorius replied as he opened his trunk to see what he would need to take with him. There were extra tunics, socks, his razor, hygiene kit, and something he had not expected to find. At the bottom, covered in dust, was a silver medallion on a leather cord. At first he did not know what it was. He grabbed the cord and held the medallion into the light. An image of the goddess Diana was engraved on one side. Artorius let out a sigh and closed his eyes as he remembered where it had come from.

"What's that then?" Magnus asked, glancing over his shoulder.

"Camilla gave this to me ... a long time ago." Indeed it had been six years since Camilla had given him the medallion. She had made him promise that he would wear it everywhere, to protect him from harm. It was a promise he had not kept. No sooner had he left Ostia that the medallion had ended up in his pack, forgotten. He was amazed that it had not been lost over the years.

"Camilla," Magnus said, his brow furrowed in contemplation, "isn't she that sultry twat you so thoroughly violated the last time we were in Rome?" Artorius gave a short laugh.

"That would be her," he replied. "One of them anyway. She and I grew up together; she promised to wait for me ..." his voice trailed off. Without another word, he absentmindedly shoved the medallion into his pack, wrapped up in a pair of his socks.

At length he and Magnus were finished packing. They each strapped on their gladius and belt; armor and helmets would not be needed. Valens and Gavius opened the door to the flat, having just returned from a road repair detail.

"I know you weren't going to leave without saying goodbye to us," Gavius chided with a grin.

"Shit Gavius, we're only going to be gone a couple months," Magnus replied, hefting his pack over his shoulder. "It will probably take a couple weeks to get home, a month of leave, and then probably another couple weeks to get back."

"At which time I'll be going on leave myself," the young legionary replied. "I'll be going with Legionary Felix."

"I thought Felix was from Ravenna?" Magnus asked.

"He is," Artorius replied before Gavius could answer. "But there is nothing there for him; not as long as he has a father who continues to hate him."

✳   ✳   ✳   ✳

At long last the port of Ostia came into view. It had been more than four years since Artorius had last been home. There had not been time to get a letter to his father through the Imperial Post, so there would be no one to greet them at the docks.

"She hasn't changed, has she?" Magnus asked, joining his friend on the bow of the ship. Artorius shook his head.

"Looks the same as when we left her," he replied. Indeed the bustling port looked exactly like he remembered. Though he had been away for years, he knew he could still find his way home blindfolded.

The boat lurched into the slip with a jolt. There were only a handful of other passengers besides the two legionaries; the boat was mostly loaded with goods from Gaul to be sold in the Roman Forum. Artorius and Magnus hefted their packs and strolled down the ramp, their legs wobbly on land as they worked to get used to being on solid ground once more.

"Well I'm off to the textile mill to see if Dad's in," Magnus said. "Hopefully Oleg's around; I haven't seen him since we first joined the legions!"

"I'll catch up with you in a day or so," Artorius replied. "Father and Juliana will be quite surprised to see me, I think. If you get a chance, come up and see us."

"Will do," Magnus asserted with a nod. The two men clasped hands and each went on his way.

It was late afternoon and the market traffic was starting to wane slightly. The crowds generally parted for the legionary, his red tunic, gladius, and pack giving away his identity. He was glad that his father lived outside of Ostia rather than in Rome, for legally he would not be allowed to enter the city armed as he was. He continued his way out of town along the paved road for a few miles until he came to an intersection. The road that ran perpendicular to his front was the Via Valeria. To the east it led to Rome; to the west it led to the coast, veering north and eventually taking travelers to Pisae, more than one hundred miles away. It was this way that Artorius went. A few miles later and he came upon a dirt road that curved up the hill that paralleled the main highway. He was now but a couple miles from home.

The sun cast its light over the eastern hills, bathing the area in a red glow. To his right Artorius saw Juliana's old cottage. He did not know if anyone even lived there now, but he saw a pair of figures-a man and woman from the looks of them-leaving the grounds and heading towards the road. The man carried a walking stick, and Artorius recognized him to be his father, Primus. He gave a laugh and walked towards the couple, his face beaming. He stopped a ways from them, his smile fading as he saw his father and Juliana's demeanor. Both stared at the ground as they walked; an air of sadness about them.

"Father?" Artorius asked, causing Primus to start. He and Juliana both felt a mixture of emotions; whatever it was that saddened them still overwhelming, and yet the joy of seeing their son standing before them.

"Artorius!" Primus cried, dropping his walking stick and embracing his son hard. "You did not even let us know you were coming home!"

"There was no time," Artorius replied. "I had just enough time to pack my things before I had to catch the boat." He then embraced Juliana, his step-mother. "But why the sad faces? Are you not pleased to see me?" Juliana looked down, the trace of a tear visible out of the corner of her eye. Primus was quick to explain.

"I am afraid I have some sad news, my son," he said, placing a hand on Artorius' shoulder. "It's about Camilla."

"What about her?" Artorius asked. "She married that rich boy-lover Marcellus all those years ago. I figured she'd still be living in high society." Primus smiled sadly and patted his son on the shoulder before they continued their walk back towards their home. Juliana remained silent, holding her husband's hand as they walked.

"Camilla's dead," Primus said at last. Artorius stopped in his tracks and faced his father, his face filled with shock.

"She died this morning," Primus continued. "Hers was a sad life at the end. About a year after you returned to the Rhine she had a daughter named Marcia. Marcellus was enraged that she had not born him a son; he immediately divorced her and left her destitute. Since there had been little political gain from their union, her family was powerless to do anything. In fact, they too abandoned her."

"She came to us soon after," Juliana said. "We still had my little cottage and I told her she could stay there; poor thing. She asked us not to tell you of her troubles and that she did not want you to concern yourself, seeing as how you had more important things to worry about."

"Like hell I did!" Artorius retorted. "The war was over; she could have come to me!"

"I think she wanted to," Juliana replied, "but she feared that like everyone else in her life, you would have turned your back on her." Artorius turned away and shook his head, feelings of guilt and regret overwhelming him.

"How did she die?" he asked, turning back to face his father and stepmother. Primus turned his gaze towards the ground. Juliana took a deep breath in through her nose before answering.

"She was never well after being so monstrously abandoned," she said. "She had but one servant living with her, and we tried to see to it that she was taken care of.

Her pride would not allow her to accept most things from us, though. She said letting her stay at my cottage was more than enough. She always swore that she would find a way to pay us back, and it hurt her badly to know that she had no means of support that would allow her to do this.

"You know she always asked how you were doing, but remained steadfast in her resolve that you not know of her plight." Juliana paused, unable to continue.

Whatever differences he and Camilla may have had, he could never forget the girl who had been his best friend in childhood and his first love. At last Juliana broke the silence.

"Your father may scoff at this Artorius, but honestly I think Camilla died of a broken heart."

"I don't scoff at the idea at all," Primus said, looking up at his son once more. "Camilla was a broken woman and nothing would have brought solace to her tortured soul."

"Except the one thing she denied herself," Artorius said. He dropped his pack and turned back towards Juliana's cottage. As he started walking towards it Juliana made a motion to stop him, but Primus grabbed her by the arm.

"Let him go," he said in a low voice. "He needs to see her for himself. The loss of his childhood love that he feels he abandoned, knowing what abject cruelty and despicable acts she was subjected to."

Indeed Artorius' emotions were torn asunder when he at last laid eyes on Camilla. The cottage was dark, a candle on a table providing little additional light as the setting sun shone through the open door. A middle-aged maidservant sat on a stool beside the bed, her eyes filled with tears.

Camilla's body lay on the bed. Her eyes were closed, and Artorius noticed her hair was considerably shorter than she used to keep it. Her face looked peaceful but worn; the torment of her loneliness and sorrow evident. Her hands were folded across her chest and Artorius took hold of one and squeezed it gently. It was cool to the touch, but yet there was still a trace of warmth. Artorius lowered his head, his eyes closed, as he fought back his tears. So much regret did he bear.

"It did not have to end this way," he said quietly to himself. He looked over at the servant, who immediately lowered her head, her own tears flowing freely. This slave, more a piece of property than a human being, was all that Camilla had left. Artorius removed his hand from Camilla's, caressed her cheek with the back of his hand and then ran his fingers through her hair.

"Will Master help me see my lady on to her final journey?" the servant asked, her voice cracking. She looked up at Artorius, her eyes swollen and red. "She never forgot you, sir." Artorius nodded in reply.

"I abandoned her once in life," he said. "I'll not abandon her now."

It was dark, the street in front of the mansion lit by a few torches. Artorius slammed the door knocker repeatedly until at last the door opened; a bleary-eyed slave squinting into the torchlight.

"What business brings you here at this hour, Soldier?" he asked, irritated but knowing his place and maintaining his manners.

"Fetch your master immediately," Artorius ordered. The slave swallowed hard, his eyes taking in the sight of the fearsome legionary. Artorius' face was hard, yet his voice was calm. Unconsciously he clenched his fists, his huge forearm muscles pulsing.

"Who shall I say is calling?" the slave asked after a short pause. Artorius lowered his head slightly, his darkened eyes boring into the man. The slave swallowed hard and quickly backed into the house, hurrying down the hall. With the way his arms were flailing with limp wrists, Artorius surmised that he must also be one of Marcellus' playthings. Slowly he paced back and forth in the entryway, clenching his hands, eyes closed and his head lowered. His pain of regret was now consumed by an overriding need to make things right, by any means necessary. Finally he heard the sound of voices coming down the hall, the slave carrying a small lantern as Marcellus in a loose robe walked impatiently towards where Artorius stood waiting.

"I didn't order any special entertainments tonight, and besides you know I have no time for those beastly soldiers!" he said in a loud voice. He suddenly stopped short when he laid eyes on the legionary. "Well what have we here? It's the legendary 'hero of the Rhine' himself! That trollop of an ex-wife of mine never could stop talking about you."

"It is about your wife that I wish to speak with you," Artorius replied, his voice still relaxed, though his face emanated pure hatred. Marcellus pretended to not notice and instead walked over to where a servant stood with a goblet of wine, which he immediately consumed.

"If it's about the funeral, it's already taken care of," he said, not wishing to look at the legionary. "A proper pyre, professional mourners … far more than she ever deserved. I myself will not be attending; pressing business elsewhere. Your father finally made me relent on paying for the ordeal; beastly expensive though it is. He said to do it for Marcia, as if she'll have any recollection of that woman!" Artorius nodded and appeared to be satisfied. He made as if to leave before turning back to Marcellus, as if he had forgotten something.

"Just one more thing," he said, walking over to him. Marcellus turned his nose up at him, as if he were offended by the smell of a common soldier.

"And that is?" he started to ask as Artorius smashed his fist into Marcellus' face, every ounce of pure hatred exploding along with the man's nose with a sickening crunch. Marcellus fell to the ground, screaming at a high pitch. The slave with the lamp panicked and swung the lamp at Artorius, who knocked it away with his left forearm, the hot metal searing his flesh. He grabbed the wretch by the neck and slammed his forehead into his face, knocking the man senseless.

"You monstrous *beast!*" Marcellus screamed as Artorius walked quietly to the door and out into the night. In spite of the loathing he felt for his ex-wife and her legionary former lover, he knew he would still have to follow through on funding Camilla's funeral, for if he did not he feared it would not just be she who made her final journey into the afterlife.

Artorius managed a short laugh at the sound of Marcellus' scream as he stepped out into the night. He took a deep breath and started back up the street when he saw Magnus leaning against the side of a building, his arms folded and a sad expression on his face. Artorius grimaced and nodded.

"I am sorry, old friend," the Norseman said. "Your father told me everything. I grieve with you."

"You know, through all the horrors I have seen in life I have always had you, Brother," Artorius replied. "Camilla had no one. I cannot think of a worse way to die than abandoned and alone." The two friends walked in silence along the street before Artorius spoke again.

"They say that crucifixion is among the most painful forms of death; death that takes a matter of days sometimes. Camilla's very soul was crucified, and her death took years."

✳   ✳   ✳   ✳

"Do you know why I saved you from those cursed mines?" Heracles asked. Radek was on his knees, head bowed, his good eye gazing at a crack in the floor. Heracles slowly walked in circles around the wretch of a man, the floorboards in the dimly lit tavern room creaking under his steps.

"No master," the slave replied. It was the truth. Radek had never been of use to anyone his entire life. He had been handsome once, though a hot poker took one of his eyes and left a hideous scar on his face. It was his punishment for raping a young girl when he had been a farm slave. He was then sold to a wealthy nobleman, who he worked for as a gardener. He had once been bound for the mines of Mauretania, only to escape and join Sacrovir's rebellion. He had been grievously wounded during the battle of Augustodunum; his one friend, Ellard, had been disemboweled by the lance of a Roman cavalryman. It was back to the mines once more, where the sulfur burned his skin and eye; his teeth completely rotted and turned black due to lack of proper food and no means of proper hygiene. He had hoped to die during his first few months, but yet somehow he was still alive.

"You are a worthless man with no purpose in life, no reason for existence." Heracles' words cut deeply, but they were true. "I will give you a reason to exist. But first you must embrace my cause with your very soul." Radek looked up him and spoke slowly.

"I live only to serve you," he said as he lowered his head once more.

"Good," Heracles replied. "You will be the instrument of our vengeance against Rome."

"Surely Master does not seek to raise another rebellion," Radek stated. "There can be no victory against the legions."

"And who says we need to face the legions to achieve victory?" Heracles asked, a wicked sneer forming. "No my friend, I have other methods for dealing with Rome. However, there are some old friends we have to deal with first. We shall purge Gaul of the traitors who fled from battle and begged forgiveness from Rome like a bunch of whipped animals."

"It will be a pleasure."

✳   ✳   ✳   ✳

A tear came to Artorius' eye as he listened to the wailing of the mourners around Camilla's pyre. It was not a tear for himself; rather he was moved by pity. Camilla had few friends and had died very much alone. At least that jackal of an ex-husband had had the decency to hire professional mourners, even if he himself did not bother to show up. He had even allowed little Marcia to attend. Artorius surmised that perhaps Marcellus felt a tinge of remorse for the way he had treated Camilla. Marcia had been taken from her mother at a very young age and would have no memory of her, except the image of her body laid out on a pyre, ready to be sent to the afterlife. Still there was an air of sadness around the child. Artorius was not one for children; he had little patience when dealing with them. Still, he could not help but be taken by this little girl. He felt almost a sense of paternal affection towards her, perhaps out of pity for her having no mother and a father who was less than a man.

The dirges nearly complete, Artorius walked up to the pyre, which was doused in oil. The stench made him gag. He steeled himself as he walked up to Camilla's body. He ran the back of his hand across her cheek and kissed her gently on the lips. His memories of her would be of the girl he had spent his childhood with, who had also been his first love; if children can comprehend such meanings. He had long since let go of whatever attachments he had had, though there was always that trace of regret. No, it was best that he remembered her for the love of his youth rather than the love who abandoned him once they were grown. He wondered if in fact they were meant to be together, and the Fates had punished her for abandoning their plan. He shuddered at the thought, knowing that they could be utterly cruel. For Camilla's sake he hoped they were satisfied, for surely she had suffered enough.

He turned to see Camilla's maidservant escorting Marcia away; not wishing for the child to have to watch the pyre burn. Not caring to see this himself, Artorius walked after them. He never looked back.

"Wait!" he said once they were clear of the scene and alone in a small side street. The two turned to face him, the servant keeping her hands protectively on the girl's shoulders. Without thinking, Artorius fumbled through his hip pouch and pulled out the silver medallion that Camilla had given him all those years ago. He knelt before the child and held it up to her.

"Your mother gave this to me a long time ago," he said in a consoling voice. "I want you to have it." Marcia palmed the medallion while the cord was still clutched in Artorius' hands. She gave a sad smile and looked him in the eye. Though she may have only been three, there was a deep sense of understanding in those eyes; she was fully aware of what had happened and was not so naïve as one would expect of a babe. Artorius smiled back, his heart breaking for her. In that moment he felt something totally alien to him; he wished that Marcia had been his daughter. He took a deep breath and composed himself. The little girl bowed her head as he hung the medallion around her neck.

"Wear this always, in remembrance of her," he said, placing a hand on her shoulder. "And know that she always loved you." He then stood and nodded to the servant, who responded with a sad smile of her own and escorted Marcia away; the child's eyes fixed on the medallion and its image of the goddess Diana.

A firm hand on his shoulder startled Artorius. He turned to see Magnus standing next to him, his eyes wet and reddened.

"Why do you cry?" Artorius asked his friend. Magnus cocked his head to the side before answering.

"Do you not know?" he replied. "You have so much to learn, old friend. Artorius, you are as much a brother to me as any of my own blood. I know your sorrow for Camilla, and your regret that life was not more kind to her; but you will not show it. You think it would be a sign of weakness; so I grieve *for* you." Artorius gave a weak smile and nodded in understanding.

"I regret not making a more conscious effort to keep her," Artorius spoke in a low voice. "She was closer to me than any when we were young. Camilla and I were closest in age, so it was natural that we would bond. Of course as we grew older, to the age where the opposite sex becomes of greater interest than just as friends, it only seemed natural that we would fall for each other. But then I let my lust for revenge consume me. The closer I came to the age of maturity, the more I longed to join the army and avenge my brother, and the less I focused on she who had always been there for me.

"When I left for the legions, I knew she would not wait for me. Had I made the slightest effort to keep her with me, things may have turned out differently. She was the youngest of her sisters and of no value politically to her family. I could have taken her with me, Magnus." He took a deep breath and swallowed hard before continuing. "You know, I have never once given a second thought to having children, as hard as that may be to believe. I have no patience with them. But when I saw Camilla's daughter today it made me sad with regret. I know this sounds stupid, but I saw today what should have been; I was *supposed* to have a daughter. That child *should* have been mine, Magnus." The Norseman placed a hand on his shoulder.

"Sadly we cannot undo the past," Magnus remarked. "And whether she was supposed to be or not, that child is not your daughter. If the Fates have any mercy, perhaps Camilla has finally found peace in the next life. Come, let us leave this place." They turned to go back from whence they came, only to see the smoke of the burning pyre in the distance.

"We'll take another way," Magnus said, echoing Artorius' thoughts.

▼

CHAPTER V

MAD OLAF

Artorius and Magnus walked in silence along the road. Their furlough would be over within a week and they would have to catch the boat back to Lugdunum. A fresh spring breeze blew gently, the branches of trees dancing in their wake. Artorius felt hollow inside, though he was glad for the sense of closure. A chapter of his life was now closed forever; a chapter that he did not even know had still been open. He had done all he could to make things right by Camilla at the end, he just wondered if his lingering sense of regret would ever leave him. He then kicked a small rock off the paving stones as they strolled on. As they approached a large shade tree, he caught sight of the large figure of a man astride a great horse.

"*Magnus you whore's tit!*" the man roared. Artorius was taken aback as his friend burst out laughing.

"Who the hell is that?" Artorius asked. Magnus shook his head, still chuckling.

"Grandfather!" he shouted and ran towards the man who was now laughing as well. The man Artorius surmised could only be Mad Olaf jumped from his mount and embraced his grandson hard. He then gave Magnus a hard cuff across the head while still laughing.

"You bloody twat!" Olaf bellowed; Artorius wondering if he was meaning to shout or if he always talked in such a loud voice. "You make your poor grandfather search all over the damn Empire trying to find you! I came down to Cologne to visit you and they tell me you are stationed in Lugdunum of all places for the next couple years. Well no sooner do I get there than I hear that you are all the way back in bloody Rome on leave! *I had just come from there!* I swear if I had gotten all the way here and found out you had left to go back to bloody Gaul I would have smashed your testicles in by the time I found you! As it is …" with that he cuffed Magnus hard across the head once more. His grandson laughed loudly as he punched Olaf as hard as he could, knocking the old madman to the ground.

"Ah I knew you had at least some fight in you," Olaf said as he struggled to his feet. "Too bad you hit like a bloody girl! Your sister hits harder than you. Oh well, come here and give your grandfather a hug!" With that he dove at Magnus, slamming his shoulder into his stomach and taking his legs out from under him. Magnus was tackled to the ground, his wind knocked out of him. Still he managed to cuff Olaf across the ear and bucked him off.

"Um, not to interrupt such an emotional family reunion," Artorius said as the two Norsemen grappled on their feet. Magnus stepped away, catching his breath. He then turned and pointed towards his friend.

"Oh, Grandfather I want you to meet …" his words were cut short as Olaf punched him behind the ear, knocking him to the ground once more.

"You wanton harlot! I didn't say we were done!" Olaf then grunted and waved his hand dismissively at his grandson before turning his attention to Artorius. "Ah, and you must be Artorius. Ye gods, but you're a big one!" Artorius laughed at the assessment.

Age had robbed Olaf of some of his height, though according to Magnus he never was very tall to begin with. He was just a hair shorter than Artorius, with a long mustache that was braided on either side of his face. His still-blonde hair was pulled back in a ponytail, underneath a skull cap helmet. Though his appearance made him look like a barbarian, he was in fact very well dressed and his grooming and hygiene were immaculate.

"And you must be the famous Olaf," Artorius replied with a chuckle. The old man gave him a friendly but hard punch on the shoulder.

"Don't be such a bastard!" he bellowed. "I know you wanted to say *Mad* Olaf. It is okay lad, I don't find the name offensive at all."

"No, in fact he relishes it," Magnus said as he rose to his feet, massaging the sore spot behind his ear that was starting to turn purple. "No other man shows such boisterous affection towards his grandchildren!"

"Hey, it keeps you sissy girls tough and on your toes!" Olaf retorted as he walked back towards his horse; a magnificent stallion that looked much too large for the old Norseman to handle. And yet he effortlessly vaulted into the saddle.

Off of one of the saddle bags hung a very old, but well-maintained battle axe. The wooden handle was sun bleached and the blade bore the scars of countless battles, yet there was not a spot of rust to be found. The two friends walked on either side of the old man as they made their way back towards Ostia.

"Your sister will be happy to see you finally," Olaf said, catching Magnus' attention.

"Svetlana's here?" he asked excitedly. Last time he had seen his sister she had been just shy of womanhood.

"No, not here," Olaf replied with a shake of his head. "She's back in Lugdunum. She had been visiting me and was accompanying me back to Lugdunum to see you. But when you were not to be found, she elected to stay and await your return, lest she should miss you. No worries, a good friend of yours is looking after her."

"Which friend?" Magnus asked with some trepidation. The term *friend* could be used very loosely, especially when it came to someone offering to 'look after' his little sister.

"I'm trying to think of his name …" Olaf contemplated. "A fine fellow, that one; told me where the best spots in the city were to relieve my swollen loins! I think his name started with a V …" A look of horror crossed Magnus' face and his stared at his grandfather wide-eyed.

"*Valens?*" he asked with a start. Olaf smacked his thigh and chuckled.

"Yep, that's the name! A good man that one!" Artorius burst into uncontrollable laughter.

"Grandfather, you left my baby sister with *Valens?*" Magnus was horrified at the thought. "He's the single biggest pervert I've ever met! The man will fuck anything that's human with a cunt between its legs! I don't want him anywhere near Svetlana!" Artorius meanwhile was laughing so hard that he had to grab a hold of Magnus in order to stop from falling over. "You're not helping things, you know!" Magnus retorted as he shoved his friend off.

"I'm sorry," Artorius replied, wiping a tear of mirth from his eye. "It's just that the look on your face …"

"Oh Magnus, quit being such a big girl's blouse!" Olaf replied with a friendly back-fist to the ear. "Your sister is hardly a baby anymore. Damn girl is taller than I am and very fit." Magnus groaned at the thought of what temptation that would be for Valens, who while very much a friend was still someone that the Norseman did not want cavorting with his sister. "Svetlana can take care of herself, no worries," Olaf continued. "The lad's been nothing but a complete gentleman to her. Now stop fussing about it; you're making young Odin here nervous!" He tugged gently on the reigns of his horse as if to emphasize his point. "At any rate, I'll be coming with you back to Lugdunum. A fine city, that! Your Uncle Gunnar is seeing to my affairs while I'm out." The two legionaries walked alongside the old Norseman and his horse for some time before Artorius elected to break the silence.

"Olaf, I understand you were at Actium," he observed. A beaming smile crossed the old man's face.

"Ay, I was," he said, his voice filled with pride. "I went back to Rome a few years ago for the fiftieth anniversary celebrations. Sadly there are but a few of us left. I cannot believe it's been more than *fifty* years. It sometimes feels like it was just last week. I was not a young man even then and yet so many of the veterans look so ... well, *old.*"

It was not until they returned to Olaf's lodgings that he continued in his story. It was a very high-class inn that only those with extravagant taste and plenty of coin could afford. So when the half-mad Norseman showed up the owners were at first keen to turn him away. Though his clothes were expensive and his hair and hygiene well maintained, he still looked 'barbaric' to them. It was then that he produced his pouch full of coin that changed their demeanor towards him. When he showed up with the two legionaries the patriarch of the inn was immediately out the door to take Olaf's horse personally and see to his needs.

"Will you need anything else?" the man asked as Olaf dismounted.

"Yes, bring us some of your finest mead!" he answered before turning to Artorius and Magnus. "Come lads, let's get drunk and tell some stories!" Magnus was still distracted, thinking about his sister and Valens. Artorius had to give him a hard nudge with his elbow to bring him back to his senses. Magnus just shook his head.

"Would you get over your sister and Valens already?" Artorius chastised. Magnus gave a short laugh.

"It's not that ... I know how Olaf gets when he's on the mead."

Approximately twenty men were lined up in front of Heracles. Hand-picked from dregs of society, they would serve him and him alone. In similar fashion to how Sacrovir had chosen his inner circle, Heracles had selected men with little left to lose. He had sought those of the most bitter and vile nature that they would do even the most repugnant of deeds for him. Some were thieves, others rapists, more murders, and some were a combination of all. Most were hiding from law and were grateful for the shelter and sense of stability that Heracles provided. It also helped that they would no longer be left starving to death in the gutters, to be feasted upon by rabid dogs. Now they would become the wild beasts that would prey upon the populace.

"What orders does Master have for us?" one man asked with his voice raspy; almost like the hiss of a snake. Radek's face broke into a wicked sneer, though Heracles remained stoic.

"We have work to do," he answered simply.

"Know that we will serve you, Master ... even unto death!" the man with the raspy voice hissed, his face kept hidden. Heracles guessed that the man was probably hideous to look upon, though in truth he had never seen what the man actually looked like.

"Of that I have no doubt," the Greek replied calmly. "And my enemy is now your enemy."

"Rome is the enemy of any who loves freedom!" one of the men snarled. "They've perverted our lands long enough. I would rather see Lugdunum burn to the ground than have it occupied by those vile imperialists for another day."

"And burn will any who stand against us," the man with the rasp spoke up. Heracles could not contain his grin. He had thought that finding men of such blind loyalty would be difficult and expensive, and yet it had been all too easy.

✲   ✲   ✲   ✲

Artorius never had much of a taste for mead; it was far too sweet for him. Even so, he took a goblet that Olaf offered him and was quite pleased. It was certainly more potent than most wines or ales he had drank in the past. Magnus downed his cup in a single pull and immediately asked for more.

"As I was saying," Olaf said with a loud belch, "it's been more than fifty years since we fought at Actium. What a day that was! Mine was among the few auxilia units honored with serving aboard Agrippa's ships! I of course was not much for boating, so I doubled my mead ration before the battle and kept a flask with me, just in case nerves got the best of me!" He downed another goblet to emphasize this point as Magnus broke into laughter.

"Grandfather, I don't think nerves have *ever* gotten the best of you!" he said with a broad grin.

"They bloody well did when I was in the middle of the sea on a rocking boat wearing fifty pounds of crap!" Olaf retorted. "It was a hard call to make; either I keep my mail on, knowing that if I went over the side I would surely drown, or remove my armor and run the risk of being felled by any weapon the enemy carried! Needless to say, I stayed fully armored.

"With four hundred vessels, our fleet had just a few more actual ships than Antony. However, ours were much smaller liburnian ships with only two rows of oarsmen. It was tales I told of the bravery of these men that prompted Magnus' brother, Oleg, to become one of them! Antony's fleet consisted mostly of the quinquereme class; ships much larger than ours. In fact, they had three rows of oars, with the top row requiring two men per oar. So even though we had more ships, as far as manpower was concerned, Antony bore a slight advantage to us. Even so, an outbreak of malaria had caused a severe shortage of rowers for his boats. This turn of events proved fatal."

"That must have been quite a sight," Artorius observed, his chin resting in his right hand, an empty goblet rolling between the fingers of the other. A servant-the master of the house in fact-quickly refilled his cup.

"Ay, it was quite a sight," Olaf recalled. "Mind you, we had our small piece of the battle to stay focused on; much like you men did during your battles against the Cherusci and Gallic rebels. Besides, by the time we engaged I was pretty well lit out of my mind! Thankfully when we took a shower of arrows from a flanking ship, I still had the presence of mind to fall into the testudo formation with the rest of the lads! I couldn't stop from laughing, even as arrows skipped off our linked shields.

"Well before that there was quite the wait, which was very tiresome since I had run out of mead and was constantly having to piss. We had encircled the harbor and were basically trying to wait Antony and the Alexandrian Twat out. Did you know there was a bet amongst every ship in the fleet as to which crew was going to capture and ravage the little harlot first? I never saw what was so attractive about that big-nosed trollop to begin with, especially after Caesar and Antony had had their old-man hands all over her … but hey, I figured I could give her a good shagging for the sake of my country!" Artorius could not help but laugh at Olaf's constant sidebars to his story. His words were starting to slur as he downed his fifth cup of mead. Magnus was pacing himself a bit while keeping an eye on his grandfather.

"At any rate," Olaf continued. "What Antony did not know was that one of his generals; a fine fellow named Delius, had betrayed him and given Octavian and Agrippa his entire scheme of battle! So when Antony had to extend his line because he could not concentrate his forces without getting flanked, he wore out his already sick oarsmen before they even got to us. We hammered them with catapult and ballista fire, staying easily out of range of their three-ton rams. Only once did we end up boarding a vessel. We sank one with our own ram; and I almost went over the side trying to board it as we backed away! When we finally did get a chance for some fighting, the enemy was pretty well spent. In fact, I think I only killed maybe one or two during the entire battle, and I was one of the lucky ones! It was from the prow of the captured vessel that we saw the Ptolemaic Twat bugger off with her entire fleet! Bloody cowards did not even try and engage us. I hate to admit it, but my most famous battle is the one I played the littlest part in."

"I've always wanted to go to Actium," Magnus said, staring into his mead. "I would like to see the monument Octavian erected on the site of the battle."

"I admit it is impressive," Olaf concurred. "The rams of enemy ships were mounted in sockets on a massive stone monument. Two in every three of Antony's ships were captured or sunk. It made for quite the display! Ah, but that was a *long* time ago ..." His voice drifted off as his head fell onto the table. Soon a loud snoring was heard echoing throughout the room.

"I thought you said Olaf went completely insane when he's on the mead?" Artorius asked, looking at his friend, puzzled. Magnus could only shrug in reply.

"Perhaps old age is catching up to him after all ..." the young Norseman started to reply.

"I'll show you old age, you sodden bastard!" Olaf yelled as he leaped over the table and tackled his grandson out of his chair. Artorius signaled for a servant to bring him some water as he sat back and watched Magnus and his grandfather roll on the floor, beating each other without mercy. As much as he was acquiring a taste for mead, he knew that if he did not drink plenty of water too he would have a headache in the morning to match the one he knew his friend and deranged grandfather would surely have.

Chapter VI

▼

All Power

At last the city of Lugdunum was coming into view once more. As good as it was to see home and his family; Artorius was relieved to be back with his men. The joy of going home had been tempered by Camilla's death. As he leaned against the railing, enjoying the cool breeze coming off the River Rhodanus, he was joined by Magnus and Olaf. The two Norsemen were looking better than they had recently, the extensive bruising on their faces subsiding over the last two weeks.

"You two are looking better," Artorius observed with a grin. Magnus snorted and Olaf waved a hand dismissively.

"You have to admit, that was some fine mead!" Olaf said boisterously. "And to think my whelp of a grandson here had the audacity to call me old!"

"I suppose it would be more appropriate to say you are advanced in years," Magnus replied, "though you'll never allow yourself to grow old."

"That's because the idea of becoming an old man terrifies the piss out of me," Olaf retorted. Artorius laughed and shook his head. Olaf had to at least be in his eighties, and yet he was scared of becoming an old man. "I've seen stooped, old men who are probably young enough to be my sons. It's not that they were crippled in battle-which is about the only noble way of becoming an invalid-but rather they just refused to take care of what the gods gave them and allowed themselves to fall into a decrepit state. Pathetic, I tell you! I'll still be fighting my great-grandchildren when I'm a hundred years old." He slammed his fist against his chest to emphasize his point as Magnus slowly walked away from him.

As the ship docked in the Lugdunum harbor Artorius saw a tall Scandinavian woman that he surmised was Magnus' sister, Svetlana. However it was not she that Magnus rushed to greet as he disembarked the ship.

"*Valens, you fucking prick!*" the Norseman bellowed as his friend stepped quickly away from his sister. Magnus dropped his pack and started after Valens, only to feel a hard slap across his ear as Svetlana quickly stepped between.

"And who's the *fucking prick* who can't even say hello to his baby sister after all these years!" she bellowed at him, reminiscent of Olaf. Svetlana was hardly a baby; in fact she was a hair taller than her brother.

"Magnus, I swear I've behaved myself!" Valens said from a distance.

"Indeed he has," Svetlana asserted. "So is my big brother going to greet me or do I have to demonstrate on you what Grandfather taught me?" She emphasized her last point with another cuff across the ear. Artorius tried to keep from laughing. It would seem that Magnus' entire family was prone to physical violence as a means of affection.

"I told you she had some spunk to her," Olaf whispered in Artorius' ear with some scarcely contained laughter.

"By Odin you've grown!" Magnus said, seeming to notice his sister for the first time. Relieved that as far as he knew Valens had kept his lecherous hands off of Svetlana he felt more comfortable embracing her. "All these years I've remembered you as an awkward little girl and now you're a woman." As he bent to pick up his pack he cringed when saw Svetlana take Valens' hand in hers. "I thought you said he behaved!"

"He has," Svetlana replied coyly, "but that doesn't mean *I* have." Magnus groaned in reply as Artorius smacked him on the shoulder.

"Hey, at least Valens finally found himself someone respectable!" The look Magnus gave him clearly stated he was *not* happy with the situation and was ready to give Artorius the beating of his life if he said one more word.

✳   ✳   ✳   ✳

"It is with a heavy heart that I come before Rome's ruling fathers today," Tiberius said, his voice carrying throughout the Senate house. The assembly shifted nervously in their seats, never certain as to their Emperor's demeanor and usually guessing wrong at his intentions. Haterius Agrippa was particularly nervous, though he felt certain that he had acted with the Emperor's best intentions in mind. He stood to voice these concerns; however, Tiberius raised a hand silencing him.

"I do not doubt that this august body acted with the interests of both me and my son," the Emperor continued. "The loyalty of the Senate is something I am eternally grateful for. However, when seeking to protect the person of the Emperor, one must be just, but temperate when dispensing justice.

"Know that I thank Senator Agrippa for his zeal in coming to the defense of my son after the insults of a foolish man. I also thank Senator Lepidus for not only his loyalty, but also his prudence and level-headed voice of reason. *Words*, good senators, are not deeds. Had Priscus spoken of treasonous plots against my person or that of my son, of course I would expect the law to exact justice in its more extreme. However, no such treason was evident in Priscus' words; written or spoken." He paused to allow the senators to absorb what had been said. As usual, there was a lot of nervous shuffling as each man tried to gather the full extent of Tiberius' meaning. In his mind he was being straightforward and expecting the senate to act on its own sense of reason. In their minds, however, the Emperor was ambiguous in his remarks and left further confusion. Finally Senator Lepidus stood to address the assembly.

"Caesar, honorable senators; whereas we seek to protect the best interests of the Imperial family, this legislative body, as well as the whole of the Empire, how then do we protect such persons to the fullest without overstepping the bounds of reason? I propose a simple measure that will rectify any further embarrassments on this house." Lepidus shot a dark look at Agrippa, who scowled at the veiled insult. "A simple stay of sentence will alleviate any rash judgments. Therefore, I propose that any sentence instituted by the Senate of Rome be postponed for nine days to allow time for cooler heads to review and implement justice that is both hard but fair." He then turned his gazed towards the Emperor, who nodded affirmatively. Agrippa had also seen Tiberius' gesture and he seized upon it in order to save any face he may have lost.

"I second the motion and move for an immediate vote!" he spoke quickly as he came to his feet. The corner of Tiberius' mouth twitched slightly, pleased as he was by Lepidus' motion. As he rose to his feet to leave the hall, the rest of the senate also stood as a sign of respect. Though Tiberius knew that the Senate would vote how they thought he wanted them to, he did not want to give the impression of influencing any vote; therefore he left before any further action on the motion could be taken. Outside the senate house Sejanus was waiting for him.

"It is done," Tiberius said as he continued walking, Praetorian guards falling in on either side of him. As soon as the Emperor climbed into a waiting litter slaves hoisted it up and started the walk back to the imperial palace. Sejanus walked beside the litter.

"If I may be so bold," the Praetorian Prefect began, "I know it is not my place to question the judgments of the senate, and even less so that of your highness."

"Sejanus my old friend," Tiberius replied, pulling the veil of the litter aside and propping himself upright onto some pillows, "you know that I cherish your candid feedback more than any; probably because you are among the few who will say what is on your mind, rather than what you think I want you to say."

"It's just that ... well to be perfectly blunt Caesar, I did not agree with your assessment that words are not deeds. Treasonable utterances can lead to wider sedition, which in turn brings about discourse and eventually threatens us directly."

"Sejanus," the Emperor replied, sighing audibly, "You know I am not one for bringing someone to trial just for speaking foolishly."

"I am not speaking of poor Priscus," Sejanus corrected. "He was indeed a fool; but a harmless one. No, what I speak of is something a little ... *darker.*" Tiberius sat up, suddenly curious.

"Have you heard such things?" Sejanus smiled internally, knowing that he had at last planted the seeds of doubt within the Emperor.

"Only traces here and there," he replied. "Nothing I would be alarmed about. However, you do have enemies; some I hate to say, within your own family."

"You need not remind me about Agrippina and her lot," Tiberius replied with a scowl, settling back down once more. All around them the city of Rome slowly moved by. People trying to catch a glimpse of the Emperor were forced back by the Praetorians on either side of the litter. At the head of the procession a Centurion was barking orders for people to move out of the way. For Tiberius it was a tedious ordeal. He could not even so much as leave the palace and go to someone's house without surrounding himself with Praetorians. And though he preferred to walk, it was Sejanus who suggested he ride in a covered litter for extra protection. Given their present conversation, Tiberius wondered if there was indeed that much of a threat to his personal safety. Even Agrippina, who was both his niece as well as one of his most hated enemies, would not dare to even think of such a thing. He put this to his Praetorian Prefect.

"Agrippina is a thorn in my side," he observed, "however; she would not dare to seek my physical demise."

"If only that were so," Sejanus replied, baiting the Emperor even more.

"What do you mean?" Tiberius asked, perplexed. "She is still friends with my son, and surely Drusus would be the first to hear of any truly treasonable talk on her part!" Sejanus' face twitched at the mention of Drusus Caesar.

While it was tempting to try and implicate his hated rival as well, he knew better. Tiberius may have had a sometimes awkward relationship with his son, but nevertheless he knew that Drusus' love and loyalty to be unquestionable. Sejanus knew that if he even so much as hinted otherwise he would quickly be on the receiving end of Tiberius' wrath. So as much as it pained him, Sejanus sought a different explanation for Drusus' lack of information regarding Agrippina.

"Perhaps the Imperial Prince has taken his father's directive regarding utterances too literally and has ignored her poisonous speech," he conjectured. "Or more likely she just keeps her tongue in check when in his presence." Tiberius frowned in contemplation and shrugged.

"Well if that little bitch or her friends do overextend their forked tongues, I would like to know about it."

"You will," Sejanus replied, beaming inside, "you have my word, Caesar."

✳   ✳   ✳   ✳

One afternoon following their workouts, Artorius decided to see what else the gymnasium had to offer. He strolled into one of the back rooms, where what sounded like men grunting and striking each other could be heard. He looked inside and saw what he thought was a boxing match. Two men were squaring off, throwing jabs at each other. Artorius was surprised to see one man throw a side kick to his opponent's body. At that instant the other grabbed the leg with his outside arm and lunged in to take out the kicker's other leg. The men were now on the ground in what had morphed into a wrestling match. Artorius was then shocked to witness the man on top smashing his elbow into the other man's face and head. He then spun around and grabbed his opponent's ankle. The combatant on the bottom immediately started yelling in pain and slapping the mat with his hand as fast as he could. He was quickly let go of, and his adversary then helped him to his feet.

"Well done," a voice said from just off the mats. Artorius looked over to see a lean and well-muscled Greek wearing nothing but a loin cloth, his hands clasped behind his back. A number of other men stood on either side of him, most sweating profusely, with more than a few scrapes and bruises amongst them. Artorius was surprised to see Camillus, sporting a rather nasty-looking black eye.

"That is enough for the day," the Greek continued. "Remember what we went over regarding submissions and strikes from the top position." He then clasped the hand of each of his students as they left. Artorius overheard them calling him *Master Delios*. The name Delios sounded familiar to him, but he was not sure from where. Then it dawned on him. He remembered where he knew the name from, and he also realized what it was he had witnessed.

"Artorius, good to see you," Camillus remarked as he walked out of the room.

"Camillus," Artorius acknowledged. "Nice mark you got there. I would hate to see what the other guy looked like!"

"Yeah, his hand did take quite a beating," Camillus laughed.

"And strangely enough, Camillus won that match," another man remarked, smacking the Signifier on the shoulder.

"I grew tired of getting hit, so I choked him out," he replied with a casual shrug. Once the men had left, Artorius walked over to the instructor, who was wiping his face off with a towel.

"That was quite the display," Artorius said. The Greek smiled at him.

"Romans love blood; they love spectacle," he replied. "What they don't love so much is the purity of man versus man combat; no tricks, no weapons. It is simply the skill of one man against another. You, on the other hand, look like one who has little use for spectacle." Artorius folded his arms across his chest and nodded.

"Blood-letting for the simple purpose of blood-letting is pointless," he remarked. "The mob loves blood. Whether it is from a gladiatorial fight, or a public execution; they always exhibit the same animalistic lust. I have no need for such things. I seek purity and strength through both the mind and body. It has been my passion in life to seek ultimate power. I know who you are; you are Delios, two-time winner of the Olympiad Pankration."

"And I know you are," Delios said with a smile. "You are Titus Artorius Justus, Legion Champion of the Twentieth Valeria and one of the most feared close-combat fighters ever to come from Rome. Yes, I do keep tabs on the more well-known legionaries in our community. But tell me; are you as skilled without your weapons as you are with them?"

"Perhaps you can tell me," Artorius replied, a smile crossing his face. Delios returned it and set his towel down.

"Pankration is an ancient form of combat. It is a conglomeration of the words *pan* and *kratos*, and it literally means *all power*. When you face a man with your bare hands, when you seek to find pankration, it becomes the quest for ultimate power." Artorius found himself utterly enthralled with what Delios was saying. He then realized that pankration was the perfect complement to his physical strength. Without another word being said, both men stepped onto the mat and faced each other.

Unarmed combat was a basic skill taught to all legionaries, though emphasis was placed on it being used as a last resort, and only until one could retrieve his weapons. Artorius knew that his training paled in comparison to what Delios had spent as a life study. Nevertheless, he settled into a fighting stance similar to that which he would with weapons. The most crucial difference was that he kept his hands up by his head in order to block against strikes. He had wrestled with bulls as a young man, and he knew that he held a dominating strength advantage over his opponent. He understood that Delios recognized this as well.

As both men advanced on each other, Delios started throwing rapid punches at Artorius. As blows bounced off his hands and forearms, Delios landed a hard kick to the outside of Artorius' thigh. This caused Artorius to panic slightly and he shot in to take out Delios' legs. Artorius was surprised that Delios actually let him take him to the ground, where he wrapped his legs around the Roman's waist; a move which isolated Artorius and hindered his movement. In spite of being immobilized, he proceeded to hammer his fist into the man's side and head, all the while Delios remained calm, trying to get a grip on one of his arms. Artorius realized what Delios was attempting, and immediately ceased in his blows. He found himself wrestling with the Greek, and strangely enough found that though on top he was on the defensive. The Greek was a master of leverage, something which negated an enormous amount of Artorius' strength. As Delios started to pry one of the Roman's arms loose, Artorius would drop his fist or elbow into his face. Delios then moved his head to one side, causing Artorius to drive his fist into the mat. With lightening reflexes, Delios let the other arm go and grabbed onto the one Artorius had punched with. He then wrapped both his legs around the arm as well, arching his back and driving Artorius onto his. The young Roman was shocked to find himself on his back, his arm stretched out in Delios' grip. He felt his elbow joint start to hyperextend; his shoulder joint being pried apart as well. He started slapping his free hand onto the mat in the same manner the defeated combatant had earlier. Delios released his arm and both men stood up. Delios had fresh bruises on his face and his ribs were red and battered.

"You are incredibly strong," Delios observed, "not to mention naturally talented. You have decent wrestling skills, and you are a respectable striker on the ground. However, you don't seem to know the first thing about submissions, and your striking on the feet is rudimentary at best. Would you like to learn these skills, as well as others?"

"I would be honored," Artorius replied with a nod. In truth he deeply respected this man. It was ironic that most Greeks were known for their art and philosophy. The warrior class of old Sparta was thought to be dead, especially after the combined Greek and Macedonian armies had been utterly routed by Rome more than two hundred years before. Many forgot the purity and masculine virtues portrayed in the games of the Olympiad. Physical contests such as wrestling and pankration were shunned by the average Romans in favor of sport that guaranteed a greater quantity of blood, if not skill.

It became routine for Artorius during their tenure in Lugdunum. When not performing his duties as a Legionary and Decanus, he could be found in the gymnasium, strengthening his body through the exertion of heavy lifting, or learning to better utilize and channel his strength through pankration. Delios became his mentor in much the same way that Vitruvius had been when he learned close-combat and weapons drill. In time he felt he would achieve *all power*. That spring the Cohort held two tournaments; one with weapons in similar fashion as the Legion Championship, and one in unarmed combat of pankration. Artorius elected not to take part in the weapons tournament, seeing as how he was the current Legion Champion and should only defend his title when the entire Legion was present. He was proud to watch as Magnus tore through the competition, becoming the champion for the Third Cohort. His friend had become a force to be reckoned with, and Artorius hoped that if any man did ever take his title from him, that it would be the Norseman.

In a surprise move, Artorius also abstained from the pankration tournament, preferring instead to train and mentor soldiers within his Century who wished to compete. Legionary Felix Spurius was one of these men. He became a mainstay at the gymnasium, and pankration became his passion. He would finish third in the tournament, behind Optio Castor of the First Century. Both men would be bested by Camillus, the tournament winner. Many were shocked to watch the mild-mannered Signifier manhandle his opponents like they were bags of straw. Spurius gave Camillus the most trouble, though even he was forced to submit when the Signifier sunk a deep choke hold on him from his own back. Castor would fall much quicker in the final match, with Camillus knocking him to the ground and then landing a series of unanswered punches which forced a stoppage of the contest.

The legionaries appreciated both styles of competition. Close-combat with gladius and shield would always be popular, seeing as how it was their mainstay and unique from the vulgar displays in gladiatorial matches. They also grew to love the purity of the pankration contests as well. Men would compete with each other in both forms of combat, often-times one man besting the other at one form, but falling short with the other. Proculus and the Centurions took note of this. Though bruises and other minor injuries were moderately increased, the sense of competition was good for the men's morale, and also kept their individual fighting skills well-honed.

Time passed as it did for the soldiers of the Third Cohort. Lugdunum had indeed proven to be quite the respite for them. They had lived comfortably in the embrace of civilization, away from the hard life of the frontier. While Proculus and the Centurions had enforced rigid training regimes to keep the men fit and busy, the sense of leisure could not be overlooked. Artorius spent much of his time at the gymnasium, which ironically was just a few blocks down from their flats and the Temple of Bacchus. There he continued to pursue his quest for physical perfection, driven by the desire for a godlike physique and power that would shame Hercules. He was always joined by Magnus as well as Centurion Vitruvius, two men who shared the same passion. In time, they grew in size and strength. All three were already fearsome to gaze upon, yet now they looked even harder, to the point that the idealized statues of the gods paled in comparison to them. His other passion, the perfection of pankration, had increased his fighting prowess far more than he had figured initially. He was more limber and agile because of his training, and in weapons drill he had become even more dangerous, much to the dismay of those who hoped to one day take the title of Legion Champion from him. It seemed ironic that even after Magnus won the Cohort Champion tournament that he had yet to face his Decanus. There would come a time for them to face each other, but not yet.

$$\ast \qquad \ast \qquad \ast \qquad \ast$$

Proculus stuffed the sealed letter underneath the cord that bound the parcel together. Nothing would have pleased him more than to take the package to the estate himself; however there was a banquet with the provisional governor that he was required to attend. He let out a sigh and walked out into the foyer, the parcel tucked under his arm. The modified Principia was always a bustle of activity. He glanced around and saw Macro talking to one of his Decanii. The young man looked familiar to Proculus and then he remembered; it was Sergeant Artorius, who had been decorated for valor during the battle against the Turani in the mountains outside of Augusta Raurica. Better still; Proculus remembered that he was also able to ride a horse.

"Macro!" he shouted as he walked up to the men who immediately ceased in their conversation. Artorius took a respectful step backwards and stood with his hands clasped behind his back.

"What have you got there?" the junior Centurion asked.

"A parcel and some letters that I need delivered to my estate in the country. I need someone who can ride a horse to deliver them for me."

"I see," Macro replied, guessing at his Cohort Commander's intent. He folded his arms and looked over his shoulder at the Decanus. "Artorius, you can ride can't you?"

"I can, Sir," he replied with a grin. Macro of course knew the answer.

"Here's your man," Macro said, facing Proculus once more. The senior Centurion stuffed the parcel into Artorius' arms.

"Excellent! Go down to the stables and requisition yourself a horse. I'll send an order to the Master of Horse to let him know that you will be doing this for me quite often and will require your own mount." Relieved, Proculus immediately turned and walked back to his office. He still had to prepare for the function that evening and his wife had not even arrived yet.

"Looks like you just got yourself an additional duty," Macro stated once Proculus had left.

"Hmm, well I would like to get out of the city every once in a while and see a bit of the country," Artorius replied. Macro grinned and snorted.

✶   ✶   ✶   ✶

"Are we seeking to employ another slave army?" Radek asked as he and Heracles walked away from the slave pens on Four Corners Road, their faces covered by their hoods.

"In a manner of speaking," his Greek master replied. "We will be more … *subtle* in our approach this time. An entire army of slaves would be too difficult to control. Besides, I told you we would not be facing the legions head-on this time." Radek allowed himself a wicked grin.

"One of our men has been keeping an eye on the legionary and urban cohorts for some time," Heracles continued. "In peace they have fallen into a pattern of predictability. I now know exactly what times they conduct shift changes; indeed there is a long period of time where the area around the slave market is devoid of any type of protection at all." Soon they arrived back the flat that Heracles had procured. Waiting for them was one of the freed slaves, a rather meek and unassuming fellow. In spite of this Heracles had at last found a use for the man.

The slave was older and going bald with a boyish face that looked like it never required a shave. But Heracles sought to exploit his services, not his looks.

"I have a task for you," he stated.

"Yes Master," the slave replied, hands folded in front of him and eyes on the floor.

CHAPTER VII

▼

LADY DIANA

It was over forty miles from Lugdunum to the Proculus estate. Artorius had tried getting Macro to allow one of his legionaries to accompany him, but the Centurion had rejected the notion. Horses were in short supply as it was, and the Master of Horse only begrudgingly allowed the Decanus to take one of his prized mounts as his own. So while he would not have the company of one of his friends to break the monotony, Artorius had a vivid enough imagination and appreciation for the natural countryside to keep his mind occupied.

Artorius was indeed glad to be away from the city for a couple days and found he appreciated the solitude. The open country appealed to him greatly, plus he knew who it was he would have to see on these trips. He grinned at the thought. The last time he had laid eyes on Lady Diana Procula had been in the Lugdunum forum the year previously. Given that he had been so distracted staring at her that he had walked head-first into a pillar was but a minor detail. He still did not know if she had witnessed his folly or not, and if so did she remember? His mind wandered as his thoughts turned to the focal point of his infatuation. He tried to sort out in his mind what he knew about Diana from what he hoped to find out.

He knew that she was of the Proculeas family, of which Centurion Proculus' family was related in some way. He also knew that Diana's little sister, Claudia, was betrothed to his good friend, Pontius Pilate. Outside of that there was not much else to know. Artorius did not know Diana's age, but surmised that she was older than him. What was puzzling then was that she was unwed; for Roman women, especially those from influential houses, almost never stayed unwed into their twenties. At least her little sister was betrothed, yet Artorius heard nothing regarding Diana. He wondered if there was a family secret; a scandal perhaps, that kept her single. He then laughed out loud at the notion of a lowly legionary taking advantage of the situation. Such a story would make for a great theater production, though that realization just emphasized the fantasy nature of what he was thinking. The theater dealt in dramatizations and exaggerations, not on reality.

"Well if nothing else, perhaps she'll let me take advantage of that gorgeous body of hers," he mused aloud. This was a far more plausible scenario, at least in his mind. Diana was indeed a striking woman with beautiful features and an extremely fit body that looked like it had not been ravaged by torments of childbirth. As he thought about what he would like to do to that body, Artorius suddenly became uncomfortable in the saddle of his mount.

✶   ✶   ✶   ✶

"I am speechless, Caesar," Sejanus said as he stared in awe at the statue. Tiberius had taken his confidant to the Theater of Pompey to show him prior to the official unveiling the statue that he had erected in Sejanus honor.

"You are the partner in my labors," Tiberius explained, "and I think the people of Rome need to have that made clear to them." The Theater of Pompey was the largest in the known world where thousands of patrons flocked to witness the spectacle that is the stage. That the Emperor would place a statue of the Praetorian Prefect in such a public place was a loud statement indeed. But Tiberius wasn't done yet bestowing honors upon his favorite.

"Yours is the highest rank that one of the Equestrian Class can ever hope to attain," he stated. Sejanus nodded in reply.

"Yes, and it is one I hope I have done honor to," he replied with mock humility. Deep inside Sejanus resented the fact that his mere birth kept him from attaining a higher office. His ambition knew no bounds and his determination was relentless. Secretly he dared to think that he could someday sit where Tiberius sat. And unwittingly the Emperor himself was slowly removing the obstacles in his way.

"You have done more than honor the post," Tiberius said. "You have been my right hand when all others have failed me. Therefore I feel it is only right that we elevate your position further. How would feel about being awarded the Praetorship?"

"I would be honored, Caesar. However, there isn't much precedent for one of my birth to hold such a lofty position."

"That is true," Tiberius conceded. "And no doubt there will be grumblings within the senate. But when I make it clear to them that my wish is for the partner of my labors to be elevated to this position, no doubt they will fold."

As the two men continued to walk around the amphitheater, Sejanus could not believe his good fortune. In the time of the Republic the Praetor was a man of enormous responsibility; tasked with relieving the judicial burden on the Consuls, as well as given the authority to field an army in dire emergencies when both Consuls were already in the field. After the rise of the Emperors, Augustus had changed the duties to those of an imperial administrator and advisor, rather than a magistrate. His power was still immense, with much focus placed on judicial matters. Twelve Praetors had served under Augustus, with Tiberius increasing the number to fifteen. Sejanus would become the sixteenth and most powerful, even though he would be the only non-senator in its ranks.

$$ * \quad * \quad * \quad * $$

At length the estate came into view. Farm fields dotted the region around the manner house. At the bottom of the gradual slope Artorius rode up to a grove of trees running perpendicular to the road. He guided his horse over to an apple tree and dismounted. He then plucked a pair of ripe red apples, giving one to the horse before remounting. He finished his own as he rode through the gates of the manor house. A twenty foot wall surrounded it, with all vegetation cut back from the outside of the wall. The only exception was a massive oak with several branches that hung over the wall on the west side. He speculated that some of the branches might support the weight of a man, if he was sure of balance.

He dismounted and handed the reins to a servant. He then removed the parcel and letters and walked slowly towards the door, taking in the sights of the estate grounds the whole time. Much had been renovated since Proculus had taken over. The manor had belonged to a wealthy Gaul, and while elaborate, Proculus sought to wipe the Gallic influence away and "Romanize" the estate. Indigenous religious shrines and relics were replaced with statues of the Roman pantheon. On either side of the large double-doors were life-size statues of Mars and Diana. Artorius grinned at the coincidence of Diana Procula having a statue of her namesake outside her front door. As if he was expected, the doors were opened from the inside, a small and balding servant pushing his way through.

"How may we be of service, noble Decanus?" he asked with a short bow.

"I bring parcels and letters from Centurion Proculus to the Lady Diana," Artorius replied.

"Of course, Sir," the servant said with a nod of his head. Artorius followed him into a well-lit entrance hall. An elaborate set of marble stairs rose off to the left; indeed everything inside seemed to be made of marble. Artorius knew that were the estate not confiscated from a Gallic rebel Proculus could never have afforded such luxury. Statues and vases adorned every niche and pedestal. They came to a side entrance with no door that led into an enclosed garden. Inside was a raised dais that was as yet undecorated with either statues or foliage. Instead there was a platter with a pitcher of wine and two brass goblets.

A large, elaborate trough for small plants ran along the wall to the left. It was here that Artorius first laid eyes on Lady Diana since that day in the Lugdunum market. Her back was to him, but still he gasped. Instead of the more feminine stola she wore a short tunic top that was open partway down the back. Though she looked soft to the touch, her back was defined with well-developed muscle. He was not aware that he was standing with his mouth wide open as the servant approached her.

"Yes, what is it Proximo?" she asked. It was the first time Artorius had heard her voice and it enraptured him. There was nothing special about it; it was after all just a woman's voice. He knew his infatuation was getting the best of him and they had not even spoken to each other yet!

"A courier from your cousin, the Noble Proculus," Proximo replied, his hands folded in front of him. Diana nodded curtly and continued working on the small plant she was pruning. Proximo then turned to address the Decanus. "My apologies, but I did not catch Sir's name."

"Sergeant Artorius of the Third Cohort's Second Century." It sounded lame, even to him. He had hoped to sound impressive, though he now felt foolish; as if a noble woman would be impressed by the rank of a mere plebian. Diana placed down her small sheers and spun around on her stool to apprise the soldier her cousin had sent. She cocked her head to one side, a slight smile forming.

"Have I seen you before?" she asked. Artorius swallowed hard before answering.

"*Possibly.*" Diana's face broke into a full grin as she addressed him once more. "I now remember where I've seen you." She turned back to her plant.

Artorius could not tell if she was stifling a laugh or not. He sighed and rolled his eyes; Carbo's favorite expression echoing in his mind. *Nice one, dumbass!*

"Just leave the parcels with Proximo," Diana said over her shoulder. Artorius complied, handing the package and letters with the servant who stood beside his mistress. Diana then turned to him once more. "There's wine if you'd care to sit with me for a while." Artorius grinned and walked briskly back to the dais. He inhaled the aroma of the wine before he started to pour. This was not cheap tavern wine by any stretch.

"Would my Lady like some too?" he asked, turning back towards her.

"Of course," Diana replied. Artorius was breathing heavily, even though he done no physical exertion. His hand trembled slightly as he set the cup down next to Diana. He caught himself breathing in deeply through his nose, trying his best to catch her scent.

"You seem a bit flushed," Diana observed out of the corner of her eye. "Please, feel free to remove your armor and relax." Artorius was only too happy to comply. While a lifesaver in combat, the lorica segmentata was a cumbersome burden at any other time one had to wear it. He removed his belt and gladius, setting them on the dais. It took him a minute to undo all the leather ties on his armor and work his way out of it. He then removed his padded shoulder covers that he wore underneath and set them next to the rest of his kit. He then tightened up the rope belt he always wore when just in his tunic and returned to his seat, wine in hand. He desperately tried to think of things to talk to this enchanting lady about.

"I take it my cousin is doing well?" Diana asked, breaking the awkward silence as she continued to work on the shrub. Artorius nodded while contemplating his answer.

"He's doing well enough," he replied diplomatically. "My Lady will have to forgive me, but I scarcely see him." He cringed as he realized the error of his words.

"Of course," Diana replied. "My apologies; I had forgotten that a Decanus would have little interaction with the Centurion Pilus Prior." Artorius closed his eyes hard as she stated the very thing he hoped she would not. His inferior status was shoved right into his face, whether the Lady had meant to or not. She was of a much higher social standing than her cousin; and Artorius did not even rate exchanging pleasantries with him!

"Well I do tend to see him more than the rest of the Decanii ... at least more so than those not in his First Century." Damn but he was pathetic! He downed his entire goblet of wine and quickly went back to serve himself some more. When he returned he elected not to sit down.

"You're a big one," Diana observed, looking his way once more. Artorius grinned.

"Why thank you; I will take that as a compliment."

"It was meant as one," she replied with a short nod to the side. Artorius then looked down for a second before addressing her again.

"My Lady, please do not mistake my being but a plebian soldier ..." his words were cut short as Diana raised a hand, silencing him.

"I think no such thing," she replied. "My cousin, while not of noble birth, is an honorable man; as I take it are the men who serve under him." Artorius nodded in response. "He speaks highly of the men who have fought beside him in battle. You have served in battle, have you not?" Artorius grimaced and looked down once more. While it was a more familiar topic, it was not one that he felt was appropriate.

"More times than I'd care to remember," he said with a sigh. Diana looked off to the side, thinking about his words.

"Proculus has said the same thing many times. And yet *you* look so young."

"I am older than I look," Artorius replied, "but yes, in the large scheme of things I am still very young. In fact, I am the youngest Decanus in the Cohort."

"That's no small accomplishment," Diana spoke with genuine admiration. "I think I now remember where I heard your name before. About a year ago I was in Cologne to see Proculus and Vorena. There was a spectacular festival going on, along with a tournament involving the legion's best fighters."

"You were there for that?" Artorius asked astonished that he had not noticed her even though the crowd had numbered in the thousands.

"I doubt that you would have seen me," Diana replied. "I sat in one of the newly-renovated covered boxes that sat up high. Vorena said she did not want to sit out in the sun; and besides, Proculus insisted on sitting with that rowdy lot of a Cohort! You looked good, by the way." Artorius felt his face turn red as he thought about Diana seeing him in one of his proudest moments.

"Thank you, my Lady."

"I mean you all do look alike, what with the exact same clothing and helmets covering your heads. You did stand out to me, though. I figure it must have been your size that gave you away. I remember watching you get practically mauled by your companions after they presented you the ceremonial gladius." Artorius grinned, though he elected not to go into further detail, especially given what he did later that evening. Granted the night he spent with those two young lasses was one of his fonder memories.

"I have to say, I was quite fascinated," Diana continued. "I've been to gladiatorial matches before, but they looked amateurish compared to the way legionaries fight."

"We did put that theory to the test one time," Artorius said. "During the Triumph of Germanicus our Optio, who was also the man who taught me how to fight, challenged a gladiator in the arena. Let's just say the end result made some men a lot of money, to include Centurion Proculus."

"I heard about that," Diana remembered. "You mentioned the Triumph of Germanicus. You are indeed older than you look if you took part in the wars against the Cherusci."

"I served in the last two of Germanicus' three campaigns," Artorius replied.

"Will you tell me about them sometime?" Diana asked. Artorius took a slow breath while he thought about it. Did he really want Diana to know about his quest to avenge his brother that brought on sheer bloodlust? While she would no doubt be awe-inspired by tales of valor against the barbaric hordes, she would be equally repelled when hearing about the utter brutality of the war that did not take place on the battlefield. How would she react, knowing that he had murdered entire families, to include women and small children, in cold blood? He elected for a more cordial and noncommittal answer.

"Sometime," he said.

"Fair enough," Diana replied with a friendly smile. "I have to say ..." She stopped in mid sentence, a strange look crossing her face. She looked away, her smile vanishing as she closed her eyes and breathed in deeply. When she opened her eyes once more they were no longer warm and inviting. She was staring at the ground, her breathing coming more quickly and deeply.

"Are you alright, my Lady?" Artorius asked, concerned by the sudden change in her demeanor. "I hope I have not offended you."

"You're fine," Diana replied curtly. She then stood and walked briskly towards the doorway. "Have whatever's left of the wine before you leave." She was gone before Artorius could inquire further. He sought to follow her, but was stopped by the servant Proximo.

"Please, Sir must forgive Domina," he said respectfully. "She can only be in the company of a man for so long before *it* becomes too much for her. She did last far longer with you than with most, I admit."

"Before *what* becomes too much for her?" Artorius asked, suddenly irritated. Proximo then raised his hands in resignation.

"It is not for me to tell Sir," he replied as he lowered his head, fully expecting to be chastised. Instead Artorius returned to the garden and finished the wine in the pitcher without bother to use a cup. He then walked over to where Diana's goblet sat. It was almost full. He finished it in a single pull and left out the side entrance, not wishing to cross through the house again.

"Well that was a bit weird," he stated out loud as his horse started out the main gate of the manor house. He wondered if Lady Diana was unwed because she was completely mental. Then again, if she were he doubted that Proculus would have asked her to oversee his estate for him.

It was almost nightfall when Artorius arrived back at Lugdunum. He stabled his horse and made his way back to the barracks flat. It was dark inside, with the only sound coming from Decimus' loud snoring. The legionary had come down with a fever earlier in the week and was confined to bed rest while doped up on the gods knew what. Artorius realized he wasn't remotely tired and that his loins needed some serious relief. Self-pleasuring himself on the road had been amusing, but by no means satisfying. With an air of determination he grabbed his money pouch and made for his favorite brothel.

He walked in to the dimly lit house, where a curtain of beads hung in the entranceway. The madam gave him a smile and walked over to him. She was certainly not an unattractive woman in her own right. She was probably in her forties, with a pleasant face and average-sized body. Artorius wondered what tricks of the trade she could teach him.

"I'm going to have to start charging you extra," she scolded, pointing an accusing finger at him, though she bore a bemused grin. "You leave my girls marked and worn to the point that they are of no use to me for at least a couple days!" Artorius shook his money pouch and smiled back.

"Oh I'm sure I can make it worth your while," he said with a wink. The madam nodded curtly and guided him through an open doorway and onto a waiting couch. The room reeked of the incense burners that hung in every corner. Here was where clients were allowed to peruse the wares before deciding on a playmate for the evening.

"Any special requests tonight?" the madam asked with her hand on her hip. She rather liked the young Decanus. He paid well, plus her girls found him exciting even when he did leave them savaged with visible bite marks apparent.

"Well you know I have my favorites," Artorius replied; his chin resting in his hand in contemplation. "However, I think I'd rather fancy something a bit more fresh and unspoiled if you know what I mean."

"Hmm, I do indeed." The madam looked up, deep in thought for the moment. Her eyes then glowed in realization. "Of course! I've got one who just came to us yesterday. Pretty little thing; don't know what her experiences were before but at least she hasn't been broken in here yet."

"Excellent!" Artorius said, smacking his hands together in anticipation. " How young is she?"

"Fairly so. I know she's of age, but yes she is a young one. Kind of petite too, so you'll have to be gentle with her. No biting this one yet!"

"Well, perhaps someone would care to accompany me to show me how to be gentle with one so delicate." There was a gleam in Artorius' eye and the madam immediately picked up on it.

"Are you coming on to me?" she asked, her face showing her disbelief. Artorius replied with a shrug.

"I might be," he confessed, his own grin broadening. The woman laughed out loud.

"Oh my," she replied. "Well you know I myself am not for sale. I simply keep this house in order and take care of the girls is all."

"Sure," Artorius conceded, "but you cannot tell me that a woman of your experience doesn't have certain … *abilities*. Perhaps you can teach both of us a thing or two. Call it a favor for an old friend." He winked at his last remark. Her face a deviant smirk, the madam grabbed Artorius by the hands and pulled him to his feet. Her ample breasts felt good pressed against him and she immediately started to massage his engorged manhood through his tunic.

"You have no idea the things I could teach you," she whispered into his ear as she flicked it with her tongue.

"I think you will find me a willing student," Artorius replied, reaching around and smacking her hard on her bottom, giving it a squeeze. He was pleasantly surprised to find that she was quite firm and not all soft and frumpy. She then guided him to the stairs and told him to wait there. She went to one of the other rooms on the bottom floor and soon returned with a rather attractive young woman, who she gently guided by the hand. She was blonde with a fair complexion. She was fairly short and thin, but at least was filled out in the places a woman was supposed to be. The last thing Artorius wanted was anything that could possibly resemble a boy.

"Now it's going to be alright my dear," the madam said to the girl, who looked like she was trembling a bit. She took a step back when she first set eyes on Artorius, her eyes wide. "This is your first client. Don't worry; I'll be there to make sure he doesn't hurt you." She then took them both by the arm and guided them upstairs. On the top floor they hear the sounds of boisterous laughter. Artorius was surprised to see both Valens and Svetlana, arms around each other, trying to fumble their way into one of the rooms. Both seemed to be a bit inebriated and having a wonderful time.

"Hey Artorius!" Valens said in a voice far too loud for how close they were. Svetlana placed her head on Valens' shoulder and waved at Artorius and his companions. "You should see the new plaything we found! These girls really do know how to have fun!"

"Yes they do!" Svetlana replied, kissing him aggressively. Artorius laughed and shook his head. It seemed as if Valens had indeed found his true partner in crime, as it were. He then wondered how Magnus would take it if he knew and couldn't stop laughing at the thought.

He was taken to one of the vacant rooms where he immediately got out of his restrictive clothes. The madam helped the young girl out of hers, who seemed almost powerless to do anything herself. Artorius apprised her with a raised eyebrow, shrugged, and then went work. The madam had discarded her own clothes and was lying next to them on the oversized bed, massaging herself. Finally she shoved the girl off the young soldier and took her place on top of him.

"Out of the way girl!" she snapped. "I'll show you how it's done. Watch … and learn …" She was a woman who Artorius could be his usual rough self with. The young girl sat at the head of the bed, her legs crossed under her, watching intently. As Artorius' deviancy came unleashed, the madam would at times grab the girl and have Artorius do to her the same things they had just been doing; only he had to be much gentler with her. After what seemed like a couple hours of pure lust and fury all three of them collapsed. Both Artorius and the madam were panting while the girl trembled slightly.

"Well that was fun," the madam said with a loud sigh of relief. She took the girl by the hand and helped her back into her clothes. She then told her something that Artorius could not hear, smacked her on the behind and sent her on her way. Artorius thought he heard the girl crying.

"Is she going to be alright?" he asked as he sat upright. The madam gave a dismissive wave.

"Ah, she'll be fine. They're all like that at first. Takes a bit for them to get broken in … kind of like a wild horse. Give her a few goes and she'll quit blubbering and getting all emotional." She then leaned down and kissed the young soldier passionately. "And feel free to come back here *anytime.*" With a spring in her step she left him alone. He then thought some more about the young woman they had just 'broken in.' He started to take pity on her, wondering what would drive someone to a life of prostitution. He then dismissed the notion. Prostitutes may have been amongst the dregs of society, but they were not slaves; no one forced them to spread their legs for a living!

Artorius then stretched his arms overhead and decided it was time for him to leave. He threw on his clothes and headed out into the night. It was only when he was halfway back to the flat that he realized they had neither negotiated nor exchanged any money. He laughed and wondered if the madam had given him a free pass, or if in her post-orgasmic glow she had simply forgotten.

Within a few days the sense of leisure for the Third Cohort would come to a brutal end.

Chapter VIII

▼

Rats in a Trap

It was well after dark when Heracles strode casually over to the slave pens, where a loan guard was posted. The man looked to be little more than a hired beggar; little more than the quarry he was supposed to safeguard while the master slept. The guard was half asleep and woke with a start as he sensed the Greek's presence.

"Hey, the bloody market's *closed*," he said with a defiant sneer, irritated that he was being disturbed. Heracles smirked in reply.

"I'm not here to buy … merely observe," he stated.

"Well there's nothing to observe either," the guard retorted, "so move the fuck along before I shove the broad end of my spear up your ass for wasting my time!"

"Oh dear," Heracles replied with mock disappointment. "I guess it will be a lesson in manners for you." As he spoke, Radek snuck up behind the guard, his butcher's cleaver in hand.

"Shit," the guard said, matching Heracles mocking tone. "How about I use you for a bit of sport like I did some of the young ones in there …" His words were cut short by the blow of Radek's cleaver that severed his head from his spine. The body collapsed to the ground, spear still clutched in the twitching hand as blood gushed from the stump that remained of the neck. After retrieving the keys to the stockade, Heracles picked up the severed head by a shock of hair. The tongue protruded through the man's rotten teeth as the lips and eyes twitched involuntarily as death took hold.

"Now there's a lesson in manners he'll not soon forget," Radek said with a grin. A mild coughing fit overtook him as Heracles tossed him the head.

"*Help, please help me; they've escaped!*" the slave shouted at the top of his lungs. He stood right outside of one of the flats occupied by Roman soldiers. Artorius had just finished tightening the straps on his belt and baldric when the man started screaming. His and Praxus' sections were scheduled for night patrol for the next three weeks and they were finishing their preparations to go on duty.

"Who the bloody hell is that?" Valens asked, perturbed. Carbo gave a sigh.

"And I thought it would be a quiet one tonight," he remarked.

"*Somebody ... anybody ... please help me!*" the man outside continued to scream. Artorius rushed outside, almost running into Praxus as both men ran down the flight of steps and over to where the slave was pacing frantically in circles, screaming at the top of his lungs.

"*What the hell is the meaning of this?*" Artorius shouted, grabbing the slave by the ear and pulling him down to his knees.

"Hey, what's going on out there?" a legionary from one of the other flats asked, still half asleep.

"We've got it," Praxus replied, "go back to bed." In his irritation Artorius cuffed the screaming man across the face.

"Shut the fuck up already!"

"Please kind sir, you must help me!" the slave pleaded. "My master has sent me from Four Corners plaza. The merchandise has all escaped! They burned down the stockade. Look and see for yourself!" He pointed frantically over his shoulder as Artorius held him down by his ear.

"Son of a bitch," Praxus said in a low voice as they caught sight of the flames that reached just over the top of the low-lying buildings in the market square. "Here!" he shouted to the legionary who was sleepily making his way back into his flat, "summon the fire watch!" The soldier's eyes grew wide as he caught sight of the flames.

"Right away!" he shouted back as he raced down the street towards where the urban cohort and the fire watch were housed.

"Let's go round up some slaves," Artorius said to Praxus as he released the frightened man.

"Yes, yes!" he spoke as he took to his feet. "I know where they went. Come with me and I'll show you!"

"Alright," Artorius replied. He then turned back towards the flat, where both sections stood on the landing awaiting orders. "Shields and javelins!" he shouted.

✳   ✳   ✳   ✳

"I'm frightened," Erin said, her hand that held the large knife trembling. Her husband, Tynan, held her close.

"It will be okay, my love," he said soothingly. Though he too was petrified at the predicament they found themselves in, he did his best not to show it.

Both were very young, in their early twenties. They had been slaves their entire lives and when their previous master had died they were sold to a procurer. Erin had been a cook and seamstress while her husband was a gardener. Neither had been exposed to the level of violence that surrounded them. Indeed it was horrific shock they felt when the men in cloaks had come and set them free ... or at least freed them from the stockades. They now found themselves huddled in an abandoned warehouse across the way from where they had been penned up. A pile of weapons had lain in the center, torchlight casting an eerie glow on the tarnished metal of short swords, axes, and other crude instruments of death. Many of the men fell upon these with lust and zeal; anxious as they were to fight for their freedom. Erin tended to forget that many slaves endured a much harsher life than the one she had lived thus far.

"Do you want your freedom?" a hooded man asked the crowd of slaves, his voice raspy and his face hidden in the shadows.

"Yes!" a young man responded with venom in his voice as he brandished a rusted spatha. "I will fight for my freedom; to the death if need be!" There were mutterings of consent amongst many of the slaves, though others were less certain.

"If we are free, then why have you taken us here?" Tynan asked, clutching his wife closer. "What do you want with us?" He could make out the trace of a sneer underneath the hood of the man who addressed them.

"It is a simple task that my master asks of you," he replied. "The stockade that held you burns, and soon the city garrisons will come."

"What of the slaver?" another man asked.

"He has been ... taken care of," came the reply. Erin swallowed hard in understanding. "You have been given weapons with which to earn your freedom. A detachment of Roman soldiers will soon be led down an alley just outside these doors. Dispose of them and you will have your freedom."

"It will be a pleasure," said the young man who had spoken so enthusiastically a moment before.

"I don't like this," Erin whispered to Tynan. "Why don't we just rid ourselves of these men and be done with it?" Before her husband could answer the hooded man swooped upon them, his face inches from theirs.

"Because it is *we* who have freed you!" he boomed. "Therefore you belong to *us* now! Do our bidding and you will be slaves no more." Before either could reply, the man strode away. He stood before the gathering and addressed them once more. "It will soon be time."

Time for what? Erin thought to herself.

✳   ✳   ✳   ✳

Beads of sweat ran down the slave's face and neck as he raced to the rally point, thirteen legionaries in tow. It was dark; the streets looked so different at night when they were devoid of life. He tripped over an upturned crate and stepped into a pile of mule dung. Though he stumbled and cursed his luck, he continued to scramble through the square until they were just two blocks from where the slave pens burned. The silhouettes of the fire watch resonated in the background as they fought to keep the blaze from spreading. He then breathed a sigh of relief as the glow cast its light on the alley.

"Here, they went down there!" he said excitedly. "They're all hiding in the building at the far end, behind the red door!" Shoving the man aside, Artorius and Praxus marched down the alley with their legionaries in tow.

"Damned runaway slaves," Valens cursed. "Why can't they just accept their lot in life and be done with it?"

"Alright, no unnecessary killing," Artorius ordered as they stumbled down the dark alley. "Beat them if they refuse to cooperate!" Valens was still cursing under his breath when he ran into a brick wall at the end of the alley.

"Ouch! Bugger it," he swore as he readjusted his helmet and looked around. In the dark all they saw was the wall. "Hey, there's no bloody door here!" The glow behind them was cast with shadows as several dozen people stepped into the alley behind them. The slave who had led them to the alley let out a laugh that was chocked full of madness.

"Oh, so sorry!" he laughed. "I guess I must have led you to the wrong alley! Please enjoy the hospitality of my friends!" Though Heracles had ordered him to return as soon as he had led the legionaries to the ambush site, he could not overcome his desire to watch. The slaves had the Romans sorely outnumbered, yet they were at best crudely armed and many had never committed an act of violence in their lives. They stood hesitant as Artorius and Praxus quickly assessed the situation.

The slaves outnumbered the Romans more than three to one, yet they hesitated. None wished to be the first to initiate combat; not even the young man who spoke so loudly about what a pleasure it would be to kill legionaries. The alley was extremely long and narrow; high stone walls on either side.

"Stay behind me," Tynan said quietly to Erin. "I'll protect you."

"Come," said one of the older men, "the least we can do in gratitude for our freedom is dispatch those who enslaved us to begin with!" He was shirtless with a body covered in scars wrought by the whips of cruel masters. Slowly the rabble started to advance, many of them still in a state of shock and disbelief, the gravity of their predicament had yet to set in. That would soon change.

"Bastard led us into a trap," Praxus said with a resigned sigh. Artorius nodded in reply as Gavius stepped forward with his javelin at the ready and filled with rage.

"Gavius, what are you doing?" Magnus asked as the rest of the legionaries fell into a hasty two ranks formation. Without answering, Gavius' eyes narrowed as he rapidly judged the distance from him to the traitor. All eyes, except those of the laughing slave, were fixed on him as he gave a shout and let his javelin fly. The slave ceased laughing, his eyes grew wide in the split second it took for the javelin to finish its flight and strike him through the center of his right femur. The man gave a high-pitched cry of terror and pain as the javelin smashed through the bone and pinned his leg to a post that he was leaning against. He started to hyperventilate and gave another loud cry as he saw his twitching leg; muscle, sinew and splinters of bone splayed out the exit wound.

"Nice," Artorius said with a brief grin before shouting his next order. "*Javelins ... throw!*" A dozen javelins sailed the short distance down the alleyway, slamming into the newly liberated slaves. Cries of anguish were heard from both men and women who had been thrust into the fray. Most of the slaves were near panic, though the thugs that blocked their escape drove them forward.

"*Gladius ... draw!*" Praxus shouted. With a shout, gladii were unsheathed and both sections advanced in two ranks behind a wall of shields and protruding swords.

Tynan had just enough time to duck, pulling Erin down with him as the Roman javelins slammed home. Screams echoed around them as each found its mark. He looked back to see a young woman, even younger than they; sprout a javelin from her shoulder. She fell to the ground screaming as the soft metal shaft at the end bent, the weight tearing bone, sinew, and flesh. They heard an audible shout from the Romans as they drew their swords. Most of the slaves responded with a loud cry of their own and charged headlong to their fate.

"Feel the wrath of Odin, bitch!" Magnus swore as the legionaries advanced. Though their opponents numbered at least three dozen, the narrowness of the alleyway worked to their advantage, only allowing roughly six to eight adversaries to engage them at a time. All Artorius saw was shadows in the glow of the flames. He brought his shield up to deflect the strike of one maddened slave. Quickly he stabbed with his gladius, catching the man in the belly. The blade embedded itself deep, rupturing bowels and organs in its wake. The slave gave a shriek of pain as Artorius knocked him back with his shield. To his left, Magnus thrust his gladius over the top of his shield, impaling another assailant in the throat; the man only able to make a gurgling sound as blood flooded his severed windpipe.

Erin hugged the wall as the slaves to her front clashed with the armored soldiers. Tynan was close by, but had released his grip on her for the moment. He was caught up in the rush of those who wished to fight for what they felt was their one chance at freedom. The flames behind them glinted off the polished steel of Roman helms and armor. Quickly she tried to back up, her hands trembling, as the slaves in front of her were quickly slain. The cries of the dying terrified her even more than the flash of legionary blades. She saw a large man in front of her wince and stoop over as the point of a gladius burst out his back. Rapidly the man fell and Erin stood face-to-face with the soldier who had killed him.

"No!" Tynan shouted, seeing the danger his wife was in. He forcibly shoved the other slaves aside as he rushed to protect the woman he loved. "*They'll not take you!*"

On the extreme left, Valens slammed his gladius home into the belly of a rather large slave. The man was huge, but slow and ungainly. The crude hand axe he carried bounced harmlessly off the legionary's shield as Valens stepped in and slew him. He then saw what looked to be a young woman armed with a crude knife. An equally young man stepped protectively in front of her, his arms outstretched, quickly speaking in Gallic. Without a second thought Valens stabbed him beneath the ribcage, eliciting a scream from the woman. The man convulsed, his eyes clouding over as life left him, and he fell face first to the pavement with a sickening crunch. The woman's eyes were filled with tears as her hand that held the knife trembled. In what can only be construed as a spontaneous act of mercy, Valens elected not to kill her; instead striking her across the temple with the boss of his shield. Her eyes rolled back into her head as she fell back and slid down the wall. He immediately brought his shield about, striking a more aggressive foe with the bottom edge of his shield.

The thugs hired by Heracles to goad the slaves into fighting realized the situation was turning against them. The slaves were being slaughtered, and still the legionaries came. One slave with a club managed to catch Decimus on the side of the helm, knocking him senseless. The man paid for this with his life as a legionary from Praxus' section quickly stepped in and stabbed him through the heart. Shouts outside the alley were heard as swarms of men from the urban cohort raced towards the scene, shields and spears in hand. The thieves shouted to each other and quickly fled. Before any of the slaves could escape the urban troops blocked their path, spears leveled.

"*Stand fast!*" Artorius shouted as Magnus ripped out the throat of another hapless victim with his gladius. The Norseman shoved the dying man to the side, his own face and chest soaked in blood. Cries of pain and sorrow echoed in the alley from the dying and their stricken companions. Carbo walked over to where Decimus lay stirring in a daze.

"You dumbass," he said as he knelt down to help his friend sit upright. He loosened up the chinstrap on Decimus' helmet and pulled it off. The legionary's eyes were glazed, a trickle of blood running out of his ear. "Damn, that guy clocked you good!"

"I guess I'm out of practice," Decimus replied, taking a deep breath and trying to focus his gaze on Carbo.

"Can you see okay?" Carbo asked. Decimus replied with a grin.

"I can see that you're still one ugly bastard," he said, prompting Carbo to raise his hand as if to cuff him on his non-injured ear. He then thought better of it and helped his friend to his feet.

As the legionaries started to round up prisoners, Valens walked over to where the woman he knocked unconscious still lay. He sheathed his gladius, leaned his shield against the wall, and knelt down beside her. She was fairly young, with a pretty face accentuated by a small nose and rather short blonde hair. He lifted her up underneath the arms, causing her to stir. She instinctively reached up to where the side of her head had started to swell and turn purple from the blow of Valens' shield. She looked around confused, her eyes then filling with horror as she caught sight of the legionary's face. The girl let out a scream of terror as she scrambled to get away from him. In her daze she stumbled and fell onto the corpse of the man who had given his life to save her. This elicited further shrieks and an unending wailing as she clutched his body and sobbed uncontrollably.

"Valens, shut that harlot up already!" Artorius shouted as he looked over his shoulder at the commotion. Valens let out a sigh and tried to coax the girl off the body.

"Come on," he said in a low voice. She refused to move and only sobbed louder.

"*Valens!*" Artorius shouted at him again, "quit fucking around back there! Get that bitch up here with the rest of them!" Valens grimaced hard, took a deep breath, and grabbed the young woman by the hair.

"I said *come on!*" he shouted as he dragged her away. She continued to scream and tried to reach for the slain man as the legionary pulled on her hair even harder. Valens cringed as he felt some of her hairs rip from her scalp as she stumbled along in his grip. The rest of the slaves were placed in a line on their knees, their hands bound behind their backs. Valens dropped the girl at the end of the line, took a length of rope from one of Praxus' legionaries, and bound her hands.

"It's going to be okay," he said quietly. The girl looked at him, her eyes swollen and stained with tears, and started to curse at him in a tongue unknown to him. Valens took a step back and turned to see Magnus watching.

"What did she say?" Valens asked, rightly suspecting that his Nordic friend understood.

"I'll tell you later," Magnus replied, smacking him on the shoulder and signaling for them to leave. The urban troopers had taken charge of the prisoners until it was decided what to do with them. Their commander came out of the house that stood next to the now smoldering stockade.

"Sergeant Artorius!" he shouted, recognizing the young Decanus, who in turn walked over to where the man stood in the doorway to the house. "You're going to want to have a look at this; bloody nasty mess in there."

"The slave owner?" Artorius asked as he stepped into the dimly lit hallway. The urban commander just shook his head.

"Down here, third door on the left." They stepped in to find the body of a man sprawled out on a bed, his head severed from his body, blood saturating the bed and pooled on the floor.

"Shit!" Artorius swore.

"It gets better," his companion replied. "We found his wife and infant child butchered in similar fashion, along with a pair of slaves." His morbid curiosity getting the best of him, Artorius walked quickly down the hall and almost tripped over one of the decapitated slaves. He then saw one of the urban troopers leaning against the next doorway, his head bowed. The Decanus then decided that he had seen enough and he turned about and walked as quickly as he could without running away from the horrific sight.

Outside, Heracles' slave who had led them to the alley was hyperventilating, his face soaked in sweat as the horror of his predicament overwhelmed him. His femur was splintered and he was pinned to the post by the Roman javelin. He knew not what to do, panic consuming him; he soiled himself as he saw a pair of enraged legionaries walking briskly over to where he stood.

"Son of a *bitch!*" Gavius swore as he punched the man across the mouth. The slave fell to the ground, his leg now twisted as it was held in place by the javelin. Gavius drew his gladius and placed the point on the side of the whimpering slave's neck. Carbo quickly grabbed him by the wrist.

"Not this way," he said as his friend struggled in his grasp. "Someone sent this bastard; we need to find out whom." As he pulled Gavius to the side he whispered into his ear, "then we can exact a little payback." Gavius nodded in reply and sheathed his weapon. He then bent down and wrenched the javelin from the post and the man's leg. The slave gave a fresh cry of pain and then rolled to his side, clutching the mutilated limb.

Legionary Felix stood panting as he caught his breath. His eyes then fell upon a brutally injured woman; a javelin had mangled her shoulder, splintered bones jutted from the gaping wound.

"Please ..." the woman whimpered, "make the pain stop." Felix glanced over at Sergeant Praxus, who nodded affirmatively. The young soldier then took a deep breath and knelt beside her. She was very young; scarcely even a woman. She was hyperventilating, her face doused in sweat, eyes fixed on Felix.

"Such a waste," he said quietly as he placed the blade of his weapon and the side of her neck and pulled back hard, slicing the artery. He stood immediately and walked away. In the past, killing had given Felix a sense of raw power, as if he were playing the role of a god. This was different. Those he had killed during the rebellion of Sacrovir and Florus had all been enemy combatants; people who had made war on Rome and had therefore forfeited their lives. This woman had not made war on Rome. She was part of an armed mob yes, but something just did not set right with the legionary. He then thought that perhaps he pitied her because she was so young, and indeed had been very pretty, even while covered in blood and gore. Felix then realized he had never killed a woman before and thought perhaps that played with his emotions as well. After all, he did not believe that women should be combatants in war; it just was not right. He further suspected that this particular woman had been an unwilling combatant.

"You alright?" Praxus asked, placing a hand on his shoulder and walking beside him. The legionary's face was covered in sweat. Felix removed his helmet and ran his hand through his hair.

"I'm confused, Sergeant," he replied. "A beautiful young girl like that, part of an armed mob. It doesn't make any sense. I think that somebody forced these slaves to attack us."

"I know," Praxus acknowledged. "But fact of the matter is they did attack us."

"I never thought that women belonged in battle," Felix said as they continued walking. Praxus gave a short, mirthless laugh.

"There are many things you need to learn then, young legionary. In parts of the world women serve as warriors; not just the men. Know that a woman's hand, properly trained, can kill you just as well as any man's."

"Well look at what we've got here," Magnus remarked as he walked up to Gavius and Carbo who both gave a wicked grin. "Bind his hands and drag his pathetic ass over to the Principia."

"You got it," Carbo replied. Magnus then walked over to where Artorius was leaving the slave master's house. His face was pale and the Norseman surmised what his Decanus had seen.

"Pretty bad in there?" he asked. Artorius nodded in reply.

"Fucking brutal," he remarked. "Someone decapitates the man, his family, and servants, releases the slaves and goads them into attacking us."

"Well I think we may have some answers soon enough," Magnus replied, his piercing blue eyes taking on a dark and sinister gaze.

Erin sat trembling, tears flowing freely down her bruised and swollen face, a trickle of blood running from the top of her head and passed her right eye, which was swollen nearly shut. Her hands were bound behind her back, her head hung low. The sight of her slain husband was burned into her mind. He was not even armed, having thrown down his club in his defiance of their 'liberators.' And yet the soldiers still killed him. All he had done was tried to protect her, and he had paid with his life. Erin sobbed and cursed her fate that he was dead while she still lived. She swore blasphemous oaths towards the legionary who killed him. His supposed mercy towards her was in reality a fate worse than death and she hated him for it. In her sorrow she wobbled sideways and bumped into another slave woman, who shoved her away hard with her shoulder.

"Ignorant bitch," the woman swore at her. "Think yourself lucky that you still live!" Erin wanted to curse the woman and scream aloud that with her husband slain all that mattered inside of her died with him. Instead all she could do was cry as despair consumed her. Her right eye was swollen almost completely shut and the stream of blood on her scalp had clotted and matted in her hair. She was living a nightmare and she silently prayed to any gods who would listen that she would wake up from it.

*   *   *   *

Heracles sat quietly in his quarters drinking warm ale while Radek stood patiently behind him. He knew by the sounds of commotion coming from the market and the slight smell of smoke that his plan had had its intended effect. Provided there were some dead legionaries, the slaves would have done their part. There came three sharp raps at the door, followed by two longer ones. He nodded to Radek, who turned and limped to the door.

"It's them," he said in a low voice as he peeked through a pin hole in the door. Heracles raised a hand, signaling him to let the men in. Three men rushed in, their faces flushed and near panic.

"Damn it man, how long did you plan on leaving us out there!" one said, exacerbated. Heracles continued to drink his ale, ignoring the man's remarks. Radek stepped over and backhanded the thug across the mouth.

"You will not speak to the master in such a tone," he hissed, his hand on the hilt of his cleaver. The three men immediately stepped back from the half-mad creature.

"I hear commotion in the streets," Heracles observed, snapping his fingers as a servant brought him a plate of figs. "I take it then that your mission was a success."

"Not as such," the first thug replied. "We burned the slave pens, just as you asked, and we got some legionaries trapped in an alley. Thing is …"

"Those bastards aren't human!" one of his companions interrupted. "They tore through that lot of slaves like a hot iron through pig fat!"

"No matter," Heracles replied casually. "We can replace slaughtered slaves easily enough. I take it there is more to report?" The three men all lowered their heads.

"Your slave that you sent to lure the Romans into the trap," the first man said.

"Yes?" Heracles prompted when the thug did not immediately continue.

"Thing is … the Romans got him. He didn't run off like you told him and one of those damn legionaries skewered him through the thigh with a javelin. Well the urban cohort shows up before we could carry him off or finish him. The Romans took him alive, sir."

"I see," Heracles replied as he let out a bored sigh. "They will torture him, no doubt. Lucky for us he knows so little. What a pity that I cannot seem to find slaves who do exactly as they are told." The servant behind him shifted nervously. The

Greek waved the men off and they quickly started for the back door. He sat and contemplated for a while, his fingers folder in front of his face and his eyes closed.

"Radek, my good man, I think we shall need to demonstrate to all what happens to those who cannot follow my orders." Radek's face grew into a smile of broken and rotting teeth.

✳   ✳   ✳   ✳

The slave was bound hanging by his outstretched limbs, his mangled leg causing him immeasurable pain. His breath was coming rapidly and he reeked of urine and sweat. Macro toyed with the dagger in his hand as he paced back and forth. The slave let out a slight whimper as the Centurion strode over and knelt beside him.

"Does this hurt?" Macro asked as he touched the exposed and splintered bone with the edge of his dagger. The slave let out a weak cry, his voice cracking from his parched throat. "I know it does. Just tell us who you belong to and I promise it will all be over." When the slave did not reply, Macro's face twisted in anger. He brought the dagger down in a hard stab into the bone. This elicited a series of fresh cries of anguish from the stricken man.

"I'll talk! I'll talk!" he shouted pitifully. Macro quickly withdrew the dagger as the slave passed out.

"Wake him," the Centurion ordered. A legionary took his water bladder and poured it onto the man's face. He woke up sputtering and sobbing.

"My master is a Greek who calls himself Heracles," he whimpered. "He was a leader of Sacrovir's rebellion. Please, that is all I know."

"Are you *sure* that is all you know?" Macro asked, waving the dagger at the slave.

"Yes, yes! I swear! He is a very private man; he only bought me two weeks ago. Please, no more pain!" Macro nodded to a pair of legionaries, who cut the bonds holding the slave up. He fell with a thud to the floor, his face contorted in agony.

"I said it would be over, and it shall." With that he snapped his fingers and walked out of the room. The slave's eyes grew wide as an enraged Artorius grabbed him by the hair with both hands and violently dragged him away, his rage overtaking him.

Out in the hall, Macro came upon Proculus and Vitruvius who both gave a start as they heard the slave screaming for mercy.

"Aren't you done with him yet?" Proculus asked. Macro nodded.

"We are," he answered. "Now my boys are executing a little retribution." Vitruvius gave a snort and shook his head.

"You're a wicked one, Macro," he said, a mildly amused grin on his face. "So what did you find out?"

"Not a whole lot," Macro conceded. "Seems he belongs to a Greek that calls himself Heracles. I've got men on their way to where his master resides, though I'm certain he will have fled once he knew his servant had been captured by us."

"Well that's original!" Proculus retorted as all three men walked down the hall and out the door that led to the courtyard. "A Greek that decides to take on the name of a god; bloody brilliant! What will they think of next?"

"He also said that this Greek was one of the leaders of Sacrovir's rebellion." Proculus stopped in midstride and turned to face Macro.

"What?" he asked. "I thought all the leaders perished."

"We only assumed they did," Vitruvius conjectured, his broad arms folded across his chest. "Truth is we never did excavate the site of Sacrovir's destroyed manor house. It is possible that some may have escaped the mutual slaughter." Proculus took a deep breath and exhaled audibly.

"The last thing we need is another damn uprising," he said. "We must make an example of all who would disrupt the peace of Rome!"

"Already being taken care of," Macro replied.

✳   ✳   ✳   ✳

Kiana saw the smoke rising from the slave market and it puzzled her. She had come into the city to purchase some fruit and bread; a task normally done by slaves, but one she had insisted on doing herself that day. She had been confined to the manor house for the last few days and she needed an excuse to go out for a while. So great was her desire to be left alone that she had not allowed any of the servants to accompany her.

She was a striking girl, and at fifteen fast approaching womanhood. Of slightly less than average height, her auburn hair reached halfway down her back and contrasted with her fair skin and deep green eyes. Her body was on the slender side, though it hinted at the curves that would come with womanhood.

Her father had sent her and her sister, Tierney, to Lugdunum as a means of escaping the aftermath of the Sacrovir Revolt. What had been a joyous time in her life had become a nightmare. She had at the time been living in Augustodunum where her beloved Farquhar had been studying at the university. Her father had approved greatly of the young man and had sought their betrothal at the earliest opportunity. Sadly Farquhar had been swept away by the poison rhetoric of Sacrovir, like so many of the young nobles. *The Noble Youth of Gaul*, as Sacrovir had called them, stood no chance against the Roman juggernaut and most were slaughtered during the Battle of Augustodunum. Farquhar had been in the vanguard, encased in plate armor meant to stop the javelin and gladius. Instead, a Roman soldier had smashed through his armor with a pickaxe. Kiana never forgot the sight of her love, his ribs punctured and smashed; his head rendered open with the skull splintered around the gaping hole.

She shuddered at the memory. Part of the reason for her father sending her away was so that perhaps not being around reminders of those devastating times her nightmares might cease. Not a night went by that she did not wake up in a cold sweat, images of death permeating her conscience. For it was not just Farquhar who she had seen maimed. So many of their friends had perished, their bodies ripped asunder by the sheer wrath of the legions.

Crucifixion was tedious work. However, Artorius was in a rage after having been played the fool by a lowly slave and he was determined to make an example of the pathetic excuse for a man. The slave cried out in pain as the Decanus drove the spikes into his wrists; securing the crossbeam to the side of the remains of the slave trader's home. Carbo and Valens had secured the arms in place with rope before Artorius drove the spikes through each wrist. Extra care was taken securing the legs, with Magnus tying an extra length of rope around the upper thighs. Often they would break the legs of their victims so that they could no longer hold the body weight and death would be expedited via suffocation. However, with the slave's one leg already shattered, they did not want him to succumb too soon.

"That'll do him," Artorius said as he climbed down the ladder. The section looked up at the slave, who was still screaming for mercy at the top of his lungs.

"Should we oblige him?" Decimus asked; his eyes on Artorius. The Decanus shook his head.

"No ... not for a while anyway. This rat bastard helped to slay the owner of this house and his family. I want him to set a firm example to any who would seek to undermine the law and stability of this region."

"Nice work," Centurion Macro stated, walking up behind the men. All turned and faced their Centurion, Artorius rendering a salute. Macro returned the courtesy before gazing up once again at the still-screaming slave.

"I like how you secured his legs so he can't suffocate too quickly," the Centurion noted with a bemused grin.

"Magnus' idea," Artorius replied, letting out a deep sigh. The screams of horror and pain were starting to take their toll on him and he had a headache. His anger had subsided and he felt a tinge of pity for the man. After all, he was little more than a slave who could not have easily disobeyed his master.

"It was a no-win situation, really," Decimus noted. "Had he disobeyed his owner, he would likely have been killed. Then again, he had the chance to seek protection when he came to us."

"Yes," Artorius said, rubbing his temples with both hands. He had taken off his helmet while they had crucified the slave. He looked over to see a young girl hunched over across the street, her hand bracing her against the stone sides of the building. Curious, Artorius walked over to her. She looked to be about fifteen or sixteen; at the age where she was blossoming from girl to woman. The sights and sounds of the crucifixion of the slave had taken their toll on her and she was dry-heaving and sobbing.

"Are you alright, child?" Artorius asked as he placed a hand on her shoulder. As the girl turned to face him, her eyes grew wide in horror, for she recognized his face while he still did not know hers. She fell to her knees, her eyes filled with fresh tears.

"No ..." she said in a low voice, shaking her head. "*No!*" With a scream she scrambled to her feet and fled down the street, seeking refuge in the crowded market that stood but a block away. The eyes of many curious onlookers fell on her as she ran, sobbing uncontrollably. Those same eyes returned to the Centurion as he beat his vine stick against the side of the building.

"*Let all bear witness,*" he began, "*to the fate of any who will seek to upset the good order of this city through sedition and murder! Behold the fate of his fellow conspirators!*" He waved his vine stick at the corpses of the slain slaves, which were laid out in a line in front of the crucified man. A butcher's shop was nearby, and the owner stepped forward, a meat hook in his hand. He was breathing rapidly through his nose, his mustache rippling slightly. He walked to within a few feet of the Centurion, lowered his eyes onto one of the corpses and then returned his gaze front. Macro folded his arms across his chest and nodded. The butcher then gave a growl of anger and slammed his hook under the chin of one of the slain. As he dragged the body away, the rest of the mob gave a shout and fell upon the rest. The Centurion shook his head and walked away.

Mob justice, he thought to himself. *So quick are they to feign their loyalty.*

"What the hell was that all about?" Magnus asked, looking over to where the girl had disappeared into the crowded market.

"I don't know," Artorius replied, "something about her looked familiar, but from where?"

"Not one of your bite victims then?" Artorius chuckled and shook his head.

"No, prefer them a little older and not quite so delicate."

Valens stood with his hands on his hips, admiring their work, when he heard a gasp behind him. He turned to see Svetlana standing with one hand over her mouth, her eyes wide.

"Svetlana, what are you doing here?" he asked abruptly, grabbing her by both arms and attempting to guide her away from the scene of death and torture. Magnus heard the commotion and immediately moved to help Valens.

"Sister, you should not see such things," he said quickly, trying to block the young woman's view. She could only shake her head in reply. "Valens, get her out of here!" The legionary nodded in reply and forcibly guided Svetlana away. Her hand over her mouth, she finally averted her gaze as she stumbled away in Valens' grip.

"Come on," he said quietly as the young woman stifled a sob. As soon as they were cleared of the scene, he placed both hands on her shoulders. Svetlana quickly composed herself.

"Forgive me," she said quietly. "It's just that I have not had to deal with such brutality before. What had that man done?"

"Led us all into a bloody trap," Valens replied. "Bastard deliberately tried to get the whole lot of us killed. I think a little crucifixion will do some good." Svetlana nodded, her brow furrowed in contemplation.

"I agree," she said at last, reason overriding the sense of shock at the horror of the spectacle. "Again, please forgive my weak constitution. I'm fine now."

"You sure?" Valens asked. "Only your brother does not want you witnessing such things."

"Then you damn well shouldn't have crucified the man in the middle of the fucking forum!" Svetlana retorted, causing Valens to wince at her rare profanity. "Besides, my brother, who I dearly love mind you, does not approve of us being together either. I think he can deal with his baby sister being exposed to some of the horrors of the world. I am of stronger stock than any of these women!"

While Valens and Svetlana spoke in the alley, Artorius looked over at his friend and realized he was very tired.

"You know we've been up well past our shift," he observed with a loud yawn.

"I know," Magnus replied, yawning in turn. "I think I'm going to go have a wash and turn in for a while."

"Sounds good to me." Artorius located Sergeant Ostorius, who was supervising the day patrols, exchanged a few details with him, and then headed to the bathhouse. All the while he kept trying to think of where he had seen the young Gallic woman before. She certainly wasn't a prostitute for she was far too well dressed. Besides, Artorius figured he knew just about all of them in the city by this time. Something continued to nag at him as he stumbled into the steaming bath; something from his past. He tried to dismiss it; he was too tired to think straight and he would figure it out later.

While the sight of the crucified man had horrified Kiana, seeing the man who had slain her lover not even a year ago filled her with abject terror and renewed feelings of pain and sorrow. She knew it was him. The image of his face staring down at her and Farquhar's grieving father was burned into her mind.

Kiana found a small alleyway and sat down, her head in her hands. Strangely enough, no one seemed to pay her any mind.

"Why?" she asked through her tears. "Why has that beast come to torment me?"

"Even the gravest of beasts can still be subdued," a voice spoke. Kiana looked up to see a man kneeling next to her. The shape of his face, along with his dark hair and well-groomed beard, led her to realize he was either a Greek or Macedonian. His demeanor was not unpleasant; in fact something about him soothed Kiana's sorrow. He extended a hand to her.

"Come child," he said softly. "Tell me what ails you."

It was but a short walk to the flat that Heracles had procured. Kiana sat down and a slave handed her a cup of wine. The young girl's hands trembled as the Greek sat across from her. She was not afraid of him. In fact she was relieved that he had come to her in her delirium.

"Animals," she said under her breath, "those men are nothing but savage animals." Heracles' face remained stoic.

"You speak of the Roman masters," he replied casually. Kiana eyed him coldly, each trying to gage the other's intentions.

"Masters of the world they may be, but they are still animals," she retorted. Something had snapped inside of her and it was consuming her conscience. Before she had not blamed the Romans for Farquhar's death. Rather she had placed the blame on Sacrovir and his minions. Now that she had seen the abject cruelty which the Romans were capable of she was starting to have doubts. Heracles could read these doubts in her face and he would exploit them.

✳   ✳   ✳   ✳

That night a group of men, their heads hidden beneath their hoods, walked quietly down the street. The tortured slave raised his head weakly, his eyes daring to hope. The men were removing torches from the walls of the alley and extinguishing them. The group passed on, leaving a single torch lit. Two men remained behind.

The slave tried to smile when he saw Heracles remove his hood. His hope proved short-lived.

"You have failed me," the Greek said in a nonchalant voice. His eyes betrayed his dark thoughts. The slave's own eyes grew wide as he shook his head, fresh tears welling up in his eyes.

"Master please, I beg you," he whimpered. "I did as you asked. Look at what the Romans have done to me!"

"Yes," Heracles replied with a nod. "The Romans have certainly caused you much pain; pain that you brought on yourself with your carelessness. I can only imagine the things you told them under torture ..." The slave shook his head once more but he knew he could not lie to his master.

"Please, have mercy on me," he said quietly. "Certainly I have suffered enough." Heracles rolled his eyes as if bored.

"I suppose you have," he replied. He snapped his fingers and raised his hood over his head. The slave started to whimper once more when the other man removed his hood. It was that vile creature Radek, who only accompanied Heracles with a single purpose. The slave caught a glimpse of the cleaver before Heracles extinguished the final torch.

Legionary Felix leaned against the side of the building. He rather liked night patrols, even if it did temporarily mess with his sleep plan. The nights were quiet without all the traffic on the streets. The nighttime breeze felt good to the young soldier. In the soft glow of the torches he could just make out some of his section mates. The horrors of the night before were still fresh in his mind; however, he was able to come to grips with what he had been forced to do. His Decanus had been right in his assessment of what had happened and though Felix still did not believe in fighting women, he knew he had done the right thing. Besides, his act of killing had been an act of mercy after all.

Sergeant Praxus had ordered them to patrol around the destroyed slave market at Four Corners Road. The slaves themselves were being held in a different location while going through interrogation. All that was left was the smoldering remains of the pens. Though the bodies had been removed from the scene, there were still the swarms of flies and other insects around the sticky pools of blood that seemed to be everywhere. Inside the slave owner's house it was far worse. Felix had decided to take a look inside just to see for himself. And though he was no amateur when it came to killing, the stench made him wretch. He let out a sigh as he gazed absently into the torchlight.

"Hey Felix," one of his companions said, startling him. "It's awfully quiet here, don't you think?"

"It always is this time of night," he answered leaning his shoulder against the building once more.

"Yeah, but it shouldn't be over here," the other legionary persisted. "The slave that Sergeant Artorius nailed to the side of the building is strung up right around the corner. Surely he isn't dead yet!"

"Well let's go and have a look then," Felix said with a bored sigh. His fellow legionary grabbed a torch off the wall and walked around to the other side of the building, which was strangely dark.

"Shit!" Felix heard the soldier swear. "Felix, come take a look at this!" Suddenly alert, he grabbed his shield and javelin and quick stepped around the building.

"Shit!" he echoed when he saw the slave. The other legionary held his torch up at the macabre sight. The slave's head was lying on the ground, his genitalia stuffed in his mouth.

"When the hell could this have happened?" the legionary asked. Felix could only shake his head.

"I don't know," he replied. "I'm going to fetch Sergeant Praxus." As he turned, the rest of his section came rushing around the side of the building, alerted by the commotion.

"Damn," Praxus said in a low voice. "Son of a bitch was spared with a quick death after all. Fetch a ladder and cut him down. Have the corpse taken away and burned."

"Right away," Felix answered as they left to find a ladder. Praxus stood with his hands on his hips and gazed at the wretched sight. He swallowed hard and shook his head.

✳   ✳   ✳   ✳

"Are you ready, old friend?" Pilate asked, walking his horse over to where Justus was inspecting one of his baggage carts. He had already sent his wife and children ahead to the docks in Ostia, where he would meet up with them. Having no family of his own, Pilate's own carts were much fewer.

"I think so," Justus replied with a sigh. "Can't say I'm too anxious to be leaving so soon."

"So soon?" Pilate chided. "You've been here for over three years, man!"

"I know, and I like it here ... well Flavia does anyway. Besides, *you'll* be coming back after a year or so. Me, I'll be spending the rest of my career in the east I think."

"True," Pilate conceded. "Still, the east is not so bad from what I hear. It's quite exotic." Justus snorted at his friend's assessment.

"It's fucking hot, dry, with inhospitable people," he retorted. "If not for the fact that Rome gorges itself on Egyptian grain I scarcely think we would bother with the place." He then looked back at one of Pilate's cart and started walking towards it. "Here, looks like one of your tie-down ropes came undone." As Justus starting to adjust the tarp, his expression showed one of surprised amusement.

"Pilate," he said. "Why do you have a statue of Sejanus in your baggage? I know you work for him, but come on man, no need to worship!"

"It's not for me," Pilate replied, fidgeting in his stance. "It's for the Legate of the Twelfth."

"What, does he worship Sejanus too?"

"Cool your tongue, old friend," Pilate scolded. "It is symbolic, so that the eastern legions may remember who it is that shares the Emperor's labors." Justus' expression fell.

"I see," he replied. "Forgive me, but I find it a little peculiar. One would almost think that Sejanus was Tiberius' heir given the way he lauds on him!"

"Will you stop already?" Pilate retorted. Justus only shook his head.

"Look, a statue of the Emperor's son I can understand, but the fucking Praetorian Prefect? That is as pompous of a gesture as I have ever seen! It is arrogance personified and the Legates will not handle it well."

"I think they will," Pilate replied coldly. "I must warn you old friend, any perceived disloyalties towards Sejanus will be interpreted as disloyalties towards the Emperor himself."

"Well forgive my impertinence then," Justus said with a trace of venom in his voice.

Justus' wife, Flavia noted the vexation in her husband as soon as he arrived at the Ostia docks with his friend Pontius Pilate. The two men had not spoken to each other since their spat over the statue of Sejanus. She went to say something to her husband, but he raised his hand, silencing her. She elected to go see how their children were adjusting to their quarters and left Justus to his thoughts. She hated seeing her husband troubled this way. He and Pilate had been friends their entire lives and it deeply upset Flavia to witness the consternation between the two men.

"Is Father alright?" her son Gaius asked as she entered the small cabin their family occupied. Flavia tried to force a smile, though the concern on Gaius' face told her that he saw through the façade.

"Your father and Pilate have some issues they need to resolve." Flavia did not wish to give too much detail, though she also knew better than to hide things from her son. Gaius was maturing fast; too fast in her mind.

"Pilate is a good man," Gaius observed, his brow furrowed, "but I do not trust his patron, Sejanus."

"Now why you say that?" Flavia asked as she ran her hands through her son's copper-colored hair and sat down next to him on a trunk that carried much of their personal possessions. The lad looked around before continuing.

"He's manipulative. I know I have never met Sejanus personally, but I see what his influence has done to Pontius Pilate. I've heard Father arguing with him over this man and the power he has over the Emperor. I know there is a statue of him on this ship—a *gift* for the Legate of the Twelfth Legion."

"Whatever their differences may be, know that your father's friendship with Pilate is stronger than any political disagreements they may have."

"I hope so," Gaius said with a nod. He was fumbling with his hands in thought, a sign his mother knew meant he was still troubled, though she hoped he would turn his talk away from Imperial politics.

"Father is a noble man," Gaius continued, "and his passion as a soldier of Rome makes him very protective of the Emperor and any threats he perceives. I just hope that someday I am able to be half the soldier he is." Flavia closed her eyes and unconsciously gripped her son's shoulder.

CHAPTER IX

▼

SLAVES AND NOBLES

"So tell me again why you feel you have to have this one?" Magnus asked as he and Valens walked over to the hastily repaired stockade. The surviving slaves were huddled inside, fearful that they might meet the same fate as the man who had goaded them into fighting the Romans.

"Macro did say if any of us wished to have one of the slaves we could buy them before he sends them to the market," Valens replied. Indeed the Centurion had hoped his men would be willing to spend a few denarii on the slaves, seeing as how once they went to market all proceeds would go to the local magistrate. Whereas the profits from any slaves sold while they remained in his custody went directly to him.

"Sure, but this woman doesn't even speak Latin," Magnus conjectured. "Plus after what she said to you after the scrap at the alley I can't imagine why you would want her." The Norseman had never told his friend what the woman had said, only that it wasn't very nice. In truth, the woman had used the names of the gods of damnation to curse Valens. Not knowing how superstitious his friend was, Magnus thought better than to let Valens think he was about to be set upon by barbarian gods.

"I have my reasons," Valens replied as they walked along the outside of the pen. The slaves had been ordered to stand by the bars, though all hung their heads low.

The young woman saw the legionaries before they reached her. She closed her eyes as fear and loathing overcame her. She heard one of the men speak while pointing at her. She started to sob and collapsed to the ground as she was forcibly removed from the pen by two men from the urban cohort. They gruffly threw her to the ground in front of the legionaries.

"Take it easy!" Magnus barked. The men ignored him and walked back inside the pen. The Norseman then knelt down and spoke to the woman in Gallic. She was on her knees, her hands resting on her legs, her good eye fixed on the ground and the other swollen completely shut. Slowly she replied to the legionary, her instincts from having been a slave her entire life forcing her to comply with his questioning.

"Well?" Valens asked impatiently.

"Her name's Erin," Magnus replied. "She was born a slave and has worked as a cook, seamstress, and gardener. The man you killed was her husband."

"I see," Valens remarked. "What else does she say?"

"I asked how she would feel about coming to work for you. She said her feelings do not matter." Valens eyed the woman, trying to gauge her disposition. If she had been a slave her entire life, then she would indeed be of the mindset that she was to obey her master, regardless of personal feelings. That was enough for the legionary.

"How much?" Valens asked. One of the urban soldiers grabbed a tag on Erin's neck and then checked his list.

"Sixty-five denarii," he replied. Magnus whistled while Valens dug into his coin pouch.

"Are you sure about this?" the Norseman asked again. "I mean that's almost an entire pay stipend."

"True," Valens replied, "but in all honesty I don't care."

"I don't need a bloody slave!" Svetlana protested as Erin stood in the corner, her hands folded and gaze on the floor.

"Well I can't keep her at the barracks," Valens observed. "Besides, I thought perhaps you could use someone to help out around here."

"That's not the only reason," Svetlana said, her eyes narrowing. Valens held up his hands.

"Hey, I'm not interested in using her for sport, if that's what you're thinking."

"Why not? She is rather attractive." A coy smile crossed Svetlana's face as Valens' turned a slight shade of red.

"If you knew the circumstances surrounding how I acquired her, you'd understand," he replied. He then kissed Svetlana on the cheek and quickly left the room. The Norsewoman apprised the girl that stood before her.

Svetlana had never owned a slave before. Her father had of course; though these had often been more for personal recreation rather than any kind of actual work. She had never really paid them any mind and was rarely even aware of their presence.

"My name is Svetlana," she said in Gallic, a language she knew well enough but had not used in many years.

"Yes Domina," Erin replied, her eyes still on the ground.

"Look at me," Svetlana directed. The face of the Gallic woman spoke of a deep sorrow that she fought in vain to conceal. Though her womanly instincts urged her to comfort the girl, Svetlana knew that she establishing the proper rapport with this slave was paramount. "I'm told you can cook."

"Yes Domina," Erin replied, her expression reverting to one devoid of emotion. This was good in Svetlana's mind. She wanted to get her into a routine immediately, distract the slave with work and she would be unable to focus on her sorrows. She then decided to see what else Erin knew.

"Can you sew and mend garments?" she asked.

"Yes Domina," Erin replied.

"What about cleaning?"

"Yes Domina." The short, almost curt answers left Svetlana a little put out, but she could honestly not expect much more from the slave.

"Can you speak Latin?"

"Very little Domina," Erin replied in Latin. This disappointed Svetlana, but it did not matter. Her Gallic was good enough for what Erin would need to know.

"Can you read or write?"

"No Domina."

"Well that is something we may have to change," Svetlana replied with a half smile. Erin did not return it. She had no idea what the point would be of teaching the woman to read and write. Since she could not speak Latin, any literacy she achieved would be in Gallic and most likely useless for Svetlana's needs.

"How's the new slave working out?" Carbo asked as Valens walked into the barracks flat. The rest of the men were inspecting and performing maintenance on their gear. Carbo was working a deep nick out of the blade of his gladius while Decimus was tapping out the indentation in the side of his helmet; a bandage wrapped around his head and covering his ear.

"No idea," Valens replied as he laid out his armor and equipment on his bunk.

"I dumped her off with Svetlana and told her to put her to work." The rest of the men looked over at Magnus, hoping to get more details from their friend.

"I think she'll be alright," he said in response to the unasked questions, running his fingers through his blonde hair. "Svetlana is multilingual, though she has not had to speak Gallic in a long time."

"So … what kind of mental state do you think she's in?" Carbo asked. He was the only one blunt enough to ask what everyone wanted to know. Everyone ceased working on their equipment and eyed the legionary. "I mean, after all, Valens killed her husband and smashed her up pretty good …" The room grew silent and Carbo went back to running the sharpening stone over his weapon.

"She's a fucking *slave!*" Valens finally barked, breaking the silence. "What does it matter what she thinks?" He was starting to question why he had even gone through the trouble of acquiring the young Gallic woman in the first place. Magnus was quick to assist him.

"Valens is right," the Norseman stated as he leaned against the wall. "She *is* a slave and is now his property. Now he must make certain she is properly maintained, like our weapons and equipment. And like our weapons, as long as she is taken care of she will serve him well."

"Is it so good to be comparing a slave to a weapon?" Decimus asked, sitting upright in his bunk. His head was bandaged and he was still feeling the effects of the fever he had had for the past couple weeks. Gavius was helping him by reshaping his helmet where it had gotten smashed during the scuffle the other night.

Artorius remained quiet the entire time. He continued to inspect the straps and rivets on his armor while taking in everything that was being said. He had contemplated purchasing a slave for the section; someone to keep the flat clean and do menial chores. He then thought better of it, not wanting to have to house a slave, plus doing details around the flat kept the men occupied and in a routine.

✳   ✳   ✳   ✳

"The girl is of noble birth," Radek observed as he and Heracles sat in the virtual dark, a lone candle lighting the table they occupied. "Quite the statement could be made with her disposal." His Greek master shook his head in reply.

"No, I have better plans for that one," Heracles asserted. "I find it more satisfying using her to do our bidding. I have planted the seeds of doubt already in her mind, now they simply need time to grow."

"I admit Master, I was surprised that you let her go."

"What else could I do?" Heracles responded. "She will not do us any good if she is a prisoner. Trust me, my friend. She will come back to us, and when she does I will own her very soul."

Doubts had indeed assailed Kiana since witnessing the spectacle of the crucified slave and seeing the legionary who haunted her. When she had first laid eyes on the soldier who had killed her beloved Farquhar on that dark day over a year before, she had not felt any sort of ill feelings at all; just sorrow, confusion, and even pity towards the young soldier. However, over time as the nightmares grew worse, his ever-present image became distorted, even monstrous.

Kiana bolted upright in her bed, sweating and breathing rapidly. She tried to catch her breath and sat with her face in her hands for a moment. It would be yet another sleepless night. Exasperated, she threw the blankets off and stormed out of the room in her dressing gown. The villa she and her sister Tierney lived in was much smaller than the grand house of their father, but it did have a pleasant garden out back that Kiana decided to visit.

As she walked past a balcony that overlooked the garden she was surprised to see the faint glow of lamp light coming from below. Quietly she walked over and looked over the edge. Seated on a bench were Tierney and a man Kiana did not recognize. What she did notice however was that he wore a red tunic, like that of a legionary. She closed her eyes for a minute and shook her head. It was not possible that her sister was exchanging pleasantries, or worse, with a *Roman*. She backed away and walked down the stairs that led to the back entrance. Without a sound she crept into the alcove that led into the garden. A glint of metal on a raised pedestal caught her attention. Her fears were confirmed when she saw a legionary gladius lying in its scabbard on the pedestal. A slave stood nearby, keeping an eye on the soldier's weapon. Kiana slowly walked up to it and went to pick it up. When her fingers were but inches away she quickly retracted her hand, as if the gladius would burn it. She clenched and unclenched her fist and then without another thought walked through the archway into the garden. Tierney's face was clearly visible, though the soldier's back was to Kiana. Her own face twitched as she heard her sister laughing out loud at something the man had said. The laughter faded when Tierney noticed they were not alone.

"Sister," she said, rising abruptly. The man turned quickly and then also rose to his feet. While Tierney looked like someone caught in a criminal act, the legionary seemed pleased to see Kiana. He was very young, probably close to the same age as Tierney, who had turned eighteen just four months prior.

"You kept telling me about your sister, and now I see we finally get to meet," he said, glancing over his shoulder at Tierney, whose face had turned pale.

"Um … yes," she stammered. "Kiana, this is Felix, a … *friend* of mine." The legionary smiled at the emphasis Tierney had placed on the word.

"A pleasure," he said, bowing slightly. Kiana returned the gesture, though her face remained blank.

"I apologize for disturbing you and I will leave you two alone," she said. Felix raised a hand and shook his head, a gentle smile never leaving his face.

"No, I really must get going," he replied. "I've gotten used to being up at night that my sleep habits are all messed up. I am sorry if we woke you." Kiana shook her head.

"Not at all; I just needed a bit of fresh air is all." Her eyes remained focused on Felix as he kissed Tierney, who remained motionless, on the cheek and then walked past Kiana and through the archway. Kiana watched him strap his gladius to his hip and follow the servant towards the front door. She then turned and faced her sister, whose face was now completely white, her eyes shut and teeth clenched.

"Kiana …" she started to say as she opened her eyes. " …Kiana I am so sorry. I wasn't sure how you would feel, knowing that my friend is a legionary."

"Your *friend* is quite handsome," Kiana replied. They remained silent for a few moments longer before she continued. "Forgive my intrusion, sister. But I have had another sleepless night." She purposely avoided making mention of Felix's status as a Roman soldier. Tierney took a deep breath and color returned to her face once more. Without another word, Kiana walked back the way she had come, suddenly tired and longing for her bed.

After the horrifying experience her sister had gone through the year before, Tierney was afraid that associating with the legionary would be too much for Kiana to bear. What she could never tell her was that Felix had fought at Augustodunum, where Farquhar was killed. Indeed she had never let Felix know about Kiana's fiancé either.

CHAPTER X

▼

HEART OF EVIL

Hoeing weeds had its own quiet appeal to Broehain. When he had been a noble with great estates at his disposal all such menial tasks were performed by slaves. But now these menial tasks were really all that he had left. As a leader of the Turani who had taken part in Sacrovir's rebellion, his lands had been stripped and his titles forfeit. The only reason the Romans had allowed him to live was because in a desperate attempt to save his family further grief and in part because Sacrovir had used his people as disposable fodder in battle, Broehain had led the Romans to Sacrovir's hiding place. For this he was allowed to live in a small farmhouse with his wife and two young sons. The boys were off playing in the woods nearby while his wife was at the market. As he wiped the sweat from his sun-baked brow, his eyes grew wide as he saw two men and a young girl in a cart riding up the dirt road towards his home. One was very haggard and at a distance appeared to be missing an eye. The other he knew immediately.

"It cannot be," he said in a quiet voice. Fear gripped him as they stopped not ten feet from him and he clutched his hoe defensively.

"Is this the way you great an old friend?" Heracles asked as he dismounted the cart.

"I thought for certain you had perished," Broehain replied, wiping fresh perspiration from his brow.

"I thought the same of you," Heracles said, a friendly smile on his face. Broehain read the look in the Greek's eyes and they were anything but friendly. "I noticed you were absent when the rest of the leaders rallied to Sacrovir's estate."

"The Romans captured me," the Gaul replied, his eyes averted. "My men were trampled and slaughtered by the Roman cavalry. I barely managed to escape with my life."

"But escape you did," Heracles asserted. "But tell me, what happened to your lands? You were a nobleman of the Turani! Surely you have more than just a small farmhouse and a patch of barren ground!"

"The Romans took most of my lands," Broehain answered, not wishing to discuss the situation further.

"But they let you live. Interesting," Heracles mused. "Or was it perhaps a little trade you did? The Romans take your land but spare your life. And in exchange for what?" He stepped in close to Broehain, their faces but inches apart. "What was it you gave the Romans in exchange for your life? All rebel leaders they captured were executed, but here you are. What was it you offered them, Broehain?" The Gaul's face was rigid, his expression unchanged. Just then the sounds of boys laughing were heard as his young sons came scampering up the hill. Their laughter immediately ceased when they caught sight of the Greek talking to their father.

"Ah, your young heirs," Heracles said, his voice kind and pleasant in front of the boys. "Heirs to a hovel, but still …" Broehain cut him short with a hard rap across the chest with his hoe.

"What do you want, Heracles?" he asked, his voice betraying the anger that simmered inside of him. The Greek glared at him, a wicked smile crossing his face.

"I want you to make things right you traitor fuck," he hissed into Broehain's ear. "You sold out your kinsmen to save your own hide!"

"You are not even of this land!" Broehain retorted, his own voice low to match Heracles'. "You are a bloody Greek and of no kin to these people who you led to their deaths!" Heracles stepped away, mocking his feelings being hurt.

"Led them to their deaths, did I? Oh no, my dear Broehain. I offered your people the knowledge with which to win their freedom. Were there any real warriors left in Gaul, you might have survived with more than just a shack for your whore and little fuck trophies." His anger boiling over, Broehain rushed towards him, his hoe raised to strike. In flash Heracles drew Sacrovir's long sword and pointed it at the Gaul's chest.

"Ah ah ah, I don't think so," he said as Broehain stopped in his tracks. He returned the sword to its scabbard and folded his hands in front. "Sad really, that you would rather rot out your existence here than redeem what's left of your sorry excuse for a life. Good day." He abruptly turned on his heel and walked back to the cart.

"A shame really," he said as he sat down. Radek gave a sickening grin as he turned the cart around and sent them back down the road.

"A shame?" Kiana asked, her face hidden beneath her hooded cloak as she sat behind the two men.

"No need to worry, my dear," Heracles soothed. "Our friend Broehain will see the error of his ways yet." Seated where she was, Kiana was unable to see the glint of evil in Heracles' eye. Radek saw it and it made him grin even broader. "It was the betrayal of those like him that led to your beloved's death." Kiana closed her eyes as the words pierced her heart. It was all starting to make sense to her. Had the rebel army not turned tail and ran like they had at Augustodunum, Farquhar may have lived. She reasoned that perhaps nothing could have saved her fiancé, though she now understood that men such as Broehain had ensured his death.

"See to it he understands his folly," she said in a dark voice that was music to Heracles' ears.

"All in due time my dear."

"Go check on your brother," Broehain's wife said to their eldest son. They were seated around the small table for their evening meal; a soft glow of a lamp providing a humble amount of light within.

"He's old enough to know how to take a piss on his own!" the boy complained, causing his father to rebuke him with a hard cuff behind the ear.

"Don't talk to your mother like that and do what you're told!" he said sharply. The lad stood quickly and left the room lest he receive an additional physical scolding. His wife stared at him for a second before returning to her supper. "I'll not have my sons disrespect their mother."

"Of course," she replied, eyes fixed on the table. Broehain then stood and kissed his wife on the forehead.

"I must go check on the goats," he said as he opened the door. "I've had to fix that bloody gate on their corral three times now and I don't want them getting out again."

As Broehain walked down the path that led to the goat pens he heard a rustling in the bushes. He started to panic; his confrontation with Heracles earlier fresh in his mind.

"Who's there?" he asked the darkness. He stepped towards the sound, only to be felled by a club from behind, rending him unconscious before he hit the ground.

"Leave him," a voice said in the darkness. "The boss said to leave this one alive."

The elder lad walked slowly down a path that led away from the house, calling out his brother's name. It was completely black outside, and his eyes had not yet adjusted to the darkness.

"I'll beat you as soon as I find you," he swore in a low voice. He walked over to the chicken coops, where a mysterious shape seemed to protrude from its side. "What are you doing over by the damn chicken coops?" He stopped short, his eyes adjusting in time to see a sight of abject horror.

His brother's small body hung from the side of the chicken coop, his limbs stretched in each direction. The boy had been disemboweled, and the stench made his brother wretch. He turned to run back to the house to find his father when he saw the form of a man in front of him. He opened his mouth to cry out but he never had the chance to utter a sound as the cleaver severed his head from his spine.

"Where are those boys at?" Broehain's wife said, her patience waning. The family had fallen on hard times since the Sacrovir Revolt had ended so disastrously for their people. So many had not returned at all; slaughtered as they were in the mountains outside of Augusta Raurica and the plains of Augustodunum. Her husband had been a chief amongst the Turani, and now they were left destitute. The Romans had only granted them a small farmhouse and few acres of land to farm, which was a far cry from the massive estates they had once overseen. With a deep sigh of resignation, she opened the door to go find her sons, only to find the way blocked by several men. One of whom she recognized as the man who she had witnessed her husband arguing with earlier. Her eyes grew wide in terror.

"What do you want?" she asked in a commanding voice. "My husband told you that you are not welcome here!"

"Your husband is indisposed at the moment," the Greek said matter-of-factly as the men forced their way into the house. "We are simply here to make him see the error of his ways." He then snapped his fingers. Two of the men grabbed her by each arm. Another, who was missing an eye, stuffed a gag into her mouth, an evil grin on his face.

"Tie her up, have your way with her, and then kill her," Heracles ordered, his voice calm and nonchalant. Radek gave a broad grin, the other two men laughing as the woman fought against their grip. For the former slave, he had not had any sort of physical pleasure since his young plaything had perished in the mines months before. He could not even remember when he had last felt the touch of a woman.

"Hush, my dear," he said in a mock soothing voice as he held his clever up to her neck. "You can play nicely and we'll make your passing swift, or you can be the defiant bitch and I can have my fun while cutting you slowly." The woman closed her eyes and sobbed in horror as her fate came unveiled. Heracles paid no heed to her sobs that sounded through the gag as he walked out into the night.

$$*\quad*\quad*\quad*$$

The day was perfect for a morning patrol outside the city. The sky was only slightly overcast, and a gentle breeze touched the faces of the legionaries. The northern road they traveled was one of the main arteries that nearly ran the length of the entire province. To their right was the River Arar, which merged with the runoff from the Lacus Lemannus, also known as the Lake of Geneva. From there it continued south out of the city as the River Rhodanus.

Artorius and Praxus usually worked together when the sections were tasked out in pairs. Macro knew how well the two Decanii clicked and so he never forced them apart. Artorius still had two vacancies in his section, which had been there ever since he took over. With seven legionaries, Praxus was only short one man. Such was the lot in any military unit; very rarely were Centuries ever at full strength. Indeed, Sergeant Rufio's section was at half strength with four legionaries.

"Beautiful morning," Artorius observed as they strolled leisurely down the cobblestone road, a gentle breeze catching him in the face. He closed his eyes and breathed in deeply. His respite was cut short by an unholy cry that seemed to echo for miles.

"What the hell ..." Praxus started to say when the cry renewed itself with even more vigor.

"Let's go!" Artorius shouted to the men behind him as he started at a quick jog up the hill. Once at the top they instinctively fell into a line formation, shields to their front, javelins protruding forward.

"I think it came from that house," Gavius observed. The same unintelligible howl sounded once more. At once they started at a dead run towards the house. The door was open and the sounds of a man sobbing were heard inside.

"Secure the area and check for any other disturbances," Praxus ordered his men as he and Artorius grounded their shields, javelins, and helmets. As they stepped quietly inside they came upon a man kneeling in a pool of blood next to the bed. He was crying without stopping, his hand clutching that of his wife. Her body lay sprawled out on the bed, signs of violation evident. What repelled the legionaries most was the fact that she had been completely disemboweled, her severed head mounted on one of the bed posts. Artorius gently placed a hand on the man's shoulder, keeping the other on his gladius in case he should turn violent.

"Sir," he said quietly, but the man just sobbed louder. He looked over at Praxus, not sure what else to do. The elder Decanus grabbed the man by the fronts of his shoulders and turned him towards him.

"Sir, you have to tell us what happened!" he ordered. The soldiers picked the man up and carried him over to a chair next to an upturned table. He did not try to resist them.

"I thought they were dead," he said between sobs. "I swore those bastards all killed themselves when Sacrovir was found." Artorius and Praxus shared a glance at the mention of the dead rebel leader's name.

"You're telling us these were Sacrovir's men?" Artorius asked. The man just started to cry once more.

"My wife ... my beautiful wife. She was *innocent!*" Praxus slapped the man across the face, causing Artorius to wince.

"Damn it man, you have to tell us; *who* did this?"

"That bastard, Heracles," he said at last. "He blames *me* for Sacrovir's downfall. Said that if I did not return to him in loyalty he would see to it I paid dearly for my betrayal."

"That's the same man the slave we tortured told us about," Artorius observed.

"Seems he's getting around," Praxus replied. They were interrupted by a pair of legionaries from Praxus' section who burst into the room.

"You're going to want to see this," one of the men stated, his face pale.

"You found my sons," the man said, his eyes on the floor. "My sons and my wife ... they have paid for my sins."

"Listen, we will help you bury your family," Praxus offered. "But then you will come with us to Lugdunum and tell us everything you know. These men must be brought to justice!"

"Justice?" the man replied, looking at the Decanus for the first time. "No, it is *I* who has been brought to justice. My name is Broehain; I was a lieutenant of Sacrovir's, until I betrayed him. I should have died with him, but instead I have brought death to my family."

"Have the men gather up all the bodies and lay them out for burial," Artorius ordered the legionaries. "We'll be out in a minute."

"Right away."

Broehain sat by idly as the Romans dug a series of graves for his wife and children with tools they had found next to the house. He had ceased crying, but now would show no emotions at all. He continued to stare at the ground and rock slowly back and forth on a stump.

"I think we're done," Decimus remarked as both sections gathered around their Decanii. Artorius and Praxus had tried to lay out the dead with as much reverence as was possible, given the severe mutilation of the bodies. Both men were covered in gore and shaken by the task.

"Doesn't he have anything to say?" Felix asked. Broehain only continued to rock back and forth while staring at the ground.

"Just get it over with," Artorius answered. As carefully as they were able they lowered Broehain's slain family into their graves. Immediately they started filling in the holes, anxious as they were to not have to observe the macabre sight any more. It was then that the Gaul rose to his feet and purposefully walked towards his house. Artorius was quick to put a hand on his shoulder.

"Where are you going?" he asked. Broehain forcibly shoved his hand away.

"Some things for my journey," he stated as he continued into the house. Artorius did not follow him, but instead continued to help his men finish their hateful task. Several minutes passed and still Broehain had not appeared.

"Hey, see what he's doing in there," Artorius directed Decimus and Carbo. "I want to get out of this place as soon as possible ... before any more citizens turn up mutilated!" Gavius and Magnus he had sent back to Lugdunum to report the situation to Centurion Macro. He hoped Macro would arrive soon. In order to expedite their message, he had ordered his men to ground their armor and equipment so that they could run back to Lugdunum. At a steady jog it should not have taken his men more than an hour and he knew that Macro would arrive on horseback.

"He's not in there, and the back door was left open," Decimus said as they rushed out of the house.

"Oh shit!" one of Praxus' legionaries shouted, pointing towards a copse of trees down the slope of the hill. He immediately started to run towards them, shouting, "*Hey! Stop!*"

"Oh no," Artorius said under his breath as the rest of them ran after the legionary. As they came around the side of the house they saw what had caught the man's attention. Broehain sat on the branch of a tree, tying a rope to it. The other end was already looped around his neck. He looked up to see the legionaries fast approaching and hurried making sure the end was secure to the branch.

"*Don't do it! Let us help you!*" Artorius shouted. Broehain shook his head and leapt from the tree, the soldiers all halting in their tracks as they heard his neck snap.

"Son of a bitch!" Artorius swore. "I should never have let him go off by himself! Damn it I should have known better."

"I'll cut him down," Decimus said to no one in particular as he walked over to the tree.

"I guess we'll go dig another hole," one of the legionaries said with dark humor.

"*Fuck!*" Artorius swore again as he walked back up the slope, Praxus by his side. "Our one chance at getting some viable information about these bastards and this is what happens!" His words came as they reached the top of the hill and were overheard by Centurions Proculus, Macro, and Vitruvius, who had just arrived on horseback. A contingent of a dozen horsemen accompanied them. He hung his head, ashamed, as the Centurions dismounted.

"So melodramatic," Macro said as he looked over at the twitching corpse gently swinging from the tree. He then gave a nonchalant shrug. "Still, I doubt that sod could have told us anything we didn't already know."

"All the same, looks like we'll never know," Artorius replied.

"It was bound to happen," Vitruvius continued. "A man loses all he's ever cared about in such a savage manner. Seriously, what were we to expect?"

"Still it troubles me what these bastards have done," Proculus added. "We're ten miles from the city. How many more will they go? And is this just a local band of thugs, or is there something larger and darker at work here?"

"There is definitely something dark at work here," Artorius answered as the rest of the legionaries came around the corner, Broehain's corpse in tow.

"Explain," Proculus persisted.

"The owner of this home was a ransomed leader in Sacrovir's rebellion," Praxus said. "We also know that his family's killers were the same men responsible for the ambush by the slave pens."

"Sir," Artorius remarked. "This is not just a band of thugs we are dealing with. I daresay we are facing the heart of evil."

CHAPTER XI

▼

INDUS' RETURN

Life had been good to Julius Indus since the Sacrovir Revolt. He had accumulated much in wealth during the raping of the rebellious nobles, to say nothing of the fact that he had his own cavalry regiment named in his honor by the Emperor himself. The Treveri cavalry regiment, now known as Indus Horse, had distinguished itself by its loyalty and valor during the rebellion. They had suffered many casualties helping a legionary cohort destroy the rebellious Turani tribe and had fought valiantly at the Battle of Augustodunum; routing the flanks of Sacrovir's army. Indus was indeed proud of his regiment and was humbled to have such brave men under the banner that bore his name. As he stood against the side of his headquarters building, one of his troopers rode up on his horse and briskly dismounted.

"Sir, message from Centurion Proculus," the man said, handing him a small scroll. Indus frowned in contemplation. While still reading he walked over to the quarters of his deputy.

"Have the regiment ready to move in two days," he directed. "I am heading for Lugdunum immediately; meet me there." He then turned to the Tribune who accompanied him. "You're coming with me."

"I'm ready to ride now," the man, whose name was Cursor, replied. Aulus Nautius Cursor was a thirty-year old Tribune who had grown bored with politics and had elected to devote his life to military study. His face bore a very pronounced nose and rather than fight his receding hairline he had elected to shave his head bald. While most men prided themselves on full, healthy heads of hair, Cursor had grown to relish his baldness as so many women found it irresistible. He had been given the cognomen *Cursor* for his ability to run great distances, and it was his obsession with speed and maneuver that led him to request a transfer to the cavalry. He had effectively led an auxiliary infantry regiment during the rebellion of Sacrovir and Florus. His men routed numerous pockets of enemy resistance in the region, though he regretted that he arrived at Augustodunum only after the battle was decided. In spite of his achievements his superiors quickly assessed his talents more suited for mounted warfare.

Legate Silius therefore sent him to Gaul under the tutelage of the legendary cavalry commander, Julius Indus. It was Silius' intent to place Cursor in charge of all cavalry assets for the Rhine Army upon his return, much in the same manner as the Tribune Pontius Pilate had been given authority of the army's artillery because of his talents in that arena. Cursor was an eager student, having seen first-hand the devastating effectiveness of Indus' regiment.

"It is as I feared," Indus said as the two men rode towards Lugdunum.

"What do you mean?" Cursor asked.

"Sacrovir's rebellion has found an heir," Indus replied. Cursor swallowed hard as Indus continued. "You know I was originally one of Sacrovir's most trusted lieutenants before turning on him and bringing my regiment to fight for Rome. That time spent in Sacrovir's camp gave me insight into the rebel army that no one else possessed."

"Who do you think this heir may be?" Cursor asked.

"I don't know for certain, but I can hazard a guess." Indus cursed himself that he had not elected to excavate the burned and crumbled remains of Sacrovir's estate. Though most of the bodies would have been charred beyond recognition, some effort should have been made to identify all of the leaders to make certain they had perished. Proculus' note had not gone into detail, but it did mention a slave under torture giving away the name of his Greek master.

Of all of Sacrovir's confidants, that psychotic Greek, Heracles had disturbed Indus the most. The only other man as wicked in soul was the Sequani chief, Taranis who mercifully had been slain during the Battle of Augustodunum. Whatever drove Heracles it wasn't love of liberty. Darkness consumed him and Indus had seen it in his eyes. He had hated being left alone with the man, although Heracles had always been polite and cordial with him. He could not imagine the turn of events had Heracles known of Indus' intentions to betray Sacrovir and Florus. If Heracles was still alive and out for revenge, Indus knew he would be among those that the Greek would try to focus his wrath.

✳   ✳   ✳   ✳

"Ah, Indus my old friend," Heracles said quietly in contemplation as he twirled the dagger point on the table. Radek stood across the table from him, hands folded. He looked up when his master mentioned that name.

"You know him, don't you?" Heracles asked, a wicked sneer forming.

"It was his cavalry that trampled us into the dirt," Radek replied, his voice venomous with hate. "Their lances rendered me the half-cripple that I am now and sent me to those cursed mines." Heracles jammed the dagger point into the table at Radek's last remark.

"Then it is time Indus paid the debt he owes to us. There is a large slaver camp about four days' march from here. We have enough men to overrun the guards. The slaves will then be freed on condition they fight for us."

"A plan similar to the one we executed in the city," Radek observed.

"Quite," his master acknowledged. "Some may view our previous sortie as a failure, given those pathetic whelps' inability to kill a single legionary. However, the civil unrest brought about made the venture a success. Citizens of Lugdunum now cringe at the thought of large slave markets within their city's walls unless they are constantly patrolled by either the urban cohort or legionaries. The Romans have not the men to spare for such menial duties, as they are tasked to the last man in a vain effort to hunt us down. The city magistrate himself has placed a moratorium on slave markets within the city's walls.

"Indus' Horse has been alerted and will soon be helping the Roman force in their search. By raiding the slaver camp they will have to send their cavalry to suppress the situation. They have not the legionaries to spare; and even if they did it would take too long for them to reach the camp." Radek grinned in anticipation of the rest of Heracles' plan. Of all the Romans he had fought against, he loathed the men of Indus' Horse the most. He could still feel the pain of the lance that hobbled his leg and rendered his back open. He thought about his companions who he had watched torn to pieces by the ferocity of Indus' onslaught. His only real friend, Ellard, had his guts ripped from his body by a Roman lance, dying a slow and horrifyingly painful death.

"When do we leave, master?"

"Tonight. We will rally at the old mill and leave by boat. The Romans have patrols on the streets at night, but they have sorely neglected to watch the river."

There was an abandoned mill down by the river. Heracles had placed a pair of men there to determine whether or not it could prove useful. They had repaired the old boats that were moored on the backside of the mill and they were now ready for use. Heracles had sent his minions to the mill a few at a time throughout the day. Daytime provided an excellent cover, what with all the activity within the city. Only he and Radek arrived after dark. There were a few buildings down by the mill, but for the most part it was away from the heart of the city and oddly enough an area that the Romans had neglected to patrol. The door was opened for the two men; they walked inside and removed their hoods.

Heracles took a moment to assess the mill and its usefulness. It was an enormous building; large enough house a couple hundred men if need be. Though it was very old, it appeared to be sturdy enough. His men had been busy cleaning away the cobwebs, dust, and rodent shit. He then smiled inwardly. When the time came he knew where he would reestablish himself.

"Is everything ready?" he asked.

"Yes Master," replied the man who had opened the door. It was the raspy voiced minion who had goaded the slaves into fighting the legionaries in the city. Heracles raised his hand and pointed towards the back doorway, beyond which the boats were moored. No more words needed to be spoken; each man knew what needed to be done.

✳   ✳   ✳   ✳

Daylight had broken an hour before Indus and Cursor arrived at the Cohort's Principia. Centurion Proculus stood outside awaiting their arrival.

"Indus my old friend!" Proculus said with great enthusiasm as he clasped the hand of the cavalry commander. A native of Gaul, Indus was a few inches taller than the Centurion; his light brown hair cut short and his face clean-shaven like his Roman counterparts. Behind him walked a man wearing a muscled cuirass breastplate and a Tribune's helmet under his left arm.

"You remember Tribune Cursor?" Indus asked, pointing to the young man. Proculus nodded and saluted.

"Sir," he said as Cursor returned the salute, "good to see you again. It's been a while."

"Yes, since Augustodunum in fact," the Tribune replied. "I was but an auxiliary regimental commander then." Cursor was a young, though highly experienced officer.

"And now Silius wants to place him in charge of the Rhine army's entire cavalry force," Indus added. "Hence why he is now working with me. It seems someone spread a nasty rumor that I know a thing or two about cavalry tactics."

"You know more than just a thing or two," Cursor emphasized. "I dare say there isn't a more sound cavalry officer in the whole of the empire!"

"Flattery will get you everywhere with me you know," Indus said with a wink. Proculus gave a short laugh.

"Well I dare say I will have some work for your men yet," he said as the three men walked over towards the Principia.

It was an odd situation for Cursor. In terms of rank and position he was the senior of the three men; however he knew his role with Indus was strictly as an observer while he tried to learn as much as he could. Regardless of rank, Lugdunum and the surrounding region militarily fell under the jurisdiction of Proculus and his legionaries. The Centurion and Indus had developed a close bond during the rebellion, particularly during a rather harrowing battle in the mountain passes west of Augusta Raurica. Their combined forces had numbered less than fifteen-hundred men, and yet they had completely routed an enemy force that had the advantage of terrain, as well as a three-to-one numerical advantage.

Cursor found he was a bit envious of the men's relationship. The position of Tribune in charge of an auxiliary regiment was indeed a lonely one. Most Tribunes held their posts for a single campaign season, and yet he kept returning to the ranks. He had held numerous administrative posts and found they bored him immensely. His only peer that he had any kind of a bond with was Pontius Pilate, but even he was gone; his friendship with Sejanus garnering him the position of Deputy Prefect of the Praetorian Guard. Cursor had been effective enough in leading his regiment into battle, and yet even there his social status had prevented him from forming bonds with any of his men, even the Centurions. That and he had never felt at home in an infantry unit.

"So what have you got?" Indus asked as he and Cursor sat down across from Proculus at a table in the room the Pilus Prior used for conducting briefings with his Centurions and Options.

"As you know, there has been a serious of murders taking place in and around the city," Proculus explained. "We think they are linked to survivors of Sacrovir's rebellion. I've got the urban cohort searching the city and my legionaries scouring the countryside; however with the size of the city and the sheer number of farms and estates in the region I just don't have the manpower. What I especially need is a mobile force. These bastards have been hitting settlements ten miles or better from the city; too far for my legionaries to react in time. How many men are you bringing with you?"

"I've placed the entire regiment on alert," Indus replied, "however with the missions already assigned to us, I can only comfortably bring about two hundred and fifty."

"That should be more than sufficient," Proculus said after a moment's contemplation. "To be honest we have no idea how large of a group we are dealing with. It could be just a handful of renegades seeking to terrorize the populace, or it could be the start of a fresh rebellion." As he listened to the Centurion's explanation of the situation, Indus traced his finger over Proculus' map, stopping just south of a group of mountains to the north.

"There are a large number of estates and settlements in this region, about three days march from here," he observed. "A prime target for the rebels, yet too far for your men to react effectively; and this terrain will work against my cavalry. What chance is there that you can dispatch some men to cover this area?" Proculus exhaled loudly.

"I can send perhaps two centuries, but no more. Thankfully the regions to the south are relatively free of settlements. If you can augment my force with one hundred of your men, the rest can be used to conduct searches of the region."

"There's a farmhouse that's just south of the mountain pass," Cursor spoke up. "It would make the perfect staging area."

"Then that's where you will make for tomorrow at dawn," Indus directed. The Tribune gave him a perplexed look; not certain if he had heard correctly.

"Come again?" he asked. Indus gave a half-smile.

"This will be the perfect opportunity for you to exercise some independent command," Indus explained. "Reconnoiter the area and start fortifying the farmhouse while waiting for the legionaries to arrive. Take a few denarii with you as well; we must make certain the owners are properly recompensed for their troubles."

"A few sheckles will buy just about anything," Cursor replied with a snort.

"I'll send Macro and Vitruvius with their Centuries," Proculus added. "Once they arrive your men can start scouring the area for any sign of the rebels. My legionaries will be your reaction force, so be certain to keep them close."

*   *   *   *

Kiana had taken to staying around the flats that housed the legionaries. Every so often she would catch a glimpse of the man she had come to know as *The Beast*. In truth the young Decanus was a very attractive man, though in Kiana's mind he was nothing more than an instrument of horror. She leaned back against the wall of an alley, her face only partially concealed by her hooded cloak. Her eyes closed, she wondered how it was she had come to this feeling of utter hatred. Inside she was torn over her feelings and could only rationalize that perhaps she had been in such a state of shock following Farquhar's death that she did not have the will to hate.

As she opened her eyes she was startled to see a group of legionaries walking along the road towards her, the beast amongst them. Quickly she covered her face and turned her back on them. She started to slip away, eyes on the ground, when she stumbled into a man, who had not seen her either.

"Hey what the bloody hell …" the man said with a start as they collided. Kiana sat upright quickly, her eyes wide as she recognized Legionary Felix.

"Kiana, what are you doing here, child?" he asked.

"Um … I, uh … I came looking for you," she said, beads of nervous sweat running down her forehead.

"Really?" Felix was perplexed as to why Kiana would need to come see him of all people.

"Yes," she emphasized, and then glancing over to where the other group of legionaries was walking away, parallel to the building they stood next to. "Tell me first; who is that man, the one with all the muscles?"

"That's Sergeant Artorius, one of the Decanii from my Century," Felix answered, still baffled by the girl's presence.

Sergeant Artorius, Kiana thought to herself. *The beast has a name.* She then spoke aloud, "come, we need to talk." With that she took Felix by the arm and led him down the alley, away from the barracks flats. So curious was the legionary as to what she wanted to talk about that he did not protest. Once they had reached a quiet corner, away from the bustle of the busy streets, Kiana turned to face him.

"So tell me," she said, a coy grin on her face, "what exactly is your relationship with my sister?" It was the only topic she could think of offhand, and one that she found she was in fact curious to know about. Felix's face turned a slight shade of red.

"You probably figured out that Tierney and I are more than just *friends,*" he admitted.

"It wasn't difficult," Kiana stated, folding her arms across her chest with her grin spreading.

"She talks about you all the time," Felix said, trying to break the silence. "I know of your loss and I am sorry."

"I've seen the standards of your unit before, haven't I?" Kiana tried to fight the urge of putting Felix on the spot like that, though she did enjoy watching his discomfort. Felix lowered and shook his head, letting out a sigh.

"Yes you have," he replied quietly. To most civilians Roman soldiers look the same and they rarely differentiated between the various legions. With a little research, though, one could easily find out exactly what unit had served in what campaign, even down to the exact actions fought. "I am sorry … not for what we did, but that you had to suffer as a consequence."

"I understand," she replied with a sad smile. "You were doing your duty and my beloved was betrayed by those who should have protected him." Felix took this as a statement perhaps against the boy's family or mentors who should have stopped him from joining the rebellion, though Kiana's meaning was more literal. She thought once more about the cowards who had run from battle, leaving Farquhar and his friends to their deaths.

"Come, I'll walk you home," Felix said, taking Kiana by the arm. She gladly accepted his offer, having found out all she needed to know.

"Tell me Felix," she said once they were out of the bustle of the main streets. "What prompted you to join the legions?" The young legionary laughed at the question.

"Your sister asked me the exact same thing. To be honest, I had little choice if I wanted to make something of my life." He then explained his father's noble birth and that he was a bastard who his father despised. He told her about his mother and how she did everything within her power to get his father to sign the letter of introduction that not only acknowledged Felix as his son, but also allowed him to enlist in the legions.

"Any siblings?" Kiana asked at length, to which Felix nodded.

"Two brothers. Granted they are practically old enough to be my father. No sisters, though. I told Tierney on a couple of occasions that I always wanted a little sister." Kiana found herself unable to stop from smiling at the veiled meaning to his words. "I just wonder how long before your father betroths her to someone else."

"I don't think you'll have to worry about that for a while," Kiana replied. "Remember, most of the nobles around our age were either killed or impoverished. Tierney was rather anxious to accompany me when Father sent me here. Her fear was that he would marry her off to one of his friends, and the last thing she wants is to be wed to some fat, creepy old man who will probably leave her a widow by the time she's twenty-five; let alone the idea of having intimate relations with one that is old, wrinkled, and sloppy in appearance."

"Such marriages are not uncommon in this day and age," Felix replied with a shrug. Kiana stared at him with a look of revulsion on her face.

"That doesn't make it right!" she retorted. "Yes, I understand that a woman's primary role is to provide heirs for our husbands and that many men reach old age before they are able to sire sons. And unfortunately, the higher a woman's social birth the more likely she will be used as a political pawn for her father and future husband. That is our lot in life and we cannot change it … but please understand that most of us would still rather at least be bound to someone closer to our age rather than our parents'."

"Well perhaps someone will be able to save your sister from such an ignominious fate," Felix ventured. Kiana smiled once more.

"Perhaps," she replied. As unreal as it seemed, she was beginning to see why her sister loved this legionary. Felix was genuinely a good person; not so very different than her friends that she still mourned. Would it be possible for her to hate Artorius and allow herself to care for Felix, or were they too closely intertwined? She did not know.

"Well this will be the last time I see you for a while," Felix said, startling Kiana out of her reverie. She hadn't realized that they had arrived at the house she shared with her sister. As Kiana turned to face Felix he continued his explanation. "I'm going to be out of the city for a while; not too long I hope." After he left, Kiana leaned against a column the supported the overhang outside the main entrance. She suspected she knew where Felix and his fellow legionaries were headed. As soon as darkness fell she left the house in her hooded cloak, for regardless of her initial fond feelings for Felix she had an obligation to pass on what he had told her.

▼

CHAPTER XII

BLACK WINGS OF DEATH

Atop a high ridge sat the stockade a half-dozen caravan style tents. The site was perfect for the slavers, for if any of their property did manage to escape there was but one way they could go, and that was along a narrow road that led into the valley. Sheer cliffs on the remaining sides of the camp prevented them from taking any other avenue of escape. The slave camp was large and cramped, most of the slaves slept on the ground. Conditions were harsh, and indeed some would die before they even reached the market. This greatly vexed the procurers, because every slave that perished or could not be sold due to ill health meant a loss of revenue. The slave riot in Lugdunum proved to be a spot of fortune for the men, because now they had a new venue with which to sell their wares. And with the competition 'eliminated' the city was rife with a need for fresh slaves and no one to supply them. The chief slave driver mused over these things as he took an evening stroll around the outside of the pens where his quarry slept.

One particular young woman had just given birth the week before and the slave owner was rather relieved. The selling of a pregnant slave was always tricky. It enticed buyers with the potential of getting two for the price of one, as it were. At the same time there was also the risk involved given the mortality rates amongst newborn slaves and their mothers. Someone making such a purchase risked losing all. On the other hand, a slave who had just given birth to a healthy baby would fetch a far higher price if sold with her child, for she had demonstrated the health and fortitude to survive the trauma of childbirth under the most austere of conditions.

"Sleep well my pretties," he said with a sneer, "for soon you will all make me very rich." He then noticed a commotion in the bushes at the outside corner of the stockade. He had recently forbidden his guards and workers from defiling his stock; however he also knew that primal lust sometimes overcame the fear of the lash and loss of employment. The slave owner was tired and not in the mood to have to discipline one of his men. He saw in the shadows what looked like a pair of legs twitching and thought perhaps the fellow was masturbating to relieve some of that urge. He was about to turn away lest he embarrass the man when he saw what looked like a flash of metal as one of the bushes trembled. As he walked over his eyes grew wide as he saw a bloodied arm flop into the moonlight. A torrent of blood was running past the post that hid the rest of the body and down the slight incline towards his feet.

Instinctively he reached for his sword, then remembering with horrific fear that he had left it next to his bed. The sound of fingers snapping behind him brought him about quickly. He could not make out the face underneath the hooded cloak before the cleaver blade severed his head from his shoulders, impacting against the post behind him with a loud thud.

Radek had grown quite fond of his cleaver. He kept it razor sharp; its added weight allowed him to decapitate his prey with relative ease. It was far easier than the mess one of the men had made murdering the guard who had in fact been pleasuring himself when his life was cut short. The thug had not realized that stabbing one in the throat did not mean an instantaneous death and the guard had struggled briefly while the man fought to slice the rest of his throat open.

Amateurs, Radek thought to himself as he walked over to the compound gate. Three of their men had assaulted the lone guard and were stabbing him repeatedly. His screams awoke the slaves from their slumber. Radek closed his eyes, tilted his head back and took a deep breath through his nose. The nearby caravan tents erupted into flames as they were set alight. Heracles had arranged for them to be doused in oil while the slave drivers slept and then lit. The tent openings had also been tacked shut to trap the occupants inside. Shrieks of terror poured forth from the tents as the slavers sought to escape. Those who managed to were quickly cut down by Heracles' waiting minions, though a few did manage to escape into the night.

"Let them go," Heracles said quietly as some of his thugs sought to pursue the fleeing men. "They will serve our cause better alive rather than dead." A loud din came from the stockade, where hundreds of frightened slaves sought to escape. The Greek calmly walked over to a raised dais that overlooked the compound, where six of his men already stood bearing torches. He knew how to quell their anguish and use their desperation for his own ends. Within the next few days there would not be a slave procurer within the province who would not fear for his head.

✳   ✳   ✳   ✳

"I am so glad we started road marching again a couple months ago," Valens stated as the section grounded their packs outside the farmhouse. "I would hate to think about having to cover a three-day stretch when we're all fat and out of shape!"

"That's the real bastard about these cushy assignments," Decimus added as he removed his helmet and set it next to his pack. "Think about it, during a campaign we cover twenty-five miles a day *and* set up fortifications when it's all done. Plus we have to have to the strength and conditioning to survive in battle during these times."

Artorius stretched his back and rolled his shoulders as he silently agreed with his men's assessment. Since the beginning of his workouts with Magnus and Vitruvius he knew he had incorporated road marches as well as pankration into his regime to keep himself limber and well conditioned. Granted, pankration left him with sore joints and the ever-present bruising on his face and body. In fact, his left eye had only opened up again two days previously after a rather nasty blow from Master Delios had swollen it shut.

At the head of the column Macro and Vitruvius were met by Tribune Cursor and his deputy, an auxilia Centurion named Rodolfo Antonius. The Centurions dismounted their horses and saluted.

"Tribune, Sir," Macro said, extending his hand which Cursor readily took.

"Good thing you men have arrived," Cursor replied. "It's the strangest thing, but the house appears to be recently abandoned. I've got most of my men patrolling the region and checking on the other estates in the vicinity, so we haven't had much time to search the grounds here."

"We'll get on it," Vitruvius replied. He then looked over his shoulder and nodded to his Optio who turned and signaled for the Century to ground its gear and start a sweep of the grounds. Optio Flaccus did the same with the Second Century.

"While your men search the area, you should come take a look at this," Cursor said as he led the men over to the stables. Outside was a pair of wagons, the horses walking along the fence line of the corral.

"Alright, I don't notice anything unusual," Macro said.

"That's the point," Cursor replied. "There is nothing unusual here. If the residents fled, don't you think they would have taken their belongings or at least rode away on horseback?"

"Perhaps," Macro conceded, "but of course we don't know how many horses they had to begin with."

"If it were me," Centurion Rodolfo began, "I would release all the horses to hinder any possible pursuit." Macro frowned in contemplation and folded his arms across his chest.

"Point taken," he conceded. Vitruvius nodded and smacked his fellow Centurion on the shoulder.

"I'm going to see how the lads are faring," he said as Macro nodded in reply.

"We'll catch up with you in a little while," the senior Centurion remarked before addressing Cursor and Rodolfo once more. "What about inside the house? Anything unusual or out of place?" Cursor shook his head in reply.

"Not really, but again we haven't had much time to make a thorough search. It took us a day and a half to get here and since then we've been searching the countryside for any sign of these people."

"And no one seems to know anything," Rodolfo added, a trace of irritation in his thickly accented voice. "Every person we have spoken to states the people here kept to themselves. In fact, most said they would not know the house owners even if they had seen them."

"What in the name of Apollo is that unholy stench?" Optio Macer asked as he and Vitruvius approached a pile of broken statues, furniture, and other rubbish.

"Smells like something died," the Centurion responded as he pulled a large chunk of broken pillar aside, revealing a trap door that led to a cellar. "Well what have we here then?"

"Looks like it was hidden deliberately," Macer replied as he and a pair of legionaries cleared the door off. The stench of rotting flesh assailed them as the lifted the trap door; the Optio gagging and letting it drop with a loud slam. "What the *fuck?*"

"Found something?" Macro asked as he and Tribune Cursor walked around the corner of the house, Rodolfo and a handful of legionaries in tow. Vitruvius nodded; his face grim.

"I don't think this house was abandoned after all."

"Get some torches and we'll have look," Macro ordered. With much trepidation a pair of legionaries pulled open the trap doors to the cellar once some torches had been lit to see what was inside. The stench of the bodies made even those with the strongest stomachs retch. There were twenty altogether in various states of decomposition. One soldier slipped on a putrid puddle as they scanned the macabre scene. Most of the corpses had been decapitated; the trademark of the rebels who were terrorizing the region. Anything that may have been of value had already been taken, nothing but the rotting corpses and some broken shelves remained.

"What do you want us to do with the bodies?" a legionary asked Vitruvius, ashen-faced.

"Burn it," the Centurion replied, much to the soldier's relief. The cellar was separate from the rest of the house and with nothing to salvage the legionaries were grateful that they would not have to retrieve what was left of the farm owner, his family and slaves.

As the flames and smoke billowed from the cellar, Artorius and Praxus walked over to their Centurion, who was overlooking everything with Vitruvius and Cursor.

"We found the offices of the owner; they have been ransacked," Artorius said as he saluted Macro. The Centurion nodded, not in the least surprised.

"Does anyone know who the owners were?" Praxus asked. Macro shook his head.

"No; we'll have to send someone back to Lugdunum to have a look at the archives. I'm guessing that the victims are yet more survivors of the rebellion."

"And since many of the rebels escaped capture we have no way of knowing how many more of them there might be," Artorius observed.

"These people must have been rather reclusive if no one reported them as missing," Cursor added.

"I would think that many of the rebels would have been that way," Macro replied, "especially if they wanted to keep their pasts a secret. It's no wonder no one in the surrounding region seemed to even know who they were." At that moment Statorius walked over to the group.

"Both Centuries have marked out positions for our tents," he said to Macro. "We're fortifying the perimeter with trenches and a stockade. Any renegades in the area won't be surprising us."

"Good work," the Centurion acknowledged.

"My men will be returning this evening," Cursor said. "I will make ready to ride again on the morrow."

"Sir, given the state of decomposition of those bodies, the rebels who did this will have long since fled the region," Macro replied.

"I know; however you should remember there is a large slave caravan encamped to the north of here. Given the trouble the rebels caused for you regarding the slaves in Lugdunum ..." he let his voice trail off as the Centurion closed his eyes in realization of what the Tribune was alluding to.

"That's all we need; freed slaves rampaging the countryside! Gods know what they would do to any of the estates they come across."

"Too true," Statorius added. "There is not one person in the whole of the Empire, slave or free, who has not heard the horror stories revolving around the slave revolt of Spartacus nearly a century ago."

"Whether or not the stories are horror of course depends on if you are slave or free," Cursor replied with a grin of dark humor. "Thankfully there is only one real way to and from the camp and it leads through a narrow valley with sheer cliffs on either side. However, there is also a little-known path that we can take and thereby avoid running into the slaves, if in fact they have been freed. Remember, we must only deal with the facts as we know them."

"How far is the passage from here?" Macro asked the Tribune.

"About three miles," Cursor replied. "Rock cliffs jut up on either side at a fairly narrow opening. Past that it is another fifteen miles to the slaver camp." Macro nodded and bit the inside of his cheek in contemplation.

"Statorius," he said, eyes still on Cursor, "tell the men to cease making camp and be ready to march. We will blockade the pass and prevent any escape."

"Right away," the Tesserarius acknowledged before turning about and issuing orders to the Decanii. The legionaries were puzzled and somewhat dismayed by the sudden change, however few complained. All knew that if they were told to break camp and be ready to march, there was a reason for it.

"It could all be for nothing," Cursor said, trying to sound reassuring. "We may arrive at the camp and find all the slaves still kept safe in their pens." He gave a smile that neither convinced Macro or himself.

"All the same, I'm not taking any chances," the Centurion replied grimly. "I'd rather have my men walk a few more miles and camp for the night at a roadside rather than finding out later that we let a thousand runaway slaves escape and wreck havoc." Cursor looked away and breathed deeply.

"Rodolfo and I will intercept our patrols and divert them to the camp via the high path," he then explained. "And we will pray to the gods that our fears are in fact unwarranted."

✳   ✳   ✳   ✳

The Caesarian coast at last came into view. This was where Justus and his family would depart and link up with Legio VI, Ferrata; the Iron Legion. He had been away from his post for over three years, and though he had thoroughly enjoyed his time spent in Rome he was secretly glad to be back in the ranks where he belonged. As he stood on the railing watching ships in the distant come and go from the harbor he was joined by his old friend, Pontius Pilate. The two men had barely spoken during the two-week voyage across the sea.

"Here is where we say farewell once more," Pilate noted. He would be taking the road by land to Raphana, home of Legio XII, Fulminata.

"Indeed," Justus replied, still gazing at the harbor as it inched closer.

"Justus," Pilate said, placing a hand on his friend's shoulder. "I don't want us to part this way. We may have disagreements regarding my patronage with Sejanus, but that should not interfere in our friendship." The Optio turned and met the Tribune's gaze.

"Many friendships throughout our history were ended due to politics," he said, his face without emotion. "Look at Caesar and Pompey. Hell, the dissolution of their friendship ended others with their bloody civil war. I mean, think about Vorenus and Pullo! Those two men were rivals, yes; but they were also brothers of the Centurionate. And yet when war came Pullo sided with Pompey and the Senate, while Vorenus remained loyal to Caesar."

"I know," Pilate replied quietly. He took a deep breath and then spoke with conviction. "But Justus, I will *not* allow that to happen with us! Whatever our political differences, we are both loyal to the Emperor and to Rome. Our goals are the same; it is how we get there that we differ. I still need my trusted friend and confidant while I am here in the east." Justus replied with a smile and leaned back against the ship's railing, his arms folded across his chest.

"What does a Tribune, one endorsed by the Emperor's right hand no less, need with a lowly Legionary Optio?"

"I need someone I can trust," Pilate responded, matching the Optio's grin. "I feel that a time will come when I will need you like I never have before." His smile was gone and he stared into the sea, almost ashamed of admitting that he was having premonitions. "I sensed the same when I last saw our old friend Artorius. I cannot place it, but for whatever reason my instincts tell me that the three of us are joined in the same destiny. Crazy, isn't it?" He looked back at his friend, whose arms were still folded but he was no longer smiling.

"Perhaps," Justus replied. "I admit it does seem strange, what with me being stationed in the east for what will probably be the remainder of my career; you doing your time for Sejanus here for a year and then back to Rome and the Praetorians; all the while Artorius is on the opposite end of the Empire bouncing between Germania and Gaul. Have you consulted with an augur about this?"

"I have," Pilate answered. "Bastard charged me a fortune and then spouted off a load of rubbish that could have meant absolutely anything I wanted it to. I think that's what they try and do; give an answer that no matter what happens they can claim they foretold it. They are no more messengers of the gods than I am!"

"I've never had a use for augurs," Justus said. "I nearly choked the fuck out of one who tried to say that my son will die in battle before he reaches a score in age! Needless to say it was most upsetting to Flavia, especially since Gaius wasn't even a year old at the time."

"Well, keep him out of the legions and you won't have to worry," Pilate observed. Justus snorted.

"The lad seems determined to follow me into the ranks. He's still got a few years to come to his senses, though. To tell you the truth Pilate, I have no faith or belief in the gods of any people. However, I cannot help but live with this sense of foreboding regarding my son. If Gaius does join the legions and in fact lives to see his twentieth birthday, then perhaps I will have found a god worth praying to."

✳   ✳   ✳   ✳

"Tribune Cursor!" Centurion Rodolfo shouted to him. Cursor road up to the slave pens, which were now empty. The bodies of numerous guards and slave drivers lay strewn about. He lowered and shook his head.

"There are only two ways to get to this place," he observed. "And since we did not run into a large mob on the way in ..." He paused and took a deep breath before continuing. "The road to the south leads through a narrow valley that opens at a large plain strewn with forests. If they get through the valley there will be no recapturing them."

"Understood," the Centurion acknowledged. "We'll make ready to ride at once."

"Send your fastest rider back by the path we took and have him alert Centurion Macro," Cursor ordered.

"Yes sir." Rodolfo saw the look of consternation in the Tribune's face and understood it all too well. Such a large number of slaves could not be allowed to escape. Word would spread like wildfire and the unrest that it may cause amongst the large slave populations of the region was a disaster they could ill afford. He also knew that they would be foolish to try to smash the mob with just their force of one hundred cavalrymen; they *needed* Macro, Vitruvius, and their legionaries.

Cursor dismounted and wearily surveyed the carnage of the wrecked slaver camp. The stench of burned corpses assailed his senses as he walked over to where the pavilion tents had stood. Unable to avert his gaze, he walked across the ash-strewn ground where bodies that had once been men lay charred and mutilated.

He then heard a loud crash in a thicket off to his right. Immediately his spatha was drawn, senses alert. A badly injured man fell out of the bushes and onto his face, his body covered in soot with numerous gashes and burns evident. Cursor sheathed his weapon and went to the man, who was lying on his side, breathing rapidly.

"They came at us," the wounded man spoke quietly, "in the night, like black wings of death they fell upon us." The Tribune placed a hand on the man's shoulder and shook his head.

"*Trooper!*" he shouted over his shoulder to the nearest of his men, who raced over to them. The auxilia muttered something in German that Cursor could not understand.

"I need water and bandages at once!" the Tribune ordered before turning back to the wounded man. Several of his men were soon kneeling next to him, bearing rolls of bandage cloth and extra water bladders.

"Fire … and death," the injured man said as the Tribune took a damp rag and started to tend to him. The man did not seem to notice Cursor or his troopers at all; nor did he wince or acknowledge his fearful wounds. "Our tent … burned. Only I escaped … a man with a cleaver … severing heads …" he shuddered fearfully and closed his eyes as the memories overwhelmed him. Suddenly his body started convulsing violently as if he were struck by a seizure.

"We're losing him," Cursor said as he frantically sought to stabilize the man. A few spasms and it was over. The Tribune threw down the blood-soaked bandage in his hand, stood up and walked away. Two of his men stood staring at the charred corpse at their feet. A shout by Centurion Rodolfo startled them back to their senses. He shouted orders at them in their native tongue and they ran quickly back to their mounts.

Within the dense woods Radek smiled evilly as they watched the auxilia cavalry ride out of camp.

"So few," he observed quietly as Heracles gave an affirmative nod.

"Yes," he replied, "but you can rest assured they brought friends with them. Our old friend Indus has returned. Time for tragedy to strike down his sacred regiment."

✳   ✳   ✳   ✳

Over a thousand slaves fled through the valley. The way behind was shut, for the mountains to the north were too steep and the weather treacherous this time of year. The only way for them to go was straight. Many of the slaves were armed, fearful as they were that Roman soldiers were in the region. The rock walls on either side proved too sheer for any but the ablest of climbers to scale; however, they knew that once they were through the valley freedom would be theirs.

A young woman clung to her baby, her free hand clutching that of her husband. Like many of their company, both had been slaves their entire lives, and now for the first time they had a chance to make something more for themselves and for their child.

It puzzled them the way that hideous man had freed them. First he had murdered the slavers and their servants, however he left the slaves themselves penned up in their wheeled cages inside the stockade. It was only when they had reached the north end of the valley had he released them. He promised weapons with which to earn their freedom, but only if they proceeded south. The slave woman was confused yet hopeful, for not a mile down the road was a large pile of axes, crude swords, spears, and other weapons. The men had fallen on them like rabid dogs. That night they sat in a shivering mass as they had elected not to build bonfires that would disclose their presence. It was but a few miles to the open plain, though most of the slaves had little sense of time or distance and had decided to camp in the valley for the night. A number had decided to keep moving, seeking their own freedom and not caring for the fate of their companions.

The woman with the newborn held the child close. She was famished and completely exhausted, for she was in no state to travel by foot as they had and the lack of food had left her feeling emaciated and worn.

"It's going to be okay," she said to the whimpering babe.

"Freedom," one of the slaves said to his companions as he pointed to where the stars lit the open plain but a mile away. Though he was starving and exhausted, he was glad they had elected to press on instead of staying the night with those old women and fools. He was quickly shoved aside by one of the more eager slaves and the mob rushed towards the plain. They knew that once they were out of the narrow passage nothing could keep them from freedom. There was no moon out this night, and the starlight did not allow for them to see well the ground in front of them. Without warning, three of the men stumbled face-first into a ditch that cut across the path. One gave a loud shriek in pain; his thigh ran through by a large wooden stake.

"What the hell is this?" the young man asked aloud as he tried to see exactly what was in front of them. Torches were suddenly struck alight in front of them and his question was answered with a horrifying revelation. They had stumbled upon a Roman legionary encampment. The slave at first had no idea as to why legionaries would place their camp in the middle of a road, but then it dawned on him. He turned to run as several javelins flew from the Roman rampart. Several of his companions were struck down with precision accuracy. The young slave then gave a shout of pain as a javelin struck him in the back. He stopped and could not fathom why his body refused to function properly. The shock of his being run through had caused his brain to not comprehend what was happening until he looked down and saw the head of the javelin protruding through the bottom of his chest. Reason and comprehension left him before his body hit the earth.

"Shall we go after them?" a legionary asked his Decanus as the remainder of the escaped slaves fled back up the valley.

"No," the Sergeant replied with a shake of his head. "They're not going anywhere; we'll see them again soon enough."

"Here! We've got a live one!" another soldier shouted from over by the ditch where one unfortunate slave lay whimpering with a palisade stake embedded in his leg. The wound was ghastly with dark crimson blood.

"He's done," the Decanus observed. "His femoral artery's been severed." As if on cue, the slave's rapid breathing became shallow and then ceased altogether. "Make a proper display out of the body to serve as a warning to other escaped slaves."

"What's all the commotion?" a voice called behind them. The Decanus turned to see Optio Macer walking briskly towards their position.

"A few ambitious slaves trying to make a run for it, that's all," the Decanus replied. In the soft glow of the torches, three of his men were seen dragging the dead slave down the path towards a dead tree that jutted out at an angle from the lower edge of the left-hand cliff. The Optio took in a deep breath as realization dawned on him.

"That slave camp is huge," he said to the Sergeant. "If these stragglers have made it here, then the rest cannot be far behind; and their numbers far exceed ours. Stay alert and sound the alarm at the first sign of the bastards."

"Yes, Optio."

$$* \quad * \quad * \quad *$$

The sun was just starting to rise over the narrow valley that the centuries had formed a blockade of ditches and palisade stakes in front of as the rider from Cursor's detachment rode up at a breakneck speed from the unseen path on the left side of the cliffs.

"I need to see Centurion Macro at once!" the man shouted to the sentries at the gate to the compound. "Tell him it's urgent!" The senior legionary nodded to his companion who set down his javelin and shield and raced towards the tent that Macro and Vitruvius had made into their temporary headquarters. The rider dismounted, took a long pull off his water bladder, and handed the reigns to the other soldier.

"Be a good man and get him some water; he's had a hard night." He then quickly raced towards the tent to catch up while the remaining sentry signaled to one of his companions to take the horse over to a nearby stream.

Artorius was leisurely wiping down his armor with an oil cloth when he heard the sound of the Cornicen's horn. His eyes opened wide as he recognized the *call-to-arms*. Quickly he looked around for the rest of his men. Decimus and Valens were sitting on stools nearby.

"We heard it," Decimus asserted as he started to don his armor.

"I'll get the rest of the lads," Valens said, though at that moment the rest of the section was seen rushing from various locations towards where they had stacked their weapons and armor.

"What the hell is going on?" Carbo asked; his face flushed as if he were out of breath.

"No idea," Artorius replied as he laced up the ties to his armor. Carbo reached down and picked up his Decanus' gladius and helped him finish suiting up. The men worked in pairs, helping each other don their equipment quickly and efficiently; a drill they had performed a thousand times before it seemed. His helmet in hand, Artorius gazed past the rampart to where the bloody corpse of a slave was left hanging upside down; its severed head clasped in the outstretched hands.

"It's almost like a contest, isn't it?" Gavius said, pointing to the macabre sight.

"What the hell are you talking about?" Carbo asked as he fought to make some last-minute adjustments to the straps on his armor.

"It just seems like us and the rebels are trying to see who can terrorize people more," his friend answered. "Every time they strike at the populace they leave a grotesque scene of death behind them. And when we strike the rebels we do the same thing."

*　　*　　*　　*

The child started to cry as his mother sought to silence him. She then became fearful, as if the cries were a warning. It was then that they heard the sound of footsteps; and not those of travelers or merchants. What they heard was a cadence of foot-falls; many men marching in step. The mass of slaves slowed to a walk as a bend in the road came into view. The sounds grew louder, accompanied by the rattle of weapons and armor. The woman started to hyperventilate as fear overtook her. The sun shone brightly as a column of legionaries rounded the bend, their armor glinting in the light.

"No," she whispered as she shook her head. She clutched her husband's hand tighter and held her baby to her chest. The husband released her hand and hefted the pitchfork he had taken.

"Not again," Decimus muttered under his breath as the mass of slaves came into view.

"If they surrender they are to be spared," Centurion Macro ordered at the head of the column. "If they choose to fight, any that we do not kill outright will be crucified." Artorius closed his eyes at the order. He was becoming rather efficient at crucifixion, though he found the task to be repugnant. Killing in battle was one thing; in fact it was something he found exhilarating. Tying or nailing people to a crossbeam so that they could slowly suffocate to death was another. In retrospect he was disturbed that he had nailed the traitorous slave to the side of a building, even though the man deserved to die. He should have just cut his throat and been done with it, but that would not have set the example needed. And here was a mob of people, both men and women, who if they made the wrong choice would also be used as an example of Roman dominance. Artorius grimaced as the slaves made their decision with a loud cry and a rush towards them, their makeshift weapons at the bear.

"*Javelins ready!*" Macro shouted as the Century hefted their weapons to throwing position. Artorius' section was positioned next to the Centurion. He watched Macro wipe his forearm across his brow before issuing his next order.

"*Front rank ... throw!*"

To Artorius the mass of humanity rushing at them was like a blur. With the rest of the men in the front rank he rushed forward and unleashed his javelin. The mob then took on distinctive shapes to him. He winced as he watched his weapon arc in the air and plunge through the bowels of an older woman. He could not hear her cries in the din of battle that was ensuing, but her face told of unspeakable agony. All around her people fell in the storm of missiles. The Decanus did not even hear the subsequent commands of Macro and Vitruvius as they ordered their men to continue to rain death down on the rebellious slaves.

"*Gladius ... draw!*" The order brought Artorius back to his senses in time to draw his weapon with a shout. It was then that plums of dust rose in a flurry behind the slaves as Cursor and his cavalry closed in from behind. The slaves far out-numbered them; however they were in such a haggard state that to fight would be paramount of suicide. The rebels started throwing down their weapons as the cavalry smashed into their companions in the back. Many would be slain by

Cursor's cavalry before the rest surrendered. The legionaries marched to within a few feet of the mob before coming to a halt. Artorius let out a sigh of relief as he saw that the fight was over. It was then that he remembered Macro's final order.

"I'll send men back to fetch the slave carts," Cursor told Macro as the legionaries started to segregate and bind the prisoners.

"Yes sir," the Centurion replied. Vitruvius walked over and sheathed his gladius.

"Pity they elected to fight," he observed as he rubbed his shoulder and worked the muscles out which had been sore for a few days.

"Pity," Macro agreed. Cursor nodded in reply.

A horrifying realization came over the slaves as dawn approached. In the early morning glow they saw their fate laid out before them in long rows on either side of the road. Legionaries and auxiliaries had been up all night building crucifixes; a cold example to suppress any hope slaves in the region may have about rising up against their Roman masters. As soon as they had surrendered they had been herded into caged wagons that the auxilia had retrieved from the slaver camp. Now any chance of escape was lost.

"*No!*" the woman screamed as she clutched her baby close. Her cries were echoed throughout each of the wagons as the cages were shaken by those within, desperate to avoid such a terrifying fate. The piteous shouts became deafening as Macro walked over to where his Decanii were gathered, awaiting his orders.

"Now the fun begins," Sergeant Ostorius said; his words devoid of humor.

"You know what to do," Macro said. The section leaders nodded in reply and set about their brutal task.

As the wagon was cleared out, the woman with the baby huddled in the corner at the front of the cage, her husband holding her and their child protectively in spite of his bound hands. Magnus and Valens approached them, each reaching for the man.

"You'll not take my family!" he screamed as he attacked the Norseman. Magnus anticipated this, but was still knocked to ground as they fell out the back of the cage. The slave had landed on top of him, his head splitting open as it struck Magnus' armor. Valens kicked the man off his friend and fell on top of him, gladius drawn. He proceeded to beat the slave mercilessly with the pommel of his weapon.

"Why … can't … you … just … fucking … *die!*" Valens was enraged at the audacity of this slave and proceeded to beat him harder. The slave's nose splattered and his cheekbone crushed under the force of the legionary's blows. Magnus grabbed his friend by the wrist and restrained him.

"Don't kill him," he chastised. "I appreciate you getting that bastard off me, but don't grant him a quick death!" Carbo, Decimus, and Gavius grabbed the now unconscious slave and dragged him over to his waiting crucifix. Magnus and Valens then turned to see Artorius dragging the woman by the hair from the cage. Her sobs and screams matched her baby's.

"Please, not my baby!" she cried as the Decanus tore the child from her arms. Artorius then drew his gladius and started to walk away. The woman tried to follow him, but was felled by her leg bonds. Magnus wrapped an arm around her waist and carried her away as Valens rushed after his Decanus.

"Artorius wait!" he called as his Sergeant walked behind a nearby tree. Artorius turned and faced him, his eyes cold and black. Valens had seen him look this way many times. Over the years Artorius had developed the ability to temporarily shut his conscience down, enabling him to perform the most unspeakable acts of brutality. Valens caught a glint of pending remorse in his eyes as Artorius' hand trembled, his gladius hanging loosely in his fingers.

"Stop," Valens persisted. "Artorius, we don't *have* to do this. The slaves are being crucified to serve as a warning to others who would rebel as they did; but what example do we set by stabbing a child?" Artorius lowered his head and swallowed.

"Do you think I like this?" he asked, his voice shaking. Valens shook his head. Artorius took a deep breath, his face contorting as he fought to remain focused on the hateful deed he had to perform. "I do this so that you men don't have to. I try to spare you the nightmares of my remorse." Valens nodded in acknowledgement. Just then Centurion Macro crashed noisily through a thicket of dead branches.

"Artorius, what the hell are you doing back here?" he asked, then seeing the child in his Decanus' arms he understood. "Make it quick," he ordered as he started to turn away.

"Sir *please*," Valens pleaded. The Centurion turned, shocked at the tone of the legionary. "Don't make him do this."

"And what would you have me do, *Legionary?*" Macro growled, his anger rising at the perceived insubordination.

As night fell it was eerily quiet along the road; the cries of the damned long since having subsided as they hung in agony waiting for death to take them. Torches hung at intervals, casting a soft glow on the scene as soldiers patrolled the area in pairs. There was no moon or stars for them to see by. The woman whose child Artorius had taken moaned quietly as she turned her head to the side. Her husband's face was a bloody, unrecognizable mess. Though he was still breathing he had yet to wake from the beating he had taken earlier. She then hung her head to the side, wondering how long it would take for death to overcome her. Her thoughts then returned to her baby as a pair of legionaries approached. Even in the faint light she recognized the brute that had torn her child from her. She started to tremble and sob at the sight of the man.

"Your child lives," the other man spoke to her soothingly. Her tears of pain became tears of relief for a moment. The soldier's eye was blackened and a long welt scoured the side of his neck; disciplinary measures from Centurion Macro for his insubordination. Artorius had not escaped the Centurion's anger either, a bruise gracing the side of his face for what Macro called his inability to keep his legionary in line. In the end though, Macro had told Artorius to deal with the child as he saw fit. The Centurion was a hard man but he was not unreasonable or inhuman. He had disciplined his men as a reassurance that they did not make their decision lightly.

"Thank you," the woman said softly, her words coming with much effort. Starvation and thirst were taking their toll on her, as was the strain placed on her lungs as she slowly suffocated. Valens looked back at his Decanus.

"Permission to execute one more act of mercy?" he asked. Artorius nodded and walked away. He had been told that they would disembowel the prisoners in the morning and start their move back to Lugdunum. Valens drew his gladius and first walked over to the husband, who was still unconscious. He thrust his weapon beneath the man's ribcage, causing him to convulse as blood flowed onto the blade. The woman's face twisted, her eyes sealed shut, as the legionary stood before her. "If you wish, I can end this now. I promise it will hurt but for a few seconds." She nodded in reply, trembling as she felt the cold point of the gladius touch her just beneath her ribs as Valens found his mark. She clenched her teeth hard as the weapon plunged into her, penetrating her heart. The soldier had been right; it did only hurt for a brief time.

Artorius hung his head as he walked away from the line of crosses. He did not notice the Tribune leaning against a tree at the edge of the torchlight.

"Everything alright, Sergeant?" Cursor asked, noting the vexation on the young Decanus' face.

"Fine," Artorius lied as he continued to walk away from the scene of death. He was anxious for dawn to come so that they could slay the prisoners and be done with it. He knew the more he hoped for morning the longer it would take, as if the gods were mocking him.

"Never a pleasant thing," Cursor observed as he walked beside the Decanus. Artorius thought to increase his stride and try and get away from the Tribune, but he knew better than to show such blatant disrespect to the man.

"It was necessary to prevent further spread of disorder," he replied unconvincingly. He then stopped and turned to the Tribune, assessing him. "Is there something I can help you with, Tribune?" Cursor allowed himself a partial smile, in spite of the grisly scene they had just walked away from.

"We share a common friend, you and I. I received a letter last week from Pontius Pilate, asking me to make contact with you." Artorius let out a short laugh.

"The world is not so vast after all," he replied. "I admit that I am grateful to hear word of our old friend. I have not written to him for some time and he probably thinks I've forgotten about him."

"There's a few issues he wanted me to discuss with you, to gauge your feelings. But those can wait for another time. Right now I am more curious to know your true feelings about what we did here."

"Why does my opinion matter to you?" Artorius asked; a trace of suspicion in his voice. His face twitched as the piteous cry of one of the crucified prisoners echoed through the darkness.

"Because I think we are of a similar mind," Cursor answered.

"It doesn't matter what I think," Artorius replied, casting his gaze downward.

"Maybe not," the Tribune said, "all the same I see you as one who sees more than just what is to his immediate front during a battle."

"You think we shouldn't have crucified those slaves, do you?" Artorius asked; his eyes fixed on the Tribune once more. Cursor shook his head.

"Not necessarily. What I do wonder is if we as leaders in warfare and in governing think through fully the consequences of our actions."

"What do you mean?" the Decanus asked, continuing on his walk and trying to put as much distance between himself and the nightmarish spectacle behind him.

"Think about it," Cursor persisted. "We conquer a region and start to Romanize the place. Over time we make the newly acquired province, as well as its people, into a likeness of us as Romans. This takes time, though. And during that time there is often periods of instability and resentment. I mean, how would you feel if you were a civilian living in Ostia and you had to witness Germanic warriors or Carthaginian soldiers patrolling the road outside your house or marketplace?"

"That's a valid point," Artorius conceded, "however; I don't see how that plays into this scenario. And besides, it was Rome that conquered Germania and Carthage, not the other way around."

"This is true. Still, one must try and understand the minds of those we fight, as well as those we conquer, if we are to ever have lasting peace and stability in this world. After all, that is the promise of Rome; a beacon to enlighten and bring the rest of the world out of the darkness of barbarism."

"And what of these slaves?" Artorius asked. "What do we see if we try to understand *their* minds?"

"That one is a little bit tricky," Cursor relented. "For with slaves, unless they are prisoners of war or convicted criminals, they have mostly been born into their place in life. Most accept this out of hand and don't question it; just as a plebian or patrician accepts their role in the greater scheme of things. Though just as a plebian dreams of ascending into the upper classes of society it only makes sense that one who is born a slave dreams of freedom. If this were not true, then you would never see plebs rise up to the equestrian class, nor would slaves ever go through the great measures necessary to earn their freedom." Artorius thought long about the Tribune's words and what they meant. It seemed so obvious, though it was also no surprise that most were blind to such revelations.

"So what we have then is a large number of slaves who were suddenly given the opportunity to be free," he said at last. "From what you said, that was no slave uprising. Rather it was a band of renegades who killed the procurers and freed the slaves, promising them freedom if they would fight for it." He paused before continuing. "*Somebody* knew we would be here. Whoever freed the slaves didn't care about giving them liberty at all! They freed them *knowing* that they would run into us and that they would have to fight."

"An unwilling mob confronts us, and we crucify the survivors," Cursor added with a trace of disgust in his voice.

"I thought you said you didn't disagree with us crucifying them?" Artorius asked, perplexed by the Tribune's tone, even though he had similar misgivings.

"This is true," Cursor replied. "A thousand slaves who've been given a taste of freedom could very well attain it through violence if they are sold to masters who don't have Roman soldiers protecting them. Slaying them in such a brutal fashion also sends a message to any who may attempt the same thing. After all, in the one hundred years since the slave rebellion of Spartacus was put down and the six thousand survivors crucified there has not been one significant attempt by large numbers of slaves to change their lot in life through force. That being said, I take no joy in what we had to do today."

Cursor was still pondering the fate of the condemned slaves as he passed by his Centurion's tent. As most of his men had since gone to sleep for the night he was surprised to see the soft glow of lamp light coming from inside of Rodolfo's tent. He pulled back on the flap and saw the auxilia Centurion seated behind his desk working away on a large block of wood with a chisel and small hammer. A carving knife sat on the table as well, and there were wood shavings covering the ground.

"Not disturbing you, am I?" Cursor asked as Rodolfo continued to work on the block, which as the Tribune looked closer was starting to resemble the bust of a woman.

"Not at all," Rodolfo replied in his ever-present Germanic accent. "Just doing a bit of wood work to take my mind off things." Cursor glanced around the tent and saw there were many carvings made of wood and small stones in the Centurion's tent. He picked one up; a small piece of basalt cut into the shape of a galloping horse. He was amazed at the finite detail.

"These are absolutely brilliant!" Cursor said with genuine enthusiasm. Rodolfo just waved his hand, eyes still on his work.

"It's a hobby," he replied casually. "My hands weren't always used for killing." Cursor gave a short nod of understanding as Rodolfo continued. "Back home, in Frisia, I made a modest living designing things with my hands. Most of my people are farmers and cattlemen, but those things never interested me."

"You could make more than a modest living in Rome, you know." Cursor was turning the horse over in his hands as Rodolfo stood and stretched his arms. "I mean look at the detail on this! The eyes, mouth, hooves, even the tail is all defined and symmetrical."

"Isn't that how it's supposed to be?" the Centurion asked with a shrug. He then reached under where one of his tunics lay and pulled out a wooden chariot. "I made this to go along with it. I figure my son would like it."

"So whatever brought you here?" Cursor asked as he spun the wheels on the highly detailed chariot.

"Better life for my family. We migrated to Gaul many years ago, and while work was more plentiful it was not always there to be had. I needed a job that had a guaranteed wage, plus I've always had a passion for horses, so I enlisted into Indus' Horse. A Centurion's pay is far greater than I could ever earn making toys and small sculptures."

"Think you'll ever be able to make a living at it again?" the Tribune asked.

"I certainly hope so," Rodolfo answered with a sigh. "I am a soldier of Rome, loyal to my Emperor and my people. But know that I long for the days when I can spend my evenings in my workshop building and fixing things, rather than destroying them."

✳   ✳   ✳   ✳

Erin was focused on her task of cleaning the crockery and she did not hear Valens and Magnus walk in. The cry of the baby startled her and she placed her hand over her heart as she caught sight of the three. She was surprised to see Valens holding the child, thinking that perhaps it was his.

"Tell her," Valens said to Magnus. Though she belonged to Valens, it seemed that his Nordic companion was the only legionary who could speak to Erin in her native tongue.

"You are to raise this child as your own," Magnus ordered. "He is now your son." Without another word, Valens handed the baby to Erin. Unconsciously her face broke into a smile as she held the child, whose eyes opened wide as he gazed up at her. Her smile held as she looked up at her master and for a moment forgot her hatred for the legionary.

"Was that your intent all along?" Magnus asked as they walked back outside.

"I admit the idea came to me rather quickly when I saw that family in the slave cart," Valens replied. "I didn't like the idea of Artorius having to kill the child; plus I thought it might help give Erin some meaning in her life." Magnus cocked a smile.

"She's a slave, what do you care?" he asked.

"She's a slave, yes; but she is still a human being," Valens replied. "Besides, she is my property and I need to do all I can to see to it she's cared for. She now has a reason to live; she will see each dawn for the sake of her child." Both men turned to see Svetlana running towards them, her face beaming.

"Oh, where is he?" she asked, excitedly. Magnus grinned and looked back over his shoulder towards the kitchen. His face then sobered. "You do know how we got him, don't you?" Svetlana gave a sad smile and nodded.

"Yes," she replied, placing an arm around Valens and kissing him gently on the cheek which bore the mark of Macro's vine stick. She then raced to the kitchen to see Erin and the child.

"Maternal instinct?" Valens asked. Magnus snorted and nodded.

"I think all women have it, regardless of whether or not they have children," he replied. They walked by the stables, where Artorius was readying his mount for another courier run to Proculus' estate.

"Damn but that's an ugly mark you got there! What's your beauty secret?" Magnus chided as Artorius replied with a rude gesture. His left eye was partially shut from where Macro had struck him; his brow and cheek a deep shade of purple. "I'm sure Lady Diana will love that!"

"Valens, you know you owe me a pankration match for this," Artorius said, pointing at the legionary sternly.

"I know," Valens replied with a sigh. "I've been sparring with Camillus in anticipation; though I think he enjoys the idea of watching you bludgeon the shit out of me!"

"The only question you need to ask yourself," Artorius stated as he stuffed some letters into his saddlebag, "is, *was it worth it?*" Valens did not hesitate in his answer.

"Absolutely."

"Then you'll take your beating like a man and we'll call it good," Artorius said with a grin as he mounted his horse. "You know the drill; Magnus is in charge until I get back. See you in a couple days."

Svetlana pulled the cloth back from the child's face as he slept in Erin's arms. The young slave looked both ecstatic as well as a bit nervous. Though probably at least a couple years older than her mistress, Erin's life as a slave had left her devoid of most of the experiences a freeborn woman of her age would have and she was rather naive and childlike herself in many ways.

"Have you thought of a name for him?" Svetlana asked.

"I haven't really thought of it," Erin replied. "This is all so sudden and a bit of a shock to me … I think I'll call him Tynan."

"A good name," Svetlana said, nodding with approval.

"It was the name of my husband," Erin replied as Svetlana lowered her eyes. Erin then spoke quickly, "I'm sorry, Domina. If it offends you, I can change it." Her mistress shook her head.

"No, it is a good name," she replied, giving a reassuring smile. "I know this circumstance is hard for you."

"I am a slave," Erin remarked, "whether I hate my master or not is irrelevant. Slaves are property, we do not warrant feelings." Svetlana cocked her head to one side in contemplation. It was true, though something she had never given much thought to. In her life she had never had any kind of rapport with a slave. They were just *there*; one did not pay them any mind. It was a strange and horrible circumstance how Valens had acquired both Erin and now the child that belonged to him. He had slain both Erin's husband as well as the parents of little Tynan. Svetlana supposed that in Rome's rather violent history such acquisitions were fairly common. Indeed after the fall of Alesia during Caesar's Gallic conquest the survivors were sold into slavery with many of the legionaries taking some of the captives as their own property.

"We still care about you," Svetlana assured her. "Valens thought that giving you a child would bring you happiness that you've been denied in this life."

"May I ask where he got the child? Slave children do not come without a price." Erin's face tightened up at Svetlana's silence. "He acquired him the same way he got me … didn't he?" Svetlana nodded.

"In a manner of speaking. Tynan's birth parents were already condemned, and the boy about to be slain. It was Valens who saved him from the sword."

"I suppose I should be grateful then," Erin replied, forcing a smile. "This does add some meaning to my life. I now have a reason to live that does not involve toil and labor. My husband was my life, and I don't know if I can ever forgive the

Master for killing him. However … I am grateful to him, Domina." A slave Erin may have been, but Svetlana found she was growing attached to the young woman. Perhaps it was the lack of female companionship and the fact that she lived in a tiny flat with Erin's presence constant. Erin worked hard to keep the flat clean, and she was a decent cook. Now she would be a mother as well; at least that brought some meaning into her otherwise empty life.

CHAPTER XIII

▼

TERROR RISING

Artorius sighed as he approached the Proculus estate. This was the fourth time he had acted as a courier for his Cohort Commander, and while he was grateful for Lady Diana's company he was becoming discouraged. The thoughts that he held were silly at best. She was always very kind to him, but also distant. How else could she be? Roman society would rather she remain alone and unmarried rather than lower herself to associating with someone of his status. It was a barrier that was ingrained from birth into all citizens.

While he was still very young and not even eligible to find a bride unless he were to reach the rank of Centurion, Artorius did not like the idea of being alone. He certainly did not lack for female companionship; however this was all purely physical. Whenever he finished his business with a lady friend or concubine, he was quickly on his way.

A slave took the reins of his horse as he dismounted. As he dug through the saddle bags Diana rode up on a dark grey mare. Her hair was unkempt from her ride and there was sweat on her brow, but Artorius was still awestruck. He quickly reminded himself that he was there on *business* and spending time with Lady Diana was just a perk. She wore a sleeveless tunic that showed her well-defined arm and shoulder muscles.

"Just some letters, my Lady," he said, trying to sound casual. Diana abruptly dismounted and walked over to him as the slave grabbed the reins of her horse with his free hand.

"I'll take them now," she said, holding out her hand. Artorius gave a glum frown and handed them over to her. He sensed she was deliberately refraining from making eye contact. What was it about Diana that made her so distant with him though she was always cordial? He had a horrible thought: she had to know of his infatuation with her. Did she find it offensive? Possibly, she was a lady. Surely she would have said so already! He never pretended to even be able to figure women out and knew that he would never find out for certain. He readied himself to remount his horse when he heard a man screaming in panic.

"*Domina! Domina!*" Proximo, dressed in field worker's garb, was racing up the road in the opposite direction that Diana had come from. His eyes were filled with tears, his face red and drenched in sweat.

"Proximo!" Diana scolded. "That is no way to behave! Calm down and tell me what's the matter." The slave fell to his knees, his hands trembling.

"It's Master Levant … he's dead, Domina … murdered …" the slave placed his hands over his face, unable to continue. Diana swallowed hard.

"Compose yourself!" she spat as she cuffed the slave behind the ear. His sobbing ceased and he fought to regain his bearing. "Now what do you mean *murdered?*"

"Beheaded, Domina," Proximo stated. This gave Artorius a start.

"Where?" he asked, stepping away from his horse. The slave had only just noticed him.

"Thank the gods," he said in a low voice, "we have Sir here to help us." Diana looked back at Artorius, and then to Proximo.

"You will take Sergeant Artorius and me to Levant, understood?" Proximo nodded meekly.

"Of course. This way, please." Artorius left his helmet in his saddle bag, but strapped on his gladius as they walked briskly behind the slave to where a grove of trees paralleled the river past the wheat fields.

"Please, not here too," the Decanus said quietly. Diana overheard him and gave him a curious stare; looking him in the eye for the first time since his arrival.

"What do you mean?" she asked.

"I'll explain later," he replied, increasing his stride. Diana was startled by his demeanor. Artorius was usually very friendly and outgoing, but now he was sullen and dark. She suddenly wondered if a soldier of Rome had to change who he was under duress or in battle.

A grisly sight greeted them as they came to the edge of a grove of trees. A headless corpse hung crucified from the branches of an old oak tree. The body had been there for at least a day, and flies were gathered in mass around the bloody stump of a neck, as well as the head which was thrust upon a makeshift spike in the ground. Artorius studied the corpse, a look of disgust upon his face.

"Who was this man?" he asked.

"Just some farmer who lived a few miles up the road," Diana answered, the sight of the mutilated body making her nauseous and faint. Artorius started to walk around the tree and the surrounding area.

"There are drag marks here," he observed, pointing to the flattened grass leading from the road, "but not much blood. Which means he was already dead and decapitated when they brought him here." He closed his eyes as terrible fear struck him. "He was brought here as a warning; a warning to you, my Lady." His eyes were dark as he turned towards Diana.

"What are you talking about?" she asked, suddenly frightened by Artorius' stare. "Who would dare send such a warning to me?"

"I can hazard a guess," he replied, walking away from the sickening scene. "Have him cut down and brought to the estate." Proximo cringed at the order.

Diana nodded, "do as he says." She had to run briefly to catch up to the fast-pacing Decanus.

"Are you going to tell me what the *fuck* is going on?" she swore. It was the first time Artorius had ever heard her use profanity.

"I need to know everything we can find out about that man," Artorius answered. "There have been a series of rather gruesome murders taking place in Lugdunum. We think they are being committed by a survivor of Sacrovir's rebellion. If this man Levant was in any way connected, we are in serious trouble." He then ceased walking and faced Diana. "I know Proculus acquired this estate from a former rebel."

"What of it?" Diana asked. "Defeated peoples often have to forfeit their lands, especially following a rebellion." They continued their walk as Artorius explained.

"We need to find out as much as we can about the previous owners. Let us see then if there is any documentation that could shed light on who they were."

As soon as they were inside the main foyer of the house, Artorius started to unlace the ties on his armor. He handed the armor and his belt to a slave, though he kept his gladius strapped to him. Diana sat on a table, one hand covering her mouth, her face still pale as she sought to comprehend what was happening.

"What happened to your face?" she asked, seeking a distraction while they waited for the servants to finish searching the archives. She had noticed the mark on Artorius' face when he arrived, but didn't have the opportunity to comment.

"Oh this," Artorius said as he placed his hand on the still tender lump below his eye.

"It looks like someone hit you in the face with a stick," Diana observed.

"Well funny you should mention that ..." before he could finish a slave appeared, bearing two dusty scrolls.

"The documents you requested, Domina."

Artorius snatched the scrolls away from the slave and signaled for him to leave. He closed his eyes and raised his head as soon as he finished reading the first.

"Have you ever looked at these?" he asked. Diana shook her head.

"No. All I know is these were the documents pertaining to Proculus and Vorena's acquisition of the estate. Why, what does it say?" Without opening his eyes, Artorius held the scroll over his shoulder for her to take. Diana gasped when she read it.

"You mean ..."

"Yes," Artorius said with a nod. "The man Levant was the owner of this estate before the Sacrovir Revolt." Diana continued reading as Artorius paced back and forth, his hands folded behind his back. "Levant was a rebel who was ransomed after the rebellion was put down. The price of his life was his estate. He was given a small farmhouse to live out the rest of his life. Your cousin, like many other Romans of rank, purchased this estate at auction."

"He told me about how he had procured the place," Diana remarked. "So why was Levant murdered?"

"The same reason as most of the others we've found slain in similar fashion. The people responsible for this are seeking retribution on those who surrendered to us rather than fighting to the bitter end. They are viewed as traitors to the cause and their lives are now forfeit. We found one former nobleman, whose life was spared, but his wife and children were butchered in the same manner as Levant. The wife was defiled before being executed and the husband hung himself soon after we arrived." Diana's face bore a look of utter disgust.

"You speak so casually," she said.

"My Lady," Artorius spoke calmly, "I have seen mankind at its absolute worst and there are some things that no one should have to see. But for now we must look to your safety." He had some doubts about his own words. How could anyone have partaken in the vile acts that he had and still be human?

"What would you have me do?" she asked, clasping her own hands behind her back. It was strange, taking orders from a mere plebian soldier; however, Diana knew that her very survival could depend upon it. She swallowed her fear and steeled herself for whatever needed to be done. She was charged with safeguarding the Proculus estate, and she would not fail.

"Do you have any weapons here?" Artorius asked.

"The slaves have some farming tools, and I have a legionary dagger that Proculus gave me a long time ago."

"Wear it underneath your stola," he directed. "Close and bar the gates and post a watch up there at all times. I'll return to Lugdunum and see if I can get some men posted here."

"And if you cannot?" Diana's face bore no emotion.

"Then I guess I will have to come back here and protect you myself," he said with a half smile. Diana smiled back as Artorius' face became sober once more. "I promise I'll not let anything happen to you." Diana gave him an inquisitive look, but before she could question him, he turned briskly and walked out of the room. With a snap of his fingers, a slave brought his armor and belt to him. In that moment, Diana found she was utterly fascinated by this young legionary. She walked slowly out to the courtyard, where he was finishing up the ties on his armor while a slave strapped on his belt. Though he was handsome and looked capable of great strength, she had never paid him much attention. She thought of him as just a courier and he seemed a bit shy around her for some reason, so she was slightly amazed at how he took charge and handled the horrible incident. She suddenly saw him not as a boy who delivered her mail, but a legionary. And a brave man he was if he was serious about protecting her himself--alone.

Artorius swung into the saddle and turned his horse towards the gates. The horse felt the excitement and pranced, ready to run. He looked over his shoulder and shouted, "I *will* protect you my Lady!"

$$\ast \qquad \ast \qquad \ast \qquad \ast$$

"Absolutely not!" Magistrate Julius snapped. Proculus stood with his hands clasped behind his back, his face hardening. "We have a group of madmen terrorizing the city and you want to send troops to protect your own personal assets? I think not! And if their numbers are as large as we fear, how many men do you think it will take to defend your estate?" While Proculus was the Commander of the Third Cohort, while attached to Lugdunum they fell under the control of the Roman magistrate.

"Look, I'm not trying to be unsympathetic," Julius continued as he poured himself a goblet of wine. "But do you realize just how many outlying estates there are in the region? It's not just yours that's at stake here. You'd be better served using your legionaries, in addition to my urban cohort, to hunt these bastards down."

"I understand," Proculus replied.

Centurions and Options sat or stood around the table in the crowded office, an oil lamp casting a soft glow on the table. Artorius and a few of the Decanii that had witnessed some of the atrocities were also on hand. Proculus sat resting his elbow on the table, his chin in his hand.

"Let's take a look at what we have," he said. "The slaver and his family aside, what do most of the victims have in common?"

"They were all paroled prisoner of Sacrovir's revolt," Artorius answered after a brief silence.

"So what then if the surviving rebels want to kill each other off?" an Optio asked. "What should we care?"

"They paid their ransoms," Vitruvius replied. "They made their peace with the Emperor and are redeemed. They are afforded the same protections as all citizens."

"That and it is unsettling to the populace," Macro added. "After all, it's not just ransomed rebels they are targeting. That slaver had nothing to do with the rebellion; though I don't doubt he profited from it. There was also the matter of the slave who led my men into that ambush."

"The slave named his master as a Greek named Heracles," Praxus spoke up.

"Yes, well there are a lot of Greeks living in the region," Proculus replied dismissively. "Some of you have befriended that Pankration teacher, Delios. Think he knows anything?"

"I don't think so," Artorius replied. "He's an Athenian, and apparently this Heracles vehemently claims to be a Spartan."

"Very nice that you want to protect your friend, Sergeant," a Centurion retorted. "Meantime we have a madman, or madmen as it may be, decapitating citizens at will. I say the man needs to be questioned at a minimum; by someone *other* than his friends!"

"I agree," Proculus said with a nod. "Vitruvius, you will dispatch two of your Decanii to question the man Delios."

"Yes sir," the Centurion replied.

"Meanwhile," Proculus continued, "I want this entire city and all the surrounding areas scoured for any signs of who may be behind this. I know this is a difficult task for our men; they are legionaries, not detectives. Regardless, as legionaries we have been charged with the protection of this province, and protect it we will.

"I want every man who can assimilate into the population to do so. I'd use the urban cohort, but they've been stationed here for years; the locals all know who they are. Many of our men are not so well known. If you have any men of Gallic ancestry, so much the better. But know that I want every man responsible for this brought before me and crucified!" He slammed his hand on the table for emphasis. The meeting over; the men rose and left the room. Only Centurion Macro stayed.

"How are you holding up?" he asked, his arms folded across his chest as he sat on the edge of the table. Proculus paced back and forth in the small room and took a rag to wipe the sweat from his brow.

"Not well at all," he replied, "especially after the news your Decanus, Artorius brought me. To tell you the truth Macro, it's not just my estate I worry about. Diana is very close to me. I was like a second father to her and her sister when they were young." He smiled at the memory. Diana had blossomed into a woman of pure beauty, and he knew Claudia was not far behind.

"I think Sergeant Artorius is infatuated with her," Macro said with a grin, trying to keep his Cohort Commander's mind occupied. "Can't say I blame him." Proculus snorted and folded his arms across his chest.

"I have been making him spend a lot of time with her, so I suppose it's my fault. He was quite passionate in his desire to protect her. And while it is appreciated, Magistrate Julius is right; the number of legionaries it would take to protect my estate would severely hamper our efforts to protect the rest of the region and track these bastards down."

Diana had hoped that Artorius would bring a host of legionaries with him; however the young Decanus was alone when he rode through the gates of the estate. He carried but a single letter, neatly folded in half with Proculus' seal.

"My Lady," he said as he handed the note to Diana. She took it and read it quickly, her head dropping slightly as the words sunk in. She swallowed hard before addressing Artorius.

"Tell my cousin that I appreciate his offer, but it would go against my charge," she said, looking him in the eye, her gaze hard. "It says you are to leave at once with my reply; well now you have it. Good day, Sergeant." She nodded curtly, turned and walked back into the manor house. Artorius let out a sad sigh.

"Good day, my Lady," he said quietly to the now empty space where she had been standing. He remounted his horse and raised his head to the sky. Gray clouds were starting to form, a cool, damp breeze brushing his face. Artorius was not one for omens, but still it did not bode well to him. "I pray the Fates do not abandon you as well."

It did not rain during Artorius forty-mile journey back to Lugdunum, which he took at a much slower pace. The clouds were gray and small gusts of wind continued to make him feel as if the Fates were trying to torment him some more. He swore they hated him, for whatever reason.

Artorius did not know if he really believed in the Fates, or even the gods for that matter. How divine forces could be so cruel baffled him. He had convinced himself that Camilla's slow and emotionally tortuous death had been brought on by their failure to follow the plans of the divine. And yet he still lived. Was he damned to lose any that he dared care for as his punishment? Diana had denied herself the personal protection of Proculus and his legionaries; was her fate now sealed?

"Damn that stubborn woman!" Proculus swore. Artorius stood rigid, his hands clasped behind his back. "Did she say anything more?"

"No Sir," the Decanus replied. "All she said was that it would violate her charge." The Centurion nodded and waved for him to leave.

"That will be all, Sergeant." Artorius saluted quickly and left the office. Magnus was waiting for him outside the Principia. Artorius shook his head as both men continued their walk.

"Too bad," the Norseman replied. "I am sorry, old friend."

"So am I," Artorius replied. "I have a problem, Magnus, and I think only you will be able to understand. Remember when I told you about how I thought Camilla had been cursed by the Fates because we violated their divine plan for us?"

"I do," Magnus replied with a nod as Artorius quickened his pace. Neither man knew exactly where they were heading.

"I wonder if I am cursed too. And will Diana suffer because of me?"

"You know what I think?" Magnus asked rhetorically. "I think you're being an ignorant, superstitious twat; that's what I think. If Diana Procula dies, it will be her stubbornness that costs her. It has nothing to do with you. Now quit getting all stupid over the things you have absolutely no influence over. If the Fates do in fact hate you, *fuck* them; you don't *need* them." Artorius stopped quickly and the two men faced each other.

"Thanks, old friend," he said with a half smile. "I needed to hear that." Magnus cracked a half smile and smacked him on the shoulder.

"I know," he replied. "That's why you keep me around I suppose." Artorius laughed and took a deep breath.

"I suppose so. Honestly though, I do feel much better. Make no mistake, I do fear for Lady Diana's safety, but what can I do about it?"

"Nothing," Magnus answered. "You've done all you can. Now we need to focus on hunting these bastards down so that you don't have to fear anymore!"

"We have not struck at our enemies for some time," Radek observed as Heracles brooded in the dark of his room. Indeed it had been many months since last they had slain one of the traitors.

"While the panic our vengeance has wrought has been productive, it has also allowed our remaining enemies to run to the Romans for protection," Heracles replied. He was wrapped in a blanket and shivering. He had not been well, nightmares continuing to plague him. In desperation he had sought out a shady chemist known for unorthodox concoctions.

"And what of the Roman garrison?" Radek asked.

"We will concern ourselves with them in due time." Heracles' head twitched and he placed a hand over his eye, trying to stifle another headache. "Where is that damned servant with my medicine?"

"He will return," Radek reassured. There was a long silence followed by a knock at the door. Radek opened it to see one of his men, the one with the raspy voice.

"For the master," he heard the voice hiss. Radek opened the door fully and let the man in. The raspy voiced man knelt before his master. "From the chemist. This is an experimental concoction that he promises will not only alleviate the nightmares, but that also has long-term health and rejuvenation benefits."

"What is it?" Heracles asked as he took the vial from the man.

"A variety of unique, yet health-promoting medicines, he assures me. The predominant ingredient is mercury."

"Mercury?" Radek asked. "What benefits come from it?"

"I am assured that it promotes long life and excellent health."

"Well once my health returns we can seek to unleash on our enemies once more," Heracles said as he leaned into the corner of the room. "Send for the girl Kiana. We will use her to garner information about the Roman troops in the city."

"Her sister has a legionary for a lover," the raspy voiced man asserted.

"That she does," Radek concurred. "However, it could take months for her to gather anything useful through this."

"Time is all we have," Heracles said.

✳   ✳   ✳   ✳

In time a sense of calm returned to Lugdunum. It troubled Centurion Proculus, as well as Magistrate Julius, that they had never apprehended those responsible for the reign of terror and their sense of justice felt violated. Still, they were glad that the troubles seemed to have passed and they reasoned that perhaps the perpetrators had been eliminated by their own kind. Such would prove to be a vain hope, and only

Kiana knew the truth as to what had happened to Heracles and his renegades. The Greek, who was growing more eccentric with rage and was becoming unbalanced mentally, decided that once he had raised a large enough force from the gutters of society he would try a more direct approach to bringing the populace against the Roman masters. Two years would pass between the time he had last struck and when he let his hate-filled soul unleash itself once more.

CHAPTER XIV

▼

HEIR TO REBELLION

The City of Lugdunum, Province of Gaul Inferior
March, A.D. 23

Tierney stood just inside the far archway, her arms folded and face stern as her sister came inside. Kiana's face was red and drenched with sweat. She did not even notice Tierney as she summoned a servant to bring her water. She downed a cupful and then stood breathing deeply, wiping her stola across her brow.

"Where the bloody hell have you been?" Tierney demanded. Kiana jumped with a start and then gave her sister a displeasing glare.

"*Out,*" she said. Tierney followed her as she walked briskly through the hall that lead away from her and out into the gardens.

"It is several hours past dark," Tierney persisted. "Not a suitable hour for my little sister to be *out.*" Kiana rolled her eyes and started to walk faster. She was nearing eighteen and still Tierney treated her like a child. "You spend many nights out; leaving by yourself without even so much as taking one of the slaves with you for protection. I tell you Kiana, if you ever plan on finding a husband, know that no man will stand for such behavior." Kiana turned abruptly and sneered at her.

"Oh, and is it my unmarried sister who thinks she can lecture me on finding a husband?" she spat. Tierney stood in shock.

"That was a wicked thing to say," she spoke in low voice, her eyes narrowing. "I have yet to find a husband because father had to send me away to look after you after your last lover sought to be some kind of damned hero ..." Her words were cut short by a sharp slap from Kiana.

"Don't you *dare* mention Farquhar!" she hissed.

Tierney was at a loss. Since coming to Lugdunum something had happened to her sister. Before, Kiana would never have even considered raising her voice to her, let alone striking her. Though only two years older, Tierney was taller and far more developed than her sister, who still retained much of her girlish appearance. Tierney growled in rage and struck Kiana hard across the cheek with a closed fist, sending her sprawling to the floor.

"I will *not* be so accosted by my brat of a sister!" she screamed, her eyes filled with tears of frustration and sorrow. Though the blow had nearly knocked her senseless and would leave a nasty bruise, Kiana refused to return any of her sister's tears. Slowly she pushed herself back to her feet. Both sisters stood breathing heavily, though Kiana refused to show any emotion. Instead she spat at the feet of Tierney.

"I am not your charge anymore," she said darkly. "I am my own woman, Tierney, and I will choose my own path in life. Go back to your fuck-toy of a Roman and see what good his pity does you!" Tierney shook her head slowly, fresh tears streaming down her face.

"What happened to you?" she asked, her sorrow deepening. "What happened to my sister that I grew up with and loved? Who is this vile creature that's replaced her?"

"This *vile creature* was spawned in the pit of hell that your lover wrought!"

"You've gone mad, do you know that?" Tierney stated, her composure returning.

"Perhaps," Kiana replied with a sneer. She then snapped her fingers and a servant appeared. She never took her eyes off her sister as she gave orders to the slave. "Ready my things; I wish to leave within the hour." The slave bowed and left the room.

"And where will you go?" Tierney asked quietly.

"I have friends," her sister replied, her face softening, her own anger dissipating. "Please understand, Tierney. I *have* to go. There is nothing left here for me. I sent a letter to Father, telling him that I left under cover of night and that he should not blame you for my disappearance. And *please* don't think about following me, or sending your legionary to track me down."

"You know I cannot allow you to leave," Tierney said as the door was suddenly flung open, a pair of burley men with their heads wrapped in rags underneath their cloaked hoods bursting in, each grabbing her by the arm. A trace of a tear formed in Kiana's eye. Tierney screamed a mixture of outrage and terror.

"Don't fight, sister. These men promised not to hurt you; please don't give them a reason to break that promise." Another hooded figure walked in and placed a hand on Kiana's shoulder.

"It is time to go," he said in a raspy voice that gave Tierney chills.

"But what of my things?" the young girl asked, to which the figure replied with a shake of the head.

"You'll not need them," he replied. Kiana bit her lip and nodded in reply. Without another word to her sister she turned and left with the hooded man. Tierney struggled in the grip of the two men, one of who produced a short club.

"Good night, love," he said sarcastically as he smashed her across the back of the head. Tierney was unconscious before she hit the floor.

$$\ast \quad \ast \quad \ast \quad \ast$$

It was a crisp, cool morning. Two sections of legionaries marched leisurely along the roads that their forbearers had built years before. The sections marched two abreast, their Decanii at the head. Artorius and Praxus had been sent out to check an old, abandoned farm house that someone had reported suspicious activity in. It turned out to be only some beggars seeking shelter from the freezing night. The winds had picked up, and Artorius had elected for their sections to remain at the abandoned house for the night.

"So how long do you think they intend to keep us here before we head back to our fortress on the Rhine? Isn't our three-year tour up yet?" Valens asked.

"Why? Are you afraid that somebody from the First Cohort has been working his way into your territory?" Magnus replied, referring to the less than savory group of women whom Valens associated with.

"I wouldn't worry so much," Gavius added, "the lads in the First have too high of standards for any of Valens' hussies to feel threatened!"

"Very funny," Valens retorted, "I like it here; and besides, Svetlana is about all I can handle anymore. Don't get me wrong, taking her to my favorite brothels has been fun ... sorry Magnus." He cringed as the Norseman glared at him over his shoulder. He quickly changed topics once more. "So again, when is our tour done?"

"August," Carbo replied. "At least that's when we had replaced those blokes from the Eighth Legion."

"I think this area is a lot more pleasant," Decimus remarked. "It doesn't get as cold, and the locals are a lot more hospitable. They are cleaner and more civilized as well."

"Which is why we are here," Magnus added. "To ensure that they stay that way, and that another Sacrovir doesn't surface."

"That guy was nothing more than a lost dreamer," Carbo said.

"Kind of like Valens and his lost dream of ever meeting a nice girl ... Magnus' sister excluded," Decimus chided. This drew a smack across the back of his helm from Valens, along with some profane remarks. Artorius and Praxus shook their heads and laughed at their men's revelry. The soldiers in Praxus' section were engaged in similar conversations.

"They never change, do they?" Praxus asked.

"No, they don't," Artorius replied. "And to be honest, I really don't want them to. At least this way they are predictable." Praxus chuckled. The sun started to shine brighter, casting its light on the frosty ground. A soft breeze made him shiver slightly. Soon the city of Lugdunum came into sight.

"Think we'll see anything interesting today?" Praxus asked at length. Artorius shook his head. It had been some time since the last sign of insurrection. The villains who had gone on a rampage of murder had escaped Roman justice and had lain dormant for nearly two years. Like his Centurions, it bothered Artorius that they had never gotten those who had wrought the most harm. In reality, those ransomed after the Sacrovir Revolt and a large number of freed slaves were the only ones to truly suffer. For the most part theirs was an unwilling guilt by association.

At length they reached the gates to Lugdunum. Life seemed to go on as always in early spring. Farmers would be planting their crops soon, the last of their stores on display in shops, awaiting buyers.

"Sacrovir was more than just a dreamer, he was a visionary! He envisioned a free and united Gaul, all peoples together in one common cause!" The words came from a nearby building and caused the entire group to halt in their tracks.

"Did I just hear that right?" Decimus asked. Artorius raised a hand, silencing him. He turned as he felt a hand on his shoulder. It was Magnus, and he pointed to the second story of a dilapidated tavern. Artorius nodded and signaled to Praxus, who took his men around to the steps at the back of the building.

$$* \quad * \quad * \quad *$$

"And what of the Roman army?" a young man asked following Heracles' outburst. "If the province rises up against Rome, their armies will destroy everything we have worked for! The Romans are gracious in their gifts that led to a better life for us. Let us not incur their wrath by showing further ingratitude. I personally am ashamed that this city gave sanctuary to Sacrovir in the first place." This type of behavior was leading to a strong sense of antipathy from Heracles. He had gathered a number of who he thought would be loyal men from around the city, and yet these were proving to be weak in their resolve.

He had snapped at the men in frustration and now sat with his head in his hand, another headache blinding him. He was beginning to wonder if the mercury he'd been taking was actually a detriment to his health.

"I agree," another man added. "The Romans were benevolent enough not to raze this city to the ground when they cornered Sacrovir here. They forgave us for the wrongdoings of our countrymen and let us be."

"Cowards and whores, the lot of you!" hissed Heracles' raspy voiced servant, who as always had his face covered in the shadows of his hooded cloak. "None will be free as long as you allow the yoke of Rome to crush you." He spat into the corner in emphasis.

As Heracles made ready to speak they heard a loud commotion from below. Words of protest from the innkeeper echoed up the stairs, as did the heavy sound of armed men running down the narrow hall in haste.

"Bastards…" the raspy-voiced thug said quietly. Heracles stood and slowly drew his sword, his headache temporarily forgotten. The frail, slat door was smashed open by the foot of a rather muscular legionary. The rest of the group leapt to their feet, though only a few were armed.

"Well look at what we found," the Roman said, his gladius pointing straight at Heracles, a deviant smile on his face.

"You will not take us so easily, *Roman*," Heracles retorted. The soldier simply shrugged.

"If you wish to die here, that is fine by me. It will spare us the hassle of trial and execution. We have been searching for you for a *long* time." Heracles gulped hard and then reached into his belt and grabbed a small dagger which he flung at the man.

The soldier deflected the weapon with his shield as Heracles turned and dove through the open window. The other rebels turned to follow suit as a group of legionaries stormed into the room.

Outside on the rickety landing Heracles saw another group of soldiers running up the steps. As the man in the lead reached the top, the dry rotted planks gave way with a snap underneath the weight of his armor. A produce cart was directly below Heracles and slaves were unloading vegetables while the owner haggled with one of the inn workers. Without thinking he jumped over the short railing and onto the cart, several of his men with him. Quickly they scrambled off the mounds of produce and onto the street. As a couple of the legionaries on the steps pulled their companion up another stepped back, turned towards the rebels, and let his javelin fly.

Heracles heard a piercing shriek and looked back to see the raspy-voiced man with the javelin protruding out his chest. His ever-present hood was flipped back, his face exposed for the first time as he fell to the earth on his hands and knees. The man was very young, his eyes looking up at his master piteously as his hand reached for Heracles, slobbering blood. He watched for the few seconds it took the man to collapse completely, his eyes bulging and tongue protruding sickeningly from his mouth. Before the Roman soldiers could react further, he and his remaining men disappeared into the throng of people that was starting to gather at the scene.

Kiana was amongst that throng that stood in shock at what they had witnessed. She had come to tell Heracles that the Romans were increasing their patrols in the area and that the time may be coming to leave the city. Grateful though she was that she was not in the inn when the soldiers arrived, she forced her way through the crowd and knelt to look upon the face of the young many that now lay dead. The javelin had bent, ripping through his torso, and he was lying face down in a growing pool of blood. Kiana gasped when she recognized the face, for she knew it well. The face belonged to Alasdair, the young lad who had been her Farquhar's closest friend and who had been ransomed by his family after being captured during the Battle of Augustodunum.

She lowered and shook her head, scarcely believing that the shadowy man whose face he had never revealed, and whose voice sounded more serpent than man, was the boy she had grown up with and had loved like a brother. So close had he been, and yet he had never revealed himself to her. Perhaps he did not want Kiana to know what he had become. Recovering her senses, she pulled her own hood over her head and made her way back into the mob. She turned back briefly; still keeping her face covered, and recognized the soldier who had thrown the javelin.

"Nice throw, Felix!" Artorius heard a legionary say as he gingerly climbed through the window and onto the balcony. His men had netted several prisoners and had slain two who tried to resist. For the first time he saw the hole in the landing where Praxus had almost fallen through. His fellow Decanus was brushing himself off, his legs covered with numerous scrapes.

"I must be getting fat," Praxus said with self-deprecating humor. Artorius snorted and grinned. His face then sobered.

"All this time we've been looking for that bastard and he eludes us once more," he uttered with a sigh.

"If it's any consolation," Magnus replied, his blond head poking through the window, "we may be able to find out from these prisoners where they are hiding now."

*   *   *   *

Proculus never took pleasure in torture and it seemed like they were doing a lot of it lately. Too often the person under interrogation would say what they felt their assailant wanted to hear, just to end the suffering. On the other hand, if one was not brutal enough they would get no information out of the prisoner. It was a balancing act, one which Proculus did not care to take part in. However he did see the need for it from time to time, especially when information was time sensitive; plus the slightest hint of rebellion enraged him.

The prisoner was an older man, long-haired, with a scraggly beard. He was nowhere near as well kempt as most of the citizens in the region, and he still reeked of "barbarian" in the Centurion's mind. The man was hanging from the ceiling by his wrists, his feet just inches off the floor. His ribs were already battered and bruised from the beating he had withstood thus far. Two legionaries stood by with clubs in their hands, ready to exact more punishment. One was a rather young soldier who had never witnessed someone being beaten into a confession, much less taking part in one. His face was pale and he was constantly wiping sweat from his face and forehead. He was by no means effeminate or weak; he had seen his fair share of fighting on the battlefield. It was just that there was an extreme difference between killing men in battle where one reacts rather than thinks; and having to consciously and deliberately cause pain and suffering, where there is too much time to think. He only hoped that the Centurion would not ask him to start cutting off fingers or limbs. The other legionary looked nonchalant, and even a little bored.

"I will ask you once again, *barbarian*, where did your friends go?" Proculus asked, his face inches from the rebel's.

"Just kill me and get it over with, *Roman*," the rebel said, his breath coming in wheezing gasps. Proculus shook his head and nodded to the two soldiers. They moved to either side of the man and in turn smashed his sides with their clubs. The rebel winced and bit his lip hard, though he made not a sound, even as his ribs broke with a sickening snap. One of the soldiers moved to the front and jabbed him hard in the groin with his club. Finally the man's will broke and he cried out in pain as he coughed up bile and blood. Proculus waved the soldiers back.

"Are you ready to speak, or am I going to have to castrate you?" Proculus asked. The rebel's eyes were shut hard, his breathing becoming even more labored.

"The old mill … on the west side of the river," he said at last. "That is where we meet."

"And how many of you are there?"

"Just a couple hundred … we came here last month … Heracles is hoping to recruit more freedom fighters …"

"Fucking traitors more like," the young legionary spat while wiping the sweat from his forehead. He hated the barbarian for forcing him to do the horrible things that he had to do. Proculus raised his hand, silencing him. He then turned and started to walk out of the room.

"What do you want us to do with him?" the other legionary asked after stifling a yawn. Proculus looked at the prisoner, who only looked to be half alive.

"Cut him down for now. If his information proves correct, you can cut his throat. If he has played us false, beat him to death." With that, the Centurion left. The old man's eyes grew wide in horror and sorrow. Had had just betrayed his comrades, and even then he was still condemned to die. The young legionary flew into a rage and beat the man across the face and head with his club until he was unconscious, blood running from numerous cuts and gouges.

"Hey not yet!" the other soldier chided as he cut the bonds holding the prisoner to the rafters. They let his body fall to the floor in a heap. The young man stood with his eyes closed, taking deep breaths. His companion bore a look of concern upon his face.

"Never had to torture anyone before?" he asked. The young legionary shook his head.

"Never," he replied. "I thought we had special detachments for that sort of thing."

"We do, we just didn't bring any with us seeing as how they are a legion headquarters asset."

"Well we should have." The younger soldier tossed his club into a corner before helping to carry the unconscious rebel into his cell. "You know I am no stranger to violence. I just don't like to witness suffering, that's all."

"Don't be such a catamite!" his companion replied. "It's not like these are innocent people here. They're bloody rebels and thieves. Crucifixion will be most of their lot. And if nothing else, that old man was an asshole!" Both men laughed at the dark humor as they locked the condemned man away.

Macro and Vitruvius were both waiting outside. They could hear the wailings of the heartbroken rebel as Proculus walked out the door.

"Ready your men," he ordered. "It would seem the rebels are using the abandoned mill as a meeting place."

"Right under our bloody noses this whole time," Vitruvius remarked.

"Quite," Proculus replied. "We will all meet at the drill field to the south just after sunset. It is about the only place we can cluster without causing alarm."

"There are a number of shops and houses in the vicinity of the mill," Macro observed. "Should we not evacuate or at least warn them?" Proculus shook his head.

"There isn't time," he replied. "Not only have that, but mass numbers of people leaving the area will only alert the rebels. Plus we do not know who may be sympathizing with them."

$$\ast \quad \ast \quad \ast \quad \ast$$

Kiana collapsed beneath a large oak tree outside the city. The setting sun and the sounds of the rushing Rhodanus River masked her sobbing. She was uncertain if Felix or any of his fellow legionaries had recognized her in the crowd, though it mattered not to her.

"Alasdair, you poor boy," she said quietly. The last time she had seen him had been after his ransom from the Romans. She had offered to accompany him on his journey home, but halfway through he asked her to leave. She had always felt a fondness for him. After all, he had been Farquhar's best friend.

"How did you come to this?" she asked, wiping a tear from her eye. "What have you become?" She shuddered at the thought of the raspy-voiced assassin and could not contemplate that he and Alasdair were the same person. The boy she grew up with was naïve and kind-hearted. He had joined Sacrovir's rebellion in a fit of youthful patriotism and Gallic pride, yet he never even struck a single blow against a Roman soldier. What had happened to him in years that followed she could not comprehend. She then took a deep breath as a realization dawned on her.

"And what have *I* become?"

CHAPTER XV

▼

FIRE AND HATE

The mill had not been used for some time before the rebels occupied it again, and had fallen into disrepair; hence why Heracles found it to be the perfect hiding place. There was a jetty with numerous boats just a short walk away as well. Even if the Romans were to find them, they would have little trouble escaping. He found it mildly amusing that they had gone so long undiscovered. Of course his men only moved at night, and the size of the city meant the Romans could not conduct an effective search with their tiny force.

Though their recruiting efforts in Lugdunum had been thwarted thus far, Heracles was far from beaten. He truly believed in Sacrovir's revolutionary ideals. With Sacrovir and Florus both gone, the young Greek felt that it was his obligation to see their dream become a reality. In truth he was a bit puzzled by his gradual change from unbridled wrath to now desperately seeking to find some good in what he was doing. His hatred for the Romans was still unabated. And yet there were days when he would try and find some nobility in his purpose, thinking that perhaps by liberating the Gauls his actions would be justified in the eyes of the gods. Then there were other days where his rage consumed him. All he wanted to do was bring pain and suffering to Rome.

It was during one of these internal tirades that he decided on his next course of action. He planned to take the boats and head south. There was a Roman estate that they could refit themselves with supplies. He was debating whether or not to burn it to the ground.

That will depend on the hospitality of our host, he thought to himself. He knew who the estate belonged to, which made him eager to exact a bit of retribution against the Romans.

Most of his men were asleep, but for some reason Heracles found that he was unable to join them. The events of the day had shaken his nerve a bit, though he dared not show it. He had come too close to getting captured, and in fact had lost a handful of his men to the Romans. He chastised himself for having even come to Lugdunum in the first place. He knew better than to try and recruit from a city that had its own garrison of Legionaries!

Heracles stood in one of the old lofts, gazing south towards the river. The cool breeze made him shiver. He then looked to his right and his gaze froze in place, his eyes unable to believe what they were seeing.

"It's not possible," he said in a low voice, yet there it was. Coming up the road at a fast jog was an entire column of Roman soldiers. They were without torches, depending upon the moonlight to guide them, not wishing to disclose their presence too soon. Heracles grimaced and raced inside the mill.

"Everybody up!" he shouted, kicking men from their peaceful slumber.

"What is it?" one of his men asked, wiping his eyes.

"We are undone," Heracles answered. "The Romans know we are here. We must leave at once!" He then directed several of his men to light torches and follow him, the rest of the men making for the boats. He stopped at the top of the landing and turned back to his men. "Burn everything you can and then head for the boats."

Proculus watched in horror as he saw men scrambling from the mill bearing torches. These were not heading to the boats with the rest. Rather they were heading towards the nearest structures.

"Dear gods," he said quietly. Buildings were quickly alight, and flaming arrows could be seen flying sporadically over the rooftops to nearby buildings.

"Gladius ... draw!" the Cohort Commander shouted. The Romans rushed towards their foe, hoping to cut off their escape, but it was too late to catch most of them. Only a small handful was too slow leaving the mill, and these were quickly cut down by legionaries. They watched helpless, as the rebels bearing torches rushed to where the boats had already started their journey down the river. People were running amok, panic-stricken as their city burned.

"Artorius take your men and clear the landing!" Macro ordered as the Second

Century stormed the mill. The Decanus nodded and then signaled for his men to follow him. They raced up a flight of steps that led to a small balcony with a door off to the left side. As he went to kick in the door, it was hurriedly opened from the inside, a half dozen rebels seeking to escape. So great was their haste that they ran into the group of legionaries before they were aware of their peril. Magnus slammed his shield into one man, sending him screaming over the short railing, his head smashed to bloodied pieces on the cobblestones below. Decimus pinned one rebel against the wall, stabbing him in the leg before knocking him senseless with the pommel of his gladius.

As the rest fled back into the building, Artorius stabbed one through the back, stumbling to the floor as the rebel feel screaming in pain. Carbo and Valens leapt over him, continuing the pursuit. By the time the Decanus regained his footing and caught up to his men, they had already slain the remaining rebels. He looked down below and saw a section of legionaries rushing in through the far door.

"They've all buggered off!" Sergeant Ostorius shouted from down below. "You catch any survivors?" Artorius turned back to Decimus, who nodded affirmatively.

"We got one," he replied with a sinister grin.

"Start forming these people up, and get these damn fires out!" Macro shouted to his men.

"What of the rebels?" Flaccus asked.

"They're gone, it's too late to do anything about them," Macro replied. "Besides, we do not even know where they may be headed."

"Actually we do," Artorius replied as he walked up with a wounded prisoner in tow. The rebel had been stabbed in the leg and could scarcely walk. Artorius had settled for dragging the man by his matted hair. "This fellow here claims to know where they are headed."

"Does he now?" Macro asked, gazing in contempt at the pathetic creature.

"Yes sir, yes sir!" the man spoke frantically, his hands clutching at his hair, his injured leg dragging behind him, useless. "I can tell you where all of them have gone. There is a Roman estate not forty miles from here. I'm sure you know of it …" The rest of his words trailed off in the Centurion's mind as he closed his eyes in realization.

"What is it, Sir?" Artorius asked as Macro took a deep breath.

"We are in trouble," he replied, turning to find Proculus. Artorius' eyes grew wide in realization. "Bring that wretch with you!" Macro called over his shoulder.

He dragged the screeching man behind him as a plan formulated in Artorius' mind. He just hoped his Cohort Commander would be of a state of mind to hear it.

$$* \qquad * \qquad * \qquad *$$

Heracles breathed a sigh of relief as the glow of the burning city faded in the distance. The current of the river picked up significantly, and he knew they would reach their destination by dawn. He smiled sinisterly at the thought. All the Romans had done was force him to expedite his departure from Lugdunum. He fancied himself that they had given the residents a fitting farewell gift. It would take days for the Romans to put the fires out, and days were all they needed. That would give them time to rest and regroup before moving on. There were numerous mountain tribes that he could hope to enlist between there and Arelate, though he dared not go as far south as Massila. That place was crawling with Roman troops. But all that would come later. For now he simply wished to enjoy the night, the ride along the river Rhodanus, and his thoughts of plunder and revenge.

"We managed to save your elixir," one of his men said, handing him a vial. Heracles scowled at the foul liquid but took a large drink of it anyway. Though he was naturally gifted and bore the appearance of being physically fit, inside his body was rotting. Hs lower back now hurt him all the time, especially when he had to urinate. The clouding of his mind had grown worse in recent weeks as well, sometimes lasting for days.

"A higher dose of mercury was supposed to cure that," he said to himself quietly.

"What have I done?" he then heard Kiana ask in a low voice that she thought no one could hear. Heracles opened one eye and appraised the young girl in the moonlight. She was wrapped in her cloak, the hood pulled over her head. In spite of this, Heracles could still make out the glistening of a tear that streaked down her cheek. He closed his eyes once more and contemplated what to do with the child. With them having to abandon Lugdunum, she was of no more use to him … well, perhaps he would have a final use for her before she could be disposed of.

$$* \qquad * \qquad * \qquad *$$

Tierney raced to the scene of the fire as quickly as she could. All along the river homes and shops burned. People were rushing from all over the city in order to help their fellow citizens, while the urban cohort sought to keep order and to prevent looting. She directed her gaze to over by the abandoned mill. A tanning shop nearby was burning and amongst those who fought against the flames she recognized the tunics of legionaries. As she walked closer, to where the heat started to make her face burn, there was a long row of hastily removed armor and weapons. There was no fighting left to do, and they would have cooked in their metal armor. A group of five soldiers stood guard over the equipment.

"Legionary Felix," Tierney started to ask, "have any of you seen him?"

"Felix," one of the men contemplated. "Oh yeah, I think he's from the Second. He should be over there, miss." The man pointed over his shoulder to where groups of legionaries were attempting to chop and clear away burning timbers before they could spread the fire further. To the right men were jumping into the cold waters of the Rhodanus to try to cool their seared skin before rushing back into the fray.

Tierney looked around for something she could use to help. Against the side of the mill was a rusted pry bar. She grabbed it and brushed away the cob webs as she raced over to help the legionaries that sought to save as much of the building as they could. The heat was unbearable as the flames threatened to engulf any who got too close. Tierney frantically pried a burning timber away from the unburned thatch roof. As the beam fell she stumbled away and caught her breath. As she turned her head to the right, her eyes met those of Legionary Felix, who was also regaining his composure before rushing back in. The young soldier at first thought to ask Tierney what she was doing there, but then realized the significance of her actions. He grimaced and nodded his approval. She returned the gesture and both rushed back into the searing hell.

Early the next morning Felix and Tierney sat against the wall of the mill, the scorched remains of the tannery holding their gaze. Both reeked of smoke, their clothing and faces blackened and sticky with sweat. Felix reached a filthy hand over and grabbed Tierney's, which was equally grubby. She looked over at him, a tear in her eye.

"Kiana's gone," she said, causing Felix to stir.

"What do you mean gone?" he asked, his face full of concern for the young girl that he had taken to thinking of as a little sister.

"She was taken by them," Tierney explained.

"She's a hostage?" Felix rose up to a knee, grasping Tierney's hand hard as she shook her head.

"Not in the way you are thinking," she replied. "It is her mind and her soul that are held hostage by those bastards. She was corrupted by them, and I could not save her."

"Well perhaps I can," Felix replied earnestly. Tierney looked up at him, wondering what he could possibly do to save her sister. "I swear on my family's honor that I will bring Kiana back to you!" Tierney reached up and embraced him hard as Sergeant Praxus strode quickly over to where the legionaries were resting.

"Grab your gear!" he shouted as soldiers started to stir and move over to where they had grounded their weapons and armor. "We're moving out!"

Felix stood with Tierney still clutching her. He gave her a quick, but affectionate kiss and whispered into her ear, "I promise." He then rushed over to join his companions as Sergeant Praxus informed them of the pending pursuit. Though he was exhausted from lack of sleep and the harrowing ordeal of the night before, Felix was grateful that he would be able to keep his oath to the woman he loved.

He came upon the rest of the Century, which was hurriedly grabbing enough equipment for the march. Men were rushing back with their packs, each man grabbing enough rations to sustain him for a few days and little else. As the Century started to make a semblance of a march formation Felix caught a glimpse of Sergeant Artorius slapping a prisoner across the face while Macro and Proculus interrogated him. When satisfied, Macro waved Artorius away, who rushed back to the barracks to grab his kit for the pending march. As the Decanus walked away Felix watched as Centurion Proculus grabbed prisoner by the throat and stabbed him repeatedly in the belly. The man slumped to the ground, twitching in the throes of death as Proculus walked back inside the building. Centurion Macro signaled for his horse, which he guided over to where his Century was still forming up.

"Section leaders, report when set!" he shouted as he and Flaccus mounted their horses. Artorius was among the last of the legionaries to arrive with his pack. Macro did a quick visual inspection of his men as the last of them reported they were ready. "*Second Century … at the quick step, march!*"

Erin was the first to see the Century leave the city. Their pace worried her. She rushed back to the little flat she occupied with Svetlana and found her mistress talking to a wine merchant. She dropped to a knee and hung her head.

"Domina, please forgive my interruption." Erin was flushed and out of breath, which took Svetlana by surprise.

"What is it, child?" she asked, suddenly concerned.

"Master has left, along with a host of soldiers." Without paying any further attention to the wine merchant Svetlana ran as fast as she could to the eastern gate of the city. She ran through the gates and almost into her grandfather, who was astride his horse, Odin.

"Grandfather, what's happening?" she asked; her voice near panic.

"They're in pursuit of the last of the rebels," Olaf replied. "Hopefully they will put an end to this sickening affair once and for all." Svetlana turned back to the scene of chaos within the city. Legionaries fought against the still-spreading fires and sought to keep the populace under control. She then turned back to where she could just make out the last of the Second Century as they crested over the side of a nearby hill. A single tear came to her eye.

"May Freyja protect you," she said quietly.

CHAPTER XVI

▼

PURSUIT

"Bloody arrogant bastards!" Proculus seethed. He removed his helmet and threw it onto a nearby bench. He then sat down in a chair, hands in his hair. The tannery had been mostly saved and the Centurion was using it as a temporary headquarters. Vitruvius stood calmly by as the light of the early dawn crept through the open window. The entire Cohort, minus the Second Century, was still helping the citizens fight the fires before they spread throughout the entire city. By dawn it looked like they had prevented any further disaster, however it would be some time before all the fires were out. The Second was pursuing the rebels, though Proculus knew there was no chance of them catching their quarry before they reached their destination. And with Indus and his cavalry spread out throughout the region he had failed to leave himself a quick reaction force to pursue the rebels. This vexed him greatly.

"Proculus, I understand your need for haste, but trust me, it will not help us here," Vitruvius remarked.

"I know," the senior Centurion replied. "It is difficult though, when it strikes close to home." Vitruvius nodded in understanding.

"A little faith in Macro and the Second will not go to waste. Remember, I served there for many years. And Sergeant Artorius I helped train. He is a resourceful individual. If anyone can pull off what he proposed, he can. Besides, it does no good to worry about it now. Their plan will work or it won't. Either way, we cannot do anything about it. The action will be decided long before we arrive. We have other matters we need to attend to."

"That we do." With that, Proculus was on his feet. Vitruvius followed him to where there were several prisoners being guarded by legionaries. They were on their knees, hands bound behind their backs. They had been thrown to the Romans as they had been abandoned by their companions. They gazed at first in contempt, and then in horror as the enraged Centurion approached them with his gladius drawn. Their legionary guards took note as well and stepped away as Proculus slammed his gladius into the belly of one of the men. The rebel gasped in pain, his eyes growing wide, blood oozing from the wound. Proculus withdrew his gladius and kicked the man to the ground, where he lay twitching and convulsing violently.

The Centurion then swung his gladius hard in a backhand slash, ripping through the throat of his next victim. This one fell over backwards, his life's blood gushing from the severed artery. Proculus stood trembling in rage, grinding his teeth hard as he sought to slay the rest of the prisoners. He was gently but firmly restrained by Vitruvius, who grabbed him by the shoulder and wrist from behind.

"Easy there," the younger Centurion said in a soothing voice. "It's going to be okay, Sir." Proculus lowered and nodded his head, his erratic breathing subsiding.

"Crucify the rest," he ordered the nearby legionaries. "Let all bear witness to Rome's answer to their impetuousness and treachery."

"Right away sir," one of the men replied as they swarmed on the prisoners, who were now screaming and attempting to fight loose of their bonds. Vitruvius, his hands still on his Commander's shoulder and wrist, slowly guided him back towards the billets. Proculus shook himself free of the Centurion's grip and leaned against the side of the building.

"Thank you," he said, unable to look Vitruvius in the eye. "I do not know what came over me, but I felt like I had lost all grip on my sanity."

"You did what any one of us would have done," Vitruvius replied. "Those men, if they can be called men, caused wanton destruction within this city. And this city is under our protection." He deliberately avoided any further mention of Proculus' estate or his cousin.

$$* \quad * \quad * \quad *$$

Diana could not believe what she saw. More than a hundred men stood outside the gates of the estate, all of them heavily armed and filthy. Among them was poor Proximo, his face battered and bruised.

"Oh Proximo," Diana said when she caught sight of the man.

"Domina, please forgive me," he said meekly. "I only wished to fetch some berries for my Lady." One of the rebels shook the slave roughly by the hair.

"Yes, it would seem our lady's taste for blueberries has cost her one slave," the rebel said as his companions laughed at Proximo's fate. Diana closed her eyes and thought hard. She was certain she would regret her decision, but she would not leave her faithful, albeit naively careless, servant in the hands of these wretches.

"Don't hurt him," she said, standing tall as she descended the steps that lead to the gate. She nodded to another servant who reluctantly removed the reinforcing brace. The rebels ran through, knocking servants aside, demanding wine and food. There was a Greek with them, who seemed to be their leader. Diana stormed over to him. As she approached, the Greek bowed low.

"My Lady," he said, "I hope you do not mind sharing some hospitality with us. We are weary and in need of provisions and rest."

"Indeed I do bloody well mind!" Diana fumed. "You come into my estate, uninvited, and you immediately start taking what is not yours and making a mess of the place! And just who in Hades are you?"

"Ah, how careless of me, how could I forget my manners? My name is Heracles, I am the leader of this group of men; men seeking freedom from Rome."

"Well you can seek freedom elsewhere! This is a Roman estate, and you are *not* welcome here!"

"Pretty little poppet isn't she?" a rather burley man said through his rotten teeth. His companions started laughing as he advanced on her. "Oh I'm sure you wouldn't mind making us feel welcome, would you love?" The man grabbed Diana by the hair as she quickly drew her dagger out from beneath her stola. She brought it down in a hard slash across the brute's forearm causing him to howl in pain. Two other men grabbed her from behind and wrestled the dagger from her. She continued to kick and struggle against their grip.

"Please, we are weary of violence, and we mean you no harm," Heracles soothed. "You will be placed in your quarters, there to wait until we leave. And you shall remain unarmed." He then reached down and picked up the dagger.

"This is a fine weapon. It must be kept safe so that the young lady does not hurt herself." With that he pointed towards the main house. The two gladiators holding Diana gruffly dragged her away. As they did so, she leaned over and bit one hard on the forearm. The man yelped in pain as blood seeped from where her teeth had penetrated flesh. As he screamed, he raised his hand back to smash her in the face. At that moment, Heracles raised a hand.

"Not a hand will be laid on the Lady," he directed, very calmly. "Nor will she be used for sport. She is of no use to us if she is spoiled. Now take her away, and be more careful!"

"I will see you rot in hell!" Diana seethed, blood covering her teeth and lips. The two men dragged her up the stairs and into the master suite which she occupied in Proculus' absence. One of the men kicked open the door and roughly threw her in. The man she had bitten smiled at her through his rotting teeth.

"I *will* use you for sport yet, my love," he sneered. As the door was slammed shut and barred, Diana was suddenly fearful. She was denied access to her servants, her weapon was taken from her, and she was all alone. Proculus was forty miles away at best. Did he even know of her dilemma?

The door was slowly opened and a small, hooded figure walked in. Once the door was closed, it removed its hood revealing a young girl of perhaps eighteen.

"I was told to come and tend to you, my Lady," the girl stated, coldly.

"I do not know you, child," Diana replied. "I take it then you came with *them*."

"I am anything but a child, *my Lady*," the girl snapped. She then swallowed hard and lowered her eyes, her composure abandoning her. "Forgive me. It has been several weeks since I entered upon this nightmare, and all I want is to go home." She pulled some small squares of cloth from underneath her cloak and walked over to the wash basin. She quickly soaked one of the cloths and started dabbing away clumsily at Diana's bloodied lip. The elder Roman gently took the cloth from her as Kiana lowered her eyes once more.

"I can take care of cleaning myself, thank you," Diana stated. "You are their prisoner then?" Kiana shook her head.

"I *was* one of their accomplices; a vile creature as my sister called me. My name is Kiana; I am the youngest daughter of a Gallic nobleman. My father sent my sister and me to Lugdunum soon after the rebellion of Sacrovir and Florus came to an end. The boy I loved was among those killed by the Romans." She took a deep breath and wiped her eyes. Diana guided her to a chair and sat down on her bed, facing her.

"I am sorry for your loss," she said earnestly. Kiana slowly shook her head.

"You don't know all of it," she replied. "I saw the man who killed my beloved. For after the battle, when families were allowed to come identify the bodies, this man walked over to me and Farquhar's father."

"Farquhar was your lover?" Diana asked. Kiana nodded before continuing.

"The man wore the ancestral sword of Farquhar's family strapped to his hip. It was then that I knew he was my lover's killer. At the time I did not hate him; or any of the Romans for that matter. I blamed Sacrovir and his poison of lies for my loss.

"But just last month I saw a sight that broke me inside. My sister and I had been sent by my father to Lugdunum as a means of escaping the horrors of what we had seen. And yet for me the nightmare was just beginning. I came to town one morning to go to market. I heard unholy screams coming from a smoldering building where there had been some fighting the night before between the town guards and some escaped slaves. Well it wasn't the town guards at all that were involved; it was a group of legionaries.

"I came upon a captive who had been horribly tortured and then hastily crucified by being nailed to the side of the building. I was appalled by what I saw; I thought I had seen all the sufferings and death that I ever would in my lifetime. Lo and behold, but who should be the Roman soldier who nailed the poor man to the building? None other than my Farquhar's slayer!" Her hands trembled as she clutched the inner folds of her cloak. Diana placed a comforting hand on hers.

"Are you sure it was him? After all, more than thirteen thousand legionaries took part in the battle of Augustodunum." Kiana nodded quickly.

"Oh yes, there was no mistaking him. See the man who killed Farquhar was big; far larger than any legionary I had ever seen. Not tall, mind you, but *thick*." Diana's eye twitched as she started to get a visual of the man. *It can't be,* she thought to herself.

"I swear, this monster had grown even larger since last I saw him," Kiana observed as she shuddered. "Here was the man who had killed the one I loved, and now he had just tortured and brutally crucified a prisoner. Thankfully he did not recognize me, for I ran from him. It was then that Heracles found me. He was kind and understanding, and when I told him my tale, he offered me a chance at retribution. I would not have to take part in any of the unpleasant things, only provide them with information. My spirit broke and I went along with it. They were good at keeping me away from what they were really doing."

"What was it they were doing?" Diana asked, fearing she already knew the answer. A tear came to Kiana's eye as she stared at the ground.

"Unspeakable things," she said quietly. "They had brought me along one night to act as a lookout for them. It was almost pitch black and I heard some noises that made me panic. I went to find the others when I saw them …"

"Who did you see?" Diana took Kiana's hand in her own. This girl may have gotten herself involved with wicked men, but Diana sensed that she was not evil.

"Boys … two boys younger than I … brutally murdered and defiled. And what those bastards did to their mother …" She broke down sobbing, her hand covering her mouth as she fought in vain to control her guilt and despair. Diana placed her arms around her and laid Kiana's head on her shoulder, rocking her gently as a mother would a distraught child.

Diana let the girl cry. She knew she had to create a bond fast if she had any hope of gleaning information about her captors. She rocked Kiana and stroked her hair. Eventually her sobs subsided, but stayed snuggled against Diana's shoulder who sighed inwardly. This was a start.

Heracles was at a loss as to what should be done with those troublesome women. Diana would serve as a valuable hostage, but for how long? And Kiana ... well he had little use left for her. He snapped his fingers and the servant Proximo came forward, his head bowed.

"Wine, and something to eat," Heracles demanded.

"Of course," the slave replied as he turned away. Heracles then signaled for Radek.

"Why don't you accompany our new friend here and make certain he doesn't have any accidents in the kitchen." Radek grinned knowingly.

"Of course, master."

*   *   *   *

It was well after dark by the time the Second Century ceased marching for the night. Having dug the required trench and set up the short palisade, the soldiers dined on cold rations, were assigned sentries and readied themselves to sleep on the ground for a few hours before they would rise and march the rest of the way to the estate they intended to save. None complained; indeed many were bitter at having to stop for the night. They were enraged that any signs of Sacrovir's rebellion still lingered so long after it had been crushed. They wished to get to where the last of the enemy was holed up and finish him. Every man took it as a personal insult that these thugs would seek out to harm the estate and family of their Cohort Commander. Artorius lay stretching his legs out when Magnus came over to him.

"I just heard Camillus telling Macro that he thinks we made over thirty miles today."

"Is that so?" Artorius mused. He could not help but be pleased with that. Twenty-five was the standard for a march, so it was good to know they had covered an extra five. That meant that they would only have to travel approximately ten to twelve miles the next day.

"We should reach the estate by midday," Magnus continued. "Then we can try to execute this half-cocked plan of yours. I still cannot believe that Macro and Proculus bought off on it." He shook his head at the thought. Artorius raised an eyebrow at him.

"What do you mean half-cocked?" he retorted. "I think it's brilliant!"

"You would," Magnus replied. "And you would also be the first to volunteer us for 'assassin' detail." Artorius sighed and rolled his eyes.

"Look, if this is about your fear of heights …"

"Angrivarii broke me of that," Magnus interrupted, referring to the Germanic stronghold they had stormed years before. "No, it's just the thought of the six of us having to sneak into a walled compound-where there will be over a hundred of the enemy-and our only hope of support is getting the main gate open, which I imagine will be well guarded."

"Have a little faith, my friend! You put too much emphasis on these rebels and their sense of tactical security. Remember, these are not Roman soldiers we are pursuing. Besides, they don't even know we are coming. They won't expect to see any of our troops for at least another week I suspect. The thought of Proculus splitting his forces has not crossed their minds, trust me. They won't have occupied the estate for more than a day by the time we get there. And let's face it, in their position what would we do?"

"Raid the wine cellars and look for some local entertainment," Magnus observed.

"Exactly," Artorius gestured with his hands for emphasis. "I imagine that any sentries they do post will have their heads buried in the old wine vats as much as the rest. Quite frankly, I think overwhelming the rebels in and of itself will be easy. The only difficulty I can foresee is cutting them all down before they do something stupid. Proculus has a cousin whom he is very fond of overseeing things there. It would not bode well if anything were to happen to any of our Cohort Commander's relatives."

Near the perimeter of the camp Praxus stood with his arms folded as he listened to the story Legionary Felix told him about Tierney's sister and how he had sworn to bring her back.

"The girl is not evil," Felix insisted as he stood rigid with his hands clasped behind his back. "Indeed I had not known of her dealings with the rebels until this morning."

"All the same, it was foolish of you to make such an oath," Praxus replied sternly. "Go and see Sergeant Artorius; he may have a few enlightening words for you."

"Yes Sergeant," Felix replied as he left to find the Decanus.

*　　*　　*　　*

Artorius knew he would not sleep well that night, not as long as Lady Diana was in danger. He lay on his side, the faint glow of moonlight making the shadows of the nearby trees dance. He has a small stick in his hand, which he drew absently in the dirt with. Over the last year or so he had grown very fond of Diana, and he sensed feeling was mutual. Were she not in some way drawn to him she would have simply dismissed him each time he completed his errands. He knew she *wanted* to allow herself to open up to him, but something inside her would not allow it. Her emotional tirades aside she had always been very kind to him. He then thought about the promise he had made to her; it was neither bravado nor false heroics. He was honor-bound to protect her.

"Sergeant Artorius?" A voice disrupted his thoughts. He looked up to see Legionary Felix kneeling next to him.

"What is it?" Artorius asked. He was not irritated with the young soldier for disturbing him; in fact he welcomed the distraction.

"I have something I need to talk to you about," Felix replied, wringing his hands nervously. "I mentioned it to Sergeant Praxus and he told me you would be the best man to speak to, since you seem to be in a similar predicament."

"Explain," Artorius ordered as he propped himself up on an elbow. Felix took a deep breath.

"You know about my relationship with Lady Tierney, the Gallic noble girl."

"Of course," the Decanus replied with a wave. "She's very taken by you and you by her it would seem."

"Yes," Felix replied, his face turning red. "Well it is not about her specifically that vexes me, but rather an oath I made to her regarding her sister."

"Her sister?"

"Yes," Felix was clearly vexed by the situation he found himself in. "Kiana is a couple years younger than her and yet she has already seen unspeakable horrors … horrors brought on by us."

"I know who she is. What do mean *brought on by us?*" Artorius was uncertain how this related to his dilemma with Lady Diana, but his gut told him they somehow were.

"You never recognized Kiana, but she knew you. You remember the young Gallic noble that you killed at Augustodunum, whose ancestral sword you now have?" Artorius nodded in reply. "The lad was named Farquhar … he was Kiana's fiancé. It was she who was with the boy's father when you confronted them after the battle." Artorius closed his eyes trying to remember, and then it dawned on him. Of course! How could he have forgotten? Granted it had been twilight when he had come upon the girl and the lad's father. He had paid her little mind, instead focusing his anger on the father who had failed his son by allowing him to fight in Sacrovir's rebellion.

"I remember her now," Artorius said at last. "I thought she was only scared of

me because she had watched me crucify that slave who led us into the ambush."
Felix shook his head sadly.

"It gets worse. Kiana's been taken in by the rebels." This last remark caused the
Decanus to bolt upright.

"What?" he tried to keep his voice down, but his anger was suddenly boiling
over. "When did you find this out?"

"Just before we left," Felix replied. "Tierney helped us fight the fire at the
tannery. It was after this that she confessed to me that her sister had run off with
the rebels. She begged me to try to save her; that Kiana was a good girl whose mind
had been poisoned by that black-hearted bastard, Heracles. I swore to Tierney that
I would bring her sister back to her safely." He swallowed hard and lowered his
head.

"You swore an oath," Artorius confirmed.

"I did."

"A foolish thing to have done; however, it is something you are now honor-
bound to fulfill. Do you know why Sergeant Praxus said I am in a similar
situation?"

"I do not," Felix answered.

"You are not the only fool here. I swore a similar oath; I promised Diana that
I would protect her knowing the dangers she would soon face."

*   *   *   *

Diana cursed her stubbornness that had led to this predicament. She knew
there would be little she could do to protect the estate against an armed mob,
and yet she still persisted in her refusal to accompany Sergeant Artorius back to
Lugdunum. He had tried to save her then, and by her own doing she was damned.
She knew he would try to save her; alone if need be, and the guilt bore into her. All
her life she had been left forgotten. Even Proculus and Vorena's kindness towards
her was borne out of pity more than anything else. Now she had no idea how to
deal with someone who genuinely cared for her. It was not pity that drove this
soldier to her, for he did not know of her afflictions. And he would risk all by trying
to save her. She walked over to the balcony and gazed out into the blackness of the
night.

"My brave soldier," she said quietly. "What have I done to you?" Though she
would never express it openly, she had grown fond of this young man who exuded
more nobility than any patrician she had ever known. His idealism made him seem
almost naïve at times, which was certainly quite the paradox when she thought
about what he had already been through in his young life. He had seen mankind

at its absolute worst, witnessing unspeakable horrors that would break all but the strongest of spirit. Yet he still believed, or at least he *wanted* to believe that there was some good left in the world. It was in her that he saw what was good and beautiful in life, and yet Diana felt that it was all a façade. There was nothing beautiful about a woman who was barren and of no use to anyone. What could he possibly see in her? She knew he was attracted to her physically, but there was more to it than that. After all, he could buy physical beauty at any of the local brothels.

She shook her head and sniffed quietly. Luckily Kiana was asleep and would not have to see her like this. Quickly she wiped a tear from her eye. It was strange these feelings she had for Sergeant Artorius. She did not see him as a potential spouse or even a lover; she just did not see him in that light, even though he was very attractive. She gave a short laugh and fought back another tear. It was then she realized that she may have lost her one chance at happiness. There was no chance of her ever finding a suitable husband, so why turn away the affections of a man who truly cared for her, even if he was but a mere soldier?

Had she left with Artorius the estate would have been taken anyway, but at least she would have been safe. Instead of allowing him to protect her, she very well could have brought about both their deaths; for she knew he would give his life to protect her.

"Are you alright, my Lady?" Kiana's words startled Diana. She wiped her eyes and tried to compose herself. The young girl cocked her head to one side in contemplation. "Who is he?"

"What are you talking about?" Diana did not wish to trouble this child, who was nearly young enough to be her daughter, with her personal problems.

"I heard you say 'my brave soldier.' I just wondered who he is." Kiana's face broke into a smile as Diana laughed nervously.

"A brave man," she said after a pause. "He swore to protect me. I did not ask for his protection, and in truth at first I resented the idea of a plebian soldier thinking it was his right to save me."

"You don't resent him now, do you?" Kiana asked, taking her hand. Diana shook her head slowly.

"No," she replied, her voice choking up.

"My sister, Tierney, had grown close to one of these Romans, and it was through them that I learned the name of that man who still haunts my nightmares."

"What is his name?" Diana asked, unconsciously clutching Kiana's hand.

"He's called Artorius ... *Sergeant* Artorius," Kiana replied. Diana's breath escaped her and she briefly shut her eyes. She quickly composed herself, hoping the young woman had not noticed her reaction. She had. "You know him, don't you?"

"I do," Diana answered with a sigh, taking her hand from Kiana's. The young girl reached out and grabbed it back, surprising her.

"He's the one you spoke of, isn't he?" Kiana was at first horrified when Diana nodded in reply.

"Tell me he is not the demon that haunts me," she persisted, her own eyes now wet with tears.

"He's not," Diana said reassuringly. "He is a soldier of Rome, and soldiers are often called upon to do barbaric things. It doesn't mean he enjoys it." What she had already said seemed enough to satisfy Kiana, who released her hand and leaned back in her chair.

"All this time I have wanted revenge until it made a black hole in me. That want became stronger than the memories of Farquhar and it consumed me. It never occurred to me to blame Heracles, who killed him as surely as if he was the one who put the sword in my love."

"Your reaction is a very natural thing," Diana said, soothingly. Kiana shook her head, her voice starting to shake.

"I have done many wicked things," she said, covering her eyes with her hand, "all in the name of avenging my lover. And yet the people that Heracles tortured and killed had nothing to do with Farquhar's death. Many were remnants of the rebellion just looking to move on with their lives. He would have none of it. Either they would follow him in his madness, or they suffered a violent death at the hands of his thugs. By the time I realized what they were doing, it was too late; I was already in this too deep. I turned my back on my sister and could no longer go to her, for she had taken that legionary as her lover! I was kept from her, lest I accidentally say anything that could be used by the Romans." Her chest heaved as she sobbed quietly. *"What have I done?"*

"What's done is done," Diana said, standing over Kiana and placing both hands on her shoulders. The girl looked up at her, her eyes red and damp. "Now we must stick together if we are going to survive. We are both hostages now, and should things turn for the worse, I daresay these bastards will not hesitate to kill us both." Kiana leaned against the railing.

"Well I intend to make amends for what I have done," she said. Diana smiled weakly and then turned back towards the open-air of the night. She leaned against the railing and let out a sigh. She knew Proculus would send troops to pursue the rebels, but how many she did not know. She then thought once more about Sergeant Artorius and the promise he made to her.

"Promise me one thing," Kiana said. Diana turned her head towards her, a curious smile forming. Kiana's own face was cold and serious. "Obviously this Artorius cares a great deal for you and I can tell by the way you spoke of him that you care for him also." Diana smiled and blushed. "Promise that you will let something come of that. I lost my love; don't throw something this precious away."

"I promise," Diana replied, a wave of relief washing over her. If Kiana could find it in her to forgive the soldier who had slain her love then perhaps redemption was possible for her.

In truth she enjoyed Artorius' infatuation with her. It made her feel wanted, which was something she had not felt in many years, if ever. She knew she was very attractive, and had often been called 'beautiful.' She was well educated and could hold an intelligent conversation with the most knowledgeable scholars. Yet for all that she was alone in the world. Her inability to bear children was black mark that erased all her qualities that would make her a very desired wife. No man of substance would have her, and indeed it had been a *long* time since she had last been in the company of a man. And even that lasted only long enough for him to learn of her burden. She sighed quietly. Was this what she was reduced to; being nothing more than the subject of infatuation for a boyish legionary?

She could not deny that Sergeant Artorius was an attractive young man, and in truth she was fascinated by the incredibly large and muscular body that lurked scarcely hidden beneath his tunic and armor. She laughed briefly, remembering his young face that made him look almost adolescent in sharp contrast to his strong body. She remembered him saying that he had served under Germanicus Caesar in the wars against the Cherusci, so she knew he had to be older than he looked. Still, she was fast approaching thirty and was certain that he was at least a few years younger than she. She took a deep breath, her fears for Artorius overtaking her. Though not a religious woman, Diana raised her head to the stars and prayed to any who would listen. She hoped that at least the goddess whose name she bore would hear her words.

"Apollo and Diana, I have never prayed to you before. But now I beseech you; please show mercy on the bravest of men who comes for me. Guide and protect him; do not let him sacrifice himself in vain." At the last of her words a sharp gust of cold wind struck her in the face. She gasped in terror at the omen. It was as if the gods were telling her, "*No!*" She started to tremble, fear washing over her.

The sound of light snoring interrupted her thoughts. She turned to see Kiana had curled up on her bed, arms wrapped around her knees, fast asleep. Diana could not help but smile sadly. Yes, Kiana had certainly been manipulated into taking part in the slave rebellion. And yet she could not help but pity her. Kiana was almost young enough to be her daughter and that brought out a small amount of maternal affection for her. She took a blanket and laid it over her before returning to the balcony to brood over their ever-worsening situation. She lowered her head and closed her eyes, thinking about the young soldier who had sworn to protect her. If the gods stood against him, what chance did he have?

✳   ✳   ✳   ✳

"Section leaders with me," Macro ordered, motioning forward. Artorius, Praxus and the others crept forward with their Centurion. The rest of the Second Century stood fast in the grove of trees. Slowly the Century's leaders made their way to where the trees broke up. The estate came into view. It was completely walled, with a gate on the south side. The local town was off in the distance, about five miles to the east.

"Well?" Macro asked, looking at Artorius. The young Decanus looked intently at the estate walls, trying to guess where the best place to breach would be. He smiled as he saw his answer.

"Over there, on the west side," he replied, pointing to a section of the west wall. There was a massive oak growing near the outside rampart, and it looked like some of its branches reached close to the wall. "Decimus could get up there easily enough. He throws down a rope, and up we go. Once inside, I will have one group dispatch the sentries on the wall, while the other gets the gate open."

"I suggest we do this close to dawn. That way Artorius' men can have cover of darkness, but we can also have it close to light once the Century breaches," Praxus observed. Macro nodded.

"I agree," he replied. "If we all get inside while it is still dark, too much chance of rebels escaping and of us killing innocents on the inside."

"I am going to have my men leave their helmets, javelins and shields behind," Artorius added. "The javelins and shields are too cumbersome, and the helmets are a dead giveaway as to our identities."

"Alright," Macro nodded, "after dark, move your men into position. The rest of us will form up as close as we can to the main gate, while maintaining cover in the trees. By the time the sun comes up, you had better have that damn gate open!"

"Yes Sir."

"Sir," a voice behind the Centurion startled him. He turned to see Legionary Felix standing rigid. "Permission to accompany Sergeant Artorius on the raid." Macro folded his arms across his chest and sternly glared at the young soldier.

"Artorius has enough men to accomplish his mission, what reason do you have for wishing to accompany him?" Macro knew the answer, but wanted to hear it from Felix personally. Praxus stood with his hands clasped behind his back.

"Answer the Centurion!" he said sharply. Felix cast his eyes downward, momentarily unsure of himself, before finding his resolve and looking Macro hard in the eye.

"I made a promise, Sir," he replied. "The girl Kiana is with the rebels, but I think she is there under duress. I swore an oath to her sister that I would personally bring her back."

"An oath you were in no position to make," Praxus observed, sternly. Macro nodded affirmatively.

"Quite," he replied. "You would have me risk one of my men for some Gallic brat who I would just as soon crucify." Felix gulped hard before answering.

"Yes sir. She was corrupted, much in the same manner as the noble youths who Sacrovir led to their deaths just three years ago. She is not evil, sir."

"Walk with me, both of you," Macro said to both Felix and Praxus. When they were out of sight of the rest of the Century he turned and glared at the two men.

"Take off your helmet," Macro said, calmly. Felix grimaced, but complied. He stood erect, his helmet underneath his arm, as the Centurion brought his fist around in a hard blow across his ear. The loud slap of his fist striking the young soldier caused Praxus to wince. The legionary surprisingly managed to keep his footing and stood rigid in front of Macro once more.

"That was for your bravado," the Centurion growled. "I will have legionaries of valor in my Century, but not glory-seeking fools who make oaths to skirts that they cannot possibly keep!"

"Yes sir, it will not happen again," Felix replied. He swallowed hard before speaking again, knowing the consequences of his words. "Do I still have your permission to accompany Sergeant Artorius?" Praxus and Macro could not keep from grinning at the legionary's persistence. The Centurion cuffed him across the ear once more, shook his head and walked back to where the rest of the section leaders were still gathered. He could be seen talking to Artorius, who nodded in reply to Macro's unheard instructions. Felix took a deep breath as Praxus patted him on the shoulder.

"I've got to hand it to you, Felix, you've got balls!" the Decanus said as he started after Macro. The legionary stood dumbfounded when a minute later Artorius walked over and signaled for Felix to follow him.

"Are you coming or not?" Artorius asked with a broad smile and a wink.

Chapter XVII

▼

Raiders in the Night

Sounds of drunken merriment could be heard from inside the estate grounds. Artorius smiled to himself. If the lot of them were drunk, then they would be easier to overwhelm. He crouched low against the base of the tree; a large oak, whose branches nearly reached over to the wall. The rest of his section lay prone on either side of him, as Decimus started up the tree. A coil of rope hung over his shoulder.

Slowly and deliberately the legionary scaled the branches of the massive oak. Like most of his section, he was devoid of shield, helmet, or javelins. Only their body armor and sword belt did any of them bring, with Gavius carrying a pair of javelins. As Decimus climbed higher, he was able to see over the wall through the branches. Two sentries stood not ten feet from him. Both were drunk, and one was passed out. Decimus gave a sadistic grin. He looked to his left and right to see if any others were on the wall. There were none that he could see.

"Get up, you drunken sod," the conscious sentry slurred, kicking his companion, who only groaned and rolled over onto his side. Decimus slowly stepped out onto the branch that reached closest to the wall. Gingerly he stepped, trying to maintain silence, as well as his balance. Five feet separated him from the wall when he reached the furthest point to where he thought the branch would support his weight.

The legionary took a slow, deep breath, as he readied himself to jump. Ignoring any pangs of doubt, he leaped as hard as he could, landing feet first on the rampart.

Without losing his momentum, he drew his gladius and lunged at the sentry. The man was laughing and had turned towards Decimus as he raised his wine flask to drink. Before his eyes could comprehend what he saw, Decimus grabbed him by the hair and with a harsh, backhand slash, sliced his throat open. His jugular seemed to explode, blood gushing in torrents. The wine flask dropped with a silent thump to the ground. Decimus grabbed his victim with both hands, slowly lowering him to the ground. He then stepped over to where the other sentry was passed out, where he rammed his gladius into the side of the gladiator's neck. The man only made a slight grunting sound, and Decimus doubted that he even woke before death took him, blood flowing freely and merging with his slain companion's.

Artorius and the rest of the section waited below impatiently, fearing the worst. Then suddenly the rope was thrown over the side, uncoiling on its way down. Artorius smiled, motioned for his men to follow him, and proceeded to climb up the wall. Once at the top, he took a second to appreciate the work Decimus had done in dispatching the two sentries. In less than a minute, the entire section was over the wall. Felix quickly recovered the rope and coiled it over his shoulder. Artorius then motioned for Decimus to take Carbo and Gavius to the right, while he took Magnus, Felix, and Valens to the left. Decimus nodded and started off with the other legionaries towards the main gate.

As they crept along the wall, keeping to the shadows, Artorius listened intently for any signs of the enemy. They hunkered down when they saw three more gladiators standing around laughing and joking, obviously drunk. Artorius looked back at his companions and motioned for them to rise. He then walked very casually towards the men, his gladius drawn, but behind his back. The men paid them little heed as they walked right up to them.

"Nice night," Artorius said, as Magnus and Valens tried to walk past the men.

"Sure is," one of the gladiators said, boisterously. "Nice night for drinking!" The others laughed at his remark.

"Say, who the hell are you guys?" one of the men asked, puzzled. As he said this, Magnus grabbed him roughly from behind, covering his mouth with one hand and ramming his gladius into his back with the other. With a flash, both Artorius and Valens stabbed their opponents underneath the rib cage. Felix stabbed another in the back of the neck as the man tried to stumble away. Little sound was made by the stricken gladiators, so great was their drunkenness and surprise. What sounds they did make were drowned out by the revelry coming from the main house.

Artorius looked to the east, and could just make out the faint glow of the predawn. The sun would be coming up soon.

"Shit," he muttered to himself. "We had best get moving."

Diana stared out her window, arms resting on the railing. Thank goodness she was their only chance at freedom; therefore, she would not be violated. Although she was a reluctant hostage, she was irrationally upset that she didn't fight harder. She rolled her eyes at herself. If she had, she still would have lost and have a few bruises at that. She sighed. Once again something completely out of her control interfered with what she was trusted. Though it would have been impossible for her to keep the men from taking the estate she had still been entrusted to take care of it. She became sad when she thought of how disappointed Proculus might be and that she would be a failure again.

As she gazed into the darkness, Diana looked upon a group of drunken louts on the rampart. She shook her head at the sight. It sickened her to watch these men violate her family's house with their vile filth. Suddenly three were viciously cut down by the others. At first Diana thought it was a drunken brawl. Then she realized the calculated precision with which the men were dispatched. In the faint light, she was able to recognize the armor the assailants wore. It was not typical gladiator garb by any means. No, these men were legionaries! Diana's emotions almost got the best of her in the excitement. It would seem that Proculus had arrived, and he would not be negotiating with these men! She then cursed herself for allowing her weapon to be taken from her. Once the rebels realized that the Romans would not parlay with them, her own safety would be greatly imperiled. Suddenly the door was flung open. Diana turned quickly away from what she had seen, moving inside so as to not draw any unwanted gazes towards the soldiers who she hoped to find her salvation in. Heracles stood in the doorway, hands behind his back. He looked sober, or at least more sober than the rest.

"I realized that I never got a chance to thank you properly for your hospitality," he said. There was no malice in his voice. Under different circumstances, Diana would have believed his words to be genuine. Heracles was not unattractive by any means. Indeed he stood out from amongst the rabble he commanded. It was the cold hate in his eyes that betrayed him. Diana simply glared.

"You have a strange concept of hospitality," she retorted, eyes narrowed, arms crossed defiantly. "You break into my family's house, hold myself and all the servants as hostages, threaten our lives, and then proceed to destroy everything I have worked for with your drunkenness!" Heracles looked down for a second before returning her gaze.

"It is a hard time my men have been through. Their spirits were broken and I needed to find a way to mend them. We know that Roman troops are headed this way, or at least they will be soon. Therefore we will not be staying long. All we want is to leave here as free men, allowed to return to our lands and our homes." It was only a half truth. Indeed, Heracles intended to burn the estate down upon the heads of Diana and all that Proculus held dear. He would have his way with her first, of course. Oh yes, she was a woman with a fiery spirit, and he would have much fun with her. What a shame it would be when he disemboweled her and left her to slowly burn to death. Such a waste. But for now, he would play the gracious guest.

"I admit that Sacrovir's revolt was a foolhardy expedition. It couldn't even gather popular support from most of the people. The Romans destroyed Sacrovir's dream with only a pair of legions. These men are all that remains of that dream. All they want is to be allowed to live. They have no hope anymore."

"So I am but a pawn for you to use in order to attain your freedom." Diana's glare turned even darker. Heracles could only shrug and raise his hands in acceptance.

"It is an awkward situation, for me as well, for I know who you are, *Diana Procula*. I know that your cousin, Valerius Proculus commands a Cohort of Roman troops not far from here. Your relation to him gives us our best hope at survival. I do hope this situation will be over for all of us soon enough." With that he turned and left.

"Oh it will be!" Diana said through clenched teeth. She closed her eyes and prayed that the men she had seen on the wall knew their business, and that they were not alone.

Kiana woke from her slumber and sat up, wrapping the blanket around her shoulders.

"What is happening, my Lady?" she asked.

"Our friends are coming," Diana said quietly, eyes fixed on the door Heracles had just exited through. Kiana allowed herself a brief smile.

There's the gate," Decimus whispered. A large courtyard dominated the area leading to the main gate. There was really no way to be stealthy once they made their way towards the gate, even in the darkness. The soldiers watched as four men laughed and joked, while leaning up against the gate. Decimus knew that just beyond, Centurion Macro and the rest of the Century waited. Another guard stood on top of the wall, above the gate. He seemed to be the only one remotely sober, and the only one who was watching outside the estate.

"That one's yours," Decimus whispered to Gavius, pointing the man out to him. The younger legionary nodded.

"Come on," Decimus said to Carbo. He stood up and grabbed a torch off a nearby wall. "Watch for the signal."

"What's the signal?" Gavius asked.

"Yeah, what is the signal?" Carbo reiterated. Decimus could only smile at them.

"You will see," he answered as he started to walk towards the men at the gate, Carbo close behind him. Gavius waited in the shadows, balancing a javelin in his hands.

"Top of the morning to you all!" Decimus said boisterously as he walked up to the men, smiling and good natured.

"Who in the bloody fuck are you?" one of the drunken men spat, ale streaming down the side of his face.

"Only a friend of the estate owner," Decimus replied, his expression never changing. Before the men could react to his words, he slammed the torch into the face of the gladiator closest to him. The man let out a scream as the flames singed his hair and scorched his face, his beard catching fire. Carbo brought his gladius down in a stab to the groin of one of the surprised rebels. Decimus swung the torch in a backhand swing, smashing it against the head of another. As the man fell to the ground, Carbo thrust his gladius underneath the jaw of the remaining guard.

As quickly as the fight ended, they looked up at the wall, searching for the remaining sentry. They then looked down to see him lying stricken on the ground, a javelin protruding from his chest, his body twitching in the throes of death. Gavius came walking into the torchlight, the other javelin in his hands.

"Alright," Decimus nodded. "Let's get this damn gate open."

The last sentries had been cleared from the wall. Artorius looked around pleased. He gazed over towards the main gate, and saw the lone sentry sprout a javelin from his torso and fall from the wall. The Sergeant smiled to himself. He was then glad that he had allowed Gavius to bring a pair of javelins. Just then he heard the sounds of shouting and watched as several men ran towards the main house from down below.

"Ah *damn it!*" he cursed. "Come on!" Quickly he descended the steps leading below, breaking into a sprint as the men made their way to the house. With all his strength, he body tackled one, knocking him into a nearby fountain. Magnus wrapped his powerful arms around another's neck, snapping it. Valens stabbed yet another in the belly. As the last one continued to run, Artorius drew his dagger and flung it at the man. It embedded itself deep into the base of his neck. The gladiator in the fountain was unconscious, Artorius finishing him with a stab to the heart from his gladius. Felix then smacked him on the shoulder and pointed towards a balcony.

"Sergeant, I saw movement up there earlier that looked to possibly be a woman. I'm going to go check it out." Artorius looked around and saw that by climbing the fountain the young legionary could possibly jump up and grab the balcony.

"Alright, but be careful. First sign of trouble, you get out of there! We'll find another way up since I don't think any of us can get up there encumbered as we are."

"Understood," Felix replied as he started to undo the straps on his armor.

Centurion Macro paced back and forth in the grove. It was taking too long. The sun would be up soon, and he had neither seen nor heard from Artorius' section. He figured a direct assault now would be extremely costly, even with the gladiators being in a state of inebriation. They still had the legionaries outnumbered, plus they had the best defensive position. No, everything hinged on Artorius being able to get the gate open. Macro watched intently, eyes never leaving the sentry he saw on top of the gate. Suddenly the man was gone. It was as if he had disappeared. Macro smiled and nodded to Flaccus. The Century was on its feet, ready to spring.

"Come on, come on," he muttered, watching and waiting. Then he saw the gate being forced open from the inside. As soon as it was open, a lone figure inside started waving a torch frantically back and forth.

"Second Century on me!" the Centurion shouted, taking off at a dead run towards the gate. As he rushed inside, he saw Decimus standing there with the torch. With him were Gavius and Carbo.

"Century on line!" Macro ordered. "Where is Sergeant Artorius?"

"He is around here somewhere, Sir," Decimus answered. "We were going to go find him now."

"Alright, go," Macro answered. "Optio Flaccus, I'll keep the blocking force here. You take the rest and root those bastards out. Drive them into us."

"You got it," Flaccus answered. He then drew his gladius. "Come on!" he shouted as thirty-four men followed him towards the main house.

Heracles had been unable to sleep that night. His plan for destroying the Roman garrison at Lugdunum had come unraveled, and yet he could not help but feel pleased with himself for what he had accomplished. Many of the traitors had been purged and he laughed at the thought of Roman soldiers trying to track down him and his men. They came close once, but thankfully Heracles had never been one to allow expendable slaves into his darkest thoughts.

What he cursed himself for was his impatience; he had failed to uphold the one virtue that had gotten him this far. He thought that after his killing spree perhaps he could rally the citizens of Lugdunum to his cause. Such a foolish notion! These Gauls were but sheep; sheep that had been frightened into obedient submission once more following Sacrovir's failed rebellion.

Ah, but what a prize he now possessed! To have captured the estate belonging to the local legionary commander was better than he could have hoped. To think that only recently he had killed the previous owner for failing to take up arms against Rome once more! The Lady Diana was a trophy in her own right, certainly. Heracles had not felt a woman's touch in many years; not since his wife had been taken from him. Would he be able to perform with Diana, should the opportunity arise? Many of his men had been eyeing the girl Kiana as well. She had pretty much outlived her usefulness to him, so perhaps it was time to give his men some well-deserved sport.

A loud commotion and the sound of many running feet interrupted his thoughts. He ran to a balcony and caught sight of numerous Roman soldiers storming the house. He sneered in rage, his eyes growing black as his hatred consumed him. The Lady Diana's fate was now sealed. She would serve as a pawn to help him escape, and then whether he was able to perform for her or not her body would be the final sacrifice to his revenge.

Dawn slowly crept in the room. Kiana was now wide awake. Neither she nor Diana knew what was happening, and they both felt helpless. Diana ran to the balcony, desperately seeing if she could tell what was happening. There were several bodies strewn around the fountain below. What she could not see was Legionary Felix directly beneath the balcony, who had just finished removing his armor and was making ready to climb the fountain. Diana rushed back inside and started removing blankets from her bed.

"Help me with this," she directed Kiana. "There doesn't appear to be any of those thugs left alive outside. We can tie the blankets to the balcony and climb down."

"Yes my Lady," Kiana acknowledged. Suddenly the door to Diana's room was flung open. She was unsurprised to see Heracles standing there and was a bit unnerved by his demeanor. His good nature had evaporated. His eyes seethed with hatred, and he held a dagger, her dagger, in his right hand. Kiana knelt in the corner behind the door, terrified.

"You are coming with me, bitch!" he snarled as he rushed towards her. She reached up and grabbed hold of his wrist with one hand and tried to push him away with the other. Heracles was startled by her strength. In a panic he swung hard with his left hand and punched her across the mouth. He then wrapped his arm around her neck and placed the point of the dagger at her throat.

"If I am to die, I'm taking you with me! So you had best be a cooperative little harlot. Now move!"

"Leave her alone, she hasn't done anything!" Kiana snapped as she stood before them. Heracles sneered and slammed Diana's head into the wall, momentarily knocking her senseless. He then grabbed Kiana gruffly by the hair and threw her across the room, where she fell next to the balcony. Before Diana could react, Heracles had the dagger at her throat once more.

"Young Kiana, you were such a fool," he said as they stepped out of the room. "You played the part so well. I release you from my service. Die in whatever manner the Romans see fit for you." Kiana heard the door being bolted as soon as it was shut.

She was then startled by further noise and commotion. Men were racing past her door, shouting in loud voices and suddenly she was afraid. These men, Heracles in particular, were inherently evil. She shuddered to think that she had allowed that man to brainwash her into believing she was helping her people when in reality it had led to murder and butchery. She knew why the men were running; they had been found, and their time of retribution had come. She then feared that she would be used as a hostage, or worse killed by the thugs in their state of panic.

She heard a clambering outside the window and saw a young man in a legionary tunic pull himself through the window. Kiana immediately recognized Legionary Felix.

"We've got to go," he said once he regained his footing. A coil of rope was slung over his shoulder; off the other hung his gladius. Felix removed the rope and started tying an end to the bed post.

"What are you doing here?" Kiana asked.

"I promised your sister I would get you out of here before something really bad happens to you," he replied while synching the rope. "Looks like I got here just in time. Where is the Lady Diana?"

"They took her away," Kiana replied, her voice shaking. "Felix … I am so sorry for all the hurt I have brought to you and my sister." Felix shook his head as he uncoiled the rope.

"It's alright," he replied, looking up at her with a smile. She smiled back, her heart full of hope for the first time. "What matters is we get you out of here and return you safe to Tierney and all those who love you." At that moment the door was kicked in.

Radek stood with a look of surprise and rage. He growled and lunged at Felix, slicing open the legionary's belly with a backhand slash of his cleaver before the young man could draw his gladius. Felix collapsed onto the bed, grimacing in extreme pain. Radek raised his cleaver to strike again when Kiana pounced on his back, vainly attempting to strangle him.

"*You bastard!*" she screamed as Radek slammed her forcibly into the wall. Her vision clouded as the wind was knocked from her. He then spun around and swung his cleaver in a rage, the blade tearing through her jugular. Kiana collapsed against the wall, her eyes wide in terror as she frantically fought to stop the torrent of blood.

"Filthy bitch," Radek swore in a low voice. As he turned back to finish the gravely wounded legionary, Felix summoned the last of his strength, drew his gladius and plunged his weapon into Radek's groin. As the stricken rebel howled in immeasurable pain brought on by his severed genitalia and punctured bladder, Felix grabbed him by the back of the head, dragging him to the ground, his own mortal wounds blinding him with agony. He withdrew his gladius and in a rough sawing motion severed Radek's head from his spine. As the floor became saturated with blood, Felix dropped his weapon and crawled on his side over to where Kiana lay dying. Her hand was still clasped to the side of her neck, blood gushing from the wound. Her eyes were wide, her breath coming in short gasps.

"Sister, I am so sorry," Felix said as he clutched her free hand. Kiana squeezed his hand and weakly shook her head.

"No," she whispered. "It is I who brought about our deaths. Oh Felix, I am so sorry ... I would like to have become your little sister ..." Her breathing became shallow and then ceased altogether; a final tear falling from her eye, her hand giving Felix's one last squeeze before life abandoned her. The legionary rolled to his back, one hand clutching his ruptured abdomen, the other Kiana's now lifeless hand. He sobbed uncontrollably as pain and sorrow overtook him.

"Over here!" Magnus shouted as he pointed to an outside door that led into the hallway parallel to the room Felix had breached from below.

"Let's go!" Artorius shouted as he rushed up the short flight of stairs. The landing inside was short, just long enough for three rooms to occupy. The last door was open; a pool of blood flowing onto the landing.

"Dear gods, no," Artorius said in a low voice. A horrifying sight greeted him as he stepped into the gore-stricken room. On the right side lay the decapitated corpse of Heracles' deputy, that vile bastard Radek. In the near corner on his left he saw the lifeless body of Kiana lying next to the stricken Legionary Felix, who was sobbing weakly as the pain of his terrible wound consumed him.

"I'm sorry Sir," he said as Artorius knelt down to tend to him. "I'm so sorry ... please ... please tell Tierney I'm sorry."

"There's nothing to be sorry for," the Decanus replied as he picked up the fallen soldier. Felix gave fresh cry of pain as Artorius laid him on the bed. He grimaced when he saw how badly the legionary was wounded. The abdomen was sliced cleanly open and was seeping blood and fluid. He lowered his head and closed his eyes, not even acknowledging the presence of Magnus and the rest of his section.

"Artorius, there's no sign of ... dear gods," Magnus stopped short when he saw the wounded legionary. He scarcely paid any heed to the corpses or the blood that was sticking to his caligae sandals. Valens shook his head sadly as he eyed to horrific sight. He knelt next to Kiana's body and gently closed her eyes.

"You have to go," Felix said between gasps. "There's … nothing you can do for me." Artorius shook his head and immediately started tearing into the bed sheets, making a hasty bandage.

"You don't die until I tell you to!" he said as he wrapped the sheets around the legionary's torso. He rolled up one section into a ball, which he placed directly over the wound before tying it down. "We'll get you help as soon as we can. You just stay alive; you hear me?" Felix nodded, tears flowing freely down his cheeks.

From the commotion coming from the courtyard, Artorius surmised that Macro and the rest of the Century had breached the gate. The alarm had been raised once they did, but it did not matter now. It was quickly getting light out, and he desperately wanted to link up with the rest of his unit. Someone had to go fetch help, lest Felix die a slow and agonizing death. The lad had come with him with the purest of intentions and there was no way he was going to let him die.

Quickly they descended the outside steps and raced towards where they knew the front gate to be. As Artorius rounded a corner, as spear flew from a nearby balcony. It had a wide blade for a head, and it imbedded itself deep into his thigh, the tip impacting the bone.

"Son of a bitch!" he screamed in pain, as Magnus and Valens caught him. As he wrenched the weapon from his leg, he saw a Roman javelin come sailing from the lower right of the balcony, skewing the thrower, who pitched over the side. Artorius looked over to see Decimus with Carbo and Gavius, who had thrown the javelin.

"Are you alright?" Decimus asked as he rushed over to his Sergeant.

"It's not bleeding too badly," Artorius observed, taking a deep breath. "It will probably start hurting like hell once this rush of adrenaline wears off!" With that he limped off with the rest of his section towards where they guessed the rest of their Century was.

"Where's Felix?" Carbo asked.

"He's hurt badly," Magnus replied as he braced Artorius upright. "We have to get him help or he's not going to make it."

"And the girl?" Decimus asked. Valens shook his head; all the reply any of the men needed.

"Let's go before my leg seizes up on me," Artorius ordered.

The main hall was filled with gladiators and rebels trying to escape the pending slaughter. Optio Flaccus and his men marched deliberately down the hall on line, swords drawn. As they came to rooms, sections would break off and clear them before the entire force would move on. Often the sounds of a scuffle could be heard inside as the rebels were overwhelmed. Many ran from the sight of the wall of men and steel, instead hoping to escape through the main gate, where unbeknownst to them Macro and the rest of the Century waited. It was Sergeant Rufio who first came upon the room where Felix lay dying.

"Praxus get up here!" he shouted. His fellow Decanus was at his side in a moment, the vision of his soldier mortally stricken with the girl Kiana lying slain wrenched at his heart.

"Sergeant," Felix said with a shallow smile, his face pale and damp. Praxus clutched his hand and looked at the sodden bandages over his abdomen.

"Sergeant Artorius," Felix explained. "He's gone to get help. I'm sorry ..." Praxus clutched the legionary's hand and shook his head.

"No," he replied. "You served honorably, you did your best. I am proud to have you as one of my legionaries." He then turned to see two of his men standing in the doorway, their faces agape in horror.

"Praxus, Sergeant Artorius has been hit too," one of the men said. "I saw his men helping him away."

"Alright," Praxus replied with a nod. "We'll have to get help for our brother ourselves then. Find Centurion Macro; get a horse and seek out the town surgeon."

"Yes sir."

Artorius lurched around the corner. Macro and his men had formed a wall of shields between a handful of escaping rebels and freedom. One of the rebels held a female hostage, his dagger at her throat. *Diana! Her lip swollen. . . bleeding.* Artorius' section--bereft of shield or javelin--fell in behind the rest of the Century.

"I'll slit her throat!" Heracles rasped. He pressed his knife against Diana's neck. As Diana struggled, he pressed the knife hard against her throat, causing a small stream of blood to escape. She immediately froze up.

"Your commanding officer would not be happy if his precious cousin died because of you! All I ask is that we be allowed to leave here as free men! Grant us our liberty and she will be returned unharmed."

Behind the wall of legionaries Artorius saw two soldiers talking frantically with Statorius. The Tesserarius pointed over to Macro's horse and signaled for one of the men to go. Artorius recognized them from Praxus' section and knew they were going to fetch help for Legionary Felix. He sighed and nodded, now focused on keeping his promise to Lady Diana.

"It is not in my authority to grant what you wish!" Macro replied. "The Senate of Rome has condemned you, only they can pardon you."

"Then her blood will be on your hands!" He started to slice the knife slowly across her neck, when he saw Artorius limp over to his Commander.

"Sir, permission to end this debacle," he stated, rather than requested. Macro looked at him and at the gaping wound on his leg.

"Damn it Artorius, where have you been? You look like hell."

"We've been busy," Artorius replied. "Now are you going to let me end this for you or not?" His eyes were cold and focused. He hardly felt the pain in his leg. The assailant paused and watched the debate, puzzled by what he saw.

"What do you have in mind?" Macro asked.

"Simple," Artorius replied, keeping his voice low, "I break this vile man with my bare hands; the lads can finish off the rest of these criminals and be done with it." Macro raised an eyebrow at what Artorius was suggesting.

"Are you sure ..." he started to say before Artorius cut him off.

"Yes, I am sure. If we don't do something now, that woman is as good as dead, if not worse." He winked at the end of his last remark, though there was no levity in the gesture. Macro nodded and stepped aside. The young Decanus then stepped rather gingerly in front of the formation.

"Stay where you are or the woman dies!" Heracles suddenly shouted, pressing his knife home. Diana groaned and tensed up. She was not sure what bravado stunt this young legionary was now attempting, and the cold steel of the dagger against her throat made her situation even more perilous. She dared not even breathe as Heracles was slowly digging the dagger deeper into her neck, the blood oozing from the wound running down the top of her chest. Artorius stopped and started to unbuckle the straps of his body armor.

"That's alright, I'm close enough for what I need to do," he replied very calmly. "What say we settle this like men? You and I, one-on-one until one of us breaks. If you win, you and your men are free to go. If you lose, then your men will surrender to face their punishment."

"But I have our survival guaranteed right here," Heracles persisted, grabbing Diana roughly by the hair. She closed her eyes and gritted her teeth; waiting for the maddened Greek to slash her throat.

"*You are a coward posing as a warrior!*" Artorius spat, momentarily ceasing in removing his armor. "You have to audacity to claim Sparta as your heritage, and yet I have learned more from an *Athenian* about true warrior culture than you will ever know!" He saw the Greek's face twitch. He had struck a nerve and looked to press his point home. "You have even taken the name of a god as your own. I'll bet that Heracles is not even your real name, is it? You want to be Heracles; then

I will be Theseus; a Theseus with a bad leg no less!" The rebels all started looking around nervously. The very thought that their fate rested entirely on Heracles and his female hostage unnerved them; but now a wounded legionary was challenging their leader to single combat. Heracles seethed in rage. The legionary had lashed at the very core of his beliefs. He threw Diana to the ground, pitching the dagger behind him. He stripped out of his tunic, revealing a well-toned body that may have lacked Artorius' sheer muscular size and power, yet did not want for overall athleticism.

"I am going to rip your heart out, Roman!" he growled in fury, his eyes completely black. "Your people have taken everything from me; now it is time I was avenged!" Without warning he lunged towards Artorius. Before the Decanus could finish removing his armor, Heracles flailed a fast kick that connected sharply with Artorius' wounded leg. The young Roman fell to his knees, biting his lip in pain, as Heracles swung his leg back to kick again. Artorius caught the leg as it came back around and brought his forearm down hard across the knee joint. Heracles gave a cry of agony as his knee popped and gave way. Artorius pushed himself off with his good leg and landed on top of the man. He smashed his elbow repeatedly into the Greek's face as Heracles fought to shove him off, while attempting to bite into Artorius' forearm. He then wrapped his legs around Artorius' waist and pulled him in close, looking to bite down on the jugular. Sensing the danger, Artorius forced himself to his feet, lifting Heracles with him. His injured leg sent a sharp spasm of pain all the way up his back, causing him to give a cry of agony. He then forced his fists beneath Heracles' jaw. In desperation he lunged forward and drove the Greek as hard as he could onto the cobblestone courtyard. A sickening crunch echoed throughout as Artorius felt the wind knocked out of him, the pain in his leg blinding him. He heard a loud gush of air expelling from Heracles' lungs as the Greek's body started twitching uncontrollably. Artorius crawled forward and felt his hands splashing into pooling blood. He sat back and saw Heracles' eyes open and lifeless, blood flowing freely from the back of his head. The remaining rebels gave cries of panic and horror as their salvation lay crushed on the pavement. One lunged for the discarded dagger.

"*Javelins … throw!*" Macro shouted as a wave of javelins slammed home into the hapless gladiators. Many gave cries of anguish and surprise, the events all transpiring so rapidly. The soldiers then drew their gladii and charged into what was left of their opponents. As they rushed past the woman, Artorius crawled over to where she lay. She was resting on her elbow, her neck covered in blood. She looked over to where her assailant lay; the body giving way to involuntary twitches in death.

"Indignant, even in death" she spat as Artorius knelt down to see if she was hurt.

"A fitting end," he replied. He felt the cut on her neck. It was fairly deep and bleeding steadily; he knew it would leave a scar. He then looked into her face. It was not the first time he noticed just how beautiful she was. Her dark blonde hair touched her shoulders; her bluish-grey eyes seemed to snare him. He had to laugh when he caught himself staring. He could not help it, even with her cut and bloodied neck, as well as her swollen lip, she was absolutely stunning. He had been right to have been enraptured by her that day when he had caught a glimpse of her in the Lugdunum forum … and he had kept his promise to protect her.

He took Diana by the hand and helped her to her feet, the pain in his leg causing him to wince as he did so and he almost collapsed. Diana caught him and helped him stand upright.

"My Lady," he stammered, his face flush and sweat forming on his brow. She placed her arms around his neck and clung to him tightly, her head resting on his shoulder. Artorius nervously placed his arms around her waist and leaned against her. He needed to take the weight off his leg, which was cramping and starting to hurt badly. He closed his eyes and gritted his teeth in pain, not knowing how he had done what he just did when at that moment he knew he would not be able to walk anymore. Diana gently laid him down, resting his head in her lap.

"I had a promise to keep," he said as Diana ran her fingers through his hair.

"And keep it you did." Her swollen lip had become puffier and blood still oozed from the gash on her neck. And yet she did not seem to notice.

The last of the gladiators had been dispatched and Macro was walking back to see how the hostage was faring. He smiled wryly when he saw her tending to Artorius. He refrained from saying anything, however.

$$* \qquad * \qquad * \qquad *$$

"My Lady, we do have surgeons who can take care of that," Artorius protested as Diana placed the damp cloth over his wound. He lay back on his elbows and winced as the medicine on the bandage caused his wound to sting. Diana just smiled.

"They're tending to your friend, Legionary Felix," she replied. She had done quite the job of stitching up his wound. Artorius had lain there, biting his knuckles as she did so, not daring to watch. Though he would never admit it openly, he was terrified of needles. It was odd that a tiny needle and thread binding his wound together unnerved him more than the spear that had filleted his leg open in the first place.

"After what you did for me, this is the least I can do," she replied. Artorius found that once again he could not avert his gaze from her. Her neck was now bandaged, and the blood had been washed from her face and chest. Her lip was swollen and cut, yet still she looked radiant. Her hands gently touched his leg, wrapping the tails of the bandage around it. Artorius found himself starting to become aroused, and he turned red with embarrassment. She finished quickly and turned, not seeming to notice, and sat on a chair beside the bed. As soon as the bandage was tied, Diana sat down on a chair beside the bed.

"What of Felix?" Artorius asked. Diana shook her head.

"I don't know. They won't allow me anywhere near that room. I heard men shouting at each other inside there ... I also saw some soldiers remove the bodies." She wiped her eyes briefly at the thought of poor Kiana.

"The wound is deep, but it should heal over time," she said at last, changing the subject.

"I hope I don't start bleeding and make a mess on your bed," Artorius said, still feeling a bit embarrassed.

"The bandage will hold, but that armor of yours is pretty filthy. It would be best if you took it off. Plus you would be more comfortable."

"Alright then," he replied. "I will just need some help undoing the straps and getting it off." As he sat up, Diana slid behind him and with much efficiency helped him remove his armor. He felt a stabbing pain in his leg as a muscle spasm ripped into the wound. He gasped and fell back into Diana, suddenly panting and sweating. She held onto him and rocked him gently.

"Shh, it's alright now," she whispered with a soft laugh as she lowered him onto the bed, seamlessly removing his armor in the process. Diana then walked over to a table, where she laid his armor next to his helmet and weapons. She wrung out a cloth from a basin of water but before she laid it on his forehead she lightly kissed it on impulse.

"Get some rest," she said as she placed a hand on his shoulder. Artorius was asleep before she left the room. His dreams were filled with images unknown to him before, things he could not describe, just feel. Radiant beauty, a world beyond that of his life on the frontier seemed to beckon him. His world would then turn fiery red as a spasm would make the wound scream in pain, waking him from his slumber. It was then that he would be haunted by images of Felix, the young man he had trained and who looked to him as a mentor. The lad was far more gravely wounded than he. Artorius was not known to pray, but at that moment he prayed to any god or spirit that would listen that the young man would be spared.

The room he was in was completely dark, save for a small lamp on the table that cast a soft glow on his armor and helmet. As the spasm subsided and he felt that any gods who were listening had already decided Felix's fate, he was immediately returned to his dreams. All the while he could feel the ghost of her kiss.

"You brought me here for this?" the town surgeon said indignantly. "The man's slashed through the guts! Give him some wine to numb the pain and let him be on his way." As the man turned to leave Praxus stood in the doorway and slammed his hand into his shoulder.

"The lad means a lot to me," he growled. "One hundred denarii if you can save his life."

"It's not a matter of price," the surgeon protested. "It's a matter of practicality. When ones guts are ripped open there is no saving them!"

"Sir you might want to have a look at this," the surgeon's young assistant said. He had removed the bandaged and was examining the wound. A legionary knelt on either side of Felix, each clutching one of his hands. The men's faces remained stoic, but their hands trembled in anguish. Felix was their brother, and they were not going to let him pass into the afterlife alone and forgotten. The young legionary simply lay there, his eyes twitching as he came in and out of consciousness. The surgeon sighed and turned back to the scene.

"What is it?" he asked, gazing at the wound.

"The guts have not been severed," the assistant observed. A glint of hope crossed his young face. "The muscles have been severed, yes. But the organs and intestines remain intact. We can save this man!"

"By Juno you are right," the surgeon said in shock. "The chance of infection means he could suffer even more, but there is hope for this lad." He then rose and turned to Praxus. "Sergeant, I will need as much clean, hot water as you can find. Also get me as many freshly washed sheets as you can." The Decanus nodded and smiled.

Several hours passed before Praxus went to see Artorius, who was dozing fitfully. Praxus placed a hand on his friend's shoulder, startling him awake. Artorius grimaced as fresh pain shot through his leg.

"Praxus you twat!" he growled. "I was about to have an erotic dream!"

"Well then I saved you from having to explain to Lady Diana why you came all over yourself and her nice clean sheets." Artorius could not help but laugh, though it made his leg spasm once more.

"You bastard, don't make me laugh!"

"I'm sorry," Praxus replied, becoming sober once more. "I came to tell you about Felix. Unless an infection sets in, he may live. His guts were still intact, in spite of the severity of his wounds. Unusual procedure that surgeon is performing.

He cleaned out the wound and then stitched up the abdomen wall. He left the outside portion of the wound open, allowing for it to air out and to keep an eye on internal infection. He said as each layer starts to show signs of healing he can continue to stitch up the rest of him."

"Thank the gods," Artorius said, forcing him to breathe slow and deeply. "I guess they don't hate me so much that they ignored my pleas for Felix's life."

"No, they still hate you," Praxus replied with a smile. "But they must like Felix, or at least the rest of us who prayed for his recovery. Just remember, he's not out of this yet. The lad still has a long road ahead of him if he's to have any chance at surviving."

"So tell me again why Artorius gets to live in plush quarters while we are here on the ground?" Optio Flaccus asked. He and some of the leadership within the Century sat around a small fire just outside the outer wall of the house.

"Would you stop complaining," Sergeant Rufio retorted. "It's a nice night out here and your bickering is ruining it."

"Besides, he *is* the one who saved Lady Diana's life," Praxus answered. "Really he's the hero of this little battle; for anyone concerned about such things."

"Which I am certain Proculus is," Camillus added.

"And besides," Praxus continued, "did you not see that wound on his leg? He definitely got hit worse than the rest of us, Felix being the exception of course, and he'll heal up a lot faster staying where he is."

"What I want to know is how he could even walk, much less thrash that Greek bastard the way he did," Camillus remarked.

"The man's a tough bastard alright," Rufio replied.

"So what happens now?" Sergeant Ostorius asked, stretching out on the ground while gazing at the stars.

"Proculus and the rest of the Cohort should be here in the next couple of days," Flaccus answered. "After that we wait for orders from the Legion. My guess is we will be off home. Our tour here will be done soon; replacements should be rotating in within the next month or so."

"To tell the truth, I kind of like it here," Camillus said, looking around at the rolling hills that he could just make out as the sun fell completely beyond the horizon.

"That's because this area is completely Romanized and feels like home," Praxus observed.

"Well at least Artorius will have some more quality time with his lady-friend," Flaccus scoffed.

"Oh come off it man. She's just grateful that he saved her life," Rufio answered, handing the Optio a flask of wine.

"Are you kidding me?" Flaccus replied as he took the flask and took a long gulp from it. "Did you see the way she was ogling him?"

"Jealous?" Praxus asked, repressing a chuckle. The old Optio's eyes lit up.

"Well to be honest, yeah. I mean when was the last time a saucy-looking woman looked at me like that?"

"Probably when you were twelve," Camillus replied.

"And that was because she was your mother!" Praxus answered. Flaccus threw a rock at him and got to his feet.

"I'm going to go and relieve myself," he announced as he walked off.

"Thanks for sharing," Camillus retorted as the others chuckled amongst themselves.

"Who is running Artorius' section for him right now?" Ostorius asked.

"Magnus," Praxus answered.

"Who I think will probably stay there," Rufio added.

"What do you mean?" Ostorius persisted. Rufio looked over in the direction Flaccus had gone. He could not see the Optio in the darkness, but he could hear him a ways off groaning loudly as he relieved himself.

"Flaccus' time with us is getting pretty short," Rufio said in a low voice. "Someone will have to replace him; and if I were a betting man, I would say that a young Decanus will be the most likely candidate."

CHAPTER XVIII

▼

REUNIONS

Diana rushed out the main gate as soon as she heard the sounds of horns being blown. She did not even try to hide her elation as she watched the rest of the Third Cohort marching towards the estate. At the head was her cousin, Centurion Proculus. She ran to him as soon as he had dismounted from his horse. He embraced her hard.

"I never thought I would see you safe again," he said. "When I was only able to send one Century to help, I feared the worst!" He looked at his younger cousin with relief.

"We are alright," Diana replied. "You obviously sent the best men you had." Proculus smiled as he took her arm in his and walked towards the house.

"And what of the young hero who saved you?" he asked. "I have heard mention of his exploits."

"His name is Artorius. He is one of your Decanii. Do you know him?"

"I know his reputation, though I have only met him a handful of times." Diana looked vaguely disappointed at the answer. "Sorry my dear, but when you have potentially around four hundred and eighty men at your command, it is hard to get to know them all personally. As I said, I know him mainly by reputation. He is the Chief Weapons Instructor for our Second Century, and one of the best close-combat fighters in the region. In fact, you may remember he won the title of *Legion*

Champion about three years ago, which he has held ever since. How is he doing? I hear he was wounded."

"He is doing better, though he won't be able to walk unassisted for some time. I have been tending to him." She looked off into the distance as she said so. Proculus smiled wryly.

"Diana, do you mean to tell me you are falling for this young legionary?" Diana seemed taken aback by the remark.

"I don't know," she replied. "I mean, he did save my life, and our house. And even with that aside, I have always found his company to be pleasant. He is extremely intelligent, and you would be surprised at the amount of knowledge he possesses outside of the army. He recited to me a dissertation by Aristotle from memory on one of his errands out here. I must say, it is refreshing to meet a soldier who doesn't completely devote his life to war."

"So you *are* a bit taken by him?" Proculus persisted.

"I enjoy his company," Diana answered with finality. "Yet he is still a plebian soldier, and I am of no use to men anyway ..." Proculus winced. He often worried about his cousin. Her husband had divorced her upon learning that she could not have children; something that had made her feel like a failure in life, though as a divorcee she was left mostly self-sufficient from a social standpoint. Of course her barren condition would be known to any potential suitor, which made any match of potential worth impossible. No man would wish to marry a woman with whom he could not pass on his line.

Diana was a strong woman, though she was very much alone, and this troubled Proculus, as he cared for her deeply. He also worried about Diana's younger sister, Claudia, who was betrothed to the tribune Pontius Pilate. He hoped that she did not bear her sister's affliction as well. Though of the Equestrian class, Pilate's career was on the rise and a match with him would benefit Claudia immensely.

"Since we will be staying here for a while, you will get a chance to continue to enjoy his company," Proculus asserted. "I will see to it that he gets to finish his convalescing here with you, as you seem to be a better healer than my best surgeons."

"I have arranged quarters in the main house for yourself and your senior officers," Diana added as they walked through the main gate. Two sentries were on duty, both snapping to attention and saluting their Cohort Commander. Proculus removed his arm from Diana's in order to return the courtesy.

"I am going to have the Cohort station itself in and around the estate. I want you to find the best cooks, butchers and bakers in town. While we are here, I want my men to be able to eat well and relax a bit."

"Of course," Diana replied. "And what of young Sergeant Artorius?" Proculus paused and frowned, pretending to be in deep thought.

"I will leave him to your care. I have to say I am rather impressed. Once I have had a bath and something to eat, I will read the full reports on everything that happened." He winked at his last remark.

"Sergeant Artorius reporting as ordered Sir." In spite of his severe limp, and use of a walking stick, Artorius still managed to assume the position of attention and snap a sharp salute. Proculus sat behind a desk in an office that he had designed for his personal use when at the estate. Macro stood off to the side, behind Artorius, his hands clasped behind his back.

"Have a seat, Sergeant," the Cohort Commander replied once he had returned the salute. Stifling a grimace of pain, Artorius eased himself into a waiting chair. Macro took a seat as well, though he remained silent. The conversation was strictly between the Decanus and the Cohort Commander. As Artorius' Centurion, he was there primarily as an observer.

"It is quite the story that I have read in the official reports, as well as what I have gathered from other sources," Proculus began. "Were it not for the fact that I saw over one-hundred dead gladiators and other rebel scum, and not one of my soldiers. It is baffling how one under strength Century can assault a fortified position, outnumbered, and yet come out victorious without a single fatality."

"We had good leadership, and a good plan which we all executed with sound judgment," Artorius replied, glancing over at Macro. Proculus waved a hand and Macro simply sat back in his chair and folded his hands in his lap.

"From the report given to me by your Centurion, the good leadership and sound judgment you speak of came from a small handful of men, led by one rather zealous Decanus." Artorius fidgeted in his seat, not certain if this was a compliment or a reprimand.

"Tell me," Proculus continued, "how is it that there were twenty men on the walls of the house, and yet your men managed to eliminate every last one of them without raising the alarm?"

"They were mostly drunk, my men are thorough, and I did not wish to face a potential beating from Centurion Macro," Artorius answered without missing a beat. Proculus raised his eyebrows at the reply and Macro cocked a half-smile. They then went over in detail the entire raid. When it came to the point where the surviving gladiators tried to escape with Diana in tow, Proculus' expression turned cold.

"Your actions up to this point were brilliant, Sergeant. *However*, at this time you elected to attempt to kill the main hostage taker with your bare hands, with an injured leg no less. Dear gods, what in Hades were you thinking?"

"Proculus, I gave Artorius permission to execute his plan," Macro replied.

"Sir," Artorius spoke up, "those men had no intention of ever releasing your cousin. So great was their malice and spite, that had we allowed them to leave, they would have cut her throat at the next opportunity. And I dare say they would have violated her in the process."

"You state the obvious, Sergeant," Proculus said.

"Sergeant Artorius is one of the best hand-to-hand fighters in my Century, even with a bad leg," Macro added. "His idea, though reckless as it may seem, was the only chance Diana ever had. What's more, it worked." Proculus looked down and nodded his consent.

"I agree," he said quietly. He then took a deep breath through his nose before continuing. "Sergeant Artorius, your daring and valor have saved the lives of Roman citizens and salvaged their property. Moreover, I am personally indebted to you for having saved a member of my own family. Under normal circumstances, your actions would have earned you the Civic Crown." Artorius' eyes widened at the very mention of Rome's highest award for valor, which was given to those who saved the life of a fellow citizen. His thoughts turned quickly to pending disappointment when he saw the downcast look on his Cohort Commander's face.

"Unfortunately," Proculus continued, "since there were no male citizens involved in the rescue, the Civic Crown cannot be awarded. Believe me Sergeant; it pains me to not be able to recommend you for this award. I received your recommendation for Legionary Decimus to receive the Rampart Crown, for having been the first over the wall of an enemy held position. Unfortunately, the Commanding General does not deem that this house met the description of an enemy stronghold, even under the circumstances. A pity really, since I have never heard of anyone being awarded the Rampart Crown four times!

"The best I can recommend is the Silver Torque for Valor for you and the men who conducted the assault with you. That I know I can get approved. I do want you to understand however, that you have my personal gratitude, and that full details of your actions will be annotated in the official reports." With that, Proculus rose and extended his hand. With much pain and effort, Artorius rose and clasped it with his own. It was only the second time he had ever shaken hands with a Cohort Commander.

"Thank you Sir," he replied. He then saluted.

"Dismissed, Sergeant," Proculus replied as he returned the salute. Artorius turned and limped out of the room. Macro stayed.

"That is a brave young man, albeit a bit reckless," Proculus remarked as he took his seat.

"I think of it as daring," Macro answered. "His actions may seem eccentric at times, but believe me; Sergeant Artorius never makes a decision without thinking it through. He is one of the best I have for thinking on his feet."

"Your Optio, Flaccus is retiring soon, isn't he?" Proculus asked, changing the subject. Macro nodded.

"As soon as we get back, as a matter of fact. And I think I may have found his successor."

"Well I hope you train him fast, because I dare say your time in your current position is growing short," Proculus replied.

"What do you mean?" Macro asked, obviously confused. Proculus produced a set of documents.

"Your Sergeant's actions are not the only ones who got noticed," he answered. "Centurion Macro, I have been ordered to advise you that you have been selected for promotion to the First Cohort, as soon as a vacancy comes open." He passed a scroll over to Macro, whose eyes lit up as he read the contents.

For conspicuous valor, sound judgment, superior tactical savvy, and leadership proficiency, Centurion Platorius Macro is hereby selected for promotion to Centurion Primus Ordo. Let it be known that Centurion Macro has been selected for promotion well ahead of his peers, thereby bypassing the rank of Centurion Pilus Prior, as a testament to his performance, valor, and fidelity. This promotion will take effect immediately upon a position within the First Cohort becoming vacant.

Signed,
Gaius Silius, Legate
Commanding General

Macro could only shake his head, astonished as he was.

"Oh come off it man, quit being so damn modest!" Proculus chided.

"Just do me a favor and don't ever call me *Sir*, ok?" Macro laughed. "I have worked for you for too many years to ever feel comfortable with that."

"Hey, you haven't been promoted yet! Gods know how long it may take for someone to retire from the First. Besides, I received a similar letter myself. There's an order of merit list that has the names of several top-rated Centurions who have been selected for membership within the First. You and I are at the top of that list.

"For now, I propose a toast." With that he clapped his hands, and in walked a servant bearing a tray with two goblets and a pitcher of wine. When both glasses were filled, Proculus raised his.

"To my old friend and former pupil, Platorius Macro, Centurion Primus Ordo *select.*"

*   *   *   *

A day after the arrival of the Cohort, Kiana's father and sister rode to the estate. They had yet to find out the fate of their beloved, and both looked hopeful as they sought out Centurion Proculus. The Roman knew they were coming and he dreaded their meeting.

"Ah, noble Centurion!" the Gaul spoke as he rushed up to where Proculus stood in the main foyer. He then looked around, puzzled. "I take it you have found my daughter?"

"We found her," Proculus replied, clasping his hands behind his back, a dark frown creasing his face. The Gallic noble's face dropped any sense of joy at hearing the news.

"Surely you have not imprisoned her!" he said emphatically. "She is but a child; a child who was manipulated by thugs and could not have done any real harm!"

"She is not imprisoned," the Centurion stated, briefly looking over at Tierney. The young woman caught his meaning and she quietly covered her mouth with her hand while closing her eyes tightly and stifling a low moan.

"Well then why is she not here to greet me?" the Gaul persisted. Proculus sighed and started to walk down a side hall.

"Follow me." Without bothering to see if his other daughter was behind him, the Gallic noble quickly fell in behind the Centurion. They came to a room with no door that led to a small, enclosed garden. A legionary stood on either side of the entrance and they snapped to attention as their Cohort Commander approached. Proculus pointed into the garden, remaining in the hall as Tierney and her father entered quickly.

They stopped just inside as they caught sight of Kiana. Her body lay uncovered on top of a dais. Her neck was wrapped, although she still wore the blood-soaked gown that she had died in. Her hands were folded across her stomach, her eyes shut.

"My sweet little girl, what have they done to you?" her father despaired as he fell to his knees in front of her. Quietly he ran his hand across her forehead and kissed her on the cheek. Tierney walked up and grasped one of Kiana's now cold hands. Her father turned to her and in a fit of rage slapped her hand away.

"Don't you dare touch her; *you* are the one who led her to this!" he snapped. Tierney backed away, frightened by her father's sudden burst of anger. His eyes were no longer cast in sadness, but fury. One of the legionaries moved as if to enter the room, only to be stayed by Proculus' hand. He would not allow the situation to become violent; however until it did he was not going to interfere.

"Father, please, I tried …" Tierney's words were cut short by her father's next outburst, his hand pointing at her accusingly.

"*Do not call me Father!*" he shouted. "I charged you with taking care of your little sister and *this* is what I get?" He raised his hand to strike, only to be distracted by the sound of Proculus and the legionaries entering the room. All three men gripped the pommels of their gladii and the Centurion slowly shook his head. The Gaul lowered his hand before addressing Tierney once more.

"I have no daughter!" he spat. "I disown you, vile harlot. *You are no child of mine!*" With that he left the garden through an outside passage, avoiding further eye contact with either Tierney or the Roman soldiers.

"She redeemed herself in the end," Proculus said quietly as Tierney turned to face him. She was in a complete state of shock and unable to speak. "She gave her life saving that of one of my men."

"Felix?" Tierney asked, swallowing hard. Proculus nodded. Tierney nodded in reply and turned back to her sister. Proculus signaled for the soldiers to leave the room so the young woman could have her moment with her sister.

Clouds cast a shadow as if the Fates sought to emphasize the sadness. A freshly dug grave dominated the scene. A small group of legionaries stood on either side. Proculus, along with the Centurions and Options, were at the head of the grave. Diana stood next to her cousin, shroud in mourning garb. It was at her request that Proculus and his men attend. Kiana had sinned greatly, but to Diana she had made things right in the end. She had sacrificed her own life trying to save that of Felix. The young legionary lay upright on a litter hastily constructed by his mates. His wounds were still heavily bandaged, but there was a trace of color returning to his face. Artorius sat next to him, his injured leg propped up on a stump in front of him. He kept looking over at Diana, but she appeared to not notice him. Instead her eyes were fixed on the grave that would soon hold the remains of the girl she had so desperately tried to save.

A Gallic holy man walked at the head of the procession that made its way to the grave. Kiana's father walked next to the man, his servants carrying the shrouded body of his daughter. His slaves carried her, for he would not allow Roman soldiers to touch his beloved child. Not surprisingly, Tierney was behind the procession, a good ten feet behind the body. Her father blamed her for Kiana's death, and she was not worthy to walk beside him. As the body was carried to the open grave, Tierney made one last gesture to appeal to her father. But before she could say a word, he raised his hand quickly, almost striking her with the back of it. She then turned and walked away as her sister was lowered into the ground.

As she walked away from the grave, Tierney turned and for the first time since arriving at the estate she noticed Legionary Felix. The young soldier gazed at her, his own eyes filled with regret. Even with the bandages, Tierney could still gauge the severity of his wounds. His face was pale, sweat forming on his brow. He should not have been moved from his room, but he insisted on saying farewell to the girl who he had loved like a sister.

Felix then reached a hand out to Tierney. At first she started to shake her head, but then when she looked back at her father once more, Tierney realized the significance of the legionary's gesture. She slowly walked over to him and took his hand in hers. She squeezed it affectionately, her eyes filling with tears as the holy man started to recite some verses from a tomb he carried with him. It was an ancient tongue that he spoke and only Tierney, her father, and a couple of legionaries who were of Gallic ancestry could understand. Even their servants could not make out the words. Tierney repeated each verse to Felix.

Gods of the earth
Welcome your daughter as she greets you on her final journey
Gods of the earth
Guide your child home
Sequana and Grannus, heal the hearts of those who loved her
As Aveta brought this child into the world, now may Nantosuelta embrace her in
death
Gods of the earth
To you we return Kiana

Tierney shuddered as she recounted the final verse. Felix clutched her hand tightly. The holy man then threw some dirt into the grave, turned slowly, and walked away. Kiana's father followed, not once looking back at his other daughter that he had now fully abandoned. The Romans started to disperse, some of the legionaries uncomfortable with having to witness a barbaric death ritual. There were others, though, who had come from similar ancestral backgrounds as Kiana and her family; and though they were Roman citizens who worshipped the Pantheon, they understood and respected the traditions of their distant kinsmen. A legionary stood at each corner of the Felix's litter and they lifted their brother up, taking him back to his quarters.

"Stay with me, Tierney," he whispered his voice hoarse. The young woman smiled and stroked his head gently.

"I promise, I will never leave you," she said as she kissed him on the lips.

"Nice one, Felix," one of his companions said as they carried him away. "Now you bloody well better survive that little scratch of yours!" Tierney laughed at the soldier's remark and walked beside the litter, her hand never letting go of Felix's.

Artorius watched as everyone left. With the exception of the slaves who were filling in the grave, only he and Diana remained. He felt himself envying young Felix. The lad had been through unspeakable trauma, and yet now he had found perhaps the greatest prize there was. Far from placing blame on him for Kiana's death, Tierney embraced the young legionary who nearly gave his own life trying to save her. The bond between them was now unshakable. And while Tierney may no longer have been a noblewoman, such a status had only served to create a barrier between her and Felix. What Felix now had was a companion who loved him; who would stay with him for the rest of their lives, waiting for the day that Rome would allow their union to be made official. It would be a long wait, one predicated by either Felix's rise to Centurion or else his retirement from the legions. It mattered not, for Tierney would still be by his side. They were both only twenty years of age, and yet it was as if they had grown up together.

"Are you alright, Sergeant?" Diana's voice startled him from his thoughts. He quickly nodded and sought to compose himself.

"Yes, thank you," he replied. "Sad affair, really."

"Quite," Diana said as she quickly walked away from him. He let out an audible sigh. Diana's emotions seemed to go from affectionate to cold at every shifting of the winds and he could not figure her out. He guessed that men and women were deliberately designed that way; as if the gods were playing a joke on them by making them inseparable and yet a complete mystery to each other.

He looked back to where the slaves were quietly filling the grave with dirt and he was suddenly uncomfortable. He pulled himself up with his crutch and turned back towards the estate. He stopped, realizing he did not want to go back, even as a cool breath hit him in the face, making him shudder. Though it would be foolish to overexert his injured leg, he decided to take a walk down to the river and let his thoughts settle. He knew the only way to figure out Diana was to approach her with the same determination he used in all other aspects of his life.

He had much going for him in his life; he was alive, on his way to recovery, and had been recognized by his Cohort Commander. And yet, in spite of all the good in his life, he felt hollow and lost inside. It was an emptiness that had consumed him for some time and he knew not if it would ever leave him. He gazed up at the clouds as he hobbled down the dirt road, not caring if anyone knew where he was going or not. Like the time he had been there before when under mental duress, the skies were dark, the wind blowing gently, but no rain fell.

CHAPTER XIX

▼

REVELATIONS

Artorius looked on as Diana gazed down the blade of the spatha. It was a good sword; a bit too ornate perhaps, but a finely crafted and serviceable weapon nonetheless.

On a table next to her was her dagger. It was honed razor sharp, as always. She hefted it in the palm of her hand. It was a standard issue legionary dagger, given to her by her cousin, Proculus, years before. Though used by many soldiers as a tool, it served as a valuable sidearm as well. For Diana it was perfect; small enough to hide, yet lethal.

Artorius stepped into the stables where Diana was examining her new weapon. He was awestruck once again when he saw her. She wore a loose-fitting shirt and riding breaches, not unlike those worn by Gallic women. Her breaches were cut off at mid-thigh, which drew his attention immediately. Her legs were well defined with muscle, though still looked soft to the touch. Her arms were similarly shaped, and her chest and shoulders looked strong. In short, she exuded both elegance and power. He breathed a deep sigh to himself.

Quietly he walked towards her, using a rail to support himself. When he was near, she spun around, her sword coming straight for him. In a flash his gladius, which he wore out of habit, was out and he blocked the blow. A sinister smile crossed Diana's face as she followed up with two quick jabs and a backhand slash.

Artorius blocked all of these easily enough, though he was surprised by her speed and tenacity.

"You have a natural skill with a weapon," he said calmly. Diana, with equal calm, sheathed her dagger as Artorius returned his gladius to its scabbard.

"When you live on an estate, you tend to grow soft. If you want to leave that estate, you must remain sharp, both in wit and physical tenacity," she replied. "I kept this weapon as a means of payment from that vile Greek you slew. A good cavalry weapon, this."

"It is indeed," the Decanus concurred.

"The hand guard is plated in gold, the pommel silver," Diana observed. "And the hand grip is not wrapped in leather. It is a rough substance, I don't know what. But what I do know is that it allows the wielder to keep a firmer grip. This weapon cost a fortune to make; a fortune I doubt that Greek had."

"I highly doubt that he was the original owner of that sword," Artorius replied.

"Then I wonder who was?" Diana said quietly as she ran her fingers along the blade. She then turned abruptly to face Artorius, cocking her head slightly as she leaned against the rail.

"They say you are one of the best close combat fighters to have ever lived," she continued. "Sorry if my way of testing that seemed a little barbaric." Artorius smiled and shook his head.

"Not at all. I too must remain sharp and tenacious, if I am to return to the legions as anything useful. I have to say, your actions against the gladiators took a lot of courage." Diana hung her head, frowning.

"I am utterly shamed by my actions, for I failed in my charge. I flatter myself that I am stronger than most and unafraid to fight. However, I am still a woman and was reminded of my physical limitations."

"What if we got rid of those limitations?" Artorius asked. Diana looked at him puzzled.

"What do you mean?" she asked.

"Brute strength alone does not make one a good fighter," he replied. She laughed as he said that.

"Kind of an odd thing for someone your size to say, don't you think?" Diana gazed at his thick, muscular frame as she said that. His tunic was tight-fitting in the chest, and his arms looked as if they were about to rip right through the short sleeves. Given the size of his powerful muscles, she figured he had to outweigh most men of his height by a good fifty pounds easily. Artorius looked himself over and shrugged.

"Well it *does* help," he answered. "What I'm getting at is that aside from strength, there is speed, agility, stamina and above all skill required to make a good fighter. When we fought in Germania a few years ago, almost all of us were dwarfed in size by the barbarians we fought. In spite of this, we still destroyed them with what some would consider contemptuous ease."

"So what are you suggesting?" Diana asked, smiling wryly. Artorius returned the smile and drew his gladius once more.

✶   ✶   ✶   ✶

Felix woke from his slumber to the sound of the door creaking open. He tried to sit upright as Centurion Macro walked in, but the pain in his abdomen prevented him from doing so. Tierney placed a protective hand on his shoulder.

"Centurion Macro, sir," Felix said through clenched teeth as he fought through the pain.

"How are you, Felix?" Macro asked as Tierney applied a damp cloth to the legionary's forehead.

"I've been better, sir," Felix replied, forcing a smile. Macro then turned his gaze towards Tierney. The young Gallic women glanced up at him and swallowed, not sure what to make of the Centurion.

"You are the one whose sister my legionary swore an oath to protect," he said after a brief pause. Tierney lowered her head, suddenly feeling like she was on trial.

"Forgive me," she replied, "I did not know who else to turn to. All I wanted was to save my little sister ... dear Kiana." She tried to force the tears back, but to no avail; images of Kiana's slain body clouded her vision. Macro placed a reassuring hand on her shoulder.

"You have done no wrong, child," he said. She looked up at him once more. "We do all we can to protect those we love. I am sorry for your loss."

"As much as it pains me to admit this," Tierney began, "Kiana brought about her own death. Her mind was poisoned beyond the ability to see reason. I only hope that she found some redemption before the end."

"She did," Felix spoke up. "She tried to save me before ..." he elected not to finish the sentence.

"The Lady Diana also said your sister made things right before the end," Macro said. Tierney tried to smile through her tears. The Centurion then motioned towards the door with his head. "Leave us; I wish to speak with Legionary Felix alone."

"Yes sir," Tierney replied eyes on the floor as she left. As soon as the door was closed Macro turned back to his stricken soldier once more.

"I am sorry sir," Felix said when Macro did not speak further. Macro looked at him inquisitively.

"What do you have to be sorry for?"

"I failed, sir. I failed to keep my oath; I let Kiana die. And I am of no use to you in my present condition."

"The doctor says your wound will heal over time," Macro interjected. "So you just might be of some use to us after all." A half grin on the Centurion's face put Felix at ease. "You did all you could, son. Your promise to Lady Tierney may have been foolish, but I cannot fault you for it."

"She's not *Lady* Tierney, sir," Felix corrected. "Her father disowned her."

"So he did," Macro replied with a contemplative frown. "His loss; she is a good woman. She would have come herself to try to save her sister, had she the means to do so. As I was saying, I cannot fault you for the promise you made. You did what you knew was right."

"Thank you sir," Felix replied, forcing a partial smile through his pain.

"Just know that if you make any more such promises of this magnitude without consulting me or Sergeant Praxus, I'll reopen that wound of yours!" Macro called over his shoulder as he left the room. Tierney was waiting outside, her head lowered, fidgeting with her hands. Macro gave her a reassuring pat on the shoulder and nodded for her to go back into the room. She immediately rushed inside, closed the door, and knelt by Felix's side, taking his hand in hers.

"Is everything alright?" she asked. Felix replied with a smile.

"Everything's fine, love."

✳   ✳   ✳   ✳

Artorius watched as the Third Cohort formed up and made ready to begin its long march back to the Rhine. Replacements from the Second Legion, Augusta had already taken over their billets in Lugdunum. He was still unable to walk without the aid of a crutch, and he knew it would be some time before he was fit to march any distance at all. He limped his way over to the Second Century, to say goodbye to his friends. It would be at least several weeks before he was fit to travel again, even by horse.

"Take care of the men while I am gone," he told Magnus as he clasped his hand. His friend nodded in reply.

"I think we may just be able to survive without you." Artorius laughed and shook his head.

"Think of it as your first chance at independent leadership," he replied. "I already told Flaccus you would assist him with recruit training as well, should we pick up any recruits while I'm gone."

"Just don't enjoy yourself too much, old friend," Magnus remarked. "Okay, perhaps just a little bit! We all know that Lady Diana has quite the affection for you. All the lads have seen it." Artorius' face turned red.

"You read too much into things, Brother. She may be grateful to me, and she is kind enough, but there is no affection there, *trust me.* You know she has asked me to teach her how to fight with a gladius?" It was Magnus' turn to laugh.

"Just make sure she doesn't hurt you too bad," he said. "She looks like the type that could give many of the lads here a run for it."

"I'd let her hurt me," Valens thought aloud. Just then Macro rode up and dismounted his horse. He stuck out his hand, which Artorius took.

"I am sorry to not be coming with you, Sir," Artorius said. Macro snorted at that.

"No you're not," he replied. "You've got a rather comfortable billet for the next few weeks. I suggest you make the most of it, because I intend to put you back to work where you belong once you get back. It's a funny thing really. Proculus was the one who insisted that you stay here to convalesce, even though Felix is coming back with us." As if on cue, a covered cart rolled by. The young legionary lay in the back fast asleep, young Tierney lying next to him, her arm around his chest. Artorius smiled, even if it was a sad one.

"Don't know what I am supposed to make of that," Artorius said with a slight frown as he turned back to his Centurion.

"Make whatever you wish of it," Macro replied. "In all seriousness, you earned the right to take some time off, Artorius. You have not asked for a single day's furlough in the eight years you have been with us, and this will do you good. I had to force you to take leave the last time …" he stopped himself as he saw Artorius wince. Macro immediately regretted his words, remembering the young Decanus' emotionally painful tenure when he went home. "I am sorry; I did not mean to bring up any bad memories. Still, it's all the more reason for you to make the most of your time here." Artorius gave a sad smile and nodded.

"I have acquired a horse for you to ride back on, to be deducted from your pay of course," Macro continued with a grin. "You've got four weeks to begin your journey back to Cologne. I want to see you as soon as you arrive. Take care of yourself." As soon as he mounted his horse, Macro donned his helmet and saluted his Sergeant in a sign of respect. Artorius returned the salute and his Centurion took his place at the head of the formation.

"*Cohort!*" Proculus shouted.

"*Century!*" all of the Centurions sounded off.

"Forward ... march!"

Artorius stayed where he was, watching the Third Cohort begin its march. As the Third Century passed by, Vitruvius leaned down from his horse and clasped his hand. No words needed to be said. Vitruvius just smiled and winked at his former protégé. Artorius did not move until the last ranks of the Cohort were out of sight. It was then that he noticed his leg was in pain once again. Even with the crutch, it hurt to stand on for any length of time. He hobbled over to the house, where servants helped him into bed. He was left restless and uneasy. He did not like being away from his friends like this. But then he heard the words of his Centurion echoing in his mind. A slight grin crossed his face as he decided he would in fact make the most of his furlough.

$$* \quad * \quad * \quad *$$

"Now, the first thing you need to do is assume a good fighting stance." Artorius was thrilled to be doing this! Here was the woman of his dreams, and he was teaching her to fight. He also reasoned that by teaching Diana how to wield a gladius or spatha, he could keep his own skills as an instructor at least partially sharp. He had acquired a pair of training gladii, and had had a training stake made out by the orchard. Padding had been added to the stake as well, so that it could be effectively used for punching. Artorius figured Diana would never wield a legionary shield, however he knew that by teaching her to punch with her left hand, she would be more than able to fend off just about any adversary. Diana stood with her feet shoulder-width apart, her right leg back slightly.

"Good," Artorius observed. "Now you want to keep your weapon close to your side, with your arm bent and the point facing forward. Remember, the gladius is primarily a stabbing weapon. We rarely slash with it, though if kept sharp it can cleave through arms and legs readily enough."

He then walked Diana through the rudimentary basics of fighting with the gladius. He had her keep her left hand up by her head, her elbow in. She learned how to effectively punch with her left hand, and to follow it up with a rapid stab with her weapon. Artorius was very much impressed. Years of horseback riding had given Diana superior leg strength and balance. She proved agile and quick in her strikes. Like he did with his recruits, he made her stand and strike her target again and again, testing her conditioning. He was surprised at how long she managed to last initially. Granted she did not have the strength or stamina of a fully trained legionary, however she did last longer than many recruits; more than enough to impress him.

By the time he told her to rest, her arms were shaking, her legs wobbly. Her hair was unkempt and sweat ran down her forehead. Indeed her entire body was drenched in sweat. She placed her hands on her knees, and found she was gasping for air. Artorius was partially aroused by the sight. He noticed that her left hand was red and battered, though Diana did not complain.

Finally, a woman with some stamina and fortitude, he thought to himself.

"That's enough for today," he said aloud.

The next days were more of the same. Diana's body felt like it was about to collapse from exhaustion by the end of it, yet still she refused to quit. Artorius demanded more from her physically than she had ever been asked to give in her entire life. She had only been training for a week, and already was becoming quicker with the gladius, with her conditioning improving as well.

At the end of an afternoon session Diana elected to take a walk through the grove to try and cool her body down. Soon she felt dizzy again, and she found herself leaning against a tree, vomiting uncontrollably. Artorius had just started to walk back towards the main house, when he heard Diana's physical distress. He smiled to himself and shook his head. Using his crutch, he walked over to where he could see her leaning against a tree, her body shaking.

"Are you alright?" he asked, walking up to her. Diana raised her hand for him to stop, and then began gagging once again.

"I'll be fine," she finally replied, taking deep breaths. Artorius walked up and ran his hand up and down her back.

"There is no shame," he told her. "Believe me; I've thrown up many a time from having overexerted myself. You have come quite a ways in such a short period of time."

"Not good enough to fight against any of you though," she replied as she leaned her head against the tree.

"Well no," he remarked as he continued to gently rub her back. "But then again, who can? I am not teaching you how to fight against legionaries; I'm teaching you … well to be honest I'm not entirely certain what I'm teaching you to fight against."

"I guess I just wanted to learn something new," Diana thought aloud as she stood upright, removing his hand from her back and quickly stepping away from him. "Thank you. I'm alright now."

As he sat under the shade of a tree by the river, Artorius struggled with feelings of awkwardness, given his latest interaction with Diana. By showing the slightest sign of physical affection towards her, he knew he had overstepped his bounds. She was a hard one to gauge. Though she had been very kind to him, there was still a barrier that existed between them. But of course this was probably unavoidable. After all, she was of the Patrician class, he a mere plebian soldier. Hell, he wasn't even a Centurion; at least then he could show that he was advancing himself well enough along to be worthy of her. He then wondered if he misread Proculus' intentions all along, that perhaps this was simply convalescence and nothing more. Diana had quite extensive knowledge when it came to medicines and treating injuries. It stood to reason that she took care for him and not risk reopening the wound on his leg by traveling too soon.

He tossed a stone into the water and gazed at the ripples. He then thought too about how neither ever referred to the other by their given names. She mostly called him by his rank, and he had always addressed her as "My Lady." It was only proper of course. He then saw her walking along the path towards him, though he pretended not to notice.

"I came to see how you are doing, Sergeant," Diana said as she approached.

"Just relaxing and enjoying the evening," he replied. At that moment he felt incredibly awkward. She sat down on the fallen tree next to him, his eyes still fixed on the current. His breathing was shaky and he could not for the life of him figure out why he was so nervous around her.

"You're quite the fascinating one," Diana continued. "You are a legionary from the ranks, but yet you appear to be as well educated as any patrician."

"My father is a teacher," Artorius explained, trying to regain control over his wavering voice. He closed his eyes and took a deep breath. It was now or never, he reasoned. He forced a coy grin and turned to face her, placing his hand on hers.

"I cannot help but wonder," he said, "how is it that someone so beautiful is devoid of a husband?" Diana's face darkened, her temper soaring. She smacked his hand away.

"How *dare* you ask me such a wicked thing!" she snapped standing up and turning to face him, her face red with anger. Artorius was beside himself and struggled to find the right words.

"My Lady, I am sorry; my intent was not to offend."

"Well offend me you have, *Sergeant*," Diana hissed. Artorius winced as she placed emphasis on his rank, driving the social wedge further between them. He was surprised that she did not storm off; rather she continued her diatribe. "Do you not know why I am alone; why the only use anyone has for me is to housesit an estate in the middle of *fucking* Gaul; of my failures to my family and to Rome?"

"My Lady please forgive me; you are no failure ..." his words were cut short as he tried to stand, a blinding pain causing his leg to spasm. His face twisted in pain as he fell back onto his seat. Diana swallowed hard, regretting her outburst. She took a deep breath through her nose before continuing.

"It is the duty of every Roman woman to help her family to pass on their line," she began. "I was married once, for a very brief time. It was a good match, and both our families looked to benefit greatly. It was soon after this that I failed in my role as a wife and Roman patrician. I am afflicted with a curse; a curse that the Fates have not allowed me to bear a child. No line can continue from my body, and I am of no use to *any* man. Every day I pray that my sister Claudia is not cursed as well."

"I am sorry to hear that," Artorius said, trying to console her. "*I* do not think you are cursed." Diana pretended not to hear him.

"Proculus is but a second cousin to me, and yet he took pity on me. I am *tired* of everyone's pity. He asked me to manage his Gallic estate while his wife is in Rome. That is what I've become; no better than a mere housekeeper, and yet I failed in that charge as well ..." Her voice trailed off as she fought to control her emotions.

"You were facing one hundred armed men!" Artorius retorted. "What were you supposed to do, fight them off by yourself?"

"It matters not," Diana replied her voice quiet, eyes lowered and arms folded across her chest. Artorius forced himself to his feet and took a step towards her.

"Well *I* don't see you as afflicted," he said. She raised her eyes and glared at him. The anger and hurt they conveyed was unnerving, but still he persisted. "It is not like you consciously asked to be this way. And besides, there are those who still care for you, regardless of your ability to bear children." Diana looked at the ground once more and slowly shook her head.

"I see you still have much to learn," she stated, her voice calm once more. To Artorius it was as cold as ice. "The idealism you frontier soldiers have the privilege of enjoying has little role in Roman society. You've become too detached by living amongst barbarians that you start to take on some of their values and beliefs."

"And are all of those beliefs bad?" Artorius asked. "I learned a lesson not too long ago; and it was most painful for me. I learned that when you love someone you do not wait for politics to dictate whether it is right or not, nor do you brush it off as meaningless. Like you, I have suffered loss; a loss that still haunts me with regret to this day. Do not allow what happened to me happen to you. I allowed she who loved me to be taken away. The Fates cursed us for it ..." He slowly sat down as Diana continued to stand in silence. "You can avoid this fate, you know; if you will only allow me to help you ..."

"I'm sorry, but you cannot help me," she said quietly, her eyes fixated on the slow-moving current. "And I do not *want* your help!" Immediately she regretted her words, for they were not true. She just could not bring herself to show her affections towards him, as desperately as she wanted to.

"You're right," he replied, forcing himself to his feet in resignation. Artorius turned and limped away and it was not just his leg that hurt him.

Diana was taken aback by his words, her eyes wide and lips slightly parted in surprise. She sat with her head in her hands, a feeling of hopelessness overcoming her. It was then that she remembered her promise to Kiana. It was a far greater thing that the young girl had forgiven Artorius and found redemption before her untimely death than it was for Diana to simply open her heart to him.

Suddenly she was tired; tired of being afraid, tired of being alone, tired of feeling like the constant failure in life. In that moment she let go of the bonds that held her soul captive.

It was an unfamiliar feeling for Artorius; one that he thought only existed in story books for children and spineless poets. His attraction for Diana went far beyond the physical, even though he found her to be more attractive than any woman he had ever known. No, this was something different, and it troubled him. Was this what his father felt for Juliana, or what Metellus had felt for Rowana? And was it what he may have felt for Camilla at one time? He certainly had his regrets about Camilla, but this feeling was not the same as what he had felt for her. There was a bond of sorts that he felt with Diana; an emotional bond that drew him to her. He knew this was a complete waste because there was no way she could ever have similar feelings for him. Certainly she probably had affection for him because he did save her life, but that was all. Diana kept an emotional barrier up that she allowed no one to get past, let alone a plebian soldier.

Artorius' heart ached worse than his leg as he sat down on a rock that overlooked another part of the stream. This part was unfamiliar to him; there was a small waterfall that he fixed his gaze on while a pair of rabbits scampered through the tall grass on the far side. He let out a deep sigh as he looked out into the setting sun that had fallen behind the hills. He shivered slightly as darkness fell on him. He heard the rustle in the grass behind him and the snap of twigs. He turned to see Diana standing behind him, her hands folded and a sad smile on her face.

"My Lady," he said turning his eyes back towards the running waterfall. As Diana slowly walked towards him, he closed his eyes and listened intently to the sound of her breathing, which was shaky. She knelt behind him, her arms trembling as she wrapped them around his shoulders and clasped her hands across his chest. He felt her breath on his neck and ear as she rested her head on his shoulder.

"Artorius, I am so sorry," she whispered, causing him to shudder. It was the first time she had ever used his given name. Without thinking, he turned and kissed her. She did not pull away; instead she kissed him back while he took her in his arms. It was impossible to comprehend what they were doing, but yet there it was. They continued to kiss for some time, and as they did Artorius' emotions soared. He caressed her back while she stroked the back of his head and sides of his face and neck. Diana continued to kiss him as she pulled him to his feet. He barely even noticed the pain in his leg. They held hands as they found their way through the woods and onto the road that led back to the estate. He used his crutch to support his injured leg while Diana held his other hand close; the fingers of her free hand gently caressing his arm. He trembled at how good it felt for he was a stranger to such affection and intimacy.

"How long have you felt this way for me?" Diana asked after a brief silence. Artorius took a deep breath and considered his reply.

"Since the first time I saw you in the Lugdunum market," he replied. "I felt a strong attraction to you from the moment I laid eyes on you."

"So all your trips to the estate were not mere coincidence then?" she asked with a short laugh.

"At first they were," Artorius asserted. "Proculus saw my little mishap in the market, where I ran into that pillar ..." Diana burst out laughing while Artorius mocked being hurt. "Anyway, he probably thought it would be amusing to have me act as a courier to you after that little incident. After that I started to request the privilege. Of course it was all under the guise that I liked to ride horses and wanted some fresh air for a few days. None of the other lads ever volunteered, so it became an additional duty for me; one I must say I always took pleasure in."

"Your company was always appreciated, even if I did not always show it," Diana replied as she squeezed his hand affectionately. "And yet it took tragedy and death to bring us to appreciate those things in each other. Sad ..."

"There were too many barriers between us," Artorius observed. "And there still are. You are of the patrician class, and I a common soldier."

"I am a divorcee as well, with an affliction that makes me an unsuitable wife to any." Diana's face fell as a tear came to her eye. Artorius stopped and turned to face her as she let out a short sob. He ran the back of his hand over her cheek.

"Well if it makes you feel any better," he said, "I have no patience for children, so I certainly do not see you as afflicted. Besides, if I get the desire to pass on my family name I'll adopt someone when I'm an old man ... preferably somebody already grown and established." Diana let out a short laugh and tried to wipe some of her tears away. He put his arm around her and laid her head on his shoulder. "Come here." Diana wrapped an arm around his waist as they continued their walk. Artorius was grateful for the added support, for his bad leg was starting to trouble him again.

"Just tell me one thing," Diana said. "Tell me that you were not drawn to me merely because you felt sorry for me."

"Not at all," Artorius replied. "I feel sorry for many, but that does not mean I fall for them. No, there was something in your aura that drew me to you … that and I admit I was quite taken by you physically!" They shared a laugh as Diana kissed him gently on the cheek. They walked in silence for some time before Diana spoke again.

"Tell me about her," she said. Artorius thought hard about what he would say.

"Her name was Camilla," he replied. "We grew up together in Ostia." He then decided if he was going to tell Diana about her, he would tell her everything. Diana held him closer as he described Camilla's death and when he gave his medallion to her daughter.

"A bit of irony that the medallion that Camilla gave to me, that I in turn gave to little Marcia bears the image of your namesake," he observed.

"I think perhaps Diana has always been a part of your life," she replied, looking up into his face.

"I wish she could continue to be," Artorius said, Diana smiling at the double-meaning of his words.

Eventually they reached the gates of the estate. Proximo came out to meet her, but smiled and walked back inside when he saw the couple together. As they walked inside, lamps dimly lit the upstairs corridor. Artorius was surprised when they kept walking past the guest quarters that he had been staying in. They stopped shortly past them; Diana taking her head from his shoulder and placing both arms around his waist.

"You don't have to stay in the guest rooms tonight," she said, a gleam in her eye. Artorius grinned and kissed her affectionately on the lips.

"Where to my Lady?"

"D … Drusus, you are not l … looking well," Claudius said as he passed his cousin in the forum. They two men had not seen each other in a few weeks, and Claudius immediately noticed the lack of color in Drusus' face. Though it was a warm day, he kept his toga wrapped close to him, as if he were cold. Their mutual friend, Herod Agrippa, accompanied him.

"I don't feel good either," Drusus replied before succumbing to a coughing fit.

"It's too much drinking, old friend," Herod chided, a look of concern on his face. Drusus looked back at him and gave a snort.

"Well look who's talking!" he retorted. "A bit of a hypocrite are we?" Herod raised his hands up, mocking his innocence.

"Hey, I only accompany you on your little debacles because your father asked me to keep an eye on you ... okay and I admit you do know where the best brothels are. Still, if you kept your pallet to simple wine and not that abominable sewage you drink every night, you might not get so sick all the time."

"Yeah, well it's all stuff that comes from your friends in the east," Drusus retorted as he resumed coughing once more. Herod glanced over at Claudius and shook his head. Though he tried to remain good-natured, Claudius knew their Judean friend was deeply worried about Drusus.

"W ... why don't you b ... both join me for dinner this evening?" Claudius asked. In truth he did not get to see his friends nearly enough. He also hoped that perhaps by keeping Drusus away from the dens of iniquity he might be able to help restore his health.

"An excellent idea!" Herod said with much enthusiasm. Drusus replied with another coughing fit.

"No, I don't think I'll make it," he said after spitting out a glob of phlegm. "I would love to, but I think Livilla has some new type of medicine she wants me to try. She said it will help my cough, but may make me fall asleep. I won't be very good company if I sleep through your hospitality, now will I?"

"You're a ... always good company, Drusus," Claudius replied. His brother-in-law smiled weakly before resuming his coughing fit.

"By Mercury, this concoction Livilla's got better work!" he said with exasperation as he walked off.

"Well I will certainly meet you tonight," Herod said. "I'm not one to pass up a free meal, you know." He winked at Claudius as he started to turn back towards where Drusus was walking away. Claudius grabbed him by the shoulder.

"Keep an eye h ... him," he said, his voice chalked full of concern. "He hasn't been well for some time and I would hate to think of something h ... happening to him."

"It would be a dark day for the Emperor, and for Rome," Herod emphasized. "Drusus is the only viable heir your uncle has. Should anything happen to him ..." He shook his head soberly and walked away.

✳   ✳   ✳   ✳

The sky was red as the sun lay low on the horizon. Artorius walked along the path, his arm interlocked with Diana's. His leg still ached, but he refused to use the walking stick anymore. Diana helped support his weight, in spite of his protests. Artorius clasped her hand, interlocking his fingers with hers.

"I'll be returning to the Legion soon," he said glumly. Diana squeezed his hand hard.

"I know," she replied quietly. The weeks had passed far too quickly for them.

They came to a patch of ground, which sloped gently upward a few dozen feet. At the top was a large oak, and beyond was a commanding view of the entire valley. The sun cast its glow on the horizon as it slowly set. Diana guided Artorius over to the oak. He leaned back against it as she set her basket down and opened it. Inside was a blanket and a bottle of wine.

"It is a pity that Rome will not formally recognize you for having saved my life, given that I am a woman," she said as she reached for him. Her fingers gripped the back of his head while her thumbs gently massaged his temples. Artorius' eyes widened in surprise, yet he was unable to stifle a moan, it felt so good. His breathing was becoming heavy, his eyes closed, his heartbeat quickening, much in the same way that it had just before battle. He placed his hands on her sides and pulled her slightly closer to him. Every fiber of him wanted her. He felt her one hand glide down to his shoulder, where it started to massage him, while her other hand caressed the back of his neck. He started to run his hands up her sides, when he suddenly stopped. He then looked down, saddened.

"What is it?" she asked.

"Diana …" he started. His mind and his heart were flooded with conflicting emotions, soaring elation and deep despair. " …I'm afraid." She looked at him puzzled, yet still continued to caress him.

"Afraid … of what?"

"Afraid that I may be falling for you." He looked her in the eyes, his own suddenly wet with emotions he had never experienced before. He had once thought that he had feelings for a courtesan that he associated with in Rome at one time. But that had only been powerful lust. He was no stranger to women in the physical sense, but this was completely alien to him. Plus, what would he do once he returned to his fortress on the Rhine? His fear was compounded by the thoughts of never seeing this woman again. He had fought so hard against building up any feelings for her. And yet he had failed, and failed miserably.

"Well I have already fallen for you," Diana replied. She then brought her lips to his and kissed him passionately. As his passion for Diana completely unleashed itself, Artorius pulled her close to him, returning her kiss firmly, yet gently and with much affection. Normally he became a savage animal when he became intimate with women, yet now he found his passion was borne out of more than just primal lust. There was a sense of affection that he had never felt before.

In spite of the impossibilities that seemed to loom over any future together, something inside told him that everything would be alright. Never in his life had Artorius been superstitious, yet suddenly he believed that everything that had happened to him recently was meant to be. He was meant to lead the attack on the residence. It was predestined that he would get wounded. And above all it was fated that he save this woman's life.

It was reckless and impossible to conceive, yet as he held her close, kissing her deeply, Artorius realized that he did in fact love Diana. Though her physical beauty was truly stunning, his feelings for her stemmed from the beauty that dominated her very soul. The invincible soldier of Rome had met his match.

Chapter XX

▼

The Journey Home

Summer was in full bloom as Artorius rode towards the city of Cologne and the fortress of the Twentieth Legion. He took a deep breath and sighed audibly as the city came into sight. It had been more than three years since he had left, and much had changed. Cologne no longer looked like a frontier outpost, but a thriving metropolis. Buildings had been modernized, the streets were now paved in many places, and the "dirty" feel of the town had evaporated. As Artorius rode through the streets, he saw that the locals had started adopting more of the Roman style of dress and appearance. There was a mix of Roman tunics, as well as traditional garb worn by the men; women of the city's upper classes could be seen wearing the same type of stola seen in Rome as well as similar hair styles.

Outside the gate were a row of houses; many of which belonged to soldiers within the legion. He saw Magnus' sister, Svetlana, walking down the road towards one, a basket full of berries under her arm. She smiled and waved at him as he rode by. Her servant, Erin, was pulling weeds from the garden in front of the house and did not notice Artorius as he rode by. Little Tynan, who had grown much in a short period of time, was running around a tree, laughing while being chased by Olaf, who had elected to stay in Cologne with his grandchildren for the time being.

Once he arrived, Artorius had no trouble navigating his way through the legionary fortress. He turned his mount over to the stable hands and negotiated with the Master of Horse a stall rental for his horse before making his way over to the Second Century's barracks. He walked into the main office to see Sergeant Rufio sitting behind the Signifier's desk. Rufio looked up from his paperwork and smiled when he saw him.

"Ah, Optio Artorius," he said as he rose to his feet, extending his hand, "good to have you back!"

"Yes, it is good to be back," Artorius replied. It was only a half-truth. Though he was glad to be back amongst the familiarity of his home in the legions, he found himself deeply missing Diana. How long had it taken him to win her over; two years? And now she was gone. He figured his feelings would fade with time, though at that moment he had his doubts. Twice in his life he had allowed himself to love, and twice it had been taken from him. Still, he knew that there would be plenty for him to do, and that by keeping busy he could more easily forget about her. Of course he knew he was merely living in denial, but what else could he do? He cursed himself for simply trading one pain for another; the regret surrounding Camilla's death now replaced by sadness at the loss of Diana.

"So what are you doing here, Rufio?" he asked. "Where is Camillus?"

"A lot has changed in the time you were convalescing," Rufio replied. "Camillus is the new Aquilifer for the Legion. He moved over there last week. I was selected to replace him. Seems some asshole told Macro about my father having been a bookkeeper and that I knew a thing or two about numbers!" Artorius grinned and nodded. He was glad for Camillus, seeing that the Aquilifer was his life's dream in the Legion; a position steeped in honor, answering only to the Centurion Primus Pilus. Artorius then furrowed his brow in thought and gave the new Signifier a hard look.

"Rufio, why did you address me as *Optio* when I walked in?" he asked. Rufio's grin broadened.

"Like I said, a lot has changed while you were gone. Flaccus retired and disappeared off the face of the planet. Macro immediately chose you to succeed him. I made a note of it on your pay chit. You will be getting about a month's worth of back-pay, minus the expense of your horse! Your promotion has been back-dated to the day Flaccus retired."

"I don't understand," Artorius remarked. "What about Statorius? He was next in line for the Optionate, I'm certain of it!"

"Yes, Statorius has moved up as well. He is working for Vitruvius now as his Optio. It's been quite hectic, what with a turnover occurring at every Principal rank within the Century; Praxus is the new Tesserarius, by the way. Oh, and you have been replaced as Chief Weapons Instructor. Macro said with as big of a shakeup as this has caused--Camillus' promotion came completely unexpected--he said no way in hell is he going to let you take on both duties."

"So who replaced me?" Artorius was concerned. He wanted to make certain that whoever replaced him was competent enough to warrant the position. Plus the total realization of his having been selected for Optio seemed surreal.

"Me," a voice said from the doorway. Artorius turned to see his Nordic friend, standing in the doorway.

"*Sergeant* Magnus," Rufio remarked. Artorius laughed out loud, reached out and embraced his friend hard, slapping him on the back.

"It's about time!" he said with enthusiasm. "I take it they made you a section leader as well?" Magnus nodded.

"I took your place, as a matter of fact. Thankfully I picked up a couple of new guys, so I've almost got a full crew. Stop by and see me later; right now I've got to go over duty rosters with Praxus. Funny how most of us were at one time in the same section and now we're running the entire Century ... Oh, and just so you know your stuff has already been moved over to the Optio's room." Artorius shook his head as Magnus walked out. Indeed everything had changed overnight it seemed.

"At any rate, you need to go report to Macro. He said he wants to see you right away," Rufio said, nodding his head towards the Centurion's quarters. Artorius took a deep breath and knocked on the door.

"Enter!" he heard his Centurion boom. He opened the door to see Macro seated behind his desk, working some polish into his armor. It was a new set of squamata scale armor; highly ornate and very expensive.

"You know, everyone tells me I should let one of the servants do this for me," Macro remarked. "However I find that there is a certain amount of personal pride to be taken in caring for one's own armor. I have a lot more faith in my own abilities, plus I'm not so lazy that I cannot take care of my own equipment. Have a seat." He motioned Artorius towards a chair in front of his desk. The newly appointed Optio readily accepted, his leg still giving him pains from time-to-time.

"So how was your journey?"

"It wasn't too bad," Artorius replied. "My leg still hurts, though it will probably always be that way. I have to tell you Macro I am completely surprised, but also deeply honored, that you selected me to replace Flaccus as Optio."

"Well you shouldn't be surprised," Macro replied, handing the armor to a servant, who carried it to the Centurion's quarters. "In my mind, there was no one else. I know this Century is going through tumultuous times, what with every senior officer moving up or moving on. And with my selection for Primus Ordo pending, we need to get this Century on its feet as quickly as possible. Truth be told, Vitruvius wanted you over in the Third, and I was going to keep Statorius. Proculus put a stop to that immediately. He said you were too close personally with Vitruvius, and that that could lead to a potential conflict of interest. So it looks like we're stuck working together." He winked at the last remark.

"So when will you be leaving us?" Artorius asked.

"I don't know for sure, but probably not for at least another year or two. Don't worry, we have time to get you and all the other senior officers assimilated. We had to promote a number of younger legionaries to Decanus as well, and they will need time to get up to speed.

"I won't lie to you Artorius; your reputation is growing rapidly. It started at Angrivarii, when you killed the Cherusci war chief, Ingiomerus. It exploded when you swept the Legion Champion tournament; and your actions during and after the Sacrovir Revolt has not gone unnoticed. Saving the life of Lady Diana was no small feat either. I must tell you though, that while this has garnered your status within certain circles, most importantly with the men of this Century, it has led to animosity from others." Artorius looked confused at the Centurion's last remark.

"What do you mean? Why should anyone bear any resentment towards me? All I have ever done is strived to be the best legionary I could be, and if that has meant taking the lead when needed, then so be it!" He felt his anger rising at the thought of fellow soldiers resenting him for doing his job.

"First off, your age is a factor," Macro replied. "I went through the same thing myself when I made Centurion, though given the circumstances; we all had more important things to worry about, what with the rebellion on the Rhine and the wars with the Cherusci. How old are you, Artorius?"

"I'm twenty-five, what of it, Sir?" Macro raised his hands, emphasizing his point.

"You have no political connections whatsoever. Fact of the matter is, you are the youngest Optio in the Third Cohort, and though I have not verified this for certain, you may be the youngest in the Legion. No one gets promoted through the ranks that quickly without some type of connections back in Rome. You are by no means the youngest to ever be promoted to the Optionate, however in almost every case of those who do make it by your age, they are either the sons of powerful magistrates, or else they have sponsors within the Equestrian or Senatorial classes who are looking out for their careers. You have none of these." This last remark was not entirely correct, as Artorius was well-connected with Pontius Pilate; though the Tribune was still very young in his own career. A sinking feeling of understanding came upon Artorius.

"What you are telling me is, there are those within the Legion who are connected as you say, and they harbor animosity towards me for having been selected ahead of them." Macro nodded in acknowledgment. Artorius immediately rose to his feet, his anger boiling over.

"*Gods damn it!* What right do any of those bastards have to say who a Centurion should or should not choose as his Optio? Is it *my* fault they have failed to earn promotion based on their own merits, that they look to someone else to make their careers for them? I cannot help it if their own abilities are so fucking pathetic that they cannot stand on their own. Who are these men?" Macro shook his head, his own expression still calm.

"At ease, *Optio.* Sit down and relax. Take consolation in that none of the dissenters are from this Century. The men were unanimous in their enthusiasm to have you as their Optio. They wouldn't stop chanting your name when I broke the news to them! I think most of them are hoping you will move up to succeed me, when my time comes to move to the First Cohort."

"Do you think that will happen?" Artorius asked, regaining his composure and taking his seat.

"If I have anything to say about it, you will rise to the Centurionate at an even younger age than I did. Unfortunately, I don't have much say in who replaces me when I go. My gut instincts tell me that they will put some political appointee in my place, just to make an example; demonstrate who has the real power within the Legions.

"That being said, once you get comfortable in your duties as Optio, I am going to start training you in how to be a Centurion. Artorius, I have watched you closely since the day you came to us from the recruit depot in Ostia. Vitruvius was the first to notice your real potential. He told me, 'Keep an eye on this one.' Statorius placed more and more responsibilities on you as time went by. You were able to seamlessly take over the duties of section leader from him, as well as Chief Weapons Instructor. Regardless of who ends up taking over this Century when I am gone, the men will know who really leads them. You were never meant to be just a rank-and-file legionary, Artorius. You are destined to *lead* soldiers of Rome!" Artorius lowered and shook his head.

"Macro, my transition through the ranks has felt like it was anything but seamless. There have been so many days that I have felt like I was going to be swallowed up by it all."

"Welcome to my world," Macro replied. "Thing is, you know your own faults and shortcomings. You acknowledge them, and you work to improve them. None of us are perfect, though where you excel is that you hide your doubts and your imperfections from the men. Where you make the biggest difference is they *believe* in you. And in the end, that is what really matters; not what those fools in Rome think, nor those who look to make their fame and fortune based on who their powerful friends are. No, the real measure of us as leaders and as men is in how those *we lead* perceive us."

Artorius lay on the bed of the room he had rented at the inn, contemplating everything that had happened that day. It seemed like his entire world had been turned upside down. He was indeed deeply honored that Macro had selected him to be his Optio, and that he had the entire Century's confidence and trust meant more to him than anything else. He was equally happy for his friends Praxus and Magnus, who were finally moving up through the ranks and coming into their own as well. It did seem a bit odd that he now outranked Praxus, though his old friend had told him time and again that he was glad to be working for him.

The political ramifications of his promotion deeply troubled him. He knew that the Roman army was steeped in politics, though he had been able to avoid such things for most of his career up to that point. Now he was stuck in the middle of it. Every move he made would be scrutinized by those who felt cheated that he had been promoted ahead of them, as well as those who sponsored them. Such was the dilemma in a peacetime army. With no real enemy to fight, they ended up fighting each other. Artorius could only shake his head. In his idealistic mind, these things made no sense to him. But whether he agreed with it or not, he could not change the way the establishment worked.

He then looked over at his lady companion, who was passed out next to him, lying on her stomach. She was a pretty young woman, one he had not met before. Of course with the city expanding the way it was, there was a huge influx of people that Artorius did not know. He laughed at the visible bite marks on her neck. Some habits died hard, he guessed. He gave her credit for having been a sport regarding his deviant savagery, though at one time he thought that he had broken her in half as he thoroughly violated every orifice on her body. While she had been mildly satisfying physically, he found himself feeling hollow afterwards. He was constantly looking for distractions to help him ease Diana from his mind, and he by no means wanted his only focus to be his duties. So he had found a fetching young lady that he thought would provide a suitable distraction. Sadly, he had found her wanting, even from a purely sexual standpoint.

To his best recollections, aside from a high-class courtesan that he had spent a night with in Rome many years before, Diana had been the only woman that was ever able to stand up to him physically and sexually. Most women were overwhelmed by his immense size, brutal physical power, and savage veracity; and if he could allow himself a bit of vanity, it was not just his muscles which were huge, or so he'd been told. Yet, Diana had seemed to revel in it. She was aroused by the beast inside him, and she had constantly goaded him into delving deeper into the depths of his brutality; so much so that he had had to push himself to the limit of his physical and sexual fortitude. No other woman that he knew of was able to withstand his onslaught. He wondered if it had been brought on by severe sexual repression from years of forced celibacy following her short-lived marriage when she was little more than a girl. He allowed himself a slight chuckle. A lady Diana may have been, but when it came to sex she bore an aggressive and deviant streak that could almost match his.

He sighed audibly, rolled out of bed, and got dressed. He left the inn and decided to take a walk in a nearby meadow outside the city that he knew so well. There was a full moon out that night, and the ground was well illuminated. He found his favorite tree, the one by the stream that fed downhill to the mills.

"I thought I would find you here," he heard Magnus say as he leaned back against the tree.

"Magnus, what are you doing out here?"

"Like you, taking a break from sowing some wild seed," his friend replied with a shrug. Artorius laughed at that. Magnus then looked at him seriously. "In all honesty, I knew at some point I would find you out here. You always come down here when things are troubling you."

"Been spying on me have you?" Magnus shook his head.

"No, but everyone knows it. When you cannot be found in your quarters, the gymnasium, the brothels, or any other place you spend time at, then everyone knows you are down here. So are you going to tell me what has been eating you up inside since the day you got back?" Artorius hung his head low in thought.

"You know," he began, "I am a bit ashamed to admit it."

"It's Lady Diana, isn't it?" Magnus interjected. Artorius closed his eyes and nodded his head slightly.

"What is wrong with me Magnus?" he asked. "I have *never* allowed a woman to inflict me so. After Camilla I became hardened towards women; not uncaring mind you, just not allowing myself to have any real feelings for them."

"Face it Artorius, you love this woman," Magnus replied.

"I do," Artorius acknowledged, "and I did not want to."

"Why would you say that?" Magnus asked, puzzled. "Diana is a wonderful woman. From what I saw, she treated you really well, she has class, social standing, is intelligent, and let's face it; she is pretty easy on the eyes! We are all looking for something in life, Artorius; whether we admit it consciously or not. I think in Diana you found it."

"I did indeed," Artorius remarked. "The thing is we can never be together. She is obligated to run the Proculus estate, and I am stuck here on the Rhine. Besides, she is of the Patrician class, I am not. I don't think I shall ever see her again, and

I feel empty inside because of it ..." His voice started to trail off as he stared into the churning water.

"You learned a hard lesson, old friend," Magnus replied. "But don't let it destroy all of your hopes about women. I see you still find them attractive at least in the physical sense." Artorius waved his hand dismissively.

"I try to find a distraction wherever I can. I have a rather voracious appetite when it comes to the sensual pleasures of women if you haven't noticed; although my tastes are certainly more refined than our friend Valens ... well maybe not anymore." He and Magnus shared a laugh before he continued. "You know, most women break under my strength and ferocity. Diana ... she held her own."

"At least you got some pleasant memories out of the whole thing!" Magnus remarked with a laugh. He then reached down and helped his friend to his feet. "Come on. Let's go find some more distractions together and we will break that spell you are under!" Artorius laughed and walked back towards the inn, his arm around Magnus' shoulder. They saw Praxus and Ostorius heading towards the inn, both men slightly inebriated and singing a song about a prostitute from Sicilia, while trying to hold each other up.

Artorius then remembered that he still had his room that he had paid for. He wondered if that little hussy would still be there or would she have run off into the night? It mattered not; she could be replaced easily enough. His friends, on the other hand ... well, they were more than just his friends, they were his brothers, and they was no replacing any of them. They were his rock that he built upon, for they never let him down. And when he was down, they were the ones to pick him back up again.

Not since the death of his brother and mother had Artorius ever felt such pain of loss. He wondered if Diana was indeed the only woman he would ever love; that whatever future relationships he may have with women, all would leave him hollow and lost. He shrugged his shoulder and figured that love was but a fantasy told by poets. After all, one did not marry for love in Roman society; it grew after the marriage, if it came at all.

Chapter XXI

▼

Sad Farewells

Isurium Brigantum, Capital of the Brigantes, Isle of Britain
September, A.D. 23

The Brigantes had been very kind to Milla since her arrival eight years previously. It was King Breogan – so named after an ancient king of legend – that had first found the young woman and her young son lost in the wilderness, terrified and half mad with hunger. He had recognized her as being of the people of the continent, but he did not ask any questions at the time. Instead, he took Milla and her son, Alaric, into his house. His daughter, Cartimandua, had taken to them almost immediately, particularly the young Alaric, who was but a couple years younger than she.

Breogan had no sons and had buried two wives; the second had died giving birth to his beloved daughter. As the years passed he had thought to make Milla his wife and adopt her son as his own, but Milla would not have it. Though she cared for Breogan deeply and had grown to think of Cartimandua as her own daughter, there was something in her past that she could not let go of. Breogan rarely asked her about it, seeing as how it upset her greatly. It was when a caravan of Roman merchants arrived that he guessed what in Milla's past vexed her so. Normally the Brigantes did their trading with the Roman merchants at the eastern coastal towns; however, these particular merchants had elected to come to Isurium Brigantum itself. When Milla heard where the men were from she ran away, sobbing in terror. Breogan and Alaric would later find her deep within a grove of trees, curled up on the ground with her head resting in Cartimandua's lap. The young woman gently caressed her hair and tried to console her.

"It is Rome that darkens your past, isn't it?" Breogan asked at length. Milla started to sob again while Cartimandua held her close and whispered into her ear that everything would be alright.

"The Romans murdered our people," Alaric said. All eyes turned to him, Milla shaking her head, but the boy was tired of keeping their past a secret. "We are of the Marsi; a tribe that was butchered by the legions eight years ago. My mother is Milla, wife of the war chief, Barholden. We are all that is left of our people." Milla placed her hand over her eyes, a host of painful memories overwhelming her. Breogan turned to face the lad. Alaric was fast becoming a man and was but a few inches shorter than he.

"But you are not the last of your people," the king replied. "Mallovendus, who I assume is your uncle, has ruled the remnants of the Marsi ever since the end of the wars between Arminius and Rome."

"He is my husband's brother," Milla said, desperately trying to regain her composure. She sat upright, Cartimandua keeping her hands on her shoulders. Milla then recounted her and Alaric fleeing their village when it was destroyed by the legions. She recalled in brutal detail the savage beating her father took at the hands of a legionary before he was slain; how her sister was stabbed in the back trying to flee, and her newborn niece drowning in the river. The Romans had been particularly cruel to the women, smashing many to death with rocks and clubs rather than granting them the quick death rendered by the gladius.

"Many tribes paid a terrible price during the wars," Breogan said when Milla had finished.

"I never heard what had happened after we fled," Milla replied. "I only wished to get my son as far away from that scene of death as I could. That is why I came here. The ocean stands between your people and Rome; and yet they still come."

"*Traders*, not legionaries," Cartimandua said reassuringly. Milla shook her head.

"A Roman is a Roman," she asserted, "and my fear is that they will find too much to their liking here; for if they do the legions will follow." Breogan dropped to a knee and took one of Milla's hands in his own.

"I must beg for your forgiveness, my dear," he pleaded. Cartimandua closed her eyes, for she knew what her father would say. "It is *I* who brought the Romans into my lands. We have had a trade agreement with them for years, as have many of the kingdoms of this isle. Many of the statues and décor you see in my city come from Rome; we trade goods and luxuries with them for tin, which this island has much of." Milla lowered her eyes, though she did not pull her hand away. In truth she did not know what Roman art or architecture looked like. She had never even seen a Roman until they came to murder her people.

"I know nothing of the Romans except the horrors they brought to my people," Milla replied. "They murder entire nations and dare to call it peace!"

"I wish to know more of the Romans," Alaric said. "If they do come to this land, then I should like to be ready for them." Breogan looked back at him and nodded as Milla lowered her head. Alaric knelt before his mother and took her other hand.

"Your mother's heart breaks at you leaving," Cartimandua observed as she and Alaric walked through the woods that evening.

Have you ever seen Rome?" Alaric asked, stepping over a fallen log.

"Once, a long time ago. When my grandfather was still king of the Brigantes he was a guest of the Emperor Tiberius, soon after his assumption of power. Germanicus was making ready to invade Germania and the Emperor wanted the reassurance of any allies or trading partners on the island that the tribes of Britain would stay out of the war."

"So your grandfather allied himself to Rome while my people were murdered," Alaric said quietly.

"It was not for us to pass judgment in the conflict between Rome and the tribes of Germania," Cartimandua replied sternly. "Rome was already a strong trading partner and our people had flourished because of it."

"You intend to remain allied to Rome when you succeed your father, don't you?" Alaric stated rather than asked. Cartimandua folded her arms across her chest and breathed in deeply through her nose before giving a curt response.

"Yes. Remember little brother; it is a brutal world that you are stepping back into. I am not unsympathetic to what happened to you and your mother. However, if I am to spare my people the same fate, the last thing I should do is antagonize the Empire that has been a valuable partner to my father and me.

"Your mother was right about one thing; Rome *will* come. Perhaps it will happen in our lifetime, perhaps not. The Emperor Tiberius has no ambition to expand the Empire further, but what's to say his successors will feel the same way? The whole of this island is volatile, with tribes constantly at war with each other. The Iceni are particularly troublesome. I daresay a Roman invasion would be a blessing!" Alaric was appalled by what he heard, but still he listened.

"Your Highness," the shipmaster said, surprised as he was to see King Breogan at his dock. "What pleasure brings you here?"

"A favor to ask, old friend," the king replied, his hand on Alaric's shoulder.

"Ah, and who do we have here?" the shipmaster asked, appraising the lad. Alaric was well-built for his age and gave the appearance being older than he was.

"This is the son of a close friend," Breogan explained. "He seeks passage to Rome."

"I'm willing to work, sir," Alaric spoke up. "I will earn my way, I promise you." The shipmaster looked him over once more and shrugged.

"I'm sure I can find work for you as an oarsman," he consented. "It's hard and tedious; but it pays a fair wage. We sail tomorrow at first tide. We have a number of ports to call upon before we head to Rome, though. We have a tin delivery to make to Burdigala in Gaul, where we will pick up wine to deliver to Brigantium in Hispania. After that it's a long ways to Ostia with a shipment of gold."

"I promise to serve you well," Alaric replied confidently.

The next morning as he sat working his oar he gazed out the small portside window and thought about his coming journey. Indeed there was little to do but think when an oarsman on a ship. Gaul, Hispania, possibly Corsica; all places he had never seen. From the sketching Cartimandua had shown him these lands were vast. And yet they were but a fraction of the Empire that was Rome. He knew not why he had to see the Imperial city; he felt as if there was an underlying force that was drawing him east.

$$* \quad * \quad * \quad *$$

The light had gone out of Tiberius' life. His son was dead. As if the gods were mocking him, they had taken from him the last person he truly loved. First it had been his father, then his brother, after that his beloved Vipsania, and now his only son. At thirty-six years of age, Julius Caesar Drusus had been relatively young, yet he had been ill for some time, the result of too much drinking no doubt. His closest friend, Herod Agrippa, was tormented by guilt, having felt responsible for his demise. Tiberius had consoled the Jew, telling him that his son had made his own choices in life, and that he had to bear the responsibilities for them. While Herod appreciated the Emperor's vindication, he still felt the guilt that always afflicted those who lost a friend and brother. Always would he wonder if he could have somehow saved Drusus?

"I could have done more," Tiberius thought aloud, echoing the same feelings that struck down Herod.

"A father should never have to bury his son," Sejanus replied. He stood off to the side, keeping a respectful distance from the Emperor. Tiberius gave him a slightly perplexed look.

"I know that you and Drusus had your differences," he remarked. To state that

Sejanus had differences with Drusus was a serious downplay of events that had transpired between the two. Indeed, Drusus had gotten physically confrontational with Sejanus on more than one occasion, prompting the Praetorians to give him the nickname of *Castor*, or *brute*. Sejanus gave a slight frown at the Emperor's remarks.

"Yes it is true that Drusus and I never did see eye-to-eye," he replied with his usual candor. "Be that as it may, I did not wish for his death; if for no other reason than the hurt I know it must bring you."

"Both of you were the only men that I could completely trust," Tiberius observed. "I needed you equally, though it was maddening to watch you fight. Now old friend, you will have to shoulder his burden as well. There is no man that can replace my son, only a close friend and confidant that I hope is up to the task of carrying on in both his own duties, as well as those left by Drusus."

"My duty is to my Emperor," Sejanus replied. "Know that my life and my talents are completely at your disposal."

Livia entered the room as soon as Sejanus left. Tiberius gave a sigh and turned his back towards the balcony. Livia gave a half smirk at the gesture. She knew her son grew tired of her, and wished for her to hurry up and move on to the afterlife. There were many days when she wished she could. She felt that her continued existence so long after she should have passed on was a mocking from the gods. Be that as it may, as long as she continued to draw breath she would continue to advise her son, even as he fought with her every step of the way.

"The Senate will wish to know when you intend to appoint a new successor," she stated as Tiberius pretended to ignore her.

"To be named a successor to the Imperial Mantle seems to be a death sentence in this family," he remarked with a touch of sarcasm. "Drusus has barely made his final journey and already you speak of politics and intrigue."

"I do it because unlike you I am still drawn to a sense of responsibility!" Livia snapped. "And don't pretend like I don't mourn for him, because I do. My heart is completely rendered; I am tired of watching my children and grandchildren perish whilst I am forced to cling to life!" She stopped in her tirade as an unexpected surge of emotion washed over her. Tiberius turned to face her.

"There is but one man whom I can turn to anymore," he began. Livia quickly composed herself, her eyes growing dark.

"Don't even think about it!" she exclaimed. "The Senate will never allow a man outside the nobility to stand as your successor!"

"The Senate is nothing but a mob of frightened sheep and old women," Tiberius remarked off-hand.

"That may be, but let us not forget that they find their courage when their precious social order is threatened. Remember what they forced you to do in Gaul." Tiberius grew angry at the underlying accusation.

"The *Gauls* forced my hand! They sowed the seeds of rebellion ..."

"A rebellion that would never have come to pass were you not so protective of the Senators' feelings regarding the opening of Senatorial membership to non-Latins," Livia interrupted. "And because of that we could have lost the province! Thankfully the people remain ignorant of such information. I should also remind you that much of the Gallic nobility was wiped out by your soldiers. Countless families either lost sons or were impoverished before it was over."

"You need not remind me of the details regarding Sacrovir's rebellion, Mother," Tiberius rebuked. "My men exacted justice and retribution as they saw fit."

"Augustus would never have allowed the entire affair to happen in the first place!" Livia found she could not help but invoke the name of her son's deified predecessor; she always comparing one to the other.

"I am *not* Augustus!" Tiberius was seething in rage. In a matter of minutes he had gone from mourning his son to entering into a venomous spat with his mother. "Augustus had plenty of opportunities to grant Senatorial membership to the Gallic nobility, but he rebuked them. Augustus left many things undone; things which he did not hesitate to leave for *me* to deal with once he was gone. Oh yes, let Tiberius play the tyrant; let Tiberius be the bad guy in order to fix his mistakes! Deified or not, Augustus was not a god while he lived. He was not infallible, nor was the woman who ruled through him!" Both mother and son took a few deep breaths as their tempers simmered. At length Livia broke the silence.

"You know the Senate will never allow you to raise Sejanus above his station," she said in a low voice.

"The Senate will do as it is told," Tiberius replied, his own voice calmer, though his temper still burned. Sweat was forming on his brow and his face was a dark shade of red. "For years I have tried to get the Senate to act as it is supposed to; like men born to rule this Empire. Instead they have become nothing but a shell of what they once were. They are cowards and fools, every last one of them; none of them is capable of making up their own minds without first wondering whether or not they will please me. They change like the winds, forcing me to play the autocrat, as if I ever wanted it! If they want me to be the sole ruler of Rome, then so be it!"

Sejanus' face beamed as he gazed at Livilla. All had gone according to plan, and with Drusus gone there was no one to stand in his way. Livilla grabbed him and kissed him passionately.

"My darling," she whispered into his ear.

"All is going well," he whispered back. "The old bastard is at last in my sole control. He trusts no one but me now. The Roman Empire is mine!"

"When shall we marry?" Livilla asked her voice giddy. Sejanus slowly pushed himself away from her.

"Patience, my love," he replied. "Your daft husband is scarcely on his final journey and you already talk of marriage. Tiberius may have complete trust in me, but I cannot do anything that would jeopardize that. As soon as you've had proper time to mourn I will approach him."

"Well don't take too long," Livilla pouted as she turned and folded her arms across her chest. "I did not damn myself with unholy sin so that I could sit back and still be nothing more than your concubine!" Sejanus grabbed her gruffly by the shoulders and spun her around so that she faced him once more. She had to admit that his brutish nature was part of what aroused her.

"Damn it woman, be sensible!" he growled. "Do you think I would have done the things that I did if I did not intend to take you as mine? I could have found other ways to bring down your beloved husband." Livilla's face contorted in a sly grin.

"Alright my dear," she said. "But I want you for my own and I want to be shown proper respect as Empress of Rome!"

"In due time, my love."

As she walked the dark, lonely corridors of the Imperial Palace, Livia wondered if this was what her family had come to; leaving its legacy to a Praetorian of questionable moral character. Sejanus cared not for the Empire and its people; he cared only about pursuing his own ambitions. Already he had concentrated the Praetorian Cohorts into a single barracks outside the Viminal Gate. Such a move had created fear and havoc amongst the Senators, who now felt as if they were living in the shadow of Sejanus and the Praetorians. Their fear of him was very real indeed, for he had the Emperor's confidence and could bring down any one of them if he chose to do so.

Livia then pondered the state of her own family, or what remained of it. Drusus had left behind two young children, Julia Livia and Tiberius Gemellus, whose twin brother had died soon after birth. Gemellus would be the next obvious choice, were he not but a child of four years. Rome had not submitted to the folly of many of the eastern provinces and their child monarchs. Germanicus had left behind six children, to include three sons; Drusus, Nero, and Gaius Caligula. However, with Agrippina having made herself such a hateful enemy of the Emperor, Livia foresaw that her children would be lucky to escape banishment or worse in the future. Any hope of the Julio-Claudian line continuing through the heirs of Germanicus was highly unlikely.

Besides Drusus' widow Livilla, Livia's only remaining grandchild was Livilla and Germanicus' brother; that fool Claudius. Livia only remembered the young man as an afterthought. She snorted at the thought of the wretch. Had he been born in a different age, he would have been exposed at birth and left to perish before he could become an embarrassment to his family. His club foot caused him to limp, his head twitched, and his speech impediment made Livia wish she could cut out his tongue. He appeared to be terrified by her, stuttering and twitching like he was having an epileptic fit. Livia then cocked her head to one side as she further pondered her remaining grandson. She remembered passing by the gardens one night, not long before Drusus' death, and overheard him talking to the Imperial Prince. She had paid it no mind at the time, but she now recalled Claudius lecturing Drusus in depth on his duties as the son of the Emperor. He had spoken articulately, with no trace of a stutter. She had not stopped to watch, so she was uncertain if his head still twitched or not. She suspected that it had not, at least not like she had seen it.

A smile then crossed her face. Claudius was no fool; everyone who took him for a fool was! All these years he had been playing them; performing a far better play than the finest actors in the theater. Oh there was no doubt that his afflictions were real; but Livia now realized that his stutter and twitching were deliberately exaggerated. While the whole of the Empire viewed him as the harmless fool, he watched and learned. Livia then gave a short laugh. Her grandson might prove useful after all.

Tiberius was now sixty-four years old, and though still in excellent health he could not deny the passage of time. Therefore a few days later he addressed the Senate once more. He had implored the Consuls to bring before him the sons of Germanicus. Many hoped that this would allay their worst suspicions regarding the imperial succession. Many nobles lived in fear of the Praetorian Prefect, Sejanus, and were terrified that the Emperor would defy Roman law by naming him his successor. Sejanus had even gone so far as to have agents plant such thoughts in the minds of the senators to stoke the fires of rumor. With Tiberius' grandson being but a child, the Senate now saw hope in that the Emperor would turn to the sons of Germanicus.

The Consuls entered the chamber, each guiding Germanicus' sons Nero and Drusus to where Tiberius sat. Absent was their brother, Gaius Caligula, still little more than a child himself. Now seventeen and sixteen years of age respectively, the lads were ready to take their place in the Roman world. Surely the Emperor would see the qualities of their father despite his hatred for their mother! Taking each by the hand he addressed the assembly:

"Senators, when these boys lost their father, I committed them to their uncle, and begged him, though he had children of his own, to cherish and rear them as his own offspring, and train them for himself and for posterity. Drusus is now lost to us, and I turn my prayers to you, and before heaven and your country I adjure you to receive into your care and guidance the great-grandsons of Augustus, descendants of a most noble ancestry. So fulfill your duty and mine. To you, Nero and Drusus, these senators are as fathers. Such is your birth that your prosperity and adversity must alike affect the State."[2]

In a rare showing of solidarity with their Emperor, the Senate broke into an ovation fraught with much emotion. Tears of joy and relief came to many an eye. It was as if a nightmare would soon be over. The sons of Germanicus would restore dignity to the Julio-Claudians. Some Senators even dared to hope that perhaps they would even go so far as to restore Republican rule to the Empire once Tiberius was gone.

✳   ✳   ✳   ✳

A week following his return to Cologne, Artorius was helping Rufio sort through letters and dispatches while waiting for a group of recruits to arrive at the Century headquarters. He had been feeling better as of late. Magnus had been right. Though he would never forget Diana, he could now allow his memories to be fond ones, rather than those that gave him the pain of loss. He had assimilated well into his post as Optio, as Macro had told him he would. Competition in sports, like his new-found passion of Pankration, as well as his continued violating of any young beauty that felt up to the challenge, kept him conditioned and eased the fire that burned inside him.

Legionary Felix was still on light duty and was assigned as his aid for the week. The young man looked to be much recovered from his terrible wound. Color had returned to his face, though he had lost a lot of weight; a far cry from when he had been an overweight recruit three years before.

"I've got the post for you sir," the legionary said as he set a satchel on the table. "I already sorted out all of the personal mail by section. This is mostly official stuff for the Centurion, though there's a couple of letters addressed to you."

"Excellent, thank you," Artorius replied, walking over with a slight limp still.

"How's the leg, sir?" Felix asked. Artorius shrugged his shoulders and opened the satchel.

"It hurts, but what can you do? How about your little scratch?"

"Getting better, slowly but surely." Felix lifted his tunic to show the Optio. The scar left behind was hideous, but the wound was mostly healed. "I've been working my stomach muscles more and should be returning to full duty within the next couple weeks."

"And how is Lady Tierney?" Artorius asked, bringing a grin to the legionary. Though she may not have been a Gallic noblewoman any more, most of the men still addressed her as such as a sign of respect.

"Well enough, sir," Felix replied, replacing his tunic. "She shares a house with Svetlana, which Mad Olaf purchased as a wedding present for his granddaughter." Artorius furrowed his brow in contemplation.

"Valens isn't anywhere near becoming a Centurion, so how exactly is it a wedding present?"

"Well Rome may not recognize it, but Valens and Svetlana did marry in a Nordic ceremony a couple weeks before you returned. It may not be legal by Roman law, but even Sergeant Magnus seemed to approve. Such practices are really not that uncommon when you think about it, sir." Artorius frowned and nodded, for it was true. He did find it strange that Roman law forbade soldiers beneath the rank of Centurion from marrying, and yet they also encouraged such common-law 'marriages.' After all, it readily helped provide the next generation of legionaries; for the son of a soldier was more likely to follow his father into the ranks than the son of a non-soldier. A good number of men within the legion had come from such unions between legionaries and local women. Valens had been sired this way, so his union with Svetlana probably felt natural to him. The marriage of his own parents had not been legalized until his father's retirement, when Valens was twenty and already a legionary himself.

Artorius felt himself grinning at the thought of Valens married as he sorted through the letters. One was addressed to him from Pontius Pilate. It read:

Hail Artorius, old friend and comrade in arms!

I do apologize for not having written sooner. It seems like I lost all track of time while I was away. I've just now returned from a brief administrative tour in Syria with Legio XII, Fulminata. Seems they were having a spot of problems over there, so Sejanus attached me to them for the last year. He said something about how it might do me some good to get a feel for the eastern provinces. Well I can certainly say I got a feel for it, _alright! Justus Longinus accompanied me to Syria; he sends his regards, by the way. His liaison tour was over and he had to return to his post with Legio VI, Ferrata. I have to say that being in the east, even for such a short time was a real eye-opener for me. The people over there are quite strange, and the climate is constantly hot. Even so, I would not mind making a return to the east some day; for all its oddities, it is quite the exotic and exciting place._

As you can tell from my boisterous introduction, I am feeling in a bit of a celebratory mood. I was finally betrothed to my lovely Claudia! Though it will be a few years before we are able to marry, we are looking forward to spending a long and happy life together; hopefully one that will include many children! Claudia's already made me promise that our first son is to be named Artorius, after you. A bit of a violation of the naming traditions perhaps, but who am I to say no? It seems that even though she has never met you, she loves you already. Can't say I blame her, especially after you rescued her sister from the clutches of those rebel bastards. Diana has told us everything, about how you slew countless numbers of those traitors, and even about the impressive manner with which you destroyed that Greek. Forgive me if I don't act surprised, old friend. Your valor and cunning will take you far in the Legions! I also understand that Diana has quite the affection for you. Too bad she cannot bear children; otherwise she would make any man a fine wife. A pity, really ...

Another spot of good news, I have been made Deputy Prefect of the Praetorians! Sejanus recommended me personally for the position. Needless to say this caused some initial anger and jealousy amongst some of the other Tribunes who have been in the Praetorian Guard much longer than me. However, Sejanus explained that I was the only one with any significant combat experience to speak of, and that the other Tribunes would learn well from it. If that did not put an end to the critics, the Emperor's hearty endorsement did. Tiberius himself came out to congratulate me on my posting and he even echoed Sejanus' remarks that there will be bigger things to come for me. Perhaps a governorship will be in my future some day? One never knows.

I truly am blessed, old friend, both in my pending marriage and in my career. Though I have grown to love the benefits of bachelorhood, Claudia and I do adore each other, and I know we will be happy together. You will have to make a trip to Rome when we are wed, and bring some of the lads with you! I trust your judgment in regards to whomever you wish to invite.

My political and military careers are set, old friend. I have the endorsement of Sejanus, to say nothing of the favor of the Emperor himself. Know that I wish you the same success and happiness. I never told you this before, but I was deeply honored to *have served with you in the Legions. I told your father as much, and he is very proud of you. Age, rank, and social status never mattered between us, and they never will. In many ways, I have always admired and looked up to you, as I still do. We have come a long way since our school days, Artorius. And while only the Fates know for certain, I feel that our paths will cross again in our careers. I look forward to that day. Until then, continue to make us proud,* 'Soldier of Rome.' *Your friend and brother in arms,*

Pontius Pilate

▼

FIVE YEARS LATER

At the Bridges over the Rhine, Braduhenna Wood, Frisia
A.D. 28

The Frisians knew it was all about timing. The Roman army was staged on the far side, overlooking the long bridges; three legions, plus massive numbers of auxilia and cavalry. Unbeknownst to the Romans, the bridges were treated with pitch and their support ropes weakened. A simple, but brilliant trick; allow the legions to start their crossing and then destroy the bridges out from under them.

The Frisians knew they could not cut the bridges too soon because the Romans would still have the bulk of their forces intact and would simply march twenty miles north to the ford and cross there. And yet if they waited too long … well the legions were a fearsome enemy and if allowed to mass their numbers they would smash through the Frisians and trample them into dust. One legion was staging to cross, followed by their auxiliaries. These particular troops looked to be strictly infantry, the Germanic auxiliary cavalry somewhere in the distance.

Hidden in a thicket a Frisian archer waited impatiently. It had rained recently, and he prayed the kindling he brought wrapped in many layers of cloth was still dry. His companion knelt next to him, flint and steel in hand. There were many such pairings in the thick undergrowth along the river bank. They would let the first wave of legionaries cross and then hit the bridges with fire while the auxilia crossed. That would trap a significant portion of their force, an entire legion at that, on the Frisian side of the river. The archer licked his lips in anticipation.

There was a fog on the far side of the river, which made Centurion Artorius apprehensive. Scouts had reported that the rebel army was huge, far larger than anticipated. One report had the enemy strength in the tens-of-thousands, though between the fog and dense woods this was impossible to verify for certain. If it was true Artorius had doubts as to whether or not their force would be large enough to defeat the Frisians even under ideal conditions. He also knew that whether they crossed here or at the ford to the north meant little. They would still be stretched thin and could only cross so many troops at a time. Speed would be the key; get enough men across to hold the far bank and allow the rest of the army to deploy.

With the possibility of battle being joined as soon as they crossed, all Centurions and Options had been ordered to leave their horses with the baggage trains. The Frisians *had* to know the legions would pursue them after breaking the siege around Flevum, and what better place to set up an ambush!

"I don't like this," he said as he was joined by Centurion Vitruvius. His superior made an assessment of the situation and shook his head.

"Neither do I," he replied. "These people aren't stupid. They knew better than to engage us in force when we liberated Flevum. No matter where we cross it's going to be a nightmare if they are waiting for us on the other side."

"My thoughts exactly," Artorius added. "And with this damn fog we can't hardly see each other, let alone what may be on the far side."

"I suspect they'll hit us with everything they've got as soon as we're across," Vitruvius continued. "It's like we are at the River Styx assaulting Hell itself." The air was damp and Artorius felt his skin crawl as a feeling of dread came over him. He then took a deep breath.

"Well if we're going to die storming the pits of Hell, we might as well get it over with," he said with a grin. Vitruvius returned the grin and winked in acknowledgment.

"*Vitruvius!*" shouted Master Centurion Calvinus, who was still on his horse coordinating final movement orders. "The Third will cross here and anchor the right. Make sure you leave enough room for everyone else to fall in on your left. And be sure you get across as quickly as you can; this place gives me the fucking creeps!"

"Yes Sir," Vitruvius nodded before turning back to Artorius, his grin returning. "Well old friend, since I've already got you here, why don't you do the honor of leading us to the other side."

"It would be a privilege," Artorius replied as he clasped his Cohort Commander's hand. Vitruvius became somber once more.

"Get over that damn bridge as fast as possible and start pushing out to the right," he ordered as he clutched Artorius' hand harder. "Dominus will follow you with the Fourth; I will take the center, all other centuries on my left." He then released his junior Centurion's hand and rendered a salute, which Artorius returned. Vitruvius then nodded to his Signifier, who waved the Signum to let the rest of the legion know they were set. In the distance, the Legion's Aquila was tilted forward; the signal to advance.

Artorius stepped onto the bridge, drew his gladius and pointed it in a high arc towards the far side. He turned back to see Rufio directly behind him with the Century's Signum, the rest of his men but a few paces behind, anxiously eyeing their Centurion. He cocked a half smile to reassure them before sounding the order in his loudest command voice.

"Second Century follow me!"

Bibliography

1 – Speech of Marcus Lepidus, as written in the Annals of Tacitus, Book Three
2 – Speech of Emperor Tiberius Caesar addressing the Senate, as written in the Annals of Tacitus, Book Four

Made in the USA
Lexington, KY
29 May 2010